The Fifth Season

ALSO BY DAVID DOCHERTY FROM CLIPPER LARGE PRINT

The Killing Jar

The Fifth Season

David Docherty

W F HOWES LTD

This large print edition published in 2003 by
W F Howes Ltd
Units 6/7, Victoria Mills, Fowke Street
Rothley, Leicester LE7 7PJ

1 3 5 7 9 10 8 6 4 2

First published simultaneously by Simon &
Schuster UK Ltd, and Pocket Books, 2003

Extracts from Ted Hughes' *Birthday Letters*
reproduced by kind permission of the publishers
Faber & Faber.
Extracts from R.S. Thomas' *Collected Poems
1945–1990* reproduced by kind permission of the
publishers Phoenix Press.

A CIP catalogue record for this book is available
from the British Library

ISBN 1 84197 626 1

Typeset by Palimpsest Book Production Limited,
Polmont, Stirlingshire
Printed and bound in Great Britain
by Antony Rowe Ltd, Chippenham, Wilts.

Acknowledgements

Dr Huw Jones of the Rothamsted Institute gave welcome advice on 'Perfect Wheat'. Michael Heywood helped me sort out the technology. All errors and exaggerations are my fault. Continued thanks to Carole Blake and Blake Friedmann for long-term support. At Simon and Schuster, Kate Lyall Grant and Ian Chapman provided valued advice and comfort. Marjory Chapman – you know what I owe. Finally, my love to my family – Kate, Flora and Polly.

For Flora and Polly

'Whatever you found
They bombarded with splinters,

Derision, mud—'

'God Help the Wolf After Whom the Dogs Do Not Bark'

Ted Hughes

'When I gave food to the poor, they called me a saint.
But when I asked why the poor were hungry,
they called me a Communist.'

Dom Hélder Câmara
Brazilian Archbishop

PART ONE

SCATTERING THE SEEDS

whatever is hidden is meant to be disclosed.

The Gospel according to Mark, 4, 22,
New International Version

CHAPTER 1

The Prime Minister handed Sam Copeland an envelope that turned his life upside down. He'd been Deputy Director General of the National Crime Squad a matter of months, but already the PM wanted him to move on.

'We're in great danger of losing this war on terror, Sam. Our attitudes are parochial but the problems are global. I've persuaded my colleagues that we need a European-wide response to policing terrorism and the European Anti-Terrorist Unit is that response.' His smile was warm but commanding. 'I want you to be the first Director.'

Sam slipped the file inside a buff folder containing the text of a lecture he was giving that evening at the London Business School.

'The Germans are happy to have you, but the French, as ever, want one of their own.' His smile was tired. 'However, they owe me and you're a cheque I intend to cash. The Spanish are deeply concerned about the whole idea, but I believe they'll see sense before the International Anti-Terrorism Conference in a few weeks' time.

I'd like to use that occasion to launch the EATU. After that, we'll talk again. Read the file and think about how you would set up this thing properly. Use all your experience.'

Sam, the former Head of Scotland Yard's Anti-Terrorist Unit, peered through darkened windows as Baker Street underground station flashed by. How do you say no to the PM?

'I've a lot I want to do at the NCS, Prime Minister.'

'I know that, Sam. I was one of the people urging your appointment, but sometimes your country needs more than you may think you're capable of giving. You've risen to every challenge we set you and I know you'll do the right thing.'

The PM reached across the car and shook Sam's hand. 'Here's your destination. I'd like to hear your lecture tonight, but sadly I have to be in Brussels in the morning.' The PM smiled. 'The London Business School is an appropriate place to talk about the rise of intellectual property crime – I wonder how many future corporate raiders passed through these doors. It's a good talk, and if I were you, I'd punch through on final peroration.'

Sam looked astonished. The PM had read his speech already. It was barely off his word processor.

'See you at the conference, Sam. Give me your answer then. Take care of yourself. We need you.'

Sam stood in the chilly London rain as the PM's black limousine splashed into the night, then turned into the warmth of the LBS building.

CHAPTER 2

The Standish Gene Technology Research Centre was silent and dark as the thief waited and watched lights sparkle in the medieval manor house at the heart of the University of Eastfield's Science Park. The sleepy town of Eastfield had been decimated by the Black Death in the fourteenth century, and the manor house, which had belonged to the first Earl, was all that was left of its former glories.

But now the Centre had brought new vitality to the area, and that evening its newly appointed director, Stef Violi, was throwing a glittering dinner for major European businessmen. Two years before, a reclusive US businessman, Johnny Standish, had founded the SGTRC, attracted by government grants and attractive land, and Violi was raising further investment to turn it into a world-class research body.

The thief depressed a detonator and heard a muffled explosion as a sub-generator blew. He'd rigged the power surge to look like an accident.

As expected, the campus guards rushed towards the blacked-out building. It would take fifteen minutes before they could boot up the back-up generator, and the celebrities would require additional security. Plenty of time, then.

He walked slowly to the Standish Centre – a new building constructed entirely of blacked glass strung on a weblike lattice of steel. It was round, like a geodesic dome, and surrounded on all sides by long glasshouses containing some of the most radical genetic-crop research in the world. In these Standish Gene Technology developed wheat designed to protect against pests, bananas containing vaccines for polio, tomatoes that would ripen slowly and give farmers a reliable crop year-round.

He crept towards the SGTRC's side entrance, a modest block of steel compared to the Ozymandian frontage, extracted a security pass from within his black boiler suit, swiped, then entered as Dr Alasdair Garner, the Head of Neutraceuticals. Garner was a fool – unlike Grace Adams. That girl had a staggering mind. A shame, really. They could've achieved greatness together. But that was behind him. Now – time to go to work.

Sam entered a long hallway filled with guests and spotted his Head of Communications anxiously searching for him among the crowd. The PM's summons had arrived unexpectedly and Sam was cutting it fine.

A deep Cornish voice boomed behind him. 'Five more minutes and you'd've been late, lad.'

Sam turned and his eyes locked with those of his boss, Ian Trevor. The Director General of the National Crime Squad was stocky and ruddy-faced and his fiercely intelligent black eyes were offset with brows that skittered across his forehead. His shock of white hair stood up as if electrified. He cradled a large Scotch and water.

'Caught up in something,' said Sam, glancing at his watch. 'Plenty of time, though.'

'How long is your speech?'

'Half an hour.'

'Keep it tight, lad. Shorter the better.' Trevor turned away and Sam heard a muffled, 'Good luck.'

The HoC's face flushed with relief as she hustled him onto the podium. He glanced quickly at the empty seat in the front row. Grace was late. Again.

His resonant West Highland voice filled the room.

'The heroin trade is nasty, brutal and short. These days, the most sophisticated organized gangs use high-tech methods to make money. Level-three criminals, as we call those who never get their hands dirty, are just as focused, just as determined, just as capable of violence, but the general public does not feel as threatened by their activities. It's easier for the new breed of super-criminal to bribe officials and lawyers to turn the other way whilst money is being laundered. If crime is virtual – what is real?'

There was a rustle at the back of the room and Grace offered a surreptitious thumbs-up as she slid into the last row. She caught her breath and tuned into Sam's speech. His long face had aged well. His thick, dark hair was expensively cut into a side parting, but still an unruly curl straggled down his forehead. He had obviously been working out, and at forty-one looked better than he had when she left the UK for Bangladesh seven years before, when a bad marriage, late nights and fast food had bulked him out.

Almost half an hour later, he reached his conclusion. 'Successful organized-crime groups work across national boundaries, exploit every weakness in the law, cooperate with one another for mutual advantage and rely on corruption to protect them. Tracking the cyber-untouchables is an expensive, specialist business requiring encryption technologies, sophisticated distance surveillance techniques and high-end database analysis. But it still needs the traditional police virtues of patience and detection. Above all. *Above all*. This country requires a twenty-first century police force of utmost dedication and unimpeachable integrity. Thank you.'

As the room erupted into applause journalists swooped forward, backing Sam against the podium. He had been big news since the capture of the assassination squad of the Levellers – a militant group of environmental activists who'd destroyed a major dam. Lights flashed as photographers grabbed pictures of him from all angles, shooting up into the shadows to make him look sinister. He moved back into the light.

On the fourth floor at the SGTR Centre, the thief navigated by memory. Halsford over there, Johnstone to her left, Pety in front of that, then Grace. Her work area was small, ten by ten. He squeezed in beside her Mac, located the security cameras, slipped plastic caps over them and then sat in front of her computer. Pinned on the partition walls were pictures of Grace surrounded by children at a farm in the north of Bangladesh, another of her with her half-brother Hal at Glastonbury, a third a collage of blues and soul musicians. He recalled that this was something she and he had in common – a love of African-American music. He preferred Parker, Coltrane, Art Blakey, Monk. Something authentic and powerful, a sound to set against the sterility of modern life. But he understood why someone like Grace would love Muddy Waters and Marvin Gaye. The combination of pain and joy would appeal to her. Something else he admired her for. Now he had to steal her life's work.

He settled in front of the keyboard, extracted a portable memory drive, inserted it into her Mac then powered up. A few minutes later, he was bypassing her passwords and penetrating her security codes, burrowing into the data she had kept secret from all but one of her colleagues.

The computer screen suddenly burst into life and a picture of B.B. King appeared as a screensaver. His white teeth gleamed as his guitar screamed out a huge chord. The noise filled the room and the thief quickly ripped the speaker from the back of the machine. As the music stopped dead, he leapt to his feet, feverishly staring into the darkness, then at the screen on which a cartoon bubble appeared from Muddy's lips.

It don't come easy.

The man hissed. *Jokes.* They greet me with jokes. Did she think me so stupid? How much did she have stored on the central network? Nothing really important. She wouldn't trust it. She would rely on local storage – burned onto a CD-ROM, a portable drive or the computer's hard disk. People think that they are so clever with their protection devices. They forget the simplest thing is to steal the disk. He pulled a screwdriver from his bag and dragged the back of the computer towards him. Seconds later, the phone next to him rang. After five rings the answering machine clicked on and he heard a Cologne accent say. 'If you carry on, you'll be electrocuted. I have that thing wired so you'll turn into barbecue. I don't recommend it. Oh, and by the way, security's on its way up.'

He recognized the voice. Brigitte, Grace's project manager. Anyway, no worries. He pulled a circuit breaker from his bag, earthed himself, then set to work.

The wire that slipped round his throat was thin and bit deep into the roll of flesh. He struggled for breath, panic suffusing him as he kicked back, struggling to free himself. His arms swung up, desperately pulling the hair of his attacker, who was short but had a grip too strong to break. The assassin put his knee in the man's back, twisted the garrotte twice more as his target gurgled, then abruptly pulled the head to one side. There was a crack as the neck snapped.

Grace gestured towards the flapping journalists busy comparing notes at the far end of the noisy reception room.

'I don't know how you can cope with those people,' she said, kissing him on the cheek. His grey-green eyes creased into a smile.

'I tell as much of the truth as I dare and hope I don't get too stitched up. It evens itself out. Doesn't pay to get too close to the media. Anyway, I'd rather do my job than parade like a pantomime horse.'

He drank her in. She'd allowed her auburn hair to grow down to her shoulders and there were a few lines around her lips that showed how tough the past few years had been. Her skin had an exhausted pallor. The thin wire glasses were a new addition, but only served to heighten the effects of her green eyes. He'd bought a piece of opal for her birthday ten years before and when he'd held it up in front of a coal fire, the suffused light playing against the stone was like looking into Grace's eyes. He'd had the jewel made up into a pendant, and was delighted to see that she was wearing it.

She seemed uncomfortable in a long, black ankle-length skirt worn for the occasion. He knew how much she preferred faded Wranglers and white shirts. Sam sipped a white wine that tasted of industrial antiseptic, then poured some still water. He felt tired but exhilarated.

'I'm sorry I was late. I had to deal with an urgent call.'

'I'm just glad you made it.'

'Fascinating speech,' Grace said, tossing down the remains of her Chianti then lifting another as the waitress passed.

His expression registered surprise.

'Don't worry.' She tapped him on the arm, 'I'm not driving. Our Head of Neutraceuticals is giving me a lift home.' She waved at a dusty-looking man in the corner, who returned her gesture. 'Besides –' she took another sip, – 'I'm celebrating.'

'What? Your birthday's not till Saturday.'

'You are coming to the party, aren't you?'

'Wouldn't miss it.'

'No. My big news is that I'm close to finishing my glasshouse work on the wheat and I've applied for a small-scale field trial. I've spent eighteen months preparing this batch of seeds and now my little babies are going out into the big bad world.

12

Those nice boys at Environment gave me a private thumbs-up today, though they want me to keep it quiet until they prepare the ground politically. So, here I go.' She raised her glass in a toast.

'That's fantastic.' He kissed her on the cheek. 'But be careful or you'll have my press friends back there on your case.'

'Oh, there's nothing controversial about me. All I'm trying to do is develop something that will make a lot of Bangladeshi women and children healthy. I'm small fry.'

'Uh, huh.' A small fry with a Cambridge First in Ecology and a Ph.D. that was described by her Head of Department as 'one of the best in a generation'. Who'd spent two weeks in jail after leading protests about the death of two women forced to leave their village to work in a slave factory in Dhaka. A positive sardine.

His Head of Communications mowed through the crowd, steering one of the guests, a small, squat, beetle-browed redhead radiating the fierce energy of self-importance.

'Looks like work.' Sam sighed, then glanced at his watch. 'This'll be over in half an hour. Let me take you out for a drink.'

'Not sure I can stand this lot for a second longer. But I've got something I want to read. I'll wait for you in a bar. Where do you know round here?'

'The Windsor Castle is round the corner. I won't be long.'

'Deputy DG.' The HoCs sonic boom reached

13

him. 'This is Angus Sommerville, Director of Television at Carnada International Media and formerly Editor of *Panorama*. He's longing to talk to you about corruption in the Force. I told him you were just the man.'

'Good luck,' whispered Grace as she melted into the crowd.

The thief's body was heavy in death. As rigidity set in, the butchers worked quietly and efficiently, quartering the torso, sawing off limbs, burning eyes and fingertips with acid, smashing teeth. When they finished, they sluiced down the borrowed meat-processing room, placed the remains in four black bags, weighted them down and drove out towards the river.

CHAPTER 3

As Grace sipped tap water, she stretched her long legs and listened to Blind Willie Johnson's haunting slide-guitar on her lightweight headphones. As Willie swayed through the mysterious 'Dark Was The Night', she closed her eyes, insulated from the bar and its chattering drinkers and slid back to Bangladesh. A pitch-black night, the stars pouring light across the millennia, rocking Nijera to sleep in her arms as they sat on the hard ground outside her hut. Nijera had just lost her second child to nutrient malnutrition that led to diarrhoea, dehydration and death. Grace felt hopeless. She had done her damnedest to help, used all the educational materials, tried vitamin A injections, and to convince the local men that their children needed more than rice and a few vegetables, but when they, too, were constantly hungry what hope had she? The children went blind, contracted rickets, or just gave up and died. And mothers struggled exhausted to hold their lives together as anaemia drained them. As Nijera slept, Grace wept and she didn't stop grieving for two weeks, by which time she was home and vowing

15

never to go back to Bangladesh until she had some answers.

'Mother's children have a hard time,' Willie growled. 'Nobody treat you like mother will.' Too right, Willie. She opened her eyes. Too right.

She tugged a letter from the bag at her side. It was from Sister Evangeline Rush – the Head of the US-based Outreach for Rural Security – a woman Grace admired deeply. The ORS was still working in Chakaria, a group of southern Bangladeshi villages. Grace had joined the ORS after a stint in the VSO.

My Dearest Grace,

We miss you here in Chakaria. Are you still playing the guitar? Not much singing around here at the moment; the floods have been severe again.

Nijera sends her love and her thanks for the money. Her son is well and prospering. Nijera's sister passed away yesterday. She was twenty-two. The Lord took her in childbirth. Please think of us here. The drought preceding the floods was intense and the rice crops are struggling. How is your research? I pray every night that Jesus inspires you to the breakthrough. Oh, how we need answers.

I do sound gloomy, don't I? As ever, the people in the district are wonderful. And I feel so inspired by their strength. I hope you are prospering and having fun. What's happening

in your life? Write to me soon, even if it's only email.
   Much, much love
   Evangeline

She saw Sam come into the pub, followed by two tall men who looked like plain-clothes policemen. As they retreated to the side of the bar nearest the door, Sam brought over red wine for her and a pint of beer for himself.

As he sipped, she grinned. 'What's happening here? You normally sink half a pint on the first go.'

'Sadly, my body started to notice that it didn't like twelve-inch Chicago pizza with garlic bread trimmings, washed down by three pints.'

'Discovering that you've started eating healthily is like finding out that the prince who built the Taj Mahal had a string of mistresses.'

'I wasn't that bad,' Sam laughed. 'Anyway, I just eat unhealthy stuff less often. As Wilde says, "The only way to get rid of temptation is to yield to it."'

Her phone trilled a version of Clapton's 'Layla' as its ringing tone. She looked down at the number; it was Brigitte, her Project Manager.

'Hi, Gitte.'

Her face tightened with worry as she listened. 'You're joking. Did they get anything?'

Relief surged through her body. 'Thank God. Thank God. I don't think I could've borne it. I know we have everything backed up. But we don't want anyone else to have it. Not till we're ready. I'll be back by midnight. See you in the morning. Thanks, babe.'

'Trouble?' he asked.

'Someone tried to break into my computer at Standish. And I bet I know who.'

'Want me to help?'

'No. It's under control, thanks.' Grace sipped her wine. 'What you were saying earlier about intellectual property theft, it's going to affect my world as well.'

He nodded. 'I read that pharmaceutical companies are already losing two billion dollars a year on counterfeit medicines.'

'No, that's not what I mean. There's a race going on between academics and scientists and the big agribusinesses. Drug companies are patenting traditional medicines like karela and jumin. They're copyrighting genes and pathways and enzymes.'

'Surely innovations would crawl to a halt if businesses weren't able to make money from their inventions.'

She swatted away the point. 'I don't object to legitimate business. But it's getting increasingly difficult just to do work for the public good. You have to hide your intentions before someone gets access to your research and slaps a patent on some or all of it. That's what whoever was trying to get access to my Mac was up to.'

He raised his glass, letting the warm beer trickle

down his throat. They had avoided discussion of her work since she'd returned two years before. 'I *was* amazed to hear that Cambridge University's Greenpeace leader had taken up GM crop research,' Sam said.

'Seven years is a long time watching kids die from preventable diseases,' she replied. 'When you're here in the UK, organic and sustainable farming sounds just the thing. But when you're there you realize that they live on the edge of existence, doing everything by hand. Poor farmers *are* organic; all they have is the most basic agriculture. But believe me, with a population rising over one hundred and twenty million, it's not sustainable just to leave nature to its own devices. Have you ever seen anyone with rickets?'

'No.'

'It's only sixty years since there were thousands of cases in the UK. It's a bone disease that can make you desperately ill. Hundreds of thousands of kids have it in Bangladesh, because rice, their staple diet, doesn't include enough iron or zinc. If the family is rich enough to afford an egg or some meat, it goes to the men. More than half the women and children are suffering from vitamin malnutrition – even those with full bellies.'

'I read something about "Golden Rice". Isn't that supposed to help?'

'Yes. Rice doesn't contain vitamin A. If boiled rice is the bulk of your diet this lack of micronutrients can lead to night-blindness and, in the worst cases, death. You get vitamin A from things like carrots – and daffodils. A brilliant Swiss researcher, Ingo Potrykus, has inserted daffodil genes into rice that make the endosperm a golden colour and turn on a vitamin A pathway. It's another part of the jigsaw. Anyway, I'm not alone in changing my mind in the face of evidence. Patrick Moore, one of the original founders of Greenpeace, is appalled at the way the debate's been going. I heard him give a speech in which he summed up the issues better than I could. Hold on –' she scrabbled around in her bag – 'I've got it somewhere. I hang on to it to show that I haven't joined the devil and all his ravening hordes.' She handed over a well-thumbed pamphlet with many markings and rapid underlings.

> *Dr Patrick Moore, formerly Director of Green-peace International, said recently, 'Genetic modification can reduce the chemical load in the environment, reduce the impact on non-target species and reduce the amount of land required for food crops. There are so many real benefits from genetic modification compared to the largely hypothetical and contrived risks that it would be foolish to ban genetic modification.'*

Sam took another quick gulp. 'How can he be so sure?' He handed back the document.

'*Come on*, Sam. You know about plants. Don't tell me you can't see the sense in what he's saying.'

Sam gazed at her sparking eyes and decided to leave the debate for another day. He'd been up half the night tinkering with his speech. Now wasn't the time to take on Grace in full flow.

Grace glanced up and noticed her designated driver at the door, tapping his forefinger on the face of his watch.

'Got to go. I'll explain in more detail on Saturday. Come down early.' She kissed him lightly on each cheek and left. Sam watched her slender body glide through a sea of admiring glances.

The arsonist turned the canister containing the homemade napalm in his muscular hands. Whereas the real thing was a mix of petrol thickened with polystyrene, this batch had been made up using soap power and turpentine. His people had followed instructions posted up on an Animal Liberation Front Web site. There were a dozen different incendiary devices listed and precise instructions as how to build them. He laughed at the injunction at the bottom of the site – DO NOT LEAVE EVIDENCE. He had deliberately used the information from the site to throw a curve ball into the police investigation. No professional arsonist would be this unsubtle. The police would assume it was someone from the wilder shores of the environmental movement rather than the arsonist.

The Web fascinated him. Free speech to the nth degree of freedom. He wished he'd had access to it as a kid. The ALF were a bunch of middle-class tossers, he thought, but they obviously knew how to plan a good ruck.

As three of his men cleaned the lock-up in which they had prepared the napalm, brushing up soap flakes, corking the turps and washing out the urns, he read the instructions on how to apply the explosive. *Take a couple of pints of the liquid, spread it out over the surface of the building in order to start a large area burning at once. Surround it with charcoal to increase the intensity.* There was also a handy tip for a time delay. *Tape a bunch of matches around the bottom of a cigarette, when the light at the tip hits the matches, they ignite and flare the napalm.* Grace's glasshouses would go up in minutes.

'Boom,' he whispered.

CHAPTER 4

Saturday was a perfect April day. Vermeer-blue light poured through scattered puffy clouds drifting lazily on a cool wind. Sam idled down white country lanes shadowed by the chalk hills of the Lincolnshire Wolds. As ever, this quiet and sparsely populated county, tucked into the east of England, soothed him. He recalled Tennyson's verse about the 'Calm and deep peace on this high wold.' He had spent the happiest days of his teenage years in these hills.

The hood was down on his ancient Triumph Roadster and he relished the sun on his face. Most of the time the TR3 sat in his garage, but he drove it today because it reminded him of the first car he'd ever owned. He'd found and lovingly rebuilt a 1960 Roadster when he was seventeen, a year in which his mother, then his father, had died. Eileen, his sister, had insisted that he live with her and her husband Tommy that summer before he went up to Edinburgh University.

He turned up Radio 3 as Elisabeth Schwartzkopf sang something by Mahler; her rich, romantic sound filled his head as he grinned at the memory

23

of meeting Grace – a gawky thirteen-year-old with long, skinny, ungainly legs. Her mother had owned White Hill House and farm – 200 acres of land adjoining Tommy and Eileen's place – and sublet the fields to Tommy for his Friesians. Sam was collecting monkshood and Grace, who tore around on a horse called Soulman, had knocked him into a ditch.

'Oh, God. Oh, God. I'm sorry. Stupid of me. No one ever comes here 'cept me and Soulman. Are you all right? What've you got there?' She took one of the flowers. '*Aconitum napellus*?'

His surprised laughter was abruptly swallowed when he saw the adolescent anger in her eyes. 'It was used to treat measles and rheumatism in the past,' she spat as she jumped on her horse and sped off.

'And it's extremely poisonous,' he shouted after her.

His sister had been cross with him when he described the incident and told him that Grace loved botany and that he should be 'ashamed of himself treating a wee lassie like that'. He felt embarrassed and by way of apology took Grace some rare yellow Nottingham Catchfly he had picked on a Scottish expedition. They had become fast friends and spent that long summer before university drifting along the fields next to the Bain documenting wildflowers. He drew and she took photographs. They were thought an odd couple, but after a lecture from his sister about 'how innocent wee lassies were', and a stern warning from Henry, Grace's dad, that he 'would break his fucking legs if he touched any part of his girl', they were pretty much left alone.

Every year, he had returned for a month after working the harvest somewhere. After weeks stuck in a threshing shed, choking on the dust, working through the night, each year he earned enough to pay for his summer with Grace. Then, one day, it ended, and opened up a gap in his soul.

CHAPTER 5

'What are you doing?' Grace asked her half-brother Hal, who was lying on the ground, grimacing.

'Staring at the sky.'

'Twit. I meant what were you doing on Sparky?' She reached over and gathered the reins of a twelve-year-old black pony she kept as a companion for her horse, Soulman the Second.

She slid from the black stallion and knelt beside Hal, who was obviously winded.

'I was teaching Ruthie how to ride.'

Grace looked across the field to the five-bar gate on which Ruthie Forester, an ash-blonde four-year-old girl, was perched. She was laughing and shouting, 'Again, again.' Her mother, Sara, was trying to shush her, with an appalled look on her pretty, pixie-like face. Sara's hair was two shades darker than her daughter's, and her body curvy but athletic.

Hal rolled onto his right side and Grace longed to help him get to his feet, but knew better than to try. It was at moments like this that her heart turned.

He crawled onto his knees. The left side of his face was frozen and impassive, but the right lit up as he watched Ruthie point and laugh. That his face was soft and beautiful, like that of his mother, somehow made its curious planes and angles all the more heartbreaking. Grace recalled the night he was brought home by her father in a small blue carrier cot. His mother, her stepmother, Sue, had died in a car accident when he was only seven months in the womb and Hal had suffered hemiatrophy when blood had stopped flowing to his brain. Grace had wanted to run from the room at the sight of the creature staring at her from the cot set up in her father's study, then Hal had cried out and reached out to grab her finger. She melted and at age eleven became his defender, mother and friend.

'You've fallen off Sparky every year for the past ten. What on earth possessed you to try again? You could've broken something.' Her voice was anxious.

'She does it deliberately. Don't you, girl?' When he slapped the pony on her haunches, she swung her head in indignation then trotted away. 'She's got this little trick. Just as I'm getting comfortable, she drops her head and shimmies to the right. Next time she does that, she's dog meat.'

'She'll hear you.' Grace grinned. 'And you know how mean she can be. She'll stand on your head. Might knock some sense into you.' Sparky whinnied a greeting to Soulman, who

trotted over to nuzzle her. The two were insepa-
rable.

Grace and Hal walked towards the spectators on
the gate, Hal's left foot dragging with every step,
leaving a snail trail across the pasture.

'Again. Again.' Ruthie giggled.

'I'm sorry.' Sara shook her head. 'I can't stop
her.'

'Who can blame the kid?' Hal rubbed the girl's
tousled hair, then wiped some of the dust from his
black shirt and leather trousers. 'Not every day she
sees a cripple pitched over the head of a pony. I'd
find it pretty funny myself.'

'Stop it.' Sara was furious. She had told Grace
that she hated the demeaning way Hal referred
to himself. Grace agreed but Hal had a stubborn
streak as wide as the River Humber. It had carried
him through tough years at the local school, where,
after innumerable scrapes and fights, he'd made
a place for himself. Now, at twenty-one, he was
poised to graduate from the Slade School of Art.
If he lived long enough.

'Heads up.' Hal leant against the fence. 'Here
comes Her Maj.'

Walking up the short gravel path to the paddock
was Hope, Grace's younger sister by two years.
Otherwise known as the Countess of Eastfield.

Lumbering along at Hope's feet were her two
aged cocker spaniels, both with long names and, in
Grace's opinion, a perfect example of the problems
of inbreeding.

Hope huffed as she made her way towards them and Grace felt for her. Her sister was nearly nine months pregnant with the Eastfield heir. Hope was hugely relieved when the scan showed a boy, after her husband's barely disguised concern at the arrival of two girls in the previous four years. The Eastfield estate passed down the male line and without an heir, the title and land would pass to a cousin. Grace knew that Hope had miscarried twice and had been pregnant or suckling for the bulk of her seven-year marriage.

'Darlings.' She blew them both a kiss. 'I've been trying to find Daddy. Have you seen him anywhere?'

'No,' they both lied, knowing that Henry, their father, was sleeping off the effects of a bottle of Scotch shared with Alf Halliwell, who had been Finance Director of the University when Henry was Vice-Chancellor. There had been some kind of fight and Henry had hit Alf. As Grace had driven their visitor to the station, she'd begged him not to report it to the police. Alf, as drunk as Henry, hadn't responded as he staggered from the car. She'd force Henry to write an apology, but if, as she expected, he refused, she would forge one. Wouldn't be the first time.

Hope was a few inches shorter than Grace and her face was finer-grained, though puffy with pregnancy. She would not be overweight for long. Three months after each birth she went to a health farm for a fortnight, leaving the baby with two nannies, and starved her body back into a size-eight dress. Her husband liked her thin.

She and Hope had never been very close; her sister had been acquisitive at a young age, demanding toys, bikes and love. Whatever Grace had had, Hope had wanted. Despite it all, Grace felt a strong affection for her sister, and understood that her absurd affectations were the product of a spoiled but troubled childhood, but these feeling were as nothing compared to the love she had for Hal.

'Tell Daddy I'll see him at your party.'

'Is Freddie coming?' asked Hal.

'Of course! He wouldn't miss my sister's thirty-fourth.' She turned to Grace. '*Thirty-four!* Goodness, what does that make *me*? We're getting ancient.' Her laughter was precise, controlled. 'Darling. We *must* find you a man before it's too late for babies.' She smiled dreamily as she stroked her bulge.

'What's a woman without a man?' asked Hal, turning to face Grace, his blue eyes sparkling.

'A horse without a bike?'

'Oh, you two are impossible.' Hope's lips smiled, but her eyes were cold. Oh God, Grace thought, she thinks we're excluding her again.

'How are the girls?' she asked.

'Fine,' Hope replied, then turned to Sara and said, 'Home.'

Hal hissed angrily as she headed towards her car, the dogs hobbling in her wake.

Grace hated the way her sister treated Sara like

a servant. Sara had been with the Delawneys since leaving school, pregnant, at eighteen and was now Hope's general dogsbody and driver. Despite her refusal to name the father, the Delawneys had stuck with her. However, her father, the Delawneys' solicitor, had cut her dead.

'No. Don't want to go home. Want stay here,' Ruthie said firmly, squirming away from her mother, and reaching out to Hal.

'We must go.' Sara lifted her protesting daughter, who burst into tears.

'There's chocolate in the car. You can have some.' Ruthie peered up at her mother through the flood, made a quick calculation then nodded and wriggled to the ground.

'Bribery and corruption.' Hal laughed. 'Won't stand you in good stead in the long run.'

She kissed him lightly on the lips. 'Easy for you to say.'

'You are coming,' Grace said.

'Oh. I didn't know I was invited.'

'But I gave your invitation to Ho . . .'

She and Hal exchanged glances and Sara's eyes slid down.

'I'd love you to come,' Grace insisted.

'Yeah. Who else is going to dance with the crip if you don't come?' Hal grinned.

Sara glowered at Hal, then smiled at Grace. 'Thank you. I'll be there.' She caught sight of Ruthie tottering towards the duck pond and dashed after her.

'Sometimes I could drown Hope,' Hal spat.

'She can't help it, Hal.'

'Oh, it's all in the genes, eh?'

'No. I don't mean that. It's – well – she's pretty much always had what she wanted. You know she finds it hard to think beyond the borders of her house, her kids, the county. Anyway, let's go and wake Dad and see if we can talk some sense into him.'

'One big happy family.' Hal hooked her arm and they trudged towards the house.

CHAPTER 6

That afternoon, Grace was staring intently at her computer screen, analysing the results of a study done at the University of Nebraska-Lincoln. One of their teams had managed to insert the two genes from the 2-5A anti-viral system found in birds into wheat, thereby increasing its resistance to wheat streak mosaic virus, which was costing US farmers half a billion a year. It was a brilliant piece of work; but it was only at the starting gate of the journey she was going on.

'What d'you think, Gitte?'

Beside her sat Brigitte Hesse, a short, skinny woman with stubbled blonde hair and a pierced left nostril. The tip of a dragon's tail tattoo snaked above the edge of her V-neck T-shirt as she peered at a row of mathematical calculations detailing the ways in which the genes they were targeting would eventually behave in their host plants.

Gitte rolled her chair over and tapped on the screen. 'Pretty impressive.' From Cologne, she had a strong North German accent, but spoke English with immaculately clipped tones. Her blue eyes were the colour of a Mediterranean noontime sky. 'What are they up to now?'

'They've gone to field trial.'

'We'll soon catch up.'

Grace smiled at her. They had worked together for two years. Introduced at a conference on sustainable development, they'd corresponded for a few months, and then Gitte turned up on Grace's doorstep with a suitcase and a dozen ideas. Grace had struggled to pay the twelve thousand a year Gitte earned. She'd had to dip deep into the small inheritance her mother had left her as well as work three days a week at the Standish Institute.

The small complex of two glasshouses had been paid for by the proceeds of the legacy. Now she was about to run out of money; but she knew, just *knew*, she had done enough to convince one of the big philanthropic funds to allow her to take it to the next level. She had grant applications in with at least a dozen, but so far had been hampered by her unwillingness to share all of her calculations and research findings in case they were pirated. And frankly, she thought, once they know exactly what I'm up to it'll be very controversial, but surely when they see the benefits we'll break through all those mealy-mouthed worries.

She looked out of the window at Hal as he laboured with a sculpture next to the big oak tree.

'How's the romance going?' asked Gitte, nodding towards Hal.

'Cautiously.'

'I like Sara.' Gitte was vigorously ringing a group of numbers with a red pen. 'She's a sweet girl. But Hal must be careful. She is very nervous about something and I would hate to see him hurt.'

'Hmm.' Grace pondered. 'She's good for him, and he's bringing something out in her. Maybe it can work. I hope so.'

There was silence as they returned to their computer screens.

'D'you think they're doing it?' Gitte asked.

'Gitte!' Grace exploded. 'That's my little brother you're talking about.' Then Gitte caught her eye and they hooted with laughter.

When Sam turned into White Hill House lane, he saw for himself the picket outside the front gate. A half-dozen people, drinking from bottles and laughing, saw him and raised a banner that screamed - *Burn the Frankenwheat.* One was Rod Leadsmith, an old acquaintance who'd bought his sister's farm. As Rod, a slight man with long, stringy brown hair and a ferrety face, strode over, Sam wound down his window.

'Good to see you, Rod. How's the old place?'

'It'd be fine if I didn't have to stay up half the night worrying about Grace's bloody contamination.'

Rod was an organic potato farmer, and as the focus of local opposition to Grace's wheat he had the support of most of the locals. Rod'll be furious when he finds out about the field trial, Sam thought, as will Freddie Delawney, the biggest and most influential landowner in Lincolnshire, who had attained national notoriety by destroying GM soya on a farmer's land in the south of the county. Since then, other than Grace, no one had had the courage to stand up to him.

'I read about your Levellers bust,' he said, referring to an eco-terrorist group Sam had rounded up the year before. 'Bit brutal, wasn't it?'

'I don't think I had many choices.'

'They were obviously misguided, Sam. But you've got to beware of becoming a police state.'

'I'll bear that in mind.' The next time someone threatens to kill a woman and her unborn child, I'll think hard about the ethics of policing whilst trying to save her life.

Leadsmith leant in, shook Sam's hand, then retreated, 'Got to go. See you at the party tonight.' So Grace had invited him to her party. Didn't expect that. Though perhaps I should. He was her second cousin, after all. Like in his own small patch of Scotland, a lot of people were interrelated in the Lincolnshire Wolds. Rod's father had been the local doctor and Grace's mother's cousin. He and Sam had played in the Eastfield House cricket team during his summer breaks. Rod had been a good leg spinner. He turned his back on Sam as he drove through.

Sam, puzzled, drove up towards the House. What was going on in Rod's mind? They'd known each other for decades and he'd always been a strange lad, but never angry like this. Not against family.

He pulled into the courtyard of a two-storey fourteenth-century farmhouse. White Hill House stretched back to encompass a half-dozen low rooms on the ground floor, and six bedrooms on the top. When Henry, Grace's father, was a rising star on the media circuit, his popular books on psychiatry had appeared regularly in the bestseller list and there had always been money around to pay for the upkeep of the House. June, his first wife and Grace's mother, had been a successful landscape gardener and had ensured that her grounds were immaculately maintained.

When Grace had disappeared to Bangladesh, Henry had stopped writing and lecturing and as Hal's medical care ate deep into their reserves, the House had been the last thing on Henry's increasingly troubled mind. Plaster had fallen off the walls, the flagstones had algae growing through and the garden, previously well kept, was unkempt and straggled unconvincingly between the house and the river. It had saddened Sam to see a place of delicious memories become so ragged. Then after Grace returned Henry had taken early retirement from his post as Vice-Chancellor of the University and poured his pension and pay-off into renovating the old place – it looked fantastic.

Sam parked beside a new feature, two long glasshouses in which he could see several strains of wheat. Outside was an expensive cooling unit. The whole lot looked as if it might've cost a hundred thousand.

A tall, cadaverous, uniformed guard asked Sam for identification. As he offered it, he checked the name of the security firm on his badge. 'Safe and Sound.' The guard scrutinized the pass identifying Sam as a police officer, seemingly trying to commit it to memory.

'Have a good evening, sir.' He walked round to check out the back of the building. In a van parked between the buildings, a second guard chattered into a mobile phone.

'Like my new chums?' Grace appeared at his elbow and they hugged.

'Sad to see them, if you want the truth.'

'There have been threats more than once to burn me out. Can't let that happen. Not now. I'm on the verge of something big.'

'I've just bumped into Rod. What's going on with him?'

She shrugged. 'He hates what I'm doing.'

'But you invited him to your party.'

'I can't spend my whole time chucking friends and relations just because I've changed my mind about GM.' She smiled. 'Rod hasn't lived my life and I've no intention of judging him. Just as I expect him to treat me like a human being and not the embodiment of some bloody personification of corporate evil. Besides, science needs the Rods of the world to stay on our backs and keep us honest. No one's going to forgive us for CJD for a long time. As far as my project is concerned, so far,' she crossed her fingers, 'so good. I'm hoping that the various threats are bluster; but I'm taking no chances. Come and see my babies.'

She passed a black fob in front of a security pad on the wall to open the glasshouse door. The corridor was cool and above them distilled water passed back and forth on thick, lagged pipes. There was a high-pitched hiss and hum as the machines kept the rooms at the exact temperature stipulated by the researchers.

As she handed him a white coat and donned one herself, she said: 'This is Gitte Hesse. She's the one really running this experiment. Gitte, Sam.' She pronounced the first letter in her friend's first name with a hard 'G'.

'Glad to meet you at last.' She extended her hand. 'Grace has spoken about you often.'

'Thank you. She has said terrific things about you,' he replied, using formal pre-war German.

'Your German is very good,' she laughed, surprised.

'My grandmother was from Berlin. Married Granddad before the Second War.'

'Sounds like a remarkable woman. I would like to know more about her. Now, if you'll excuse me, I must get ready for Grace's party.'

'She's fantastic,' Grace said as Gitte left. 'A great mathematician. Totally dedicated to running the project. I'd be lost without her. This way.' She directed him towards a small room around which were arrayed half a dozen wheat plants. The ears were thick and looked ready to harvest.

'This is it, Sam. "Perfect Wheat". This is what I've been working on. I've transferred in a gene from a strain of rice to enable it to survive drought stress, boosted the micronutrients, especially a massive increase in iron, and thrown in resistance to nematodes for good measure.' She pulled off a seed and picked away at the top of it, revealing a small piece of material the size of a pinhead. 'This is the embryo. I've manipulated it to switch on different pathways at different times in the plant's cycle, then shut them off again.'

'I thought that whatever DNA you inserted was switched on in the whole plant?'

'Not now. That's the joy of the new technologies. We can target different parts of the plant and switch DNA on when and where it's needed. Most of what you see in Perfect Wheat will be the usual commercial plant that turns up in bread the world over. But at certain crucial points it will generate different characteristics that will help feed people the stuff they need to be strong. This'll grow in the lowlands in Bangladesh. And it should be a good cash crop for export. They call this my Frankenwheat. It's more like Frankincense. A gift to set before God.'

Sam turned over the grains in his hand, feeling their rough surfaces.

'"And the Lord had regard for Abel and his offerings, but for Cain and his offering he had not regard."'

'What?' she asked.

'Genesis 4. The Lord was keen on Abel's fatted lamb, and not very on Cain's fruits of the earth.'

'Was that before or after Cain bumped off Abel?'

'Before.'

'Bit unfair.'

'Not necessarily,' he replied. 'The Lord was looking into Cain's heart, not at his work. It's why you do things that's important, not what you do.'

'Very impressive memory you have for the Old Testament.'

'You forget my dad was a Church of Scotland minister. And his father before him.'

She touched his hand. 'No. That's something it would be impossible to forget.'

The DJ cranked up the volume on the PA and the sound vibrated against the glass.

'Come on up to the House. Hal's longing to see you.'

Arm in arm they crossed the drive, then ducked down through a low entrance into the long living room that led to a red-and-white-tiled Edwardian veranda. This in turn opened onto a lawn that tumbled towards the river sparkling below. A large tent was pitched in which caterers were milling around finalizing the details of supper. A fireworks specialist was preparing the display that would crown the evening.

He whistled. 'Pushing the boat out.'

'Told you.' She grinned. 'Big, BIG, celebration.

41

Blowing the last of Mother's inheritance. Most of it went on the glasshouses and the experiment. Look, there's Hal.' Her brother was chipping at a massive wooden head he was carving from a large piece of oak. It was a bust of Grace, and captured her energy and humour. Hal turned and a lopsided grin spread on his face.

'Sam. It's good to see you.' All the 'S's were slurred. As they hugged, Sam recalled playing with Hal when he was a baby. He and Grace had changed his nappies more times than he could remember.

'See you later, I've got to dress.' Grace disappeared up the low set of stairs onto the terrace.

'I love the piece.' Sam ran his right hand across the intricate but muscular carving.

'Dunno. I think it's a bit literal. Should've cut something a bit more abstract. Cosmic.'

'But your sister's rooted in *this* world.'

'Sometimes a bit too much.' Hal looked thoughtfully at his work, then put down his tools. 'Drink?' he asked.

CHAPTER 7

Sam sat on a bed in the sloped attic room when a surge of emotion hit him. He had almost kissed Grace here. He had been twenty-two, fresh from a bad love affair, this time with a hypnotic but dangerous graduate student five years older than himself. Mad. Grace was rising eighteen and extraordinarily beautiful, but hid beneath baggy jerseys and even baggier trousers. She'd spent most of that summer on her own, riding, with occasional forays into Virginia Woolf, Sylvia Plath and, for reasons only a teenager would understand, P. G. Wodehouse.

He lay back on the bed hearing rich, romantic chords in his head. Ravel. They had been playing Ravel on the portable CD player whilst watching the sun burn out over White Hill. She had put her head on his chest and he had laced his fingers through hers. As shadows crept down the valley he had bent down to kiss her lips, then hesitated, fatefully. A half-second later, Hal had hammered on the door lisping at the top of his voice. 'I know what you're doing. I know what you're doing. I'm going to tell Father.'

They tumbled from the room and down the stairs to escape Henry's wrath. The moment broken, they felt foolish and awkward. He was angry with himself, realizing how young and vulnerable she was. The following day, he left for London and threw himself into his studies, calling Grace occasionally. When he returned to White Hill six months later, she was engaged to Freddie Delawney. She refused to tell Sam why she broke it off, but when she and Freddie met animosity still cracked in the room like electricity.

How many times had he played 'what if?' What if he hadn't hesitated? What if Hal hadn't banged on the door? What if he hadn't married on the rebound later that year? He had been reading Burns at the time and recalled the couplet that played on his mind for years to come:

> 'And mourn in lamentations deep,
> That *life* and *love* are but a dream.'

'Sam.' Grace knocked firmly on the door. He leapt to his feet.

'Coming.' He opened up and his heart raced. A short black jacket hugged Grace's body and her drainpipe trousers were tucked into short black velvet high-heeled boots.

'Time to party,' she said.

Hours later, Gitte waved to Sam as she drifted across the lawn towards the glasshouses. She was happier than she'd ever been. The years of hell had given way to a time of peace and she wanted to be alone with the seeds. Every night before going to bed, she spent time alone in the glasshouse – meditating and reading.

As she turned the corner, she expected to be challenged by the guards, but they were nowhere to be seen. Damn.

As Grace led her band into a rousing climax of 'Your Love Keeps Lifting Me Higher', the arsonists worked quickly, smearing napalm on the floor and lower walls of the seed room, piling charcoal on top, then positioning the makeshift detonator. In a few minutes, the building would be engulfed.

Gitte saw the shadows of three figures flickering in the glass. Who the hell? She ran to the door, pulled it open and shouted, 'What are you doing in here? Get out.'

'Fuck, it's the German bitch.'

'Get out. Get *out*,' she yelled, then spotted the burning charcoal. 'My God. What're you doing?' She grabbed the fire extinguisher, switching on the flood of foam and screaming for help.

'Shut her *up*, for Christ's sake.'

'Please join me outside for the fireworks,' Grace shouted into the mike and then jumped down from the makeshift stage.

She stood next to Sam and Hal, holding their hands as fireworks music boomed from giant speakers and the night sky exploded – rockets flooding the darkness and Catherine wheels throwing tangled spinning sweeps of sparks. Her face glittered with excitement. 'Where's Gitte?' she asked Sam. 'I want her with me.' She scanned the crowd.

'She told me she was going to check the seeds,' he replied. 'She'll be back in a second. It's a fab . . .' His words fell as he saw a tall security guard stumble across the lawn, then collapse, vomiting.

Sam ran to him. 'What's wrong?'

'Fire. The glasshouses are on fire,' he groaned. 'I think there's someone in there. A woman.'

'Gitte!' Grace shouted, then sprinted towards the house, reaching the first building just after Sam and screaming with anger and distress as the glass shattered and sheared. Peering inside, they saw sacks of burning seeds and beside them Gitte's body, curled in a foetal position, blood streaming from her head.

Sam plunged his jacket into the rainwater barrel, covered his head and crawled into the fire. The heat was intense and he could feel his skin singe and the acrid smoke tear at his eyes. Even on his belly, inching forward, his lungs were searing, burning. Blindly, he crawled along the floor, trying desperately to remember where she was, but he'd lost his bearing. Smoky tears flowed down his face as his mind screamed at him to retreat, to save himself.

His fingers groped ahead like blind crabs, feeling burlap, seed, matches. Where was she? Where *was* she? He held his breath for ten seconds – twenty, thirty. Dizzy. Getting dizzy. Got to go back. Got to breathe.

Suddenly Grace was beside him, desperately pulling a mask across his face and turning on a cylinder. As he sucked air into his lungs, she slipped goggles over his eyes. He saw a piece of the roof cracking, shearing, and tumbling towards them. Pushing Grace backwards, he spread his body across her and felt a thousand splinters cascade across his legs.

His hand made contact with flesh. Gitte. He grabbed Gitte's shoulders and with Grace's help hauled her towards the door, his jacket burning and the heat on his face unbearable. The next seconds felt endless as they stumbled hunchbacked across the room into the fresh air.

Grace dragged off her mask and vomited as Sam lifted Gitte and carried her towards the House.

'Oh, God, tell me she's OK. *Please.*' Grace came running alongside, pleading.

He placed Gitte on the ground, far from the flames, then felt for her pulse. At least she was breathing.

'Has someone called a doctor?' asked Sam.

'Chris. Where are you, Chris?' Grace yelled for her GP, a guest at the party.

'Here. I'm here, Grace. I've got an ambulance coming.'

As he knelt beside Gitte, Grace glanced back at the glass houses in bleak despair, and Sam watched Rod glaring at the collapsing buildings – transfixed by ecstasy.

47

CHAPTER 8

Malkie Collins stood by a trailing willow as Johnny Standish reeled in a flailing trout and killed it with a quick gesture. Even to Malkie's untutored eye, Standish looked as if he knew what he was doing. They'd been in business together for four years and Malkie never ceased to be surprised how many things his partner could do well. He could cook, paint, shoot and ski. And most of all, Malkie reflected, Johnny ran a money-laundering operation that he'd managed to keep hidden from the filth on both sides of the Atlantic. It still made him laugh. Hundreds of millions of dollars pouring out of Colombia, New York and Los Angeles and being spun through legitimate academic institutions – one in Brazil, the second in Italy, and now the third in England. Brilliant. Really brilliant. 'These days, an army of lawyers is more powerful than real soldiers,' Standish had told him not long after they hooked up.

Standish gazed out over the sluggish but clear river-waters of the Bain as the sun dipped towards the hills. He was lost in meditation. In contrast to Malkie's wiry, short, muscular frame, boxer's quick gestures, and sandy hair, Standish was tall, six two, his hair was white and his face thin, tanned and lifted. He looked ten years younger than the fifty registered on his birth certificate. He lived for moments like this. At peace. He wanted more of it.

'Perfect day,' he sighed. 'Just perfect. Don't you think?' Malkie had been thrilled the first time he heard Standish speak – he sounded just like all those American movie actors he'd loved when he was growing up – and it was only later, as Standish took him to the US on the occasional trip, that he began to understand that Standish's accent was shared mainly by members of his class, namely, people who went to Harvard and looked down on the Kennedys as Irish upstarts. Malkie knew that Standish's contacts made his double life possible.

'See this?' Standish asked, holding up his dry fly. 'It's a cinnamon sedge. Scientifically proved to be the number one fly for trout fishing.'

'I wouldn't know. There wasn't much fishing tackle in the Gorbals when I was growing up. The line would've been useful for pulling the gear up to the first floor, though.'

'You wouldn't like this sport, Malcolm. Far too slow for you.'

Malkie picked up the large umbrella and the picnic hamper. 'It's not that.' He shook his head. 'I just don't believe in killing things for pleasure.'

Standish wore an immaculate sweater, cap,

green jacket and boots. His hair was beautifully cut and fell in a floppy side parting.

'I agree with you, Malcolm.' He was the only one allowed to call him by his full Christian name. Malcolm had been his da's name. The bastard. 'You should always eat the things you kill,' Standish continued. 'Anything else is the act of a barbarian.' They walked back to the Range Rover and dumped the paraphernalia. 'And I'll cook a meal for you tonight that you'll never forget.'

As Malkie drove, he stole glances at Johnny, who had his eyes closed and was humming along to a Pet Shop Boys song. Killing Johnny would be hard. But the alternative was worse. I have to kill him because he is going to sell me out. He's going to give me up to the filth in return for amnesty. Johnny's Basque paymasters had made it clear to Malkie that when they gave the signal, either he killed Standish or they would assassinate him – and his family.

It mattered to Malkie that his actions were rational, not emotional. He had fought as a teenager and young man – all the way through two years in the army and three in Glasgow's notorious Barlinnie jail. His balled up anger was alternately fuelled and calmed by the drugs he had used until cleaning up his act eight years before.

His mind drifted to the time when the prison chaplain had dragged him to the Citizens' Theatre to see Marlowe's *Edward II*. He had been stunned by the performance; the king had been an all too credible mixture of arrogance, fragility and, at the end, dignity. Then, like the rest of the audience, he had shuddered at the final attack, when the assassins, aware of Edward's homosexuality, impaled him on a fire iron. His paymasters had demanded that Johnny should similarly suffer for his betrayal.

Malkie was infatuated with the theatre and when he left prison he bought dozens of videos. He locked himself in his office watching Gielgud, Olivier, Branagh, Welles. He loved Shakespeare's histories, especially *Richard III*, thought the comedies dull and *Lear* bemusing. Why would he give up his kingdom in the first place? Mad.

He glanced again at Johnny. Any move he made against him would have to be as subtle as if Johnny had planned it himself. Keep learning, his mother had told him. Life comes to a man who knows the world. During his years in prison for dealing ecstasy, Malkie had studied law and accountancy. When he left, he called in his debts. Using boxing contacts from the days when he was a pro, he started a security guard business that turned into a legitimate front for handling half the ecstasy consumed in central Scotland. It was then that he came to Standish's attention. Well, I've spent four years with a great teacher, he thought, and now I want my degree. And there are friends willing to pay for the graduation.

Malkie could taste the money. He had promised himself he would be worth five million by the age

51

of forty. And he had three years and two million to go. That would be enough. Then he'd bail out. Disappear with his wife and child. He glanced in the mirror at the Range Rover following them. Inside were two well-paid bodyguards. Each of them trained by some of the world's best security forces. He had been told that someone close to Standish had been turned by the Basque and would aid him in Johnny's assassination. But he had no idea whom. Malkie nodded in time to the music.

Both cars stopped at a towpath and all four jumped down onto a richly coloured canal boat. On the roof lay Raul Rodriquez, a lithe, athletic Spaniard in his late twenties. He wore a loose-fitting black shirt, blue slacks and black loafers. A book lay beside the blanket on which he rested – a Spanish translation of Hemingway. Malkie had a rudimentary grasp of Spanish, and translated the title, *For Whom the Bell Tolls*.

Raul stretched, his back muscles arching through the thin material, then rolled to his feet and stepped towards them. He kissed Standish tenderly on the lips.

'Nice time?' asked Standish.

'Hmm,' he replied, his English lightly accented, 'it's a beautiful day. I like England like this.'

'You remember Malcolm, Raul.'

Raul ignored Malkie's extended hand and headed down the hatch towards the kitchen.

'Still not forgiven you, Malcolm. He's a young man. Doesn't like humiliation.'

Malkie had been forced to shut Raul down one night in a bar, when the latter, high on coke and Scotch, had been boasting about 'business' to a friend. Standish had raised his eyebrows and Malkie had taken it as a sign to hustle the young man from the club. A scuffle had developed and Malkie had dropped him with one punch.

'Now, boys and girl. Chow time.' Standish unpacked the fish.

'Lottie, you're on 'erbs. I think some parsley, coriander and dill.' Lottie Grun had taught martial arts in the German Security Service. She was a lean redhead, with a strong face and profound black eyes. She moved gracefully to the cupboard, extracted the herbs and chopped them with speed and precision, the blade so close to her fingers it was impossible to believe she was not cutting them off.

'And Malkie. Given we're in jolly old England, I think we'll make fish and chips. You're Scottish. You practically live on the stuff. We'll entrust the task into your capable hands. Ah –' he accepted a martini – 'thank you, Raul.'

Standish handed the fish to a large white guy, who lifted a serrated blade from the counter and expertly gutted them. Louis Highfield had been an undercover drug enforcement officer in the US, and had probably killed at least fifteen dealers until he was dropped for sampling too much of the merchandise. He always left a calling card. He cut off his victim's tongue.

More than once he had performed this service on Standish's behalf.

Not that Johnny would acknowledge the deed, thought Malkie. Johnny insulated himself from all violence. He had never ordered a hit in his life. Nor would he discuss any operation in terms of the violent means used to achieve their ends. 'I'm just a businessman, Malcolm,' was his usual refrain. 'I'm providing a service. The quickest way to prison is through violence.'

It was a clever trick, the way Johnny identified the target without explicitly mentioning a name – a little comment here, an irritated snort there. It all added up to one thing. Sort it. Standish had only ever made one glancing reference to the dark actions his words unleashed. 'Never, ever hurt a civilian, Malcolm.' Malkie had always guarded against collateral damage, as the army taught him to call civilian deaths, and Johnny knew he would ignore any hint that he do otherwise. Malkie had severely reprimanded his guys for almost killing the German researcher. They would have brought the wrath of God on their head for a simple arson job.

Since prison, Malkie had worked hard to control himself. Sort out your temper, his da had told him when he'd lost his first boxing match for head-butting the opponent – a bit rich coming from the old man. Malkie's eyes turned hard, remembering the welts on his back the evening the police had arrested him for stealing lead from the school roof. His father had beaten him for getting caught and he hadn't been caught very often after that. And now his fury was under control; he'd learned to use it as a weapon, the way he had with his right hook when he was Scottish bantamweight champion. He unleashed his anger infrequently and only when he knew there was absolutely no alternative. There was no going back once the mist flooded his mind.

'You're lost in thought, Malcolm. Where are those fries?'

'Sorry, Johnny. Chips coming up. My ma's secret recipe.'

'And what was that?'

'Oil and potatoes.'

'I do love your sense of humour, Malcolm. Really, I do.'

After the meal, they sat on the deck drinking coffee. Malkie sipped camomile tea whilst the others savoured twenty-five-year old armagnac. First class all the way with Johnny. He had style. Malkie had to admit that. But, he was going to betray them, and would have to go. Downstairs on the Djinn vinyl deck Johnny had brought with him from New York, T. Rex belted out the choppy opening chords of 'Telegram Sam'. Johnny liked the soft, mushy tone of old albums more than the clinical sounds produced by CDs.

'Good stuff, that music,' Malkie said, drumming his fingers on his muscled thighs.

'Don't lie to me, Malcolm. You hate it. It's too camp for you. And we all know what you think about the gay life. Don't we, boys and girl?' Johnny blew out the smoke from his Monte Cristo. It almost made Malkie want to start smoking again. He loved those big Cuban cigars. But there was no point in going back. That expensive bloody therapist and the AA sessions had been for a reason. He wasn't returning to skag, and one thing always led to another. That was a mug's game as far as he was concerned. Staying off it had been the best thing he'd ever done. He'd made more money in each of the past four years than in his whole life, and now the big pay-day was coming. Below deck, Bolan hammered out 'Twentieth Century Boy'. Well, this was the twenty-first century, and it was up for grabs for anyone with the balls to take it.

'That was a long time ago, Johnny. I was brought up wrong. Taught to see difference as dangerous.' Malkie shrugged. 'People should follow whichever path they choose.'

'Very Zen.' Raul sneered into his brandy, then drew deep on the cigar and blew in Malkie's general direction. The smoke drifted off into the trees.

Malkie watched him lazily over his tea. It would take a lot more than Raul to send him over the edge.

'How's our situation shaping up?' asked Johnny. 'Has our German friend gone on a long research trip?'

Malkie nodded. Habermas had been stupid. And

greedy. Trying to play Standish off against some other company also trying to steal Grace Adams' data. Sometimes old-fashioned muscle was the only answer to a problem. Malkie had ensured four degrees of separation from the squad that pulled off the operation. But they still knew who gave the orders. And they knew better than to fuck up.

'And Dr Adams? She's a selfish girl, not sharing her work with the rest of the team. I wonder how we might persuade her to bring her research into the Centre now that she has had such an unfortunate accident with her glasshouses?'

'I think she's probably in the mood by now,' replied Malkie. 'I might have a wee word with her.'

Standish blew smoke into the sky, where it curled around the moon and drifted lazily into the darkness.

'I think that would be an excellent idea,' he said with his eyes closed.

CHAPTER 9

Burhan al Imam sat peacefully in his study in a tall house that overlooked London's Regent's Park. His long, elegant fingers held a fountain pen that scratched left to right across thick, creamy paper as he completed his last testament. He wrote in English to avoid misunderstandings when his intentions were finally revealed.

He loved the written word. As a development economist, his books had been praised around the world. But after fifteen years on the international lecture circuit, he had retreated to a modest house in the dusty city of Aleppo and written a three-volume history of Jerusalem. It had taken him ten years and had been universally praised for its scrupulous moderation and, in the end, hope. Finally, in his late sixties, he had turned to short stories and his intense miniatures spoke of desolation, loss and redemption. There were regular whispers that the Nobel committee intended to offer him the prize for literature – an honour that he would in any case refuse.

Western reporters spoke of his other-worldliness,

of his passion for the poor and the dispossessed. They compared him to Kahlil Gibran, which always brought a wry smile to his face when he read the interviews. The Lebanese, Gibran, was the only mystical Arab religious thinker the interviewers had heard of. Otherwise the Arab voice was that of Osama or Arafat – loud, strident, insistent, violent, bringing the wrath of Israel and the US on the heads of our children.

Few people penetrated his reclusive existence. He lived with his niece, a placid girl of nineteen who ran his household and ensured his work was undisturbed.

He placed the pen carefully on a blotter, then laced his fingers. Behind him, his library of books stretched to the high Regency ceiling.

'This must be the last time you come here, my friend. From today, we will communicate in code.' His voice was light and soft, barely more than a whisper. 'It will be based on this.' He passed over the paper. 'It's my last testament. There is no copy in existence. Have it translated into Sanskrit and then use every second letter, every second day as the basis for our code. Do you know Sanskrit? It is the mother of the world's oldest poetry.'

'Sadly, no.' Standish folded the paper and tucked it into his jacket.

'It will repay your study a hundredfold.'

Al Imam paused for a second, then dreamily quoted from the Upanishads,

'From the unreal lead me to the real!
From darkness lead me to light!
From death lead me to immortality.'

Standish studied him. He had first met the Syrian in Jerusalem twenty years before but had been extremely cautious when his old contact had called him out of the blue two years before to discuss his exciting new research on antioxidants in wheat. Slowly, the Syrian had revealed his hand. His contacts with the intellectuals who supported ETA ran deep and he played his hand carefully, treating Standish with respect, almost deference, as he plunged into the research provided by Standish's team. Then the Syrian dropped his bombshell.

Standish stood by the window watching a young woman in a smart blue suit – Prada, he guessed – stop by a tree and light a cigarette. It had taken the tobacco companies fifty years to own up that their products might cause slow agonizing death, and he wondered how long it would take for the GM agribusinesses to own up that one of their products was slaughtering a generation.

Al Imam smiled, then said, 'Do we have Dr Adams' work?'

'We have worked out a plan,' Standish turned back into the room, admiring its richly coloured rugs and restored cornices and pilasters. 'We should have her data within weeks.'

'And when will we have control of Aventis?' asked Al Imam.

Standish was advising a consortium of Saudi businessmen in a bid to gain control of the world's third largest agribusiness.

'I would say it will be yours very soon.'

Al Imam sipped thick, bitter coffee. 'No problems?'

'Not at the premium your people are offering.'

'Good. We need Aventis. "Perfect Wheat" is our Trojan horse and Aventis will sell our seeds into the breadbaskets of America and Europe.'

And the Syrian will make sure that the wheat is carcinogenic within two years, thought Standish. Give us this day our daily death.

'We will produce the bread of heaven,' said Al Imam, his face grave, his eyes filled with mixture of fear and hope. 'Do you trust your people?'

'Totally. Grace Adams is a clever woman, but I'm sending in someone much more sophisticated.'

'Good, Mr Standish. Excellent. There will be one hundred million dollars in payable bonds waiting for you in a hotel room in Manila once we have Dr Adams' research.'

They shook hands.

'It'll be soon,' said Standish. 'Trust me.'

CHAPTER 10

The following afternoon Malkie read a story to Lilly, his daughter. At four, she was blonde like Roni, her mother, and had the sunny and positive disposition that drew him to Roni in the first place. 'One more,' she pleaded as he finished a funny storybook about clever Polly and the stupid wolf.

'Sleep time, little one.' He inhaled her unique aroma of sandpit and Coco Pops. She was always exhausted by lunchtime and slept for an hour.

'One of *your* stories.'

He slipped from the large double bed she had commandeered from the spare room. She surrounded herself with Barbies, bears and assorted plastic cups, saucers and pans. 'No. I've got to work.'

'Per-lease.'

'No.' He grinned.

'*Please.*'

'You're a bully, Lilly. Budge up.' He sat with her head in the crook of his arm.

'Close your eyes.'

She screwed them tight.

'Once upon a time, in a deep dark forest near the highest mountain in the world, there lived a dragon and a wolf.'

'Nice dragon?' she asked.

'Nasty.'

'Was its name Lilly?' She loved appearing in the deep dark forest stories.

'No, Johnny.'

She opened her eyes and glanced up at him.

'It's Johnny,' he reiterated.

She thought for a second, weighing up the chance that Malkie might call off the story if she interrupted too much. 'It's a boy dragon, then?' she asked.

He nodded.

'That's different then. Johnny's a nice *boy's* name.' She shut her eyes and snuggled deeper into his arm.

'The wolf was called Malkie.'

Lilly smiled.

'And Malkie was an angry wolf. The dragon had stolen all the treasure and locked it up in the biggest cave at the top of the highest mountain in the whole wide world.'

'Nasty dragon,' she murmured.

'Very.' He thought for a second. 'Malkie and his friends wanted to get back what was rightfully theirs, so one night, while the dragon was at flying practice, they crept into his cave. They were astonished at the beautiful things in there – a golden phoenix, red rubies the size of footballs, silver plates that Malkie could see his face in.'

'Chocolate eggs?' she asked.

He kissed the top of her head. 'And all the chocolate eggs in the world.'

'*Very* nasty dragon.'

'Very,' he agreed, and continued: 'But the wolves ignored all the lovely things, because what they really wanted was the dragon's magic dust. Without it, the dragon couldn't make fire come out of his mouth, and without flames in their tummies dragons can't fly. The wolves searched for hours and hours, and then they could hear the dragon coming back, its big wings beating the air outside.'

'Oh, no. Don't hurt the wolves, Daddy.'

'Malkie and the other wolves slunk back into the shadows as the dragon came over to inspect its treasure. Then, looking around, it sniffed the air, trying to detect strangers. Malkie and the others were protected, though. They had bathed in the magic stream.'

She smiled in relief.

'Then the dragon pressed his paw against the wall and out popped a chalice full of magic dust.'

'What's a chalice?'

'It's like a big silver Lilly cup.' He indicated a large plastic beaker filled with apple juice. 'And then the dragon put it back and went to sleep on top of all his lovely, stolen things. In the middle of the night, shivering with fear, Malkie edged very, very slowly across the wall and climbed up next to the dragon's huge red scaly body. Its right eye was wide open!'

'Daddy.' She gave him a warning look. All the stories had to end well.

'But that was all right because dragons are only ever awake when they have *both* eyes open.'

She settled again. He glanced at his watch. One thirty. He needed to fill Johnny in about his plans for Grace. He had better wrap this up.

'Malkie stole the chalice. When morning came, the wolves attacked the dragon and forced him out of the cave and down towards the big swamp. The dragon tried and tried to fly, all the time screaming and crying. It blundered into the muddy water and began to sink.'

'Did the dragon die, Daddy?'

'Oh, yes.'

She grinned. 'Good.' She turned over and drifted off to sleep.

CHAPTER 11

Two days later, Grace stopped her old black Toyota at the security gates of the EA Science Park and remembered when all that had been there was some scrubby setaside. She admired what Sophia Mortimer, the new Vice-Chancellor, had pulled off since she'd taken over from Henry. Fifteen companies on the cutting edge of the high-tech industries had clustered together with the University's Computing and Software departments on this empty patch of land. It helped that there were two motorways fifteen minutes away, tucked helpfully behind the low Wold hills, and a local airport that could accommodate private planes and helicopters.

The Glaswegian security guard tapped on her window. She zipped it down. 'Hello, Dr Adams. I'm sorry for your trouble.' He knelt beside her door, his strong, milk-white face impassive. 'I'm ashamed that it was our guys guarding you.'

'Are they OK?'

'Got their marching orders and a kick on the backside. Quite right, too. Drinking on duty. They claimed that one of the waiters had brought them a beer with your compliments. Bloody unprofessional, if you ask me.'

The fire brigade report was due in that day, but off the record they had already told her that it was arson. Looked as if a homemade incendiary had gone off. Sam had told her he recognized the approach – activists of some kind.

'The reporter on local radio says you intend to replant the wheat. Good luck and have a nice one.' She had been bullish with the interviewer, but she felt less than confident that she could raise the money to proceed with the experiment. She was wiped out. Her phone rang.

'Grace. It's Sam. How're you doing?'

'Been better.' She glanced in the mirror at her ragged hairstyle; she had managed to get most of the singed bits off. Apart from the cut on her left cheek, she looked OK. 'But I'm fine, really.'

'And Gitte?'

'Not bad considering. She's out of hospital. Bit shocked, as you would expect.'

'The local CID says that she was attacked and passed out. When she woke up outside the glasshouse she tried to rescue the wheat.'

'You don't know how much it means to her, to us. I'd've done the same thing. How're you?' she asked.

'Doctor says I'll never play the saxophone again.'

'That's lucky.'

He laughed. 'Seriously, Sam. I can't thank you enough.'

'I'm sorry I couldn't stay longer. There are some problems here.'

'I understand, honestly. Can you come up here soon? I want to take you out for dinner.'

'Will do. Call me if you need to talk. Trauma creeps up on you quietly. Don't bottle things up as you usually do. See you.'

She stepped from her car and took a deep breath of crisp morning air, trying to avert her gaze from the Standish glasshouses and other people's experiments. She would've finished her preparatory work months before if only they'd supported her. It's all about money – bloody money, just because she would not assign them her patents. They had even tried to bribe her by offering to set up an independent company in which she would be a shareholder. She knew that several of her colleagues were paper millionaires on similar deals. Christ, she was giving Standish fundamental theoretical work on the wheat genome, building the ultimate clickable computer model that would tell them the innermost secrets of one of the world's most commercial crops. *Wasn't that enough?*

She'd been tempted to leave the previous year, when they'd turned her grant application down for the second time. And yet, she knew she had to stay. She needed access to the computing, to the worldwide support network of biochemists, biologists, ecologists and ethologists. And she needed her salary to support Gitte. She looked at her battered car in some disgust. Sam had introduced her to fast cars when they were growing up and it had been one of her great pleasures when coming back to the UK to buy something to burn up the motorway. But she'd had to sell her beloved MG to pay for the down-payment on the cooling unit. God, I *miss* that car, she thought as she turned towards the domelike building.

When she reached her workstation, she adjusted the Mac, tidied her desk, and fiddled with the bunch of Casablanca lilies Sam had sent. *Hope you enjoy the Lilium speciosum*, read the card. She smiled, recalling their first meeting, when she had been pompous about the Latin name of a plant. How she had wanted to fall in love with him. Then Freddie Delawney had turned up, with his flattery, his extraordinary good looks, expensive dope, charming, feckless friends and endless parties, and she had fallen for it.

Although they were second cousins, she had seen little of Freddie when they were growing up. He had been at school or with cousins in Scotland. And his father had not approved of Henry, calling him 'that teacher'. Henry, for his part, had despised the insular county set, with their endless talk of horses, horticulture and Highgrove, and pointedly ignored the infrequent invitations from Eastfield's mansion.

With Sam in retreat and Henry at his most bitter, Freddie had been an explosion of pleasure in her life. They had met when she went up to Cambridge, he was in his final year and she was little Miss Country Mouse comes to town. It had taken her six months to see the emptiness of their relationship. Then when Freddie, coked out of his head, staggered in after a party and tried to rape her, she walked out. They never talked of the past. He never apologized or tried to explain.

Freddie's older brother, Andrew, had died in a car accident and Freddie had inherited the title then married Hope. Grace had tried to talk her sister out of it, but the pull of the House, the title, and Freddie's beauty had been too much for her. Even now, she would not divorce the rat no matter what he did. Couldn't leave it all behind. Good to his kids, though. Grace had to admit that. And he poured effort into the estate and as far as she knew no longer took drugs. Perhaps even bastards grow up. Eventually. Pity he was so vehemently against her wheat. It was another bone of contention between the two sides of the family.

Grace swivelled on her chair and picked up Hal's carving of a sheaf of 'Perfect Wheat'. It was beautiful and detailed and she stroked its delicate curves, then put it down and fired up her Mac. The case was still scratched from the thief's attempt to steal her hard disk. She guessed it had to be Kurt Habermas, although no one could pin anything on him. Whoever had been here had been using someone else's card, had worn gloves and disabled the security camera. Although there were no fingerprints, Habermas had means and motive. He had tried to move in on her the second he arrived from the University of Berlin. She knew of his reputation, brilliant when young, burnt out at forty, but still capable of flashes of genius. He, too, was working on the clickable plant project, trying to unlock the mysteries of DNA, of the pathways in the genome. They had the map, now they were trying to understand the journey. He had tried to draft her on to his team. But because she was doing theoretical work she wanted to work alone. It suited her, she explained to Helen James, her dry stick of a boss, and Helen, for once, had backed her. It helped that Habermas had made a barely disguised attempt to steal James' job from under her nose.

Last month Habermas had been banished from the Standish buildings and then from the Park altogether as his behaviour had become more and more intolerable. She ran her finger across the beautifully designed transparent casing of the Mac. Yep. Had to be Habermas. The police had been round to his rented house in Garton, but there had been no sign of him – he must've gone to ground, probably back in Germany annoying the hell out of some other research team.

She was typing up fund-raising options when the phone rang. She stabbed the speaker button.

'Grace Adams.'

'Stefano Violi here.' It was Standish's new Head, who she had only briefly been introduced to at his inaugural party. He had an extraordinary reputation as a researcher and, she had to admit, was pretty easy on the eye. He was the same height as her, with a thick shock of black hair and large brown eyes. She had read his biography in the university magazine. He was forty-five and had been a rising star at Harvard before being poached by Standish to run his research institutes. This was his third. He had been brought in when the previous director resigned without explanation.

'I've heard about your shocking loss,' he said. 'Violence on that scale is appalling. These people don't seem to realize that behaviour like that is on a par with Nazis burning books.'

'You've got that right,' she replied with feeling.

'Can you spare me ten minutes? I've a proposal to put to you.'

'Sure. When?'

'Now. My office.'

She stared at the wheat.

'Sure.'

CHAPTER 12

Johnny Standish's smile flashed as he stared at a picture of Lilly playing with another child. She was the only chink in Malcolm's armour. The man was fearless when it came to his own safety.

As he threw the Polaroid into the fire and watched it shrivel, he reflected on the dangers posed by his clever and increasingly powerful number two. Not only am I playing off three government agencies across two continents, Malcolm has a deep suspicion that I intend to sell him out. I can see it in his eyes. Standish knew that knowledge might have come from his primary paymasters, the Euskadi Ta Askatasuna, the violent Basque independence movement whose name meant 'Basque Country and Liberty'.

Standish's relationship with ETA went back twenty years and he had made them a great deal of money for their revolution. He had long shared their intense desire for liberty and their violent credo that freedom was to be taken, not given.

He had moved to Bilbao when he ran from his privileged upbringing. He'd had enough of private schools and colleges and life lived on the scale of a postage stamp and disappeared from Harvard before the end of his first term as a freshman. His journeys took him to Colombia as a journalist, where he provided covert financial support for various revolutionary factions. Then, when the police gave him no alternative, he fled to the Basque country, where his new friends in ETA put his talents as a spy and drug runner to good use.

But now he wanted out. He needed to be at peace with himself – to disappear and never be found. But no matter how careful he had been about his exit strategy, he knew there was always someone who would leak. It was impossible to coordinate the CIA, MI6 and the GEO, Spain's Anti-Terrorist Police, without some informer leaking to his pay-masters in ETA, or their friends among dissident Irish republicans. That's why he had his cover and his counter-bluff. If his plans failed, he would tell the Basque that his approach to the security agencies had been to draw out a traitor. Malcolm would take the fall. Afterwards, it would be a challenge to make his contacts in ETA continue to trust him.

As he peered into the fire, he weighed the risk that they would simply track down and assassinate him for his breach of security; then his thoughts turned, as they did most days, to the Syrian and the biggest pay-off he had ever seen. The Syrian was offering enough untraceable cash for him to escape beyond the reach of the most dedicated assassin.

He could barely allow himself to recall the Syrian's name, let alone commit it to paper. A bead of sweat ran down his back. The man's vision operated on a grand scale. 'The West will choke on its own greed,' the Syrian had told him. 'And *our* civilization will once again be its equal. Then we shall reveal our courage, our wisdom – our renaissance. We will show the depth of our culture and of our people.'

Standish smiled, grimly. The West deserved its fate. Not that he intended to share it.

He sipped Montrachet as he surveyed Eastfield House's smoking room. A dozen comfortable chairs circled two sofas and above the fireplace was a large painting of three of Delawney's dogs attacking a pheasant. High bay windows allowed a golden light to play gently across crystal, glass and ormolu. The thing he liked about the English display of wealth was the lack of ostentation. Things that would be the object of adoration in New York or Boston were scattered around like so much bric-à-brac. Glancing references could be made to the historical provenance of possessions, but only as an assertion of their emotional wealth. Only when in financial trouble did the English aristocrats' teeth appear as they negotiated with Christie's and the government about exporting large parts of England's inheritance.

In the great square hall hung dozens of paintings of Freddie Delawney's ancestors. The house looked in a lot better condition than it had the first

75

time he had seen it, four years before. Then it had been faded and crumbling, with leaks in the roof and buckets on the floor. Freddie had done well out of drugs.

Delawney swept in wearing an old tweed jacket over a frayed shirt, the collar rumpled at the back. His tie was thin and green and his baggy cords were well worn, as were his brown brogues. His thick hair tumbled down over a ruddy face that hauntingly retained the memory of a beautiful young man. Delawney thrust his mane back as he stuck out a vigorous hand.

'Good to see you again, Johnny. Take a seat.' He motioned vaguely to a three-seat sofa whilst he threw a couple of logs on the fire. 'Bloody cold for the time of year,' he moaned. 'Never get the bloody wheat going at this rate.' Standish knew that on his large organic farm Delawney grew wheat and barley. He also had a prize herd of beef cattle, praised for the texture of their meat. Free-range geese, duck and hens had the run of the pond a quarter of a mile from the house.

Delawney poured a glass of wine, took a gulp, then slumped into a long, comfortable armchair by the fire that seemed to fit around him like an old handmade shoe.

'Have you heard from Malcolm recently?' Standish asked.

'Good God, no. Collins keeps to himself. Very secret squirrel, is old Malkie. Good man, though. Good man.'

Standish could smell a side-deal between Malcolm and Delawney, but could make no sense of it. It had nothing to do with the cocaine they had collectively been importing using a combination of Eastfield students and Delawney's organic food company. But he needed to know the details as further insurance. He knew better than to spook Delawney who, for all his bluster, was terrified of prison and disgrace.

'When is your baby due?'

Delawney smiled. 'Today.'

Standish could hear children on the lawn outside and Delawney walked across to the window and waved.

'It's like getting a kick in the gut, every time you see your children growing up. It's the most powerful emotion there is. I'm looking forward to having a boy. We're going to call him Hesketh.' He turned back to Standish. 'I feel an almost moral necessity to hand this place over to young Hesketh in better nick than it came to me. Two sets of death duties in one year crippled the place. You see?'

Most interesting justification of drug running that I've ever heard, Standish mused, but, then again, was it so different from ETA, the IRA or the UDA selling drugs to pay for a murderous fight for their homeland? Wasn't that about the next generation? Our blood, our land, our people. And the peasants who sold the opium did so for no other reason than to protect and feed their children. I'm the only childless figure in the chain

77

and I sell drugs because people want them. I'm no different to McDonald's or mining companies, or automobile manufacturers, and yet the CIA is not hounding the executives who run these companies. They're allowed to live their lives unmolested, he thought bitterly. Well, the Syrian intended to take the fate of the West into his hands and Gold Card citizens would not live in their comfortable worlds for long.

'Are you staying for lunch? Chicken soup and crusty bread with apple tart to follow. Everything's pure. No pesticides used round here.'

'You forget, I sponsor gene technology at the Standish Centre no more than five miles from your home.'

'That's an evil thing, Johnny. GM crops are poison. Virtual poison.'

Standish smiled at him. How can this man live such a compartmentalized life? He's selling drugs to subsidize his house and lands, and yet he has the gall to lecture me on genetic research.

'I'm afraid I can't wait for lunch. I just wanted to tell you there's a little gift waiting for you in Brazil.' He had just deposited two hundred thousand pounds in Delawney's account as his cut of the payment for their last shipment.

Delawney walked across to the wine and poured his glass to the brim.

'Isn't it about time I had a pay rise? Workman worthy of his labour and all that.'

'What did you have in mind?'

'An additional ten per cent.'

Standish's eyes turned hard and Delawney stepped back.

'Negotiable. It's negotiable. Maybe seven and half?'

'I'll think about it.'

'You do that.' Delawney's eyes briefly flashed and Standish could see the bully lurking behind. Standish almost regretted agreeing to Malcolm's idea of hooking him into their scheme. But who was going to believe that an organic food company would be a front for a world-class drug-running chain? It appealed to his sense of irony.

'Give Malcolm my regards.' Standish shook his hand. 'Oh, by the way, how is your old friend Alfred Halliwell? I haven't heard from him in a while.'

Delawney's features sagged into crags that would shape his face when older. If he ever got that far.

CHAPTER 13

Grace waited outside Violi's office on the top floor of the building. He had a corner location and she could see the hills sweeping down into the valley. The river twisted and turned, cutting a slithering pattern into the landscape, before gathering itself into an estuary and being absorbed by the sea. She shaded her eyes and searched for White Hill Farm. Yes. There it was, abutting the outer reaches of the wood that separated it from the Science Park. And beyond that Eastfield House.

She studied a large painting on the wall. A timeless Italian square, the moment frozen, empty. She was sure it was a Chirico. It must've set Standish back at least a couple of million – the kind of money that would fund her research for years.

The door opened and Violi appeared. He looked at her for a moment, seemingly perplexed she was there. There was an awkward silence and she was about to introduce herself when an open smile lit up his face, illuminating its handsome, sculpted contours.

'Dr Adams.' He pulled the door wider and

stepped back. 'Come in. Come in. I'm delighted to meet you again. I've heard so much about you and your work.' His American accent still retained echoes of Italian. She recalled that he had been brought up in Palermo until his teens and then sent to stay with an uncle in New York.

'Please sit.' He pointed at a long blue sofa and she sank into its cushions. The room was huge and light, with corner picture windows to the south and west. There were at least a half-dozen more significant canvases and sculptures. Was that a Pollock?

'Tea? Coffee?'

'No, thanks.'

He turned to his PA, who had followed them into the room. In her early forties, she was beautiful in a Californian-blonde way, and dressed in a well-cut suit. 'Double espresso for me, Julie. Thank you.'

He took a seat across from Grace, put his hands together as if in prayer, then bumped his fingers on his lips as Julie put the coffee on the table, with a warm smile for Grace.

'Thanks, Julie. Kind of you,' he said as she closed the door behind her.

Grace noticed a buff folder on the table beside the elegant white coffee cup. It had her name written in large letters across the top, and her photograph neatly clipped to the side.

'I can't believe you are happy with us, Dr Adams. We have not treated you properly.'

She almost fell from the sofa in surprise. He

raised his cup to his lips, regarding her with his large, warm, tawny-brown eyes through the wisps of steam.

'I . . . In what sense?' Was he about to terminate her? Her stomach churned.

'If I were you, I wouldn't stay here.'

Oh, God. Here it comes.

He tugged at his left ear with his thumb and forefinger, never for one second taking his eyes from her. She held his gaze, then decided to tell the truth.

'Yes. It's true. I have been unhappy. I came here because I'd heard that Standish was well known for supporting state-of-the-art research.'

He nodded.

'And yet you didn't want to support the "Perfect Wheat" project.'

He flipped open the folder, ran his finger down her previous application form, studying it intently, then looked up and held her increasingly hostile and hurt stare. 'As I understand the situation,' he replied, 'we agreed to fund the work, in return for the patent and the right to exploit the wheat through our commercial companies.'

'But that was missing the point,' she said. 'The reason I came back from Bangladesh, and the reason I stay here rather than helping families there, is because I want the wheat to be made available at the lowest possible cost. I want the research out there. Not locked up by some patent.'

'Hmm. I admire your idealism, Dr Adams.' He

82

smiled again, laughter lines creasing around his eyes. 'But I wonder if you have quite thought through the many options open to you.' He rubbed the side of his nose, then reached over to a pack and extracted a thin cigar.

'D'you mind?'

There was a universal no smoking policy in the Centre. Either he hadn't heard of it, or he was ignoring it.

'No.' She forced a smile.

'It's a disgusting habit, and I keep meaning to quit.' He leant back in the chair, a sense of satisfaction settling over him. 'My father smoked these all his life.' The smoke lifted and gathered around the ceiling, motes dancing through it. 'Still alive at eighty. Extraordinary man. I ration myself to three a day.'

He stood and her eyes followed the line of his beautifully cut black jeans and blue open-necked shirt. Now what? Violi riffled through some files on his ash-wood desk.

'Ah,' he muttered to himself. 'Good. Here they are.'

He returned to his seat and passed her two pamphlets. 'Have you heard of the Global Seed Development Project?'

'No.'

'I'm not surprised, really. It was only established at the turn of the year.'

'I've been a bit preoccupied,' she replied.

He grinned again, that same disarming, open

gesture. 'It's a small research fund and could be right up your street. They are prepared to finance fundamental crop work. Johnny Standish pulled together a group of ten individuals, each of whom pledged ten million dollars to the fund. It will exist for no more than ten years. Some people call it the 3-Cube project, for obvious reasons. Three times three. Investors times dollars times years equals success.'

Her head was spinning at the scale of the money involved.

'Although I would like you to believe that this is purely philanthropic, I'm afraid that is only partly true. It is also a complex tax-avoidance scheme dreamed up by Standish's lawyers. Nonetheless the money will do good and that's the important thing.'

'Why haven't I heard of this fund before?'

'It's very much word of mouth. The men and women behind it don't want too much publicity in case the IRS decides to change its mind.' His laugh was delightful, rich. 'But there is no secret. It has a closed Web site and once a year the recipient of a grant gets to meet either the donor or a nominee at a dinner. They take a very personal interest in the work.'

'And you think they could give me some help?'

He leant back in the chair, folded one leg over the other and waved his cigar like a conjuror.

'I'm certain of it.'

CHAPTER 14

As his boss stomped into his office, Sam quickly shuffled a report under a pile of memos on his low glass coffee table.

'You should get yourself a proper bloody desk,' Ian Trevor said. He thumped down onto the black Conran sofa Sam had installed when he'd thrown out his predecessor's large desk and assortment of hard wooden chairs. 'A bit poncy, all this stuff.' Trevor waved a dismissive hand.

Let's not start that again, Sam thought. 'I like people to be comfortable in my office, not sitting to attention all the time.'

Trevor's eyebrows scuttled upwards. 'I'm sure you know what you're doing. But in my experience people like to know where they stand.'

Yep, right in front of *you*. Sam smiled, then replied, 'If I feel that my sofa is compromising my command and control responsibilities, I'll immediately replace it with something more appropriate. I will, of course, ask your advice.'

Trevor scrutinized Sam's face for irony and finding nothing but a thoughtful smile, changed the subject. 'How's the security for the conference?'

Trevor was President of the European Association of National Criminal Services and was angling for the part-time post of director after his retirement. He had set up a major conference on 'anti-terrorist security in the twenty-first century' and had called in a lot of Sam's contacts. And he was relying on Sam to organize security.

'I'm looking forward to it,' Sam replied. 'Be good to see some old friends.'

He wondered how to respond to the PM's request that he move to Paris to take over the new European Anti-Terrorist Unit. He had so much to prove here – to himself above all. And then there was Grace.

Trevor crossed his thighs and his eyebrows settled into a bridge across his nose.

'The conference is going to take a lot, and I mean a *lot*, of organizing. Providing protection for Europe's top coppers on top of everything else means I'm going to be a bit preoccupied for the next few weeks. I don't want anything, and I mean *anything*, going pear-shaped around here.'

Sam maintained his thoughtful nodding and Trevor ploughed on.

'I know you're new around here, but your predecessor has left everything working pretty ticketyboo. And I like it that way. None of your grandstanding necessary. Time to buckle down to some real work. Running things well and being a great manager is the most important thing you can learn in this job. Keep it steady over the next few months, Sam, and I'll make sure that you're in the running to succeed me. But you've got to earn it. Understand? Your golden bollocks status can only take you so far. You help me; I'll help you. Do we understand each other?'

Sam smiled. 'Totally, Ian. Expect my absolute concentration on making the Squad look well managed.'

Trevor paused as he rose. Again, his shrewd eyes probed for mockery. 'Good lad.' He lumbered from the room.

Sam exhaled. Have I made a mistake taking this job? He'd been talked into applying by many of his colleagues and by the Chairman of the NCS. But it was a different world from the operational role he'd loved with Scotland Yard's Anti-Terrorist Branch. If the PM stuck to his timetable, Sam would have to make his mind up about the new job in a few weeks. He would be back on the front line. He parked the thought for another day, then pulled the file from beneath the mountain of memos. He'd asked one of his boys in Garton to get up close on the investigation.

Attack on Dr Adams' Glasshouse
The attack is clearly arson. It showed all the hallmarks of an extremist group. The bomb's signature suggests the Animal Liberation Front or some anarchist group.

Sam scratched on the side of the paper in red ink.

Yes, but anyone could have copied the mechanism off the Web. Do we have opportunity?

The report continued.

> *There are three possible means by which the bomb was planted:*
>
> *(a) By a guest at the party,*
> *(b) By a security guard,*
> *(c) By a person or persons unknown who slipped through the security cordon.*
>
> *We have checked the guest lists. A smattering of memberships of Greenpeace or similar legitimate organizations in their past. (Including Dr Adams herself.) But nothing on the surface to suggest alliances with extremist groups.*

Sam wrote: *MUST DIG DEEPER.*

The investigating officer noted:

> *The Earl of Eastfield has, of course, led protests in the past and is a vocal opponent of his sister-in-law's work, but has never been involved in terrorist activity.*

More scribbling. *ALWAYS A FIRST TIME.*

> *The security guards are from a firm with a good track record. Nothing to suggest they are dodgy. They have sacked the guards in question. We have both men under surveillance, but nothing*

untoward as yet. No major movements in or out of their bank accounts. Police interviews and the examination results on the drugs in their bloodstream support their claim that they were doped.

FAKED IT? CHECK OUT SAFE AND SOUND, THE SECURITY FIRM. WHAT ABOUT TIM ALLEN, THE SECURITY GUARD?

Seems most likely that it was a stranger. Drugged the guards. Did the glasshouse.

Sam gazed into the middle distance, then quickly noted – *TOO SOPHISTICATED FOR OUT-SIDERS. NEEDED TO KNOW TOO MUCH. INSIDE JOB.*

Sam slipped the note back into a folder, then extracted another sheet of paper.

Preliminary Report on
Rodney Charles Leadsmith

Rodney Charles Leadsmith (40), Hanging Wood Farm, Earl's Langley, Lincolnshire.

Convictions: Traffic violations. Tax evasion. Both minor. Tax paid off.

Financial situation: Close to bankruptcy two years ago. Seems to have recovered. Bank manager happy with the business plan for the farm.

Politics: Broadly Conservative. Anti-Europe, pro-hunting. Very pro-organic farming. Invited to Highgrove several times to meet the Prince of Wales. Joined the picket outside Dr Adams' farm six months ago. Is a frequent visitor but has a reputation as a non-violent moderate.

NOT WHAT I SAW IN HIS EYES, wrote Sam. *NOT AT ALL.*

CHAPTER 15

Grace and Gitte had set up office in her mother's cramped attic study. It was filled with her mother's design books and garden magazines and the roof slanted sharply down at the far wall. But it was quiet, and they wanted to be out of Henry's way. He never came into this room. These days he spent a lot of time on the hills, sometimes sleeping in an old hut in the woods.

Light drifted in from the skylight and illuminated Gitte's bandaged face. She was seated on a frayed Persian rug, her legs crossed in a half-lotus; her white T-shirt, two sizes too big, was pulled over her knees and her long green trousers were tucked into black DM boots.

Grace sat at the computer filling in the application form for the seed development fund, 3 Cube.

'I don't like it, Grace.'

'I'm not thrilled myself, babe. But I can't think of any other way of getting started again. We're totally out of cash.'

'Can't Henry help?' Gitte asked, biting the edge of her bottom lip.

Grace shook her head. 'He's living on a retired academic's pension. His book royalties have pretty much dried up. Besides, you remember he didn't want me to do the project in the first place. It was only because Hal backed me up that I managed to force it through the trust's management committee.'

The farm and the house were managed by a trust, of which Grace, Hope and Hal were beneficiaries. Each had equal voting rights. Henry had been explicitly cut out of her mother's will after the divorce and had no control. When Hal had reached sixteen, Grace had insisted that he was included in the trust, despite the fact that the house had been her mother's. Grace and Henry had talked Hope into it with the promise that the farm and its buildings would revert to the Eastfield heir if Hal and Grace died without having children. White Hill House had belonged to the Earls of Eastfield for three centuries, until 1910, when it was sold for death duties to a cousin, Grace's great-grandfather. Recently, Freddie Delawney had made several offers to buy it back, but the Adamses had no intention of selling.

Grace continued. 'What money Henry had, he ploughed into the house when I came back from Bangladesh. I can't be sure what he's got in the bank. He never talks about money, and I would never ask.'

She turned back to her portable Mac and the keys clacked rapidly as she filled in the electronic form. Stef had told her to email it to Julian Porter, the Director of 3-Cube, who was planning to be in London in a few days. Stef had phoned an hour before to say that he was going to talk personally to Porter to speed up 3-Cube's response. He had no doubt that they'd say yes.

She'd weighed up the need to secure the grant against the secrecy she required to protect the research.

'I'm not sure I can go back into a structured institution, Grace. I . . .'

Grace swivelled round and knelt beside Gitte, hugging her close.

'We're in this together. *We* know why we're doing it. They won't undermine us. But unless we try this fund, we're a busted flush.'

She lifted Gitte's head.

'I need you,' Grace said. 'The work needs you. We must be strong.'

Gitte's smile was tender, troubled, but resigned. She rubbed her eyes. 'I'm being pathetic.' She levered herself to her feet. 'Let's get this application finished. What shall we say about the real source of the recombinant DNA?'

'As little as possible.'

CHAPTER 16

Malkie picked up the bottle of vodka from beside the chair on which his wife, Roni, was slumped. It was seven o'clock in the morning and on the stereo U2 blared out 'I Still Haven't Found What I'm Looking For'. Roni was addicted to the song.

Malkis stroked her gentle face, coarsening as the alcoholism gripped, then kissed her forehead.

'I'm fine,' she mumbled.

I used to know how to make you laugh, he thought. How could I have forgotten how to do that? Soon, we'll get out. Go somewhere warm. Buy a house with a stream running by. You, me and Lilly. No one else. I'll make it happen. There can be happy endings.

He carried her to bed. As she crawled under the duvet, blocking out the hazy morning sunlight, he went into the kitchen to make her a cup of weak tea. As it brewed, his mobile buzzed.

'It's me,' a slurred, electronically disguised voice crackled.

'I guessed,' Malkie replied. 'Who else sounds like a Dalek?'

94

'Don't fanny around,' the voice hissed. 'We've got problems.'

'Do you mean *we* or you?'

'Same thing.'

Oh, I don't think so, thought Malkie. 'What's the issue?' he asked.

'Mole.' They had adopted a name code drawn from *The Wind in the Willows* in case their calls were being monitored. Malkie was Ratty, Delawney was Toad. Mole was their financial expert, Alf Halliwell.

'What's wrong with him?'

'His conscience.'

'Troublesome thing consciences. I subscribe to St Augustine. "Make me good, Lord, but not yet."'

'Yes, yes.' The voice was impatient. 'What are we going to do about it?'

'You mean what am I going to do about it?' Malkie replied.

'Same thing,' said Toad.

Oh, I don't think so, thought Malkie. I don't think so at all.

CHAPTER 17

Grace closed her eyes, allowing the model of wheat pathways to play around in her mind; searching for entries, light at the end of tunnels. Something was tantalizingly close. The walls of her cubicle had disappeared and she was afloat on pure speculation. Free. She wore sound-reducing headphones, blotting out the rest of the Standish team as they set about their work. Where? Where?

She started in shock as someone tapped her insistently on the shoulder and pointed at her ringing phone. She took off her headphones and picked it up.

'Grace. Good to hear from you. It's Alf Halliwell.'

She pictured him last time they had spoken. A stout man, with thin, sandy hair and fine hands. His nose was bleeding from Henry's punch. Alf and her mother had been friends of a sort and he'd helped in the garden when Henry had first disappeared. He had tried but failed to get them to call him Uncle Alf all those years ago.

'I'm so sorry about Henry, Alf.'

'Not your fault, love. What's between your dad and me is our business. And thanks for the letter. It was kind of you to pretend to be him. But I know *he'd* never apologize.'

'I, well . . .'

'Listen,' he said. 'I need to talk to you about your bloody wheat.'

'Why?'

'Don't replant it, love.'

'What?'

'For your own sake, don't. For the sake of your family. It's too dangerous. And there are things you don't understand.'

'What are you talking about?' What can he mean, 'the family'? All the death threats are aimed at me.

'Look, I must see you somewhere. Do you know the Whistle and Flute?'

'Isn't that in the Garton shopping centre? That's ten miles away.'

'Would you meet me there at twelve? What's your mobile number?' She gave it. 'Wait outside the pub,' he said. 'I'll phone you, then pick you up in my car. We'll go somewhere quiet and have a chat.'

'But . . .'

'Please, Grace.'

'OK. Twelve it is.'

Grace glanced at the pendulum clock in the middle of the shopping centre and pulled her leather jacket tight. She was cold and the wind whipped through the post-modern alleyways thrown up in the 1980s. She glanced at the buildings around her. What would've been a fine architectural joke when executed in marble in the City felt absurd and horrible when rendered in concrete in a struggling shopping area. Still, struggling was better than drowning. The town was doing a lot better than it had. New money was beginning to lift the economy and although all she could see were chain stores, restaurants, pubs and fast-food joints, it was better than the decaying 1960s hole that had been here before. *Where was Alf?* He had given her the creeps.

She tried his office again.

'I'm sorry, Ms Adams,' the PA replied tersely. 'I've tried his mobile, but there's no response. Could you call back this afternoon?' Grace wondered how often she had to cover for Alf. He and Henry had been known to take the occasional five-hour lunch.

Her mobile registered an incoming call. At last. She quickly said goodbye to the PA and hit OK to accept the call.

'Alf? It's Grace. Where are you? Alf?'

Silence.

CHAPTER 18

Hal was standing in the yard with a bunch of wildflowers in his hand when she arrived home. Beside him were Sara and Ruthie, who ran to Grace for a hug.

'We've been picking flowers. And I got on Soulman's back and he smiled at me. He did. Didn't he, Mum? Tell her.'

'Hmm.' Grace put her down with a grin. 'Don't think I like a rival for Soulman's affections. You're far too cute. Just be careful, though. He likes running *very, very* fast.'

'You're the proud auntie to a new nephew,' Hal told her. 'Ten-pound boy. Hesketh Delawney. Sara came over to tell us.'

Hope and Freddie had named the Eastfield son and heir after Freddie's father, a forbidding, austere man whom Grace had met only occasionally. She felt a curious leap in her stomach at the news. Mixed with her happiness was a strange sensation. She glanced at the house. If she and Hal failed to have children, Hesketh would own this, too. He could never love it as she did. And Hal.

'How's Hope?' she asked.

'You know her.' Sara tugged nervously at the red ribbon in Ruthie's hair. Untying and retying it. 'Already asking for her makeup. She's seriously happy, though. She asked if you would go over this evening, all three of you.' Grace stole a glance at Hal, who pulled a face at the thought of Henry and Delawney in the same room.

'What time?'

'Before supper? Seven thirty?' She gathered the flowers from Hal.

'We'll be there. I take it Freddie's happy?'

Sara's shy smile faded and her eyes seemed to close in slow motion.

'Of course. He was at the birth this time. And why wouldn't he be happy? He's finally got what he wants.'

Grace wasn't so sure, but held her tongue.

'Let me walk you to your car.' Hal escorted them down the lane, Ruthie skipping ahead. Grace watched Sara let Ruthie into the back seat, close the door, then turn and kiss Hal passionately. Well, she thought, that *is* going well. She smiled to herself, then grimaced as she recalled Hal's face when Henry was mentioned. He was obviously depressed again. Oh, God. When would it lift? And still he wouldn't see anyone, get help. Too bloody independent.

She needed to talk to him about Alf Halliwell's phone call. Her stomach turned queasy again. What *was* that about? She had phoned his mobile and his PA several more times and was seriously thinking of calling the police.

Her father was asleep on the sofa in his study, his hair wild on the white cushion. He'd obviously been out on the hills again: his muddy boots were tumbled in a heap next to his blue jacket. On the floor were the remains of a bottle of white wine and a half-eaten Cheddar cheese sandwich. She picked up the glass and the bottle.

'What're you doing home at this time of day?'

'Alf Halliwell invited me to lunch, then stood me up.'

Henry sighed. 'Silly old fool, I appointed him in a moment of weakness. I knew your mother was fond of him. What'd he want?'

'It was weird, really. Creepy. Told me I had to stop the "Perfect Wheat" project.'

'I've been telling you that for eighteen months.'

'This was different. He told me there were things I didn't understand. That you and Hal were in danger.'

He opened a lizardlike eye. 'He was always an old wife. Don't worry about what he says.'

She nodded, but she still intended to track Alf down. He wouldn't have worried her without reason. He'd always been kind to her.

'Want some coffee?' she asked.

'No. I'm fine. You get on with what you want to do. I'll just sit here and read.'

'Good news about Hope.'

'Lovely.' He closed his eyes again.

When she returned, he was sitting up, an old battered copy of Yeats' *Collected Works* face down on his lap. She put the coffee on the occasional table.

'Poetry is all I can be bothered with, these days.'

She looked around his study at the volumes that were the tools of his former trade. First editions of Nietzsche, Freud, Jung, Kline, Skinner, Chomsky, Weber; review hardbacks of his contemporaries, heavily broken and scored with his damning comments, editions of his own five works in dozens of languages. And now piled beside him were paperbacks of Heaney, Yeats, Hughes. Dark, emotional poetry from men he'd ignored or despised as paper Celts in his Radio Four review programme when at the height of his fame.

'All other writing is so transient.' He turned the book over. 'Your mother gave me this as a honeymoon present.'

Grace studied the portrait of her mother above the fireplace. She looked stern and severe. The painting caught none of her energy or enthusiasms. She had been devastated when she found out about Henry's affair with Hal's mother. The doctor said that she died of breast cancer, but when she was young Grace had believed she simply gave up. Although her will had left the farm to Grace and Hope, as their father he had guardianship over them and had married Hal's mother and moved in with them.

'Come on, Henry. You're only sixty.'

'Age shall not weary – eh?'

She shook her head.

As her mobile rang, she glanced at the number. Alf. 'Where have you been?' she asked.

'Who is that speaking, please?' a female voice asked.

'What?'

'May I ask who is speaking, please?'

'Dr Grace Adams. Who's that?'

'Where do you live?'

'What? Look, I'm cutting this call now unless you tell me what's going on.'

'Don't do that, please. It's Lincolnshire Police, here. DS Lovett. I'm afraid Mr Halliwell has been in an accident.'

'Oh, God.' The colour drained from her face. 'What kind?'

'Fatal, I'm afraid. I would be grateful if you were available this evening for questioning.'

'How did you get this number?'

'It was the last one he dialled.'

CHAPTER 19

Henry stared absentmindedly at the TV set as Mickey and Donald silently went through their paces. Poor Alf, he thought. Poor, poor Alf.

He reached for the bottle of Valium. As well as lecturing on psychiatry at Eastfield, Henry had maintained a high-profile private practice in London and he'd been prescribing antidepressants for himself in a fictitious name since Hal's mother died. He felt a familiar sick and shivery feeling. He hadn't slept much since Alf Halliwell's last . . . final . . . visit.

His former finance director had been tense, sallow. Skin weighed heavily on his jowls. Henry seldom got drunk these days, but he'd put away a bottle of red wine, followed by four double Scotches, and Halliwell had matched him glass for glass.

'I've got to go to the police, Henry.'

Through the fog of drugs and alcohol, Henry recalled punching Halliwell, and Grace rushing in to separate them. Halliwell had intended to confess to his organizing role in the Eastfield drugs ring.

But Henry knew that in turn this would reveal the corrupt sale of land earmarked by the University and the local Council as a nature reserve. This was the property on which the Standish Centre was built and Henry had authorized and benefited from the sale.

He swallowed four pills, aware that his addiction was getting worse, but feeling powerless to deal with the depression and fear overwhelming him. Halliwell's death haunted him.

When his finance director had first approached him with the bribe, Henry had laughed at him. But Halliwell had worked on him for months, promising amounts of money that would protect Hal for ever. Their bank account was empty – Hal was in and out of hospital and the treatments had eaten up his savings. But still be had held out, prepared to struggle on. Then Grace had tearfully phoned to say she was returning home. After the call, he'd wandered round the house, painfully aware of the squalor and decay, seeing it through her eyes. White Hill House represented all that was good about his life – stability, continuity, family. And all that was bad – betrayal, hypocrisy, decay.

He had spent the rest of the night drinking, then phoned Halliwell and capitulated. Later, Henry justified the corruption to himself – the Centre was world-class, putting Eastfield on the intellectual map. And his successor had validated his strategy by attracting serious money to build the Science Park around it. Everybody benefited.

How dare Halliwell get a conscience? How dare he?
Henry asked himself time and again during the
night of Halliwell's last visit. Serpents and pimps
cannot afford such luxury. Forgiveness comes only
with death.

As Donald hit Mickey with a large saucepan,
Henry mourned, staring at the screen and wondering if he should tell the police what he knew
about Rod Leadsmith. He was certain that he
would strike again. Would be compelled to.

CHAPTER 20

Grace sat on a chair in the kitchen, nursing a cup of breakfast coffee. She'd had a bad night, sleeping fitfully, and felt sick. What had Alf wanted?

Hal dropped a thick padded envelope on the table. 'Some motorcycle messenger just dropped this off.'

She looked at the return address written on the top left of the envelope. It was from Alf Halliwell. She stared at it for a moment, then ripped it open. Inside was a series of photographs. She stared at them, then retched as they dropped to the floor.

Hal picked them up. Someone had taken the press photographs of Halliwell's mangled corpse and digitally superimposed Grace's face. There was a simple, typed message inside the envelope.

PLANT THE WHEAT. WE KILL YOU NEXT.

Sam stared at the pictures of Halliwell's bombed-out car and then passed the file to Lindsey Hamilton, a detective inspector in his High-Tech-Crime Unit. 'What do you think?'

Lindsey was small, wiry and carried herself like the t'ai chi expert she was. Her hair was dark red and bobbed, her eyes brown and clear. At twenty-eight she was a rising star in the squad. She and Sam went back to his days in the Met's Anti-Terrorist Branch. He had recruited her straight out of Imperial College after reading about her research on MI5's porous online security and had been delighted when she'd been picked a few years before as the number two in the NCS's new technology team. He trusted her. She represented the new breed.

Lindsey chose her words carefully. 'Did Halliwell support the "Perfect Wheat" project?'

'Not visibly.' He'd met Alf a few times over the years and he'd never struck Sam as a man with many deeply held principles.

'It's possible that the person who burnt down Grace's glasshouse is the car bomber,' he said and passed her the images Grace had faxed over that morning. 'But equally, this might be an opportunist use of Halliwell's death to scare Grace.'

'When in doubt, start with the obvious,' said Lindsey. Sam nodded. She was quoting a maxim he called Copeland's razor – never multiply the hypotheses beyond the point necessary to make sense of the crime. Stood him in good stead in the hall of mirrors in the Anti-Terrorist Branch.

'The absence of doubt is the beginning of prejudice,' Sam muttered to himself. 'Do we have any of our people in Garton?'

'We've a syndicate tracking a heroin-dealing network around the port. Good bunch.'

'Thanks.' He jotted down a quick note. 'Do me a favour, Lindsey. Get someone to run a production order for Halliwell's bank details. Also let's dig into his background. See if there's anything strange. Oh, and do it quietly, don't want to raise any hackles with the Lincolnshire or Garton lot.' The last thing he wanted was an irate Chief Constable fighting a turf war.

'Will do.'

Later that afternoon, Lindsey handed Sam a printout of Halliwell's bank details and he hummed a Mozart horn part softly to himself as he studied it. 'Five million quid is a lot of money for someone earning seventy grand a year,' he said.

'He wasn't that great at hiding it. His systems were as secure as a baby on a banister. He bought a new holiday house in Mallorca last year, a million pounds, cash on the nose. The money was wired to the local Banco España from the Banco Industrial de Brasilia in Florida, which is currently under suspicion for laundering large amounts of drug money from the Colombian cartels. I called in a few favours and we found out that our boy had stacked up large deposits in the English Commerce Bank in Dominica, from where it was wired to Florida. The first payment was two years ago.' She checked her notes. 'Nine hundred K, followed at irregular intervals by other payments.'

'Cash?'

She nodded.

'Does Mr Halliwell have an explanation for this sudden rush of good fortune?'

'Says he had an inheritance from an aunt with which he started to play the stock market.'

'Hmm. A miniature Warren Buffet. What was he investing in?'

'We found some PEPs and ISAs, and a couple of hundred thousand quid's worth of shares in blue-chip companies, but nothing that would give him a thousand per cent return.'

'I think I might pay Agnes Halliwell a visit.' Sam tapped his keyboard and checked his electronic diary. The day was packed, as usual. A breakfast meeting at 8 a.m. and nonstop until a drink with a rising politician at 8 p.m.

'Jo.' He put his head round the door and smiled at his PA, a smart woman in her twenties who had more common sense than most of the DIs in his department. 'You're going to hate me.'

She was sitting behind a long counter that served as the reception point for the NCS Directorate. The room was long and thin and stiflingly hot. The original contractors had failed to install any equipment to regulate the heat and when the NCS inherited the building from the Home Office, no one had bothered to tell them that there were only two temperatures – freezing and roasting. The whole building was a scruffy, low-rent office block, not exactly an appropriate setting for England's high-tech crime squads, but somehow very British. Into one of the interior walls that led to the Directorate Board Room was etched a relief map of England and an image of the Squad's motto, the Scarlet Pimpernel.

Across from him was the large, cluttered office of his boss, with the crests of dozens of foreign police services mounted around the walls. Thankfully Ian was in Paris for a planning session for his conference, because he certainly wouldn't've liked what Sam had to say next.

'What am I up to tomorrow?'

'Let me guess.' Jo swivelled round, her lips stern. 'You want me to clear the diary.' She'd been with him for five years and knew what his questions meant. 'You're supposed to speak at a seminar on modern police methods in the afternoon.'

'Lindsey.' He turned. 'You're the future round here. Would you take my place?'

'Well . . .'

'Go on. A bit of profile'll do you good. Besides, they've all heard me do this stuff before. They're longing for a new face.'

She hesitated again, clearly anxious about something. 'Sir. Are you sure about this Eastfield thing? It's a bit close to home and personal, isn't it?'

Sam looked at her, thoughtfully. She was a good officer, but on occasion ran the rules too tight – didn't trust her instincts. 'True,' he acknowledged. 'On the other hand, your dossier certainly suggests that Alf was up to something murky. It has all the marks of an organized drugs ring, and, for some reason, it ties back to Grace. It's my neck of the woods. I've met Agnes Halliwell a few times. She'll trust me. I'm going to be more valuable down there than riding a desk up here.'

Jo grinned at her boss. 'What desk?'

'So, it's a deal?'

Lindsey nodded.

'I owe you one,' he said, and she nodded again.

CHAPTER 21

S am pulled into Earl's Langley village – a couple of dozen ancient cottages with a social housing estate of a hundred houses tacked on the fields at the back. Sam had been a frequent visitor to the most famous Langley of all – the town that played host to the CIA's headquarters in the US – and he wondered how many of the spooks knew that word 'langley' was an Old English word for 'a woodland clearing'.

Another clearance, this time by Garton Council, had created the uneasy social mix of farmers and urban families. Grace had told him there was increasing tension between the newcomers and the original Earl's Langley villagers, many of whom could trace their lineage back several hundred years. In one thing they were united – both sides hated Grace's experiment.

Sam smiled when confronted by the two pubs, the Black Bull and the Green Man. Whilst the older inhabitants drank in the latter, the former had been colonized by the 'soshies', as they were locally known after the council's description of them as socially challenged tenants. And in the middle of a small patch of grass was the War Memorial, dedicated to 'The Men Who Fought in the Great War'. This small village had lost seven – every family lost someone – including the great-grandfather of Jenny Appleyard, the landlady of the Green Man since her husband Jerry disappeared with an in-comer. She kept the best beer in the county. And knew most of the secrets.

As he entered the bar, there was a darts game going on in the corner. He noticed a muscular man in his mid-thirties who turned, ran an enquiring eye over Sam, then threw his dart, hitting double top.

'Deputy Director General.' Jenny, small and wiry with a shock of black hair, rushed forwards and grabbed him round the waist. 'You're losing too much weight, Sam. You need one of my pies. Ellie, get Sam a pint of Peculier.' She bustled off.

A few moments later, Sam was drinking the thick, gooey liquid and watching with a mixture of dismay and pleasure as Jenny returned with a plate loaded with two pork pies, a mountain of homemade chips and a token piece of lettuce. He tried mentally to work out how long he'd have to spend in the gym to work it off, but gave up as the first crisp piece of potato hit his tongue. Jenny joined him, sipping gin and tonic.

'How are things, Jen?'

'I'm thinking of packing it in, to be honest.' Her hand flicked nervously at her hair. She lit a cigarette and drew deep. Not like her. She's normally a joy.

114

Must be the disappearance of her husband. More strain than he thought.

'Things aren't the same round here since *that* terrible winter. Tommy dying, the soshies getting the upper hand. And to top it all, since Grace started on that Frankenwheat stuff most of the locals have frozen her out.' She sucked fierce smoke down into her lungs. 'I can't stand to see my friends at each other's throats. *And* there's more and more strangers around the place. We don't see Grace in the pub any more. Not since that bastard Griffiths tried to punch her.'

'What?'

'Him over there.' Her voice dropped to a whisper. 'The hard-looking one.'

Sam glanced at the huddle of men laughing in the corner. So that was Roy Griffiths. He'd heard of him from the Garton syndicate. Former Special Boat Service, highly decorated, drummed out for cigarette smuggling, returned to Earl's Langley and became Delawney's head gamekeeper. Sam had known his father, Ted 'Three Bellies' Griffiths, who'd worked for the old Earl as a general dogsbody and been a nasty, violent bully. The syndicate believed Griffiths was running a team of coke mules, but nothing could be pinned on him.

'You know he helps a bit up at the House?' She referred to Eastfield House. 'Well, he also does a bit of "security" on the side, if you know what I mean. Organizes the bouncers round some of the Garton clubs and over at the other place.' She nodded in the direction of the Black Bull. She never called the pub by its name.

'What's he got against Grace?'

'He was picking on Hal, claiming that the lad owed him money for some dope Hal'd scored. You know what Grace's tongue's like when she's angry. Stormed in and gave him all sorts.' She drew deep on her cigarette, her hands unsteady. 'He lashed out at her, but she poured a pint of beer over him and then she and Hal did a runner. Had to ban her, though.' Jenny's laughter stopped. 'That bugger threatened to put me out of business if I didn't. And I've had to hire his services.'

Griffiths sauntered over, hands in the pocket of his low-slung jeans, taut belly and well-defined chest under an England soccer shirt.

'Hello, Mr Copeland.'

Interesting. Knows my name.

'Don't see you round here very often these days. Thought you'd forgotten us,' he said, his soft Garton burr belying the hardness in eyes.

'Oh, I'd never forget Earl's Langley, Mr Griffiths. Not for a second. I take too much of an interest in the welfare of its inhabitants. And I probably get a bit too emotional if I hear about anything bad happening to them.'

Their eyes locked, then Griffiths grinned.

'I'll be back for my pay later, Jen, my love. Have it in tenners, if you don't mind. Can't be doing with coins. Bye, Mr Copeland.'

As he pushed through the door, Jenny whispered, 'Scum.'

'Want me to do something about him?'

'Not worth it, Sam. Your local boys don't have time to worry about low-life rats like him. He'll just ignore them and carry on as normal. No, you stick to the big stuff.' She stubbed out her cigarette.

'On another subject, Jen. Do you know anything about Alf Halliwell that might help me with this case?'

She thought for a second. 'He was a nice man, Alf. Always helpful. Bit of a handful with the how's your father, but decent with it. Not aggressive.' Her voice dropped again. 'He was having a fling, I think. I saw him a few times here. Blonde woman in her thirties. Don't know her name.'

Sam filed away the information. 'Hang in, there, Jen. You love this place. Lived here all your life.'

'I know. I know. But sometimes . . .' She seemed to drift. 'Anyway.' She cupped his hand. 'It's grand to see you back. You see if you can talk some sense into Grace.'

Sam sat on the sofa drinking tepid Earl Grey from a china cup. On a green chintz chair opposite sat Agnes Halliwell. She was a big woman, around sixteen stones, but took an obvious pride in her appearance in her black, well-cut dress. In the dozens of pictures around the room she was with her three children and husband, and had developed from a slim, fresh-faced girl to a grandmother of five. A decent life lived with personal dignity.

Sam looked into her watery blue eyes. They were drained of emotion, the lids puffy from tears and lack of sleep. She'd put on some foundation and makeup, but still looked wrecked.

'I'm sorry to ask you more questions, Agnes.'

'I'm glad you're here, really. The kids mean well, but they're tiptoeing around me as if I were sick.'

'Can I get you some more tea?'

'No. No.' She shook her head and stared at her lap.

'I miss him, Sam. I really do. I've spent most of my life with Alf. We talked every day, wherever he was he'd phone. And we'd just gossip. I've no idea what we talked about. No idea. Can't remember a single thing. Isn't that ridiculous?'

Sam smiled, remembering his parents, whose love affair had lasted from the age of fourteen until they had died, within months of one another. They were buried side by side. 'No. It's not. You were lucky to have a marriage like that.' Unlike my own wretched affair. Five years of volunteering for overtime to avoid going home to face whatever emotional coil she'd wound herself into. Thank God we didn't have kids.

'You and Alf seemed to be doing well these past few years.'

'It was a real surprise to me. Alf was always interested in the stock market. Most finance people are, I suppose. Never held any fascination for me.

He had an imaginary portfolio and every so often would tell me that we were worth a million or had dropped a few hundred thousand. And then one day, he said he'd made some real investments and we had some money in the bank. He told me that for tax purposes he'd put it offshore. Jersey, I think.'

'Your solicitor can't find any such account. Have you any idea where he might have left the password or any details?'

'I can't bring myself to look through his things yet. Is it important, Sam? Nobody knew we had any money. We both decided that we'd stay here. We've been here over twenty years. Alf was Head of the Planning Committee on the council and you know how tongues wag about bribes and suchlike. You know what I mean?'

I do indeed, he thought.

'Did he ever talk about someone called Rod Leadsmith? Did they know each other?' he asked.

'Vaguely, I think. Not bosom buddies or anything. Opposite side of the political spectrum. Alf didn't mix with Greens if he could help it. Thought they were irrational.'

She walked to a mahogany cabinet and opened the bottle of sherry. 'I need a bit of Dutch courage. Would you like a drop?'

'Love one, but can't, I'm afraid.'

She sat down and gathered herself. 'I loved that man and thought I knew him. But when you trust someone as much as I trusted him, you turn a blind eye to some things at first. But he wasn't himself. He wasn't right or happy. I didn't want that bloody house in Mallorca. I was perfectly happy with our timeshare. It was as if I was married to a different man. He was involved in something that scared him.' She stroked a picture of Alf taken thirty years before. 'Silly old sod.'

Sam's driver put his head round the door and mouthed – 'Sorry. Call.'

CHAPTER 22

Sam sat with Grace in the garden. She had been silent for several minutes, sipping the gin and tonic he'd brought her, rolling the ice round with her fingers. She was wearing shapeless overalls, and had spent the morning digging out a large bush. Her face was marked with sweat, grime and weariness. The plant was stubborn and still half buried, its roots deep in the earth. On the ground was her Gibson semi-acoustic, which she'd been playing when Sam found her – a dark blues number by Blind Willie Johnson. At her feet was a photograph of her head superimposed on Halliwell's body.

'Want to help me?' she asked.

'Of course.'

Grace handed him a pickaxe. 'Let's get that bloody juniper up. It's sucking the life out of everything around it. Been wanting it out for ages.'

He looked down at his dark suit trousers. Oh, well. The sod thudded as he dug in.

'You're so lucky,' he grunted. 'You've got good earth around here.' He bent over and fingered the reddy-brown loam; a fat worm slithered away from

121

his fingers, digging blindly back to safety.

'Yeah. I know I'm lucky.' She hacked viciously at a root with her sharp-edged spade and the gnarled, knotted line burst open. 'Two to go.' She grabbed the rough leaves of the evergreen bush between her hands and tugged. She felt it budge.

Sam pummelled one root and it gave, then repeated the exercise with the final one.

'Good. Great.' Grace breathed. 'Now, then. Together.' As they grabbed the large, ugly plant and hauled it out, it gave quickly and they landed with a thump on the muddy lawn.

She looked at Sam and giggled. 'You look terrible.'

'I've got a change in the car.'

Her giggles turned to hiccups, then to sobs. 'Who's doing this, Sam? Who killed Alf? Who wants to kill me?'

'That was too drastic.' Toad was on the phone and he was angry. Malkie was waiting in his car to pick up Lilly. On Thursdays she spent a full day at St David's, a small private school. He always picked her up afterwards and took her for a burger and fries at McDonald's. He hoped that her mother would be sober by the time they returned.

'Don't know what you're talking about.'

'Stop fannying around,' Toad hissed. 'You know what I mean. Why did you kill Halliwell, I mean Mole?'

'It was nothing to do with me.'

122

Malkie glanced out of the window at the sun flooding the compact playground, the old Victorian schoolhouse and the cool, restful woods beyond. He and Lilly had often gone hunting for fairies in the grounds.

'*What?*' Toad was incredulous.

'Happened before I got anywhere near him. I was on my way to have a wee chat to him when I heard about his accident.' Malkie had a receiver in his car that monitored police calls.

'I don't believe you. Don't play fucking games with me. What're you up to?' Even through the electronic scrambling, Toad's voice was startled and shaking.

The other parents began to turn up in people carriers, Mercs and Beemers. He preferred something anonymous, a second-hand Volvo. Sara Forester emerged from her beat-up car and he wondered how she could afford the school. Didn't think her salary as Hope Delawney's assistant would be up to it. Nice girl. Her kid, Ruthie, and Lilly were great mates. She was with a man he didn't know. Tall, skinny, acne. Hang on, he recognized his face. Alex Cross. Worked with that psycho Roy Griffiths. What's he doing here? Sara waved and he nodded.

'Stay calm,' Malkie said. 'Nothing can be traced back to us. We've got at least five degrees of separation from the front-line guys. Chill.' He cut the connection. Toad was becoming a serious nuisance. But there was nothing he could do about it – for the moment. But with Johnny gone, maybe Toad was a loose end that would have to be tied up. He stepped from the car.

'Hello, Sara. How are you?'

'Pretty good.' She looked troubled and weary.

'This is Alex. My cousin.' She smiled at him. He'd been the only one to help her when the rest of the family deserted her. They'd known each other since childhood and he had been her best friend until Hal turned up.

She asked, 'How's Lilly?'

'It was one of her good days, according to Mrs Staples.'

'Must be really hard for you. I don't know if I could cope.'

'She's a great kid. And it's only a mild form of autism. Give her a lot of love and attention and she's a treat.' His heart froze as he recalled the doctor giving her diagnosis on his vulnerable little bundle. At first it sounded like a death sentence, but then he thought, Screw it, she's my kid. That kind of love is unconditional.

Lilly came rushing towards him in tears. 'Daddy. That lady called me stupid.' Malkie looked across at a flustered-looking plump woman who was trying to mop up her two unruly kids.

Holding Lilly's hand, Malkie walked across and stood in front of the mother, who straightened her back.

'*She* hit Vienna. It was rude,' the woman huffed.

Malkie smiled at the little girl, who was pulling

faces at Lilly, then he hunched down beside her.

'That true?' he asked.

'She stood on my toes.'

'Did she mean to?' Malkie's gaze was direct, but his voice was gentle.

As the child drew a line in the gravel with her foot, her mother grabbed her by the arm. 'You'll ruin your shoes. Stop it.'

The girl looked up at Malkie, then down again and shook her head.

'What are you trying to say?' asked Malkie.

'She didn't mean to,' Vienna whispered.

'Give her a hug,' Malkie took her hand and she and Lilly embraced.

He stood and leant towards the mother, his eyes hard, piercing.

'Don't ever call my child stupid again.' His voice was even. Each word picked out in emphasis. Her gaze slid away, looking anywhere but at him. 'Please apologize to Lilly.'

'What? She's just a kid. They never notice anything. Anyway, she shouldn't be in a normal sch . . .'

'Do it,' he ordered, picking Lilly up in his arms until she was the same height as the woman.

'Oh, for God's sake. Sorry. OK? Sorry.' She turned on her heels, dragging her kids towards a Mercedes.

'Say goodbye, Lilly.' Malkie kissed her on the cheek.

'Bye,' she waved shyly – worried that she had

caused the anger she could sense in her father.

Sara came to his shoulder.

'Terrible snob,' she said.

Malkie turned. 'Fancy a burger, girls? Strawberry milkshakes?'

'Yes, please,' chorused Lilly and Ruthie.

'We can't, really,' Sara said. 'I've got to get back. They need help with the new baby.'

'Let them sort themselves out for a while,' Malkie insisted. 'Let's give *your* girl a treat.'

'Go on, then,' laughed Sara. 'God. McDonald's. I haven't had one since I was at school.'

'You go,' said Cross. 'I'll take a raincheck. Got stuff to do at the House.'

Malkie opened the door to the car and wondered how Grace had reacted when she received his note. When he heard about Halliwell's murder, he had turned it to his advantage and sent the terrifying picture to Grace. There was no way she would try to mount the experiment on her own land again. She would be safely inside the compound, where they needed her.

As he fired up the car, a worry tugged at his gut. Who *had* killed Halliwell? And why?

CHAPTER 23

Sam was back at his desk by eight the next day. His restless night had left him tired. As he tipped back his third espresso of the morning, Lindsey popped her head round the door.

'Morning, early bird,' she said.

'Got any worms?'

'Actually,' she dropped a file on his desk, 'I have. Seems like some UE students got themselves into an accident in Barcelona earlier this year.'

'Bad?'

'They were fried in a camper van. Nothing left but cinders. Had to be identified from their dental records.'

'What were they doing in Bilbao?'

'Field trip on Basque history, was the official reason. Rumour has it, there were six kilos of cocaine hidden in the chassis.'

'Rumour?'

'Our Basque chums are playing the silent game.'

'Maybe some of it went missing. There are a lot of rumours around that counter-intelligence agents are feeding the dealers who are working with ETA.

Keeping them sweet and picking up intelligence.'

'Guess who was in Bilbao the week before the blast?'

'Our dead friend?'

'Uh, huh. Halliwell personally authorized the trip.'

Sam stared out of the window at a watery London, looking grey and grimy in contrast to the emerging life around the farm. What was going on? Why was Grace part of this?

'All quiet at the University?' he asked.

'People are very nervous, as you would expect.'

None of it made sense. He felt as if he were doing two jigsaws simultaneously, but uncertain which pieces fitted which puzzle.

'I think I'll put in a call to Sergio.' He noted her quizzical look. 'Sergio Colinas, Head of Spain's Anti-Terrorist Unit, the Grupo Especial de Operaciones. We worked together on a few Europol things years ago. He's a friend. Good guy. Straight as they come. He might nod us in the right direction. Thanks, Lindsey. Good stuff.'

Sam clicked his mouse, repositioned his Webcam, and Sergio's face sharpened on the screen. He was near retirement age – his face lined and papery from too many cigarettes – but his eyes were as clear and focused as ever. No wonder his colleagues dubbed him 'The Hawk'.

'Sergio. How're Real doing?'

Sergio was a serious football supporter and

travelled the world ostensibly on Interpol business, but miraculously a great many of the trips coincided with Real Madrid's European Championship games.

'Don't ask, my friend. That Russian we bought left his right foot back in St Petersburg. I don't doubt that the Russian Mafia is paying him to throw games. What's new with you, Sam? Found yourself a woman yet?'

'Oh, they're queuing up for a workaholic divorcee, Sergio.'

'I'm serious, Sam. You need a good woman to take your mind off the work.' Sound advice from a man with three divorces under his belt. 'You got trouble your side of the water?' Sergio lit an unfiltered cigarette and drew deeply.

'You remember Grace Adams?'

'Difficult to forget, my friend.'

'Have a look at this.' Sam emailed an attachment with one of the images of Grace's head superimposed on Halliwell's body.

Sergio scanned it. 'Not nice.'

'I think,' Sam tapped on the table with his pencil, 'that somehow or other she's caught up in crossfire – something to do with this guy Halliwell. He was on his way to see her when he got hit.'

'Could be coincidence. Most things are.'

'Maybe. But . . .'

'But you have a feeling in your gut. I know, I know.'

Sam continued: 'Halliwell was in Bilbao when

129

a group of students from UE were burnt to death in a car. There are rumours that they were coke mules, but your colleagues in the Guardia Civil are being coy.'

Sergio pursed his lips. 'Juan Fernandez is due in London in a few days on business. Why don't I ask him to meet you? If anyone knows, he will.' Sam had met Fernandez, Bilbao's Chief of Police, quite a few times over the years.

'Thanks, Sergio. I owe you one.'

CHAPTER 24

Two security guards marched beside Grace and Gitte. Violi had called to ask her to come to the Institute to talk about the 3-Cube application and when she reached the campus, the men had insisted on accompanying her. She was grateful for the protection.

As they stepped from the lift, they were met by Julie, Violi's PA.

'Lovely to see you again, Grace. Stef will be a few minutes, then he's all yours. Coffee?'

'Not for me.' She felt jittery enough.

'Dr Hesse?'

'Water, please.' Julie smiled and poured a Pellegrino. Gitte's 'thank you' was formal and restrained and Grace could sense her friend's tension.

Stef Violi emerged from his office, his arms spread in greeting. 'Grace. What a delight to see you. Thank you for coming in at such short notice. And this must be Dr Hesse. I admired your piece on string theory in the Fachbereich Mathematik und Informatik in Berlin.'

Grace stole a glance at Gitte, who could not

conceal her surprise. Stef reached across and shook their hands, then ushered them into the room. A cigar butt smouldered in an ashtray. He picked it up and dumped the remains into a bin.

'Disgusting habit,' said a light, amused, Californian voice behind Grace. 'You've no willpower, Stefano. None whatsoever.'

'Ah, Julian, there you are.' Stef nudged Grace lightly on the arm and she swung round to see a short, tubby, well-tanned white man with a snowy beard and thick shock of hair. He looked about fifty and was wearing a casual blue shirt under an immaculately cut black two-piece suit.

'Grace, Dr Hesse. Julian Porter, Director of 3-Cube and, as you can see from his girth, chronic overeater.'

'Gave up smoking five years ago.' He patted his stomach. 'Put on three stones. Comes in handy with the grandkids at Christmas. I make a convincing Kris Kringle. Please, sit. You're making me nervous.' His smile was infectious, and returned by both Grace and Gitte.

'Do you have a proper drink around here?' Porter asked. 'A drop of Scotch. Malt, if you have it.'

'It's eleven in the morning, Julian.'

Porter indicated his watch. 'Not in California, it ain't.'

Stef laughed, and turned to Grace. 'He's relentless when he wants something.'

Five seconds later, Julie turned up with a thick tumbler holding two fingers of Scotch.

'You're a mind-reader, Julie. Why didn't I marry you when I had the chance?' Porter laughed.

Julie poured some water into the glass. 'It's Glenfarclas. Your favourite.'

'She's a wonderful woman, Stefano. I think it's time to move her to the States. What'd'you think, Julie? Come live with me in the mountains. Beautiful, clear air, wonderful people, skiing in the winter. And, who knows, I might grow on you.'

'I don't think the current Mrs Porter would approve.' Julie offered her small, enigmatic smile and closed the door.

Porter turned to Grace. 'Tell me why I should give you a million bucks.'

Two hours later, the table was littered with papers, cups, glasses and computer printout. Gitte was in full flow on the mathematics underlying the project and Porter was nodding enthusiastically.

Gitte finished and he sipped his second Scotch.

'Very, very impressive,' he said.

Stef smiled across at her, his eyes sparkling. Throughout the presentation he had caught her attention, urging her in certain directions, then halting her from plunging off into tangents by asking pertinent and penetrating questions.

'You gals are holding something back. What is it?' Porter stroked the rim of his glass.

It was the moment Grace was dreading. She had given Porter more than anyone else – but she was determined to keep key information to herself.

'Nothing that would stop you making a decision about whether to fund the project,' she replied.

'Hmm,' he responded. 'Where are you getting the DNA from?'

'Molluscs,' replied Grace.

'That all?'

She paused, knowing the controversy ahead. She'd had to use oxygen-carrying animal molecules, rather than those normally found in other plants. It would have been easier if her modification technique had been plant-to-plant, rather than a trans-species operation, but her detailed research threw up consistently negative effects on the wheat from anything other than her own cells or those of other animals. After all, she'd thought in some irritation, *we* get most of our dietary iron from meat and fish, why can't we allow those who can't afford meat access to the same privilege?

'It's early days,' said Porter. 'I have no ethical problem with your work, but there are a few issues, not least security and PR. If it got out that you were experimenting with animal DNA, even your life would not be safe.'

'But that's mad. I'm not *experimenting* with animal DNA. I'm inserting a precise gene into wheat to do a specific and beneficial job. "Perfect Wheat" will save hundreds of thousands of lives a year.'

'Grace, Grace.' Stef leant over and placed his hand on hers. 'There is no question about the validity of your research. Julian was simply pointing

134

out a fact of life. They've already burned your glasshouses to the ground.'

'This is work of the highest calibre,' Porter tapped the paper. 'You gals heard of Alaina Prokovitch?'

They glanced at one another. Of course they had. She was on track for a Nobel in a few years' time. They'd attended a conference in London at which she was the plenary speaker, and hung on to every word.

'Alaina owes me a few favours. I helped her out when she was your age. If I could persuade her to come over and work with you for six weeks or so, would you be interested? I'd feel a lot happier signing a cheque if Alaina was around for a while.' A slight, knowing smile played around Stef's lips.

Grace turned to Gitte, her face taut with excitement and tension. 'What d'you think?'

'I think we should reflect on it.' Gitte stood and stretched out her hand to Porter, then Stef. 'Thank you,' her voice was tight. 'We have a lot to think about.'

CHAPTER 25

Juan Fernandez was waiting for Sam in Regent's Park, just before dusk. The park was left to a few joggers and winos bedding down for the night. Fernandez, his arms wrapped around his body, gazed meditatively at the statue of a small brown terrier.

It was a blustery, cold evening and both wore thick overcoats. They clasped one another by the upper arms. Juan had aged since they had last met, but he was still handsome, with fine features, a long nose and nut-brown eyes.

'Amazing story, this, my friend,' said Fernandez is his light, slightly accented baritone. 'The dog was subjected to vivisection operations for two months at University College. Every time a wound healed, the dog was opened again. And you English call bullfighting cruel.'

'There used to be an older statue here,' said Sam. 'Taken down in 1906 after it provoked riots between "brown doggers", who were violent anti-vivisectionists, and medical students who were pro. The new one was erected in the 80s. The old one is now in Battersea Park – a pilgrimage for vegetarians.'

136

'Why do moral causes provoke such hatred?' asked Fernandez.

'For some people, violence is continuation of conscience by other means,' said Sam. 'Democratic countries need intense alternative voices to shock them out of their lethargy. But it's our job to make sure that legitimate protest doesn't descend into terror.'

Wind lashed their faces and Sam's teeth ached with cold. 'I'm all for fresh air, Juan, but it's a bit brisk out here. Shall we find a pub?'

'You're going soft, Sam. The desk job is thinning your blood. Let's walk. ' Fernandez turned towards the formal gardens. 'I love this park. So much to see and do. You are lucky, you Londoners. You have a green city.'

As the huge golden dome of the Regent's Park Mosque began to dominate the skyline, Fernandez exhaled slowly.

'Your Halliwell case may be tied into something we're investigating. You know about the 'Ndrangheta?'

'Sure. Italian organized crime outfit. Based in Calabria.'

Fernandez stopped and breathed air deep into his lungs.

'Did you hear of the Messina story?'

Sam racked his memory. 'Something about a university and the Mafia?'

'Absolutely. For twenty-five years, the 'Ndrangheta ran Messina University. Eventually, the corruption gave off too much of a stink and the Italians arrested one hundred and sixteen professors and students.'

Sam laughed. 'You're not really suggesting that the University of Eastfield is a hotbed of Mafioso activity?'

'Are you mocking me, my friend?' asked Fernandez.

'No, of course not. But you've got to admit it's a bit far-fetched.'

'Not really. Such corruption happens a lot in India, and another organized crime ring was broken up a few years ago in Eastern Europe. They were issuing fake degrees in dentistry at thirty thousand pounds a time.'

They walked in silence for a minute, and then Fernandez said, 'I asked about your friend Halliwell. He had contacts with the Barracuda, and we think they are running drugs on behalf of ETA.'

The Barracuda, as Sam knew, was a loose co-alition of criminal gangs stretching from Colombia down to Venezuela then across to Bilbao, and on to Paris, London and points north until they ran up against the Russians somewhere around Prague. They moved a billion dollars' worth of cocaine each year.

'You must be joking,' said Sam.

'At Sergio's request, I lightly touched on the subject with the Drugs Unit.' He stared up at the night sky. 'It was as if I'd threatened the Ministry of Justice with a bomb. I've been warned off this investigation by people very high up. And they are not playing games. So, this is our only meeting on the subject. And that meeting is now over.' He took Sam's hand and held it tight. 'I've heard through the grapevine about the job offer. I hope you take it, Sam. We need you.' He turned and walked quickly into the dark.

Sam invited Lindsey and another of his squad, DCI Bobby Neil, for pizzas in his office. As he mulled over Fernandez's oblique warnings, he wondered how many other people had heard about the offer of the European Anti-Terrorism Unit. Good grief, has it reached Ian or the General?

Bobby was a big man in every sense. Almost as tall as Sam, he'd played second row for Wasps in his twenties, and even now at thirty-eight turned out for the thirds. His father had been in the Jamaican police force before coming to England and Bobby was a believer in muscular Christianity.

'Thanks for joining me.' Sam handed round the American hot and opened a Tiger lager for Lindsey and himself and a diet Coke for Bobby. 'Both of you up to speed?'

They nodded, acknowledging that they had read his report detailing the conversation with Fernandez.

'It's clear that I have a personal stake in the firebombing case, but I think I can carry my objectivity into the operation.' He glanced at Bobby, who conspicuously tucked into his food without acknowledging the look.

Lindsey looked at the files piling up in his in-tray and replied, 'Uh, huh.'

'You remember Sergio Colinas, Bobby?'

'Yeah. I met him at your fortieth birthday party.'

'He and I have done each other a lot of favours over the years. Never compromising our investigations or organizations, but helping each other out. I phoned him after my meeting with Fernandez. I've never known him so cautious. Must be major political heat coming down on both of them.'

He took a chunk of pizza, enjoying the heat of the chilli on his tongue. The Tiger cooled him down and began to soften the edge of his simmering temper.

'Bobby. I want you to head this up. I intend to go down there tomorrow and I want you with me. Don't worry, Lindsey,' he turned to her, 'I haven't gone mad. The work up here'll be done first. Eastfield'll be a day trip and then I'll leave it to the lads and lasses in the field.'

'Have you squared this with Lamond?' asked Bobby. Alan Lamond, one of the squad's assistant chief constables, had jurisdiction over Lincolnshire and Garton. He had been very unhappy with the idea of Sam going on a 'fact-finding' mission, as he put it. But Sam had overridden

140

his objections, telling him that it would boost morale for senior staff to be seen around the regions.

'Alan's fine with it,' replied Sam.

'Have you run a search on new employees at the University?' he asked Lindsey. 'Anyone who might be a front for the Barracuda?'

'Uh, huh,' she nodded. 'Have you heard of Stefano Violi?'

Sam shook his head, then said, 'Hang on, Grace told me something about him. He's just taken over as Director of the Standish Centre.'

Lindsey read from her file. 'His brother Anthony's a lawyer who does a great deal of work for the Di Gambetta family in Agrigento in southern Italy. The Gambettas, I need hardly remind you, are some of the leading drug dealers in Europe. However, there's no evidence that he's involved in Mafia activities. Smoke and fire, though. Violi's father, Luca, was caught up in a corruption scandal at his university. He was rolled up in a syndicate that issued fake degrees, but wasn't charged, and there was little to go on, really. His older brother was killed in a car accident when Violi was fourteen. There were suspicions that one of the Gambetta factions carried out the hit. But it was covered up.'

'It's hard to get away from that kind of thing in Sicily and Calabria. You don't know who you're dealing with half the time.'

'Except anyone involved in private protection

businesses,' Bobby responded. 'You know with unvarnished truth that they're the bad guys.'

'Violi was sent to the US after his brother died. Stayed with relatives in New York. Became an upstanding citizen. A whizz at biochemistry, he worked with one of the leading Nobel guys. They were into some brilliant stuff. Then the old guy died and Violi seemed to get caught up in nasty academic politics. He lost his funding and threatened to quit. Then, suddenly, the money starts to flow again and he becomes a blue-eyed boy with Standish.'

'So what's he doing at UE,' asked Bobby, 'it's hardly what you would call Ivy League?'

Is this what Fernandez is pointing me towards? Sam wondered.

'Did you check out Safe and Sound, the security firm that protected Grace's glasshouses?'

'Now they *are* interesting. It's a shell company, whose ultimate owners are St Kentigern Financial Services, registered in Guernsey,' said Bobby. 'We think the main man behind SKFS is Malkie Collins.' He flipped a photograph over to Sam, who studied the intelligent but tough-looking face. A torrent of memories flooded through his mind – fragmented moments of the last time he'd met Malkie. He'd been in the middle of Argyll Street in Glasgow's city centre on a freezing January night. Wind was howling through him as he fought the heroin running through his veins. He was naked, tarred and feathered. The last words he remembered were those of one of Malkie's guys. 'Tell your gaffer not to fuck with us. Next time we won't be so gentle.'

Sam had spent four months undercover in Malkie's gym, becoming his weight-training partner, burrowing into the gang, getting closer to the drugs. Then someone in HQ had slipped a note to Malkie's lawyer, and that period of Sam's life drew to an agonizing close. Even now, twelve years and a lot of dangerous situations later, he shivered at the humiliation he'd felt that night.

'You OK, guv?' asked Bobby. 'You know this creep?'

'Yeah.' Sam nodded, then gathered himself. 'Lost touch a while back. I tried to nick him.'

'A lot of people have. Collins was behind a lot of ecstasy and cocaine dealing, but we never managed to get him on anything. He set himself up as a legitimate businessman. Bought a security firm, put in some of his best thugs and some good management, and on the surface is making good.'

'But?'

'But he's a nasty thug who should be behind bars.'

Amen to that, thought Sam. He understood Bobby's anger. Hidden behind a protective veil of friendly bank managers, diligent lawyers, compliant family and hardened gangsters, the criminal elite were looked after like a silk-spider in the middle of a web. He'd seen Malcolm Collins up close and personal. He'd felt the man's intensity.

'What's the connection with Violi?'

'None. His firm was hired to manage security at the Science Park. Guess who signed the contract?' Lindsey produced the document.

'Halliwell?'

'None other.'

CHAPTER 26

Grace looked down on the wreck of her glasshouses. She and Gitte had been debating for hours.

'I can't see any other route forward,' she said.

Gitte sighed, then sipped red wine. 'I've just enjoyed the freedom too much.'

'But it's still our research. The difference is that we've got access to real money and we can finish the project in half the time. And we get to work with Alaina Prokovitch, babe.'

Gitte drank some more. 'You're as good as she is.'

'No, I'm not, you know that. I'm getting there, but she's world-class. Six weeks of her time'll be like two years of anyone else's.'

'But what do 3-Cube get out of it?' Gitte asked. 'What's their motivation?'

Grace thought for a second. 'Same as the Rothschild Foundation supporting "Golden Rice" or the Gates Foundation curing Aids. To mark their place in history, to do some good, guilt about their wealth.'

'So why do they keep their names hidden? Why the secrecy?'

'It's a tax-avoidance scheme, according to Stef.'

'Is that what we want to be involved with?'

Grace sat down on the floor beside Gitte.

'We can spend our whole life wrapped up in cynicism, fighting the machine. Or we can *use it*. We can trust to hope. Stef's obviously a good guy. I've checked him out with at least half a dozen people.' She stopped as Gitte's chin slowly dropped forwards onto her chest and she fell fast asleep.

Sam rubbed his eyes. It had been a long haul, but he'd cleared the in-tray. He settled down in the back of the car and slept all the way to Garton, Lindsey pounding away on her laptop next to him. He woke, startled, from a nightmare. The piercing cold Glasgow wind whipped his face as Malcolm Collins' words echoed in his dream. 'Don't fuck with me.'

His car pulled off the motorway and into Exodus Park, a suburban business zone, with an ugly, red-brick head office for a cable company in the middle, surrounded by various call centres, insurance offices and a massive curry wholesaler. On the ground floor of a bleak two-storey building was the location of Bobby's syndicate.

He and Lindsey entered a long room littered with PCs, laptops, half-drunk cups of coffee, and piles of CD-Roms and videocassettes. He had brought Lindsey with him in order to give her a feel for the investigation on the ground. Locked in with her computer, she would in the end just see the numbers not the flesh and blood reality.

Sam's approach was noted by half a dozen DCs and DSs – it wasn't often the brass came this far down the food chain. Must be something big. He had tried to disguise his interest by pretending it was an unofficial visit; but he knew the canteens and pubs would be humming with gossip unless he did something.

Bobby clapped his hands and shouted, 'Prayer meeting, people.' As his team formed a semicircle, leaning on desks and walls, Sam surveyed them – some young eagle scouts, other faces battered by experience, all forged by Bobby into a top-class team. He didn't tolerate weakness.

'Listen up,' Bobby said. 'Among other things, we're sniffing around Malkie Collins again.'

A few faces lit up and someone muttered, 'About time.'

'Those of you who don't know about Malcolm John Collins should consult your more knowledgeable brethren. Now, here's the thing. We have no idea how he ties into the murder of Halliwell. But he's here, and wherever he is, there's trouble. There's something happening around Dr Grace Adams that we don't understand and we don't like.'

Sam stepped forward, looking directly into the eyes of as many of the team as he could scan. He had to trust these people and he wanted them to feel his presence. He was new to the squad and some would owe their allegiance to the other three assistant chief constables and their supporters. He hadn't time to build up the kind of automatic support that a Guv'nor would command. Certainly nothing like the total commitment Ian Trevor could summon.

'You're wondering why I'm here,' he said. 'Well, it's simple. Grace Adams is a friend. A close friend. But I don't expect that to influence you one way or another. You are a brilliant team of dedicated pros and I know you'll work this one out. I'm here because I need to feel what's going on, so I can make sense of it back at HQ. You all understand that need.' Nods all round. Few of them wished to be pulled off active service for a desk job. 'It goes without saying that tongues would wag if others knew of my interest in this case, and it would get back to whoever is behind this, one way or another.'

'In other words,' Bobby intervened, 'the guv'nor's got his rights, just like the rest of us. And I will bring hellfire and damnation down on anyone who even hints about this to anyone else. Understood?' His rich preacher's voice filled the room. More nods. 'Now let's get to work. I want a team on the university staff records. Any unusual movements in or out. I want another doing the same thing with students. John,' he waved at the white-haired finance specialist, 'you're on Halliwell and Malkie. I want to know who, what, when and why. And the rest of you start fanning out in the pubs around the university. And let's pray for good luck.'

'One last thing,' Sam said. 'You've all been on dangerous operations, and been around hard men. But Malkie Collins is one of the most intelligent men I've ever met. And among the hardest. Do not, I repeat *not*, put yourself at undue risk.'

As the team dispersed, Sam turned and strode to the door. 'Come on, Lindsey. I want to pay a visit to Dr Violi. Find out if he knows anything.'

Gitte was still fast asleep on the sofa in Henry's study. Grace knelt in front of her with a bottle of water, two aspirins, three rounds of toast and a worried frown. It wasn't like her to drink so much. She was surely going to pass on the 3-Cube funding if it was going to cause Gitte this much pain. As she reached over and pushed a straggly clump of hair out of Gitte's eyes, Gitte's hand stretched out and touched her face.

'Thank you,' she whispered. 'You're a good friend.' She popped the pills and drowned them with water.

'What time is it?'

'Ten.'

'Not much time, then.'

'For what?'

'To go to Stef and tell him that you are accepting the 3-Cube money.'

'Are you sure, babe?' asked Grace. 'Really, really sure?'

'I'm sure.'

'Fantastic. You and me against the world.'

Grace bear-hugged her.

'You and me,' Gitte echoed. 'Just you and me.'

She stared into space, and then, slowly, she smiled.

CHAPTER 27

Sam appraised Stef Violi. Handsome, clever, good taste. The art confirmed that he was connected and cultured. As no academic could afford the pieces, they must be on loan from some collection. Private or public? He would get his art expert to track them down. The black jeans, open shirt and unlit cigar told him that Violi was a man at ease with himself. Despite his rise to the top of an important research centre, Violi was not one for ceremony or hierarchy. Sam wished he could be as relaxed. The cigar remained unlit, but occasionally found its way to Stef's lips. So, a touch uneasy. But was it anything other than the normal worries that beset people when faced with the police? We shall see.

'So, you can think of no obvious reason for the arson attack and the car bomb?' he asked. 'Do you think it has anything to do with the Standish Centre?'

Stef sucked in air. 'Possible. We're all open to threat these days. But there's been no specific attacks against us before, either here or around the world.'

Sam looked over his shoulder at the group photograph on the desk. It showed Violi as a teenager with his arm around the shoulder of a beautiful woman with a smile like silver. A boy, who looked like a younger, more haunted version of Stef – presumably his brother, the one working for the Gambettas – flanked him. Another brother, older, fresh faced and open hearted, held his mother's hand. He was the one who had been killed.

'Have you had any concerns about your staff recently?'

'Other than Grace?'

'Other than Grace.'

Stef slowly shook his head. 'Can't think of anyone. Oh, hang on, there was someone I had to let go in my first few weeks here. Professor Kurt Habermas. He was causing great disruption.'

'Can you tell us where he might be?' asked Lindsey, Palm Pilot out and ready.

'I'm afraid I can't. He lives in Germany. Hanover, I think. He may have returned there. As you might expect, he and I were not on speaking terms. In fact, the last person he talked to was . . .' He cupped his hand to his mouth. 'Alf Halliwell. He was handling the payoff and Habermas was pestering him. You don't think . . . Good God.'

Sam maintained a level gaze. Stef's eyes were large and expressive. They looked troubled. Either this was a bloody good act, or he had just made an unwelcome connection.

'Does your personnel department have any

further details on Professor Habermas?' asked Lindsey.

'Of course,' Stef replied as he opened the door. 'Julie. We need the files on Habermas. Would you personally see to it?'

Stef sat on the sofa, his face suddenly pale. 'I can't believe it. Habermas is a difficult man, but he's not, he's not . . . a killer.'

Leaping to a lot of conclusions, Sam thought. Or trying to lead me to them.

'On another track,' Sam said. 'Have you heard of UE students being involved in drug dealing?'

Stef closed his eyes, apparently still troubled by his revelation about Habermas and Halliwell; then he sipped his drink and looked thoughtfully at Sam, his brown eyes steady.

'Oh, there's the usual campus gossip. Some dope. E. Nothing serious. Why?'

Sam baited the hook. 'I have evidence that some of your students were involved in a major drug bust in Bilbao.'

Stef shook his head. 'Heard nothing about it.'

'Sure?'

'Of course I'm sure.' He proffered a lazy smile. 'Am I being accused of something?'

Sam let a grin play at the edge of his lips. 'I'm just surprised. Unusual for someone to be part of the senior management of an institution and not be aware of something like that.'

'I'm afraid like most academics my interest in

the world is limited to my own subjects and teams. I don't take much notice of the wide world of Eastfield University.'

Sam acknowledged the point. 'Do you mind if I have a look at your paintings?'

'Of course not. But don't run away with the idea they belong to me. They're on loan from a private collection.'

'Oh? Whose?'

'It's a *very* private collection, I'm afraid.'

Sam paused in front of a painting with hard planes and edges. It looked Italian. He recognized the style.

'Is this a Boccione?' he asked. A girlfriend had once taken him to a small Futurist museum in Canonbury Square.

'Very impressive,' Violi acknowledged, surprised.

Sam continued, 'The only thing I remember about the Futurists is that Marinetti, their leader, became a hard-core fascist.'

'True,' noted Violi. 'But is art above the politics of the artist? Should we no longer play Wagner or Richard Strauss? Kipling supported imperialist oppression in India. Men are creatures of their time.'

Lindsey, padding along beside them, was clearly impatient and itching to ask more questions. Sam shot her a warning look and she chewed her lip in silence.

'I've always believed that great men and women

rise above their circumstances. They can make choices,' Sam replied.

Violi shrugged.

Sam continued his tour until he reached the photograph that had been his intended destination since entering the room.

'What a lovely picture,' he said, pausing at the family group. Stef picked it up and rubbed a thumbprint from the glass.

'My mother and brothers,' he replied replacing the frame on the table next to his computer.

'Do they live in the States?'

'No, no. Calabria. That picture was taken at my grandfather's farm. We spent a lot of time there as boys.'

'Are your brothers academics too?'

'No, my younger brother's a lawyer. A good lawyer and a good man.' Stef laughed. 'A hard thing to be in Calabria, let me tell you – an honest lawyer.' A cloud passed over his face. 'My other brother died some years ago.' He paused, glanced at the picture then said, 'Let me show you this wonderful Chirico.'

As they chatted about the eerie stillness of the Italian's work, Sam suddenly asked, 'Was Alf a friend?'

Stef paused, looked deep into Sam's eyes and replied: 'Everybody loved Alf. But I only met him a few times. He dropped in with a bottle of very good malt for a chat a few days before he was killed.'

'Did he ever mention any Spanish friends?'

155

'No. I don't think so. But then again, why would he?'

'He had a holiday home in Spain and was a regular visitor to Bilbao.'

'I'd never have taken Alf for a Gaudí fan.'

'I'm not sure he was, Dr Violi.'

'Look,' Stef replied, stealing a glance at his watch, 'I'd love to chat more, but I have a meeting due. Is there anything else you wish to ask?'

Sam extended his hand. 'No. You've been most helpful. If I think of anything that still concerns me, I'll be sure to ring.'

'You do that. I hope you catch the terrorists soon.'

So do I, thought Sam.

As they descended in the lift, Lindsey asked, 'What do you make of him?'

'He's hiding something.' Sam rapped a frustrated drum roll on the wall, his intuition pinging like a Geiger counter. Violi had handed over something unexpected – a link between Halliwell and Habermas, whoever he was. So why do I think the good professor's doing a snow job?

As they reached the car park, Grace's Toyota screeched to a halt and she jumped out.

'I've got the money. I can carry on with the research.' Her face was bright with excitement and pleasure, her eyes sparking.

'Congratulations.' He, too, grinned.

As she tried to kiss him on the cheek, their

lips collided. Lindsey turned away and walked to the car.

'Where's it coming from?' Sam asked.

'What?' she asked, flustered.

'The money.'

'3-Cube.' She registered the puzzled look on his face. 'The Global Seed Development Project. It's a charitable foundation the people at Standish put me in touch with.'

'Who's behind it?'

'A couple of good guys. I've checked them out. Besides, Stef Violi, who runs this place, vouches for them.'

Oh great, thought Sam.

The long syndicate room was flowing with a bustle of noise and energy as officers reviewed the videotapes from the security cameras in front of the Science Park's entrance, chased leads on the phone, ran database checks on the University records and financial analyses of Malkie's businesses.

Sam stopped by John Woodland, the white-haired financial specialist. John was code-named Casper by the rest of team, after the cartoon character, Casper the Friendly Ghost. For protection, each of them had nicknames they used when running surveillance. Bobby was Gabriel. Lindsey, never having been operational, had no nickname.

'How's it going?' Sam asked.

Casper swung around to a PC and hit a few keys.

'Our old friend Malkie is undoubtedly up to fun and games.'

A bunch of figures ran down the screen showing massive cash transfers from an obscure timeshare company in Mallorca. 'This was set up last year, with Malkie as a non-executive director. It's run by a couple of Spanish guys who were supposed to build on a plot in the mountains.'

'Let me guess,' said Sam. 'The land's about the size of a postage stamp.' He checked the numbers. 'Twenty million quid cash went in, twenty out, presumably to the Cayman Islands.'

'I reckon this is the money that landed up in Florida, and it's also the cash that Halliwell was bagman for.' As Casper chewed a double cheeseburger and chips, Sam's stomach grumbled.

'You reckon he was the courier?' Sam asked Lindsey.

'Among other things.'

'We had the final report on the car,' said Bobby. 'Turns out he was a keen gardener.'

'I remember him at White Hill,' said Sam. 'He turned up to help when Henry went AWOL.'

'I don't think whoever blew him up intended to. The bomb was quite small. But unfortunately Halliwell had a bag of lime in his boot.'

'Good grief,' said Sam. 'It would've compounded the explosion a hundredfold in a confined space.'

'Exactly,' said Bobby.

'Are you sure the lime wasn't part of the bomb?'

'According to his wife, their garden was a bit acidic and lime was the cure.'

Sam brooded. Now what? Someone had tried to frighten Halliwell and it had gone horrifically wrong. Was he killed because of his connections with the Barracuda? Did he phone Grace because he knew something about the attack on the wheat?

'How is Mrs Halliwell holding up?' he asked.

'Turned the whole house over to us,' replied Bobby. 'Made the guys endless cups of tea and bacon sarnies. Reckons that whoever turned her husband into one of the bad guys should have their unmentionables crushed. Can't say as I blame her.' He shook his head sadly at the memory of the tough old bird trying to cope with the chaos around her. 'One of the blessings of Christianity, Sam, is you can reassure yourself that eternal damnation awaits these people, even if we miss them.'

'It's not much consolation, Bobby.'

'It's the best I've got, sir.'

Sam turned to Casper and patted him on the shoulder. 'Good work. Keep it up. There's something that ties Malkie to Standish and then there's a thread that pulls this whole thing together. We just have to keep tugging away.'

'Thank you, sir.' Casper stole a look a Lindsey, then sipped his Coke and swung back to his machine.

CHAPTER 28

Sam had one more trip to make before returning to London. Henry had sent him a note saying that he needed to talk. Sam found him down by the paddock feeding the pony.

'Gets a bit of a raw deal, old Sparky,' said Henry. 'Companion to the stars and all that,' he nodded at Soulman, 'but never the centre of attention unless she's playing the straight man to Hal's cripple act.'

Sam produced an apple, which the pony happily crunched before trotting off to join the stallion.

'Devotion is overwhelming, isn't it?' said Henry. 'Whenever Grace takes Soulman out, Sparky is half crazed. Spends hours whinnying with loneliness.' He watched Soulman nuzzle Sparky. 'Perhaps it's a price worth paying.' He turned towards the house. 'Let me make you a cup of tea.'

Later, they sat on the veranda sipping Earl Grey.

'This is the kind of day that almost makes atheists believe in God,' said Henry. 'Not that you need much persuasion, Sam.'

'When you see new life everywhere, evolution seems sacred. Each seed is an everyday

160

miracle. That's why I sometimes worry about Grace's work.'

'Science replacing God?'

'Something like that. It's almost as if she is creating a fifth season.'

They fell silent once more, enjoying the tea, the sun, old friendship. Henry seemed more at ease with himself. His lined and creased face was a handsome but pale facsimile of the sensuous, some said cruel, features that Sam had feared in his teens.

The man Sam had grown up with had been capable of ripping someone apart with a caustic, well-chosen quote. Sam's memory had always been good and was honed by his fascination with wildflowers, but he'd quickly had to put it to defensive use in the face of Henry's onslaught, and memorized huge chunks of Shakespeare, Freud and Dorothy Parker to protect himself.

'Who are you reading at the moment?' asked Henry.

'You won't approve.'

'I didn't ask for a recommendation – just a fact.'

Sam smiled. That was more like the old Henry.

'R. S. Thomas.'

'The rector?'

Sam nodded. Thomas had been a Welsh Anglican priest as well as carving out poems as dark as Welsh hillsides in winter. Henry, too, was Welsh, though seldom admitted it.

'I met him once,' said Henry. 'Tried to interview him for the wireless. I thought he was another useless old Celtic windbag. Christ, the bloody Welsh! I ask you.'

Sam grinned, then quoted:

'*To live in Wales is to be conscious at*
Dusk of the spilled blood
That went into the making of the wild sky.'

'Is that Thomas?' asked Henry, running a thumb down his cheek.

Sam nodded. 'A poem called "Welsh Landscape".'

'Better than I remember,' said Henry.

'I'll send you some of his stuff.'

'How are things in London? Still enjoying it?'

'Oh, you know . . . Been there a long time. Come to an accommodation with the old girl.'

'I never could,' replied Henry. 'Tried it before I met Grace's mother. Did a spell at LSE. Too anonymous for me.'

Sam had to get back to HQ, but Henry and Halliwell had worked closely together and he hoped that Henry had some answers. But he didn't want to push his depressed friend too hard.

'Can you tell me anything about Halliwell?' he asked.

'He was a bit of a lad,' said Henry. 'Liked a drink. Bit of a gambler. Very attentive to the ladies. I think he tried it on a few times with June. Did a bit of gardening here when I . . .' He seemed to lose the thread for a second. 'When I was otherwise engaged. But we rubbed along together. He was a great finance director and helped me build the university. You should've seen the mess we inherited.'

'Is it possible he was less than virtuous?' Sam sipped his tea, listening to the ensuing silence.

'There were rumours. He was on the council's Planning Committee and people gossiped. But I don't think so. As I say, he was larger than life, but the university's books were very closely audited and nothing was ever out of place. If I'd done half the things people gossiped about, I'd be in my grave by now.'

Sam finished his tea.

'Bit more?' asked Henry.

'Can't. Love to. Got to go.'

As Sam stood, Henry placed his hand on his arm. 'You know I can't breach patient confidentiality?'

'Of course.'

'But I'm really torn.'

'Why?'

'You know I retained my private practice until a few years ago.'

'Sure.'

'I think it's possible that one of my former patients killed Halliwell and is desperate to kill Grace.'

CHAPTER 29

Sam answered his emails with simple commands – Yes. No. Please do. Tomorrow. Monday – as he dispatched his in-tray. The chairman had asked to see him and wanted to cover his bases.

When he finished, he pulled out a sheet of paper and began to doodle. At the top he wrote:

Habermas

Grace had told him that she suspected Habermas of trying to infiltrate her computer data, and Sam's instinct told him that Halliwell had been a bagman for Malkie. Who else was in Malkie's pocket? Was there a connection to Habermas?

There was a knock on the door.

'Come in.'

Lindsey entered and placed a buff folder on the desk in front of him. Habermas's Stasi file.

'Where did you get this?'

'Oh,' she smiled, 'you know.'

He did indeed. A back channel.

164

'He was a Senior Research Fellow in Molecular Biology at Danzig University in the 80s,' said Lindsey.

Sam stared at the picture of a small, squat ugly figure, a severe short haircut, hard grey eyes.

'He ran with the hare and with the hounds. Stasi and BND,' continued Lindsey. Sam had a lot of contacts in German security and had put her on the trail. 'He was greedy, unstable and had a cocaine habit. Eventually, they dropped him.'

'Cocaine,' Sam wondered. 'Does that connect him to Malkie Collins?'

'Could do.'

'Anyone with a grudge against him?'

'According to our contact, half of his colleagues in Danzig, when they discovered what he'd said about them in their Stasi files.'

'Good work.' Sam handed back the file. 'Need more, though. Need to find the guy. He's one of the keys.'

He glanced up. She looked frail and tired. 'It can wait till morning. Get some sleep. That's an order.' After she left, Sam called his driver and told him to offer her a lift home.

Sam stared at the name at the top of the list, then jotted down the few facts that he now knew.

Habermas –
German. 54. Born in Danzig. Stasi informer.
Still connected to security?????

165

He drew a line down the middle of the page and put Grace's name at the top of one column and Malkie's on the other.

Grace   Malkie

Then he began to tally up the connections.

Habermas   Habermas???
Halliwell   Halliwell.
Violi   Violi?

Where was Rod Leadsmith? Henry had given him very little to go on, other than a litany of psychospeak about Rod's intense desire for Grace. Sam had had him pulled in for questioning about the glasshouse attack, but could make nothing stick, then he had disappeared.

His PA stuck her head round the door. 'Sir Charles would like to see you in ten minutes.'

Sir Charles Lambie looked every inch the general he once was. At sixty-one, his figure was still trim, his Prince of Wales check suit immaculately cut and his black brogues polished. He had an equine face and almost comically bad teeth. But he commanded attention.

Sam sat in a hard green leather chair in the spartan office and watched as the Chairman of the NCS, and the man to whom he was ultimately accountable, poured him Sri Lankan green tea.

After handing Sam the cup, he pulled his swivel chair from round the desk and sat opposite. You're a clever old bird, Charlie, thought Sam. You know how much I hate unnecessary displays of status.

'So. You've been here, what? Five months?'

'Six.'

'How's it going? Living up to your expectations? Getting on all right with Ian? Bit of a stickler for the rules, Ian. Not too restrictive, I hope?'

'It's certainly different.'

'More bureaucratic than you expected. I *did* warn you, Sam, when you asked me whether you should apply. You're managing an army of fourteen hundred people. It's as much about logistics as leadership.'

'So I'm finding out.'

'But the reasons you came here hold good. We need your strength and determination to take on this new breed before they worm their way even deeper into cyberspace. Your predecessors began the process, but we need to go much further.' He sipped his tea and glanced at Sam, his grey eyes clear and direct. Sam could sense another agenda. Charlie didn't often ask him over for elevenses.

'Biscuit?' He opened a barrel and offered Sam a chocolate digestive.

'No, thanks.'

'Quite right. Young man like you should look after his body.' He took a bite. 'I'm too old to care. Tell me about Grace Adams.'

So that's it.

'I know you must be asking yourself whether the Garton case is too personal. Ian will be unhappy, you know.'

'How did you hear about it?'

'You cancel a speech at short notice, correspondence is slower coming out of your office than it might be and you're disappearing off to Garton at a moment's notice with our best DCI. Word spreads, Sam. And eventually it gets to me.'

'Grace Adams is a close friend. But there's something big going on down there that we must get to the bottom of.'

'That's what you have syndicates for, Sam, and operational line managers. Your job is strategic, not tactical. I'm compelled to say that it would be a mistake if you lost sight of the big picture in the pursuit of a personal vendetta.'

'You know me better than that.'

'Do I? I can only go by your actions. The squad and the Home Secretary, whilst they respect your commitment to the operational side of the business, want you as a thinker, Sam. You are Ian's natural successor, and I want you to get there. Your days chasing people in fast cars are over. You must move on. There are several more rungs on the ladder, you know. Don't want to put up a black mark on the way. You owe a debt to those of us who supported you.'

Sam put down his tea, untouched. He wanted to tell Charlie about the PM's job offer, but was sworn to secrecy.

'I understand what you're telling me, Charlie,' he said as his mobile beeped and he glanced at the message.

Found Habermas

'Got to go, I'm afraid.'

'Good, good.' Sir Charles rose to his feet and escorted Sam to the door, a slight pressure from his hand on the small of Sam's back, then he stopped and, almost as an afterthought, said: 'Dr Violi.'

'What about him?' asked Sam.

'I have a favour to ask of you. Any communication with the good doctor should be routed through me.'

Sir Charles opened the door and looked into Sam's eyes.

'He's off limits.'

CHAPTER 30

A tall man, thin as a hair-clip, dug a speck of dirt from under his manicured finger-nails, watched two girls play hopscotch and checked the Colt automatic sitting on the passenger seat of his car. He glanced at his watch. One thirty. For two days now, the woman and two children, accompanied by a cripple, had had lunch at McDonald's. Afterwards, the kids played in the small swing-park, whilst the odd couple held hands.

The man appraised Hal. He would be useless in a struggle. After one last glance at the target, he put Lilly's photograph back inside an envelope, started the Renault 11, and slid into the afternoon.

PART TWO

STONY PLACES

Behold, a sower went forth to sow;
And when he sowed, some seeds fell by the
way side, and the fowls came and devoured
them up:
Some fell upon stony places, where they had
not much earth: and forthwith they sprung up,
because they had no deepness of earth:
And when the sun was up, they were scorched;
and because they had no root, they withered
away.

The Gospel according to Matthew, 13, 3–6,
King James Version

CHAPTER 31

Stef beamed proudly as he introduced the elfin figure next to him. Her thick charcoal hair was worn in a plait and her jet-black pupils and pale skin gave her a translucent beauty. 'Grace, Gitte, this is Alaina Prokovitch.'

'Pleased to meet you.' Her English was good, her Moscow accent transformed by a Boston twang. 'I've heard a great deal about you and your work. It sounds very impressive.'

Grace glanced at Gitte, a twinkle of pride and disbelief in her eyes. Alaina Prokovitch admires our work, she thought. *Unbelievable.* She could see Gitte thinking the same thing, a smile tugging at her lips.

'Now,' said Stef, 'I think it's time we showed you what our friends at 3-Cube have delivered.' As they followed him out of his office, down three flights and across a glass bridge, the Standish building billowed out behind them. At the end of the corridor, the group passed through a detailed security check, then the metal door opened and they were greeted by a security guard.

'Dr Adams,' he smiled, 'I've been permanently

assigned to your new Unit. I'm looking forward to it.'

Unit, thought Grace. What Unit? She peered over the man's shoulder and a surge of shock ran through her body. They were in a large white rectangular room filled with gleaming Apple Macs, flatbed scanners, cytogenetics equipment, two Unix workstations, and an ABI gene sequencer. Equipment she had dreamt of when she and Gitte were locked in her mother's little study with secondhand computing and lashed-together equipment. And the lab was humming with people, who looked up and smiled as she entered.

The next few hours were a blur of introductions as Alaina walked them round the lab. They met an Indian man in his twenties who specialized in quantitative genetics and biometrics, a Chinese woman in her forties who had developed a new generation of analytic techniques capable of measuring thousands of proteins in less than an hour. Half a dozen young worker bees researching their doctorates completed Alaina's team.

Over coffee and tea in a small office at the side of the laboratory, Alaina, Gitte and Grace discussed the next few months.

'I hope you didn't mind me bringing in my SWAT team.' Alaina sipped hot, sweet tea. 'You will of course recruit your own people, but we thought you'd come so far on your own that you'd appreciate some immediate help.'

Grace's head was spinning. She would be able to

send the wheat to true commercial trials two years earlier than she expected.

'It's fantastic, Professor Prokovitch.'

'Please, my dear, call me Alaina. Bureaucratic formalities are the preserve of men, I think. Don't you?'

Grace caught Gitte's eye and they both grinned. 'It all looks so professional, I don't know where *we* fit in.'

'You, my friends, have a rare gift. You belong to a select band of scientists who combine intuition with application. I can see it in the patterns of your work. The leaps that you make in logic, the things you see that others don't, the risky experiments. Come.' She stood and they followed, puzzled, as she led them into another room, this one with two workstations side by side. On each sat a vase of white roses she recognized as 'William Salisbury', their sweet scent filling the room.

'I love flowers,' said Alaina. 'Our workplace should be filled with beauty. Otherwise we would live in such a dreary world and we would not be able to ride the waves of our intuition. Science and mathematics are beautiful, soulful pursuits. If we allow ourselves to fade into the mundane then the sterility of our thought will turn us into philosophers, and as Karl Marx noted, "Philosophers have only tried to understand the world, the point is to change it."'

She grinned at Gitte. 'Ten years of Marxist

dialectical training and this is the only quote I choose to remember.'

Gitte returned the smile, her pupils large and illuminated by inner light. She could feel sexual curiosity flowing from Alaina towards her, and she reflected it back with interest.

Grace shook her head in amazement that someone had brought all the things from her office and replicated their exact position around her Mac. On the round chill-out table in the middle of the room sat a bottle of Krug.

'I hope you don't mind the intrusion,' said Stef, flowing into the room.

Grace stood. 'No. Of course, not.' On impulse she hugged him. 'I can't thank you enough.'

Stef stood back and held her by the arms, his eyes dancing. 'Of course you can. Create your wheat. Save a lot of children.'

'And gain a Nobel Prize for Standish, eh, Stef?' Alaina chuckled.

Stef popped the champagne. 'Cynic,' he laughed as he poured four glasses.

'To you,' he offered a toast.

'To "Perfect Wheat",' Grace replied as they chinked glasses.

'To success,' Alaina responded.

'To hope,' Gitte raised her glass.

An explosive roar ripped across the car park and they watched as Grace's Toyota rose as if in slow motion, turn in the air, then shatter into piercing fragments of glass, metal and plastic.

CHAPTER 32

Sam pulled on his battered Brooks Beast running shoes and hit the rain-soaked road, pacing himself so he could think. Regent's Park was quiet on a wet Saturday afternoon.

Whoever had bombed Grace's car had sent her a note – *Welcome to the mystery of hatred, bitch. Nobody wants your dance. Don't plant the wheat.* They had puzzled over the message until Sam recalled the quote. It was from Ted Hughes' 'God Help the Wolf After Whom the Dogs Do Not Bark'. He'd looked up the full stanza.

Nobody wanted your dance.
Nobody wanted your strange glitter – your floundering
Drowning life and your effort to save yourself.
Treading water, dancing the dark turmoil.
  Looking for something to give –
Whatever you found
They bombarded with splinters,
Derision, mud – the mystery of that hatred.

Hughes' poem about his doomed wife, Sylvia Plath, seemed a weird choice, but consistent with

177

Henry's view that Leadsmith was locked into some intense love–hate relationship with Grace.

Why are the attacks intensifying? And what about Habermas? A local fisherman had pulled his torso from a reed bed in the river. His guys had identified him from the bare remnants of the tattoo of a lion on his shoulder. Who had killed him and why? Something to do with the drugs deal? Was he involved in the shipments? But why tamper with Grace's data? Were the two things linked?

Then there was Violi. Where did he fit in? And, more to the point, why did Charlie Lambie warn him off the investigation?

Sam skirted the pond, scattering a gathering of ducks, and headed towards the zoo, offering his customary nod to the black bear isolated at the top of its ziggurat-shaped hill. Is Violi under investigation by another agency – CIA? FBI? – and they don't want me to queer their patch? Sam knew the General was incorruptible, and therefore discounted any sense that he was being leant on for criminal reasons. He turned for home, quickly discounting the last alternative; but if someone was on the General's radar, and for the hint to be so strong that he was off limits, Violi had to be a player.

'Spare me a minute, Sam?' Shocked out of his stride, Sam turned to face Sergio Colinas, huddled on a park bench drawing deeply on a cigarette, a long, black coat covering his emaciated frame.

'Good grief, what's going on?' Sam asked. 'What's wrong with you?'

Sergio's hack came from the depth of his being. As he fought for breath, he extracted another cigarette from his pack. 'I have a head cold. It's nothing.'

'Some head cold. C'mon, I'll take you back to the flat. Get you something to eat.'

'No, no. Sam. It's too . . .' He hesitated.

'Too what?'

'Too kind of you. I'll go back to my hotel soon. I'll be fine. I just need a word. I saw you leave your flat and followed.'

Sam reached down and lifted his friend to his feet. 'We're both getting soaked. Let's go to my place. Get you some dry clothes and warm food. *Then* you can go back.'

Sergio slipped from his arms, unconscious.

Hal laced his fingers through Sara's and smiled as Lilly Collins and Ruthie teetered on their bikes, the stabilizers doing enough to keep them upright. Roni, Lilly's elegant mother, had dropped off a top-of-the-range green Raleigh Malkie had bought the week before, whilst Ruthie had a worn out hand-me-down boy's bike that Sara had found in the stables at Eastfield House. When she had seen the condition of her friend's cycle, Lilly had immediately swapped. On each other's bike, the girls twisted through the trees and down a concrete path, the park's wooden fence protecting them from the odd car that drove lazily towards the village.

Parked in the street opposite, engine idling, was a Renault 11. Inside, the thin man lit a cigarette. It was nearly time.

'This statement is false.'

'What?' asked Sam, slicing pizza, the gooey cheese sticking to his knife.

'You of all people must remember *that* from freshman classes in logic,' Colinas insisted.

Sam glanced up at Colinas; some of the colour had returned to his cheeks. He was lying on Sam's dark green Conran sofa, sipping Carajillos, a Catalan cocktail of espresso and brandy. On the floor sat an ashtray filled with violently crushed butts.

Sam thought for a second, as he slipped the food onto a large white plate.

'Of course,' he replied, 'the Liar.'

'I knew I could rely on that extraordinary memory of yours. Exactly. The Liar – Eubulides' paradox.' Colinas attacked his Fiorentina with the gusto of a man who had not eaten in days. Sam was worried about his friend's condition. But with Sergio, you waited until he was ready to talk.

'I hated the Liar at University.' Sam swallowed his Tiger beer. 'It seemed trivial in a way, but maddening in its circularity. If it's false to claim that "This statement is false" then the speaker is telling the truth. On the other hand if the speaker

180

is telling the truth, then he's lying.'

'Exactly. If it's false it's true, if true, false –
a facile but deadly argument. But this is the
world you and I have inhabited these many years.
We live in a whisper chamber in which the words
of friends, colleagues and partners echo, mix and
refract.'

'You've been reading too many spy novels,
Sergio. The Cold War's over. Smiley retired.'

'Smiley's universe was simple compared with the
way we live now. Then the enemy was clear. But
now there are no sides – merely angles. And all the
time people like you and I try to serve our masters
in the war against terrorism, not knowing who our
masters serve.'

Sam poured himself some coffee. 'What's eating you?'

Sergio scratched nervously at the stubble on his
chin then he dropped his head back on the sofa.

'I've been retired.'

'*What?*'

'As good as. They've put me on sick leave after
my call to Fernandez. Something about a risky
psychiatric profile.' He spat out his words with
undisguised venom. 'They suck you in, destroy
your ability to love and trust; then, when all you
have left is *them*, they crush you.'

As Sam moved to comfort his friend, he was
flushed with a vision, a revelation of himself as an
older man being comforted by a younger colleague,
telling him that life was more than the job, and

that the howling waves of loneliness would pass. His heart thudded against his chest as he pulled Sergio into his arms.

Ruthie laughed as a large blob of ice cream slithered onto Lilly's white shirt, almost smothering a bright red hand-stitched ladybird.

'No reply.' Hal hit the disconnect button on his mobile. Roni Collins had promised she would pick up Lilly at two o'clock and it was now half past.

Sara felt nervous. She was twenty minutes late for an appointment with Hope Delawney. 'What shall we do?'

Hal kissed her, relishing her softness.

'Don't worry. You go back to Her Maj and I'll take Lilly home. Perhaps a neighbour can look after her.'

'There are no neighbours. They're renting Summerhouse.'

'Wow,' he said. Summerhouse was a neoclassical house surrounded by two hundred acres of woodland that used to belong to the Eastfield estate, but was sold in the 1920s.

'Malkie mentioned a housekeeper.'

'There you are, then,' he answered. 'Simple.'

They kissed again. 'Thanks. I'll see you later?'

'Without a doubt.'

'Girls,' she shouted. 'Home time.'

'Nooo . . .'

Hal walked over and lifted Ruthie onto his hip. 'Oh, yes. Otherwise no treats tomorrow.'

Lilly stretched out her arms, eyes gleaming. 'Me. Lift me.'

'Sorry, sweetheart,' said Hal.

'He can't,' explained Ruthie in a matter-of-fact voice. 'He's a cripple.'

'*Ruthie*!' exclaimed her horrified mother.

Hal hugged Ruthie, then dropped her to the ground.

'But you are,' Ruthie pleaded with Hal. 'That's what you told me.' Her lips trembled. 'And you laughed.'

Hal knelt down, ignoring the pain in his leg.

'That's true, sweetheart. Thing is, and this is a big secret between you and me, friends don't call each other cripples. If I say you're gorgeous, what'll you reply?'

'I'd say you're funny?'

'Give me a hug,' he replied. 'Now, get your bike.'

'Race you,' shouted Lilly and jumped on Ruthie's bike.

'Don't go on the road,' yelled Sara.

'Course not,' replied Lilly.

As the girls pedalled furiously towards the wrought-iron gates, the thin man crushed his Gitane, put it carefully into a plastic package, revved the car and signalled to the driver of the green Range Rover behind him. Some metres ahead, a black Transit van waited. The kidnapper glanced at his watch. They were half an hour behind and the contingency time had been eaten up. They had to do it now and their mission had to be achieved calmly and efficiently. He pulled a brown bear mask over his face and glanced in the mirror as his colleague became a lion. It was time.

'C'mon, little monsters.' Hal pointed Lilly towards the Cherokee Jeep, and Sara steered Ruthie towards her ancient blue Citroën.

Hal lifted the bike into the back, then smiled at Lilly.

'Where's Mummy? Is she drinking vodka somewhere? She's always drinking vodka. Daddy tells her she'll die. Do you think she'll die?'

'Of course not.'

'Good. I don't want her to die. I love her. Is your mummy dead?' As Hal strapped her in, his phone rang. 'That's probably your mummy now.'

He answered. 'Hi.' Silence. 'Who's there?'

A second later, he watched as Ruthie broke free of her mother's grasp and ran towards them. 'I've got your bike, Lilly. We forgot to swap.'

She ran onto the road and the Range Rover, swerving to block Hal's jeep, threw her into the air like a rag doll. She thudded onto the pavement; the sound of her cracked skull lost in the squeal of brakes and screams of her mother.

The thin man realized that this was going to be messier than he had planned. The key was to get in and get out fast. If anything held him up for more than two minutes, he always called off a mission.

He threw his car into a spin, blocking Sara as she ran towards Ruthie, then pulled a gun, fired and

184

caught Sara on the shoulder. She spun, collapsed, then crawled towards Ruthie, who lay motionless. 'Please,' Sara mouthed. 'Please.'

Hal was rooted to the tarmac. Seconds before his life had been wonderful, now it was disintegrating in front of his eyes. Then suddenly a green Range Rover slewed in front of his Cherokee. Two men leapt out and ran towards the passenger side. As one unbuckled Lilly, she bit him on the cheek.

'Little bastard.' He slapped the child.

The action jerked Hal out of his terrified stasis. He hauled open the driver's door, dragged out a baseball bat, and his first swing cracked the man's head, splattering blood across Lilly's face as she fought free and ran towards Ruthie.

The second kidnapper thrust a gun into Hal's temple and hissed, 'Back off.'

'Do it, Hal.'

He snapped his head around. It was Malkie. Hal recognized the face from a photograph in the newspapers that Sara had shown him.

Malkie cradled a shotgun.

'Lilly. Come here, darling.' As she ran towards her father, the thin man's car sped towards her. Metres from impact, Hal threw himself on the girl, clipping her to the ground and smothering her with his body. While he braced himself, the windscreen of the Renault exploded inwards under the impact of Malkie's shells. The car veered off, bounced high on the kerb and smashed into the park railings. The thin man staggered from the wreckage, yelling into a thin microphone strung round his neck. 'Out. *Now.*'

As the Transit van reversed, tyres squealing on the unforgiving tarmac, Malkie ran towards Lilly and Hal was suddenly conscious of a long howl – 'Ruuuthhhiee.'

CHAPTER 33

Sergio Colinas watched a young black winger jump a tackle, swerve to the left then strike a sweet shot that dipped inside the top right-hand corner of the net.

'He's good,' he muttered, rubbing his hands vigorously.

Play resumed on the referee's whistle and the players churned up the red gravel pitch. Beyond them, St Alban's Abbey perched on a hill, two thousand years of Christian faith peering down on the small town. Sergio had spent an hour wandering around the building, devouring its past. He had put off this meeting for as long as he could, wary of an uncharted future.

'You didn't bring me out on my day off for a chat about football,' said Ian Trevor. 'What do you want?'

Sergio watched the black kid slide a perfect pass to one of the centre backs. He envied the child's talent, knowing when to release the ball was the highest skill in the game.

'We have a problem,' he replied.

'What kind of problem?' enquired Trevor.

'The worst. Ten of our guys. Could be the same with you. Rotten. Running protection for the Barracuda cartel. Making files disappear. The works.'

Trevor peered out at the thick blue cloud sitting on the horizon and breathed slowly.

'How high do yours go?' he asked.

Sergio was silent, brooding, watching the match unfold. Finally, mournfully, he said, 'Fernandez.'

Trevor absorbed the information that so powerful a figure was corrupt. Decades of experience in bureaucratic struggles ensured that he maintained his cool. Underneath he was speculating furiously. Who of his men? Which bastard has gone over?

Sergio's head shook. 'We believe one of your most senior men has—'

'Thank you, Sergio.' Trevor cut across the other man's accusation. 'We can take it from here.'

In his mind, he checked off names of his three Assistant Chief Constables. Alan Lamond was due to retire next month. He and Trevor had started on the same day at Hendon Police Training School. Fiona Cassell was on her way to the top and had passed every test asked of her in the eight years they had worked together. Tommy Hacket would have been his chosen successor if the General hadn't insisted on Copeland. There was no way that they were crooked.

'All I know is that our informant is reliable.' Sergio handed Trevor a file. 'Do with it as you please. We wanted you to know and to give you the chance to clean up your own stables before we announce our arrests.'

Over the years at least sixty NCS officers had gone over to the other side, but no one had ever suggested that the problem had gone this high. This is Burgess and Maclean. No, he corrected himself, feeling queasy. This is Philby – the highest-ranking traitor in the history of British intelligence. Then he thought of Sam – what do I really know of the spook?

'Thank you,' he said, standing. 'I will ensure that we pursue this with maximum speed. I'm sure that we will clear all of our officers.'

As he walked towards the squabbling geese and swans, he heard Sergio say, 'We are relying on you.'

Trevor headed for the Six Bells, where he downed a large double before phoning his wife, cancelling dinner and travelling to London.

Tears coursed down Sara's face as she listened to the consultant. Her right arm was in a sling; the bullet had passed clean through. She and Hal gazed at Ruth's motionless figure.

'She lost consciousness for a while,' said the consultant.

Hal squeezed Sara's hand, which was wet with tears.

'Will there be brain damage?' whispered Sara.

'We'll know more by this evening when we do the scan.'

CHAPTER 34

R oni Collins' face was frozen as she stroked her daughter's hand and sang their special song:

Golden slumbers kiss your eyes,
smiles awake you when you rise;
sleep pretty loved one do not cry,
and I will sing a lullaby.

She used to have a good voice, good enough to sing in the University Choir, then a rock band, where her addiction to cocaine and drink began. She had met Malkie at an AA meeting the first time he had tried to clean up. He was different from the others – powerful, fascinated by everything. One day he carried a copy of Shakespeare's Sonnets into the quiet church in which she, too, sat, struggling with her demons.

He smiled. She returned it. Nine months later they married. Six months on, Lilly was born. Her child's autism seemed somehow to represent the curse Roni had placed on herself as little by little she understood more of her husband's business, especially after she met Standish. The man terrified her. As did Malkie's commitment to his daughter. There was no way he'd let her run, just take Lilly and go live with another man. He loved his girl too much.

She no longer knew what to think. What to do. She had felt crushed by the weight of Malkie's disappointment when she returned to the bottle, but it was either that or slit her wrists. She ran a finger through her daughter's hair, fingering it gently. The only way to calm her down had been to let her watch *Kipper's Snowy Day* half a dozen times and eventually Lilly had fallen into a shallow sleep in her arms.

Roni rocked on her heels. I've become a stereotype, she thought. And yet this was no film, no easy fiction to be resolved like Diane Keaton walking away from Al Pacino in *The Godfather*. Keaton just took off her makeup and went home to Woody Allen. She longed to phone her lover, to have his voice soothe her, make promises, caress her. As Lilly groaned, Roni sighed. I've got to stay here. For her. She wiped her eyes with her hands and reached for the bottle. I need a drink.

'Daddy, Daddy, wake up, wake up. You're screaming.' Malkie felt the small fingers on his face, dragging him back from a dark place – a world of torments in which she had been killed by the kidnappers. A life without Lilly. A life not worth living.

191

'Are you crying, Daddy?' She wiped the tears from his eyes onto the pillow.

'No, sweetie.' He kissed her hair, absorbing her scent. He could never understand child-abusers. How could they rob children of this innocence? This pure unencumbered soul. And he wondered again about how his father, his *father*, had beaten him, stubbed cigarettes on his flesh, broken his arm. What did I do wrong? Why didn't he love me as I love Lilly?

'I'm fine, darling, go back to sleep. Where's Blankie?'

'Blankie's happy,' she smiled, hugging a thread-bare old blanket, the stuffing falling from the inlaid blue dolphins. She'd slept with it her whole life and refused to travel anywhere without it.

She turned her back to him, thrust a thumb in her mouth and snuggled down.

'Daddy?' she asked sleepily.

'Got to sleep, menace.'

'Mummy won't die, will she? I don't want her to. I love her, Daddy.'

'Me too,' he said.

He'd found Roni on the floor beside the bed, impossible to rouse. The nanny had been distraught. As he had been undressing Roni, Lilly had come into the bedroom filled with night fears. They had made hot chocolate and then he told her a story about Lilly and the magic rabbit. He'd fallen asleep fully clothed on top of her covers and drifted down to the dark place.

He waited until Lilly's breathing was slow and regular, then tiptoed downstairs to the kitchen.

'Hi, boss. You OK?' Frank Brown, one of his guys, sat at the table drinking hot, sweet tea, an Uzi sub-machine gun on top of a copy of the *Sun*'s Page Three pin-up. Outside, patrolling the walls, were another four of his men, each hand-picked. Any one of them could be a traitor. But not Frank. He could trust his life to Frank, and did.

'Fine, Frank. A bit restless.'

'Understandable. Anyone messing with one of my kids, I'd rip them apart. Don't worry about a thing, boss. We're on the case. And we're the best. You should know, you taught us.'

'Thanks, big man.'

Malkie trudged upstairs, undressed and settled in next to Roni. He tried to wrap his body round hers, but she shrugged him off. He fought off his nightmares as he, too, drifted off.

CHAPTER 35

Al Imam placed the glass of cold lemonade against his cheek. He was feeling feverish. His doctor had been telling him to rest, but there was no time. Soon he would be dead. And the dead have nothing but rest. His stomach cancer was eating him from the inside.

He coughed bloody phlegm into a handkerchief and then turned to the oxygen mask. As the pain dulled, he wrote his political testament.

> *By the time the West finds out that I have taken revenge for two hundred years of humiliation, I will have become dust. But I will have left a legacy. The West will be weakened by a disease as bad as AIDS. It will suffer as Africa is suffering.*

Standish's scientist had told him that there would be 30 per cent adult mortality across the West as the stomach cancers spread by 'Perfect Wheat' took hold. They would engineer a promoter for carcenoid tumours, a rare form of intestinal cancer that targets men and women over the age of forty.

The wheat would take generals and presidents, teachers and clergy, lawyers and crooks. But the young would remain and the West would be reborn with fresh ideas, to meet on equal terms a resurgent Islam, no longer caught between corrupt Arabian kingdoms and religious fanatics.

His own cancer had been his inspiration. At first he had been bitter that Allah had inflicted such pain on him. He read widely about his cancer and its possible cures, increasingly filled with despair as his body and mind disintegrated.

His last collection of published stories drew parallels between his physical weakness and the collapse of Arab culture. His misery at the inability of his people to break away from corrupt regimes, or to develop tactics other than the suicides of teenagers or the idiocy of the child Bin Laden, bit deep in his soul. Had the Arab nation come to this?

His research had led him to the possibility that GM wheat might produce a cure for some cancers. But, day by day, the life had drained from him and he realized that his disease was incurable. On September 11th, 2001, he watched from a London hospital bed as his dream of a tolerant Islam crashed to the ground. The West and its allies had turned his people into barbarians.

That night, lost in a miasma of painkillers, he had dreamt the Patriarch Joseph's dream of seven lean years and seven fat years. He had seen America humbled. He realized deep in his subconscious that

Allah had called him to a higher calling by allowing the illness to ravage his body. Allah had provided him with a means of turning back the clock on the West. He must rein in America's arrogance and allow the world to return to some kind of balance. Only then would Arab culture flourish once more.

When he woke up, he began to plan and to organize.

'Ebola is a stupid disease,' he'd told Standish on his last visit, 'just like the tactics of that fool Bin Laden. Both strike hard and visibly and then are forced to retreat when they rapidly kill their hosts. The Taliban would still rule Afghanistan if Bin Laden had not drawn American wrath on their heads.

'AIDS is smart. It takes time and consumes its host slowly. It mutates and hides, constantly probing for an opening. It kills generations by infecting their pleasure. The wheat will be like AIDS. We'll take Dr Adams' work and within two generations the seed will promote tumours. But it'll take five years before the source will be traced and then it'll be too late. Our brothers and sisters in Bangladesh will receive Dr Adams' pure wheat, the West ours.'

As he coughed into his handkerchief, he wondered again about Standish. What was the man's motive? It went beyond money. He seemed to despise his family, his country, his race. But any man who allowed himself to be rootless hated

196

himself. He would have to be careful with the man. For Standish, betrayal would be as natural as breathing.

He returned to his last testament.

In 1944, Henry Morgenthau, the US Treasury Secretary, proposed a final solution to the problem posed by a hundred years of Prussian militarism. He had no faith in the German character or the morality of its people and wanted the Reich stripped of its entire industrial base and turned into 'a country primarily agricultural and pastoral in character'. Similarly, the Arab nations have no patience left. Western arrogance has left us no choice but to attack your body to enable you to rediscover your soul. We are your equals.

His niece gently entered, carrying a tray loaded with pills.

'You must rest, Uncle.'

'I am too weak to rest.' He opened the first of his painkillers and swallowed deep.

CHAPTER 36

'I've no idea why someone would try to kidnap my daughter,' Malkie told the detective sergeant as he shielded his eyes from the early morning sun. *They* could come for him, Lilly or Roni at any time. Whoever *they* were. He had to be prepared. If his housekeeper hadn't called him, Lilly would already be dead or gone.

Either Johnny had found out about his deal with ETA, or his Basque handlers were taking out extra insurance that he would actually kill Johnny when they ordered him to. It just might be some old score being settled by a domestic rival, but he doubted it. He was strong, and packed a lot of support. It was only when you were weak that the weak turned against you.

'I seriously have no idea,' he repeated.

In a car parked in a small lane at the bottom of the drive, Sam and Bobby Neil listened to the conversation via the wire the DS wore. Later they would examine Malkie's voice to monitor stress, trying to detect patterns that would reveal when he was being evasive or lying. But Bobby had no need of high-tech solutions at this moment.

'He's lying through his teeth,' he muttered.

Sam wasn't so sure. If Malkie knew the identity of the would-be kidnappers, then by now someone would be dead and the word would be on the street as a warning to others.

Lilly sat on the lawn, pulling clothes from a Barbie and laying it beside the other naked dolls. She was obsessively tucking each one into a box, then taking it out again and carefully dressing it. She had eaten nothing but bananas since the accident. Just as she had as a baby.

Next to Lilly, Roni sat on a low-slung deckchair, working her way through a large orange juice, with, he suspected, a shot of vodka. He smiled in her direction, but her black sunglasses gave no indication of the emotion in her eyes.

'Coffee?' he asked the DS.

'Not for me, thanks.'

Malkie retreated to the kitchen and filled a large mug. He assumed the policeman was wired and wanted to make sure he was sending the correct messages to the NCS. He had a well-paid informer inside the squad who had told him they'd launched an investigation into the Halliwell connection, and of the unusual interest shown by the new Deputy Director General, Sam Copeland.

Malkie had followed Sam's career with interest. He was the only undercover cop ever to get close to breaking through Malkie's defences. He'd never forgotten his shock at discovering Sam's betrayal. His first instinct had been to get his guys to slash the infiltrator's throat and dump him in the Clyde. Couldn't do it in the end. Too easy a fate for Sammy boy. Malkie guessed that the humiliation of being trussed to a lamppost and exposed to post-club crowds howling abuse would live long in Sam's memory.

The word on the street was that Sam was sophisticated and tenacious. Well, thought Malkie, he's got a real problem this time, because even I don't know what's going on.

'Lilly, darling.' He walked back into the garden and his daughter looked up, a dull stare. 'What present would you like to give Ruthie when we see her?'

He'd been on the phone to Sara on the hour every hour and knew that Ruthie's scan was clear. He planned to take Lilly to see her that afternoon. His little girl needed to be shaken out of her terror, needed to see Ruthie alive, to share secrets. He'd told Hal and Sara that he'd had kidnap threats from a Turkish gang. 'The danger of working in security,' he'd said. They were too worried about Ruthie to think very deeply about the reason for the attack.

Lilly scampered back into the house.

'You got kids?' he asked the DS.

'Seven, five, three.'

'Bit of a handful?'

'Totally.'

'I love my kid more than anything else in the world.'

Lilly returned with her blanket.

'I want to give her Blankie.'

'You can't give her Blankie, sweetheart.'

'Want to. Want to. Want to.'

The policeman turned away. Lilly's tense mono-tone rhythm was troubling for everyone who heard it.

'Tell you what.' Malkie hugged her tight. 'Why don't you loan her Blankie till she gets out of hospital? Cause I think Blankie would be really unhappy if he left you for too long.'

'Blankie's a she, not a he, Dad. You know that.' She giggled and his spirit cautiously rose. Once she was through this phase, it normally took no more than a good night's sleep to get her back to what the outside world would see as normal.

As Sam listened to the conversation, he realized that Malkie was making it clear that he wasn't going to back down. He was taking his daughter to the hospital irrespective of the attempt to kidnap or kill her. And he was telling him that he loved his daughter more than his own life. He wanted protection. A way out. Sam was sure of it.

'Pull out our guys,' Sam said.

'What?'

'Nothing to be gained.'

'But, Sam . . .'

'Out.'

'Shhh.' Bobby exhaled.

Malkie's mobile rang. He let it ring for a few seconds, as the DS, too, answered a call.

'Hi,' Malkie said.

'The old up and down. Seven fifteen.'

As the phone went dead, Malkie gathered his daughter in his arms. 'You finished with me?' he asked the DS.

'Looks like it . . . sir.' There was undisguised hatred on the other man's face.

'Good. C'mon, madam. You and I are going for a swim. And I'm going to throw Blankie in the pool.'

'Noooo,' she screamed in delight. He thought of the bite she'd inflicted on one of the kidnappers. Tough kid. I'll protect her. But can I stay alive while trying?

CHAPTER 37

Ian Trevor needed someone to trust. Four times he had reached out to phone the General and each time had cut the connection before completing the number. The General was too fond of bloody Copeland. He wouldn't countenance an investigation. Would find the whole idea daft.

Trevor opened the file again, and there it was, evidence of a long-standing relationship with Malkie Collins. And a bank account that was too healthy for a copper on Copeland's salary. Over the past four years, tens of thousands of pounds had been spent in lump sums on restoring his father's old manse and farm. He was losing a great deal of money on the farm, and yet somehow found enough to survive. Every six months Copeland paid twenty thousand pounds in cash into his account. Where was that coming from?

Underneath the financial information were the transcripts of a single conversation between Copeland and Barcelona's bent Chief of Police, Fernandez. The Spanish had obtained it illegally and it would not be admissible in court, but it was damning.

He scanned it for the tenth time, trying to take it at face value. If Copeland was guilty they were going to need a lot more proof than was furnished in this folder.

Copeland – *We must be careful.*

Fernandez – *Always. But they are not on to us. I would swear it on my mother's eyes.*

Copeland – *Have you sent my latest instalment?*

Fernandez – *Waiting for you at Big Planet. A double helping.*

Copeland – *I need it. Running tight on resources at the moment.*

Fernandez – *Tell that to the Barracuda.*

The sound of laughter, followed by Copeland cutting the connection.

Beside the transcript was the tape, and beside the tape a set of headphones and a cassette player. He looked into the eyes of Hacket, Lamond and Cassell, his Assistant Chief Constables. They were clean; nothing in the files incriminated them. Ian Trevor believed he was a good judge of people. He had spent forty years studying eyes, hands and gestures. Listening for weakness, for evasion, strength. And he had recruited good men and women around him. Always. But not Copeland.

204

Copeland was a mystery. His deputy had been foisted on him by the General and the Home Office. Trevor believed him to be arrogant, a weak manager, and an inadequate organizer. Bloody sofas and no bloody desks. What fucking sense was there in that? Only confused people.

Trevor was filled with resentment that Copeland might have compromised the squad and feared that the cancer might have gone deep in his organization. Even if there was an innocent explanation for all this, he glanced again at the transcript, Copeland should not have contacted Fernandez without first telling him. But if he had gone over . . . A sick feeling welled up in his gut. The squad would be discredited yet again – this time a hammer blow.

He had taken out twenty corrupt DIs and DSs eight years before when he had become DG. He had hunted them with precision, ruthlessness and cunning. No early retirements, no excuses, no cover up. But this, he tapped his pen on the desk and glowered at his ACCs, what a mess. What a fucking mess.

'What do you think?' he asked his ACCs, arrayed on hard upright chairs around his desk. He showed them the pictures of Sam with Fernandez in Regent's Park that Colinas had dropped off that morning.

'It smells like double crap,' replied Hacket.

'Sam has high-level support and an unblemished record,' said Cassell, her body leaning away from

Hacket, whose face, shaped like a split lemon, she found unnerving.

Trevor handed her the transcript of a long conversation between Sam and Malkie. On the corner was the time and date, *02 AM*, the previous December. Sam had told his team he hadn't met Collins since his days in Glasgow, and yet here was a wiretap of Collins telling him about Barracuda shipments into Liverpool. The dialogue was stilted and careful, nothing that would incriminate either man, but nonetheless proof that Sam had a relationship with Collins.

'You know what Sam's like,' she said, handing back the file as if she wanted nothing to do with it. 'He could be running solo with something. Malkie could be a snitch. What happened to the shipments?'

'Disappeared. Never took place. They had a tip-off that the Spaniards were on to them.'

'Fernandez?' she asked.

Trevor nodded. 'Fernandez had a clean record. Rising star,' he said, then added, 'Like Copeland. We know ten of the Dagos are bent. We might have the same number. We need to know.'

'I agree,' replied Lamond, the ACC in charge of Lincolnshire. 'Sam's taken too close an interest in this case. He dropped Collins' tail. Bobby tried to pretend that he ordered it himself, but he's incapable of lying. And I'd asked Sam not to intervene in the Halliwell case.'

Cassell noted that his brown hair was darker

than usual. He was touting for jobs in the private security sector, and taking down Malkie Collins would make a huge difference to the CV.

Trevor snapped shut the file. 'Someone in the squad has gone over.' He slapped the folder. 'There's too many examples of our information ending up in the hands of people like Malkie Collins. Copeland may be innocent, but we can't be too careful. People were talking of Philby as a future Chief of the SIS, until he suddenly turned up in Moscow. Let's not be fooled by Copeland's reputation, let's judge him on the facts. I'll take personal charge of this. Tommy,' he turned to Hacket, 'you back me up. Hand over the day-to-day stuff to your deputy.'

'Have you told the General about this?' asked Cassell, her face tense and white. She had most to lose from a cock-up, and most to gain if Sam took the drop. She would be first in line to take over. The General, or his successor, would never appoint Hacket – they'd never be able to put him in front of the media. 'Copper's copper', 'rough diamond', all the usual clichés attached themselves to Hacket – and she made sure they stuck. She was already casting around for a shadow team to keep tabs on Trevor's gang. She needed to be on the inside track. And she knew the ideal person, Lindsey Hamilton, the squad's surveillance specialist. Nothing would escape *her*.

'The General has no need to know, because there is nothing yet to know,' said Trevor. 'Fiona. I want you to lead on the bomber case.' That'll keep her busy, Trevor thought. Her mouth dropped. The car-bomber case could take years and still not add up to anything – most such cases were broken by luck rather than judgement. Not much glory there. Not like taking down Copeland.

'Keep your eyes and ears open,' he said. 'Keep this in the family. I'll put together a small task force and we'll start at the top, weeding through everyone's accounts. Clear out the bad apples. Any of your men are remotely whiffy, I want to know. Understood?'

He glared at them.

'Yes, Guv,' they replied in unison.

As they trooped out, Trevor ordered his PA to track down Lindsey Hamilton. He had watched the wheels turn in Cassell's mind. She was summoning the girl club. No chance. Hamilton was *his* for the duration. He turned grimly back to the file.

CHAPTER 38

Malkie waited at the top of the tree and watched his contact park a large brown Ford sedan in the clearing. He was half an hour early. And alone. Sound man. Malkie peered through powerful binoculars, scouring the countryside and woodland for any sign that there was backup. He was 99 per cent certain, but taking no chances, he clung to the tree and waited another fifteen minutes. There was no sign of movement, other than the contact sitting on the bonnet, taking out a Thermos and pouring a cup.

Malkie climbed quietly and slowly down the oak, hesitating with each branch crack. He was dressed entirely in greens and browns, and a soft wool ski-mask covered his head and chin. At the bottom, he headed into the increasingly gloomy woods. A few minutes later, he crouched at a safe distance. He saw the driver check his watch, reach into the car and switch on the inside light. Malkie felt for his weapon – a Smith and Wesson .45 automatic – as the contact's head sat up like a melon waiting to be hit. Malkie took aim, a perfect target; the bullet would whip the top off his skull.

Then he slid the gun back into his pocket, edged round the back of the car and slipped inside the left-hand rear door.

'Hello, Malkie.' Sam handed him a cup of tea. 'This is a bit colder than it should be. I'd've brought some vodka but I'm told you no longer drink.'

'Sadly true, big feller. You must've cut back yourself. You're looking good. Given up the condensed milk?'

Sam grinned. 'You're not too bad yourself. Still pushing weights?'

'A wee bit. Nothing like the old days, eh? Don't have anyone to compete with me the way you used to, big man. Let's see your muscles.'

Sam took the hint. Malkie wanted him to show that he wasn't wired or carrying a Nagra tape recorder. He took off his jacket.

'How's Lilly?'

Malkie patted Sam's chest and quickly ran his hands down his back.

'Better, thanks.'

'Seems a sweet kid.'

Malkie placed a mobile jamming device on the seat beside him.

'I fancy a wee bit of music,' he said. 'What've you got there?'

'Beethoven. Fourth symphony.'

'Just the ticket. Sling it on.' That'll take care of long-range listening devices. He leant forward, very close to Sam's ear, and could feel the heat from his skin.

'I love my girl.'

The statement was simple and true. Sam picked up the message. If I'm in trouble and can't care for her, I'll trade.

'How can I help? Witness protection?'

'That's a bit unsubtle, big guy,' laughed Malkie. 'You're offering me a new name, a crap council house in Dorset, and all the unemployment benefit I can spend. Oh, and a million-pound contract on my head. Very good offer, Sam. Must've sent you on a training course for that one.'

'I thought you might want to live like a civilian. Bring your kid up like the rest of the world, rather than behind big iron gates.'

'Better than behind big iron bars, Sam. Or in a big wooden box.' No chance, thought Malkie. There's no way I'm going back to the world I grew up in. No way. Lilly won't have to endure the same struggle. I'm getting out of this. Somehow.

Silence fell between them, then Malkie asked, 'Any idea who pulled the job?'

'None.'

'C'mon, Sam. It's *my* kid we're talking about.'

'Last time I checked, it was someone else's child who was lying in a hospital bed. And I'm not playing games with you. We don't know who's behind this. Apart from the fact that they behaved like the Keystone Kops at the kidnapping scene, they were bloody good at disappearing.'

Malkie was silent, then said, 'They won't stop.'

'Who do you think it is?'

'I wish I knew,' replied Malkie.

'Checkmate, then,' said Sam.

'Help me, Sam. And I'll make it worthwhile.'

'How?'

'I'll give you the bomber.'

'Are you connected?' asked Sam.

'I'll find him.' He thought of Halliwell's ripped body. 'I've a few ideas.'

'And what do I give you in return?'

'Whoever did the job, Sam. And I want the information as soon as you get it. There's every chance you won't get them before they get me.'

Sam started his engine. 'I'll think about it.'

'Don't think too long, Sam. The offer's open for a short time only. You understand my options. They're none too pleasant. But you know me. More lives than a cat.'

'You've used eight, Malcolm. Give me the guys in the Eastfield drug ring; I'll put the kidnappers away for fifteen years and I'll get you the lightest possible sentence. Nothing much can be pinned on you, I imagine. Give them up and you'll be out in two years. We'll put you in WP.' Another offer of witness protection.

'Not going to happen, big guy. I don't have the vaguest idea what you're talking about.' Shell companies, managers, solicitors and barristers insulated Malkie; it would be impossible for anyone to make a legal case against him that would stick.

'Ever heard of a guy called Kurt Habermas?'

Sam asked, listening intently for any change in the rhythm of Malkie's breathing.

'Kurt who?'

'Scientist up at Standish. It is your firm that has the Standish contract, isn't it?'

'Middle management takes care of stuff like that, Sam. I'll see you at the party.' He slipped from car, into the woods and out of sight.

CHAPTER 39

Sam watched Hope Delawney move gracefully through a throng of guests. When he looked closely, he could see the twitching exhaustion in her pupils, but in the middle distance, it would have been impossible to tell. A long blue dress swirled gently around her postpartum curves and around her neck was a simple, beautiful string of pearls that for five generations had been awarded on the birth of the heir.

For an hour, she had moved people from conversation to conversation. The most awkward of guests were made to feel at home and that they were the most stimulating company.

'Darling Sam.' She'd greeted him with an air-kiss on both cheeks. 'Let me introduce you to the Contessa d'Almovar, the wife of the Spanish Ambassador. I know how much you love Spain.' The Contessa was, as Sam expected, a delight. Charming, beautiful, interested in Sam and his job. If she had been bored or boring, Hope would have swooped and redistributed them to other more deserving or interested partners. As it was, she stirred the pot every ten minutes or so

214

anyway, ensuring a constant buzz of pleasurable conversation.

Champagne, still water and delicately flavoured canapés circulated on silver trays carried by waiters dressed as Pierrots. Sam stepped onto the wide terrace and watched clowns juggling, a stilt-walker picking cranelike steps across the flowerbeds, fire-eaters breathing flames into the black sky. To his right, a quartet played a selection of classical music.

Malkie passed him, sipping water from a thin glass.

'Garden,' he whispered without breaking stride.

Sam listened for a few more minutes to the luscious music, picked up a glass of champagne and headed into the night air. He waited by a fountain, surrounded by a high hedge as Bach gave way to a Mozart dance.

'How did you and Freddie meet?' asked Sam into the darkness.

Malkie, sheltering behind the shadow, said, 'We both liked the odd flutter. Bought a nag together.'

From the terrace above the Palladian entrance, a photographer using the latest in digital surveillance cameras snapped pictures of the two men as they talked.

'Does the name Stef Violi mean anything to you?'

'Why?'

'Don't mess me around, Malkie.'

'I wouldn't go there, if I were you, Sam. You'd

just embarrass yourself. Standish has nothing to do with this.' He needed to keep Sam on the wrong track until he could work out what to do. 'Here.' He passed Sam a slip of paper. 'My drop-point. Safety deposit box, Garton branch of Barclay's. Leave anything there you want me to pick up.'

On the terrace the photographer fired off more pictures.

CHAPTER 40

Rain fell softly against the windows of the old hut Henry had had built in the woods twenty years before. He sat at his desk and compiled a dossier on Rod Leadsmith, his former patient, who'd had all the characteristics of a disturbed teenager. Leadsmith had confessed to him that he'd killed small animals when young, was a regular bed-wetter into his teens, and had set fire to several sheds and derelict buildings. *These traits*, he wrote, *would be compounded by the subject's frustrated sexual desire for Grace Adams. He'd channel his aggression into intense opposition to Grace Adams' wheat.* He put his notes into an envelope and addressed it to Sam.

On the wall above him was a group photograph from his period as Vice-Chancellor. He was wearing black tie for the Founder's Dinner and was sitting next to Delawney and Halliwell. Henry thought again of Delawney's grin the night they'd closed the deal to sell the land to Standish. As Henry'd drained the second bottle of expensive claret at Ramsay's, the implication was clear – 'I own you now.' And now Halliwell was dead. Who would be next? It was unravelling. Henry put down his pen and reached for the Valium.

Drizzle forced the party indoors. The circus people followed the guests into the great hall and the library, performing feats of small magic. Sam watched intently as a clown untangled metal rings with a few strokes of his hand.

'Like to try?' asked the Pierrot, his white face gleaming in the candlelight.

'Sure,' said Sam. He closed his eyes, felt the rings, called back to mind the man's gestures and with two quick flicks released the knot and handed the puzzle back to its astonished owner. He wished he could solve the Eastfield cases with such ease.

'Pretty impressive, Sam.'

He turned towards Grace. She looked tired. 'Party trick,' he shrugged. 'Not terribly useful in the great scheme of things.'

'Oh, I don't know. Everyone needs magic. I know I do. Have you seen my nephew yet?'

'He's beautiful.'

'You're an old softie, really, aren't you, Deputy Director?'

As he escorted her through the crowd, she murmured, 'I owe you dinner.' They ate once a month, alternately in Lincolnshire and London.

'Tuesday night. MoTo's. Eight?'

'Be great.'

Out of the corner of his eye Sam saw Sara enter via the terrace, wearing a simple pair of blue jeans and a yellow windcheater that bunched round her injured arm. Her fair hair was plastered to her face, her eyes wild.

As she brushed past several startled revellers, knocking a Pierrot's tray clattering to the marble, an eddy formed in the crowd.

'Sara. Are you OK?' Grace rushed over.

Moving with surprising speed, Hope cut Sara off.

'Where is he?' whispered Sara, her head swinging furiously around the room. 'Where is the bastard?'

'Make a fuss, and I'll never forgive you,' Hope hissed into her ear. Then she turned towards Sam and Grace. 'She's unwell. It's understandable, poor girl. Would you escort her back to the flat.'

'Come on, babe,' Grace hugged Sara. 'Let's get you out of here. Not the place for you.'

Hope circulated, calming and reuniting the party.

'She's distraught, poor girl,' she told the Contessa. 'Her daughter's been in an accident.'

As Delawney and his clique, mainly first cousins and friends from Oxford, emerged from the billiards room, Sara broke free of Grace's grasp and hurtled across the room. Delawney, shocked, attempted to withdraw, but before he could do so, Sara stretched onto her toes and slapped him hard on the face, the echo filling the suddenly silent room.

'Ruthie's *your* child, for God's sake,' she hissed. 'She's been in hospital for three days, and you

219

couldn't even phone to find out what was happening. You're lower than scum. No *real* father would behave this way.'

'Oh, my God,' groaned Hope. 'Get out of here, you hysterical tramp.'

'And as for you,' Sara reached across, scooped up a glass of champagne and threw the contents in Hope's face, 'consider this my resignation.'

As Grace and Sara drove back towards White Hill House, Sara was silent, her face grim, then she broke down. 'Oh God, what am I going to do?'

'You'll stay with us,' replied Grace, decisively. The family owed Sara. Big time.

'But your sister'll . . .'

'Don't worry, I'll talk to her,' she said as they pulled up at the front door. Five minutes later, Sara was shivering in bed and Grace was downstairs fixing a large gin and tonic for herself and a Coke for Sam, who'd followed in his own car.

Oh God, Grace thought, poor Hope. Humiliated in front of her friends. Hope's face had turned to a mask when Grace had scooped Sara up and practically carried her to the car. She remembered that look from their childhood. *Caught.* How much did Hope know? Grace tried hard to believe that her sister was not aware of her husband's behaviour.

Grace had called Hal earlier and he'd rushed back from the hospital. 'Where is she?' he asked Grace.

'Sleeping in your room. She's exhausted.'

Hal's face was grim as he made for the stairs.

'She's a strong woman,' Sam said to Grace. Night had fallen rapidly, chilling the land and enclosing the woods. An oak stood out against moonlight that flared like phosphorescence on its branches. 'I'd better go. Got a lot to do in London. Look after her well.'

Grace followed him to the front door, then shuddered and wrapped her arms round her body.

'I couldn't've done what she did. Stay with Delawney.'

'You don't know what you would have done to protect your child,' he replied, thinking of the time he had seen a mother throwing herself in front of a bomb to save her son. 'Look at Hal,' he said. 'Could've died taking on the kidnappers.' He kissed her gently on the cheek. 'You'd've done as much.'

His phone buzzed. 'Got to go.' They hugged briefly and brushed cheeks. 'See you at MoTo's,' he said.

She watched his retreating frame – big against the moon, casting large shadows. 'Sam,' she whispered. 'Where are we going?'

Hal held Sara's hand, afraid to disturb the stillness that had descended on the room. What had she gone through, living in the same house as a man who treated her as a servant? He had a thousand questions to ask her.

Sara reached up and stroked his face.

'I know what you're thinking. I don't think I can explain. I thought I . . .' She paused, trying to find the words. 'I thought I was helping. I thought . . .' She stopped again, then shook her head. 'I was an idiot.'

'You were young.'

This time her shake was more vigorous.

'Not too young to see him for what he was.'

What is he? thought Hal.

'I'll clear out Hope's old room. Used to be Mum and Dad's, so it's the biggest in the house, and it's got a dressing room with a connecting door. Ruthie can sleep there.'

She reached across and ran her hand down his face.

'How can I thank you?'

'By marrying me.'

Sara kissed him, tears running down her cheeks and onto his lips.

'Who else would have a cri . . .' He stopped himself just in time 'Who else would have me?'

'Half the women in the world.'

CHAPTER 41

Ian Trevor watched as Lindsey Hamilton read the detail of the report on Copeland.

Copeland – *Have you sent my latest instalment?*

Fernandez – *Waiting for you at Big Planet. A double helping.*

'Do we know what "big planet" is?' asked Lindsey.

'If you follow the logic of the transcript, then "Big Planet" would be the code name for a bank account and "double helping" would be the size of the take,' replied Trevor, his eyes hooded.

'But surely not . . .'

'Judas was trusted with Christ's treasury. Never forget that. Here.' He handed her a production order for Sam's bank accounts. 'See if you can make sense of the irregular flow of funds.'

This can't be happening, she thought. Sam Copeland was one of the best guys she'd ever come across. He was the future. She stole a glance at Trevor, could sense him reading her like radar, and closed down her emotions.

'Certainly, sir. May I have these tapes as well?'

'If you're worried about them being fake, don't. We've had people poring over them. They're more kosher than a Stamford Hill deli.'

Lindsey stood, maintaining her stillness. 'I'll do what I can, sir.'

'I know you will, Lindsey. This is on a need-to-know basis. I'm putting together a small task force. I'll lead. ACC Hacket will take day to day.'

Heavy-duty team. Whatever secrets Sam had would not be hidden long.

Sam's sister, Eileen Daniels, locked the ancient door of the small chapel of St Martha's. She smiled as she ran her hand across the fourteenth-century stone. Sometimes when clear sunlight spread across the warm walls after rainfall she closed her eyes and felt for the hands of the medieval builders. The carving undulated and curved as it had when the original mason had shaped the block.

Their practical piety was her example. She had crawled over the building for thirty years – organizing repairs, flowers, Harvest festivals. Then as the Church opened up to women like her, she had become a deacon and now a priest. Her God was compassionate, and she was known throughout the county for her commitment to the poor. No one was turned away on the first three occasions, but when she felt the charity of the Church was being abused she did not hesitate to inform the petitioner of her anger.

Her faith had not lost its mystical but hard Celtic edge. Jehovah took vengeance on behalf of the children of God. She despised gentle-Jesus-meek-and-mild icons. Her Christ was a revolutionary leader who despised the social order of his day. His was a love that demanded devotion.

Grace watched Eileen from the gate at the end of an ancient cemetery marked with lichen-covered headstones and encaged stone effigies – the great and good revealed in a frozen act of eternal piety. Eileen was like an aunt to Grace; had seen her through many bad times, celebrated with her in the good. As Eileen turned into the afternoon sun, Grace was stuck again by her likeness to her brother – the same big frame and unruly black hair. Her makeup, unchanged in style since the early 1970s, was perfect.

Grace thought of her own face. Ageing. She felt worn, threadbare. Scared. The enormity of the challenge at Standish rolled before her like a dust storm in the tundra. And then there was Sam. Where *am* I going?

'Grace. How are you?' They embraced, Grace lost in the folds the jacket of Eileen's black trouser suit, feeling small again, safe.

'Let's have a cup of tea and maybe a cake or three.' She pinched Grace's cheek. 'You're too thin. You'll be passing yourself off as one of those daft models next.'

They turned into the path of a sixteenth-century cottage across the road from the imposing Victorian vicarage. The house, sold by the Church twenty years before, was currently a weekend home for an investment banker.

Eileen's cottage had belonged to the warden of the old almshouse and it retained an air of sparse charity. A rickety staircase led to three bedrooms, one, Eileen's, overlooking the chapel. Downstairs, two small, cosy rooms gave way to a fair-sized kitchen from which the warden's wife had dispensed frugal meals a hundred and fifty years before. In this room, Eileen lived and worked. Her computer clung precariously to one end of a long wooden table, surrounded by theology books and papers.

She scooped up a baking bowl encrusted with dough and dropped it in the dishwasher, then extracted a tray of scones from the oven.

'Got them just in time,' she said, as she toppled them onto a plate. 'Fetch the jam, please.'

Grace found homemade plum, apple and raspberry and took them to the table, along with a large slab of butter. She was feeling better already. So many times, she had sat in Eileen's kitchen and set the world to rights. They would discuss everything from Rwanda to liberation theology, cheating men to recipes for apple crumble. And now Grace wanted to talk about Sam. She felt her stomach tighten.

'Ahh.' Eileen sat on an old armchair, slipped off

her black leather shoes and put her feet on an old, cracked rest. She dipped a scone in her tea, then munched hungrily on the contents. 'That's better. Forgot to have breakfast again.'

She looked across at Grace, who had settled into a deep cloth seat, pulling both legs underneath her, picking nervously at the scone.

'Eat,' ordered Eileen.

'I am eating.'

'That's air eating. Put it in your mouth and swallow.'

'But . . .'

'Now.'

Grace raised her eyes to the ceiling, but did as she was told. The warm cake melted on her tongue and she began to relax.

'What's going on at Standish?'

'We're doing well. We have a new research team. Some brilliant people. We're ahead of the game. I reckon we can have commercial trials sometime next year.'

Eileen started on a second scone loaded with plum jam.

'I wish I could be more confident about the morality of your wheat, Grace.' Her deep blue eyes registered the love and concern she felt for her friend.

'You know I've wrestled with this, Eileen. Done so with you.' She waved a hand. 'Right here. But I can see no alternative.'

'You've got a good soul. I'd never question that.

But you're going to face opposition all your life. There was a Brazilian archbishop called Dom Hélder Câmara, a beautiful man. Fell foul of the authorities. He said once, "When I gave food to the poor, they called me a saint. But when I asked why the poor were hungry, they called me a Communist."'

An awkward silence settled as Eileen waited for her friend to speak. Grace wrestled with the words, finding it difficult to form a sentence – to speak would be to release her fears into the world, and would open up the possibility of pain as well as hope.

'Is this about Sam?' asked Eileen.

Lindsey Hamilton sat in her study, nervously scrubbing the edge of her thumbnail, watching dawn creep up like an unwelcome visitor.

The other task force members had set up shop in the bleak modernist government building across the piazza from the NCS, but she had been granted permission to work at home, away from the distractions and noise. She had established a firewall to keep out hackers and maintain her own security. By contrast, she maintained a virtual private network that would allow her to penetrate NASA if she felt so inclined.

She felt sick, wounded, as she replayed part of Sam's conversation with Fernandez.

Lindsey had discovered that 'Big Planet' was an account registered with a financial investment agency on the Channel Islands. More precisely, Big Planet was an account with the sorting code 1986 10 404, and she had come across it only after an assiduous search.

Always begin with the obvious, Sam had taught her, and she'd decided to see if Big Planet was a simple code for an account named after a planet. She had tracked the outflows from the banks the Spanish claimed were clearing-houses for Fernandez's money, then data-merged the account names with NASA's on-line galaxy search.

Ten hours later her speaker had pinged, telling her that her search had thrown up a result. She cursed when she read the cryptic result. She had expected a natural language response – the Global Bank, or Jupiter Investment Systems – and thought her software was malfunctioning when it pushed out a series of numbers.

Lindsey double-checked and then the result made sense. The figures referred to a newly discovered moon circling Jupiter, the largest planet in our system. The moon was waiting for a real name, meanwhile it was identified by a number. For hours, she followed the trail of dealings from 1986 10 404 across three continents and dozens of fake businesses that washed the money cleaner and cleaner until it turned up in the Channel Islands again. This time in a respectable account registered in the name of Clyde Security. The company secretary was Roni Collins.

She triangulated the flows of cash from Clyde

with the dates of pay-offs to Fernandez and those of Sam's phone calls to Collins. There was a distinct pattern. A phone call from Fernandez to Sam, a logged message from Sam to Collins, then two days later a payment into 1986 10 404. 'Shit.' She punched the computer. 'Shit, shit, shit.'

CHAPTER 42

S am had sensed something wrong in the
office. It was in the flow of air around his
room, like a barely perceptible drop in the
temperature. It was there in Trevor's greeting, in
Lindsey Hamilton's sliding eyes, and in Hacket's
abrupt tone. All day it had tugged at him. Trevor's
hiding something from me. Playing politics. But
why? The bomber case? Were they trying to work
round me because I'm too close to Grace? Was this
about Violi? Had the General given instructions
that I'm out of the loop?

He reached for the remains of a bottle of beer and
pushed away the spaghetti con vongole he'd cooked
for supper. He and Sergio had talked about going
to Madrid together, hitting some of the old haunts
and having a good time. Sam was deeply worried
about his friend, whose eyes seemed to be sinking
further and further into his skull.

'What are these?' asked Sergio, sitting at the
table, sipping brandy.

'Scene of crime pictures. That's the bomber's
first victim.' He pointed to Halliwell's wrecked
car.

'He the one with business in Barcelona?'

Sam nodded. 'A couple of days after that, Grace's car was blown to bits. He followed up with some mumbo-jumbo about saving the planet and some references to a poem. Since then, nothing. The second bomb was more sophisticated, so the guy is learning his trade.'

'You think it might be eco-terror?'

'But why kill Halliwell? He wasn't tied to Grace's work,' Sam mused. 'But he did know something was wrong and was trying to warn her.'

'Did they hit Halliwell to throw you off the scent?'

Sam picked up his car keys. 'I must go. Help yourself to whatever you need. You know where everything is.' He scooped the pictures into a bag, gathered his coat and headed for the office. He needed to think.

Gitte yawned, then looked at her watch. Nine p.m. 'I'm tired. We've done an eighteen-hour stretch. Let's hit a Chinese restaurant. I would die for prawns and black bean sauce.'

'I think Gitte's right.' Alaina shut down her computer. 'The morning's problems are those of the night before.' She lifted her jacket, a rich red velveteen affair with a dozen zippers. 'Let's eat.'

'You two go,' said Grace. 'I want to answer some emails. I'll catch you later.'

They glanced at one another – shy, uncertain – and Grace offered them a silent blessing as she reflected on dinner with Sam tomorrow and on his sister's advice. According to Eileen, Sam had been badly burned in his first marriage and felt contempt for his own behaviour in those years. But now he was ready to commit, wanted kids. Is that what I want? What kind of mother would I make?

As dark silence floated over the room, Grace switched on a lamp and rubbed her face. It had been an exhausting week. She dialled Hal.

'Hi, darling. How are Ruthie and Sara?'

'Good. They're watching *The Sound of Music*. You coming home?' Hal asked. 'Sara's cooked a fish pie. She only used three pots. Amazing. Didn't think it was possible to cook real food without using everything in the kitchen.'

'Mmmmm.' Grace was noncommittal. There was so much to do.

'Come back,' Hal insisted. 'Get some sleep. You're looking like the Bride of Dracula. Pretty soon, even Sam won't fancy you.'

'Cheek. Hold some supper for me.'

She hit the disconnect button, swivelled to the keyboard, pulled down her music menu looking for something upbeat, found it in Robert Cray, clicked on a half-dozen tracks and let the software do the rest. Then she opened her emails. She had set up a filter to dump the abusive messages, so at least the people who wanted to reach her were genuine researchers. She opened an email from Amir Rahman, from the University of Dhaka in Bangladesh.

Dr Adams,

Greetings. I can see from your work you are on the verge of great things. I'm puzzled though. I cannot see from your findings the source of your genes. It cannot be plant based. Can it be you are using animal material? You are obviously familiar with Craig Nessler's work on transferring rat genes that encode for vitamin C into lettuce. It increased the level of vitamin C by seven hundred per cent.

Using your calculations, I've factored in the micronutrient boosters that you are relying on, and the only way you can get iron in "Perfect Wheat" at the levels you are suggesting is to use animal genes. Human?

Oh, Christ, thought Grace. I didn't expect someone to be onto this so quickly. This guy was either clever or lucky. She didn't recognize the name and quickly consulted the list of approved contributors to the group. No Rahman. He's either hacked in or used someone else's password.

Dr Rahman,

I'm not sure how you gained access to these data. And I'm disappointed that you've taken the liberty to use information to which you are not entitled. How fascinating that you should come to these conclusions. Is this pure theory or have you some experiments we might share?

That should smoke him out, she thought, then began to pack up. As she did so, her speaker pinged and Rahman's reply came through.

I have most of the idea. He offered a page of statistics, as well as educated guesses as to how to fill in the gaps. She dropped her bag to the floor. His calculations described 90 per cent of her work. That was impossible. She stared at the screen, bemused. What could she say?

She checked his calculations again – what an extraordinary mind – then breathed a sigh of relief when she saw that his analysis of the iron pathways was out by a factor of a thousand. Anyone following his research would be barking up the wrong theory.

It's the wrong time to reply, she thought. I'm too tired. Guy's lucky, that's all. Got nothing. Good brain, though. She'd email him in the morning, see if she could enlist him as a contributor. 'The morning's problems are not necessarily those of the night before,' she mumbled, then snapped off the light.

CHAPTER 43

'Couldn't sleep either, huh?' Sam asked Lindsey Hamilton. A small circle of light illuminated her desk, phone and computer. Her soft grey blouse and elegant, simple cotton trousers were a far cry from her normal, tough, business-suited persona.

She twisted her body from side to side, easing the tension from her muscles and bones. He admired the way she understood and controlled her body, but then everything about Lindsey screamed order and discipline. And yet, her approach to numbers was hugely creative.

'Got the bug,' she replied, not catching his eye. 'Can't get the Eastfield thing out of my mind.'

'Join the club. I feel as if we're being turned round six ways on this. Fancy a break? Let's grab a coffee at that all-night place over by the tube station.'

She hesitated, then, 'Sure. I'll get my jacket.'

As they set off into the gathering morning, the sun's early rays illuminated office blocks.

'I love this time of day,' smiled Sam. 'London is a different place. It seems cleaner, less frenetic, more companionable.' He had planned to retire to his grandparents' old manse that he'd bought ten years before. But retirement was a long way off and he could not imagine being anything other than a policeman. The life appealed to something deep within him, a sense of justice imprinted by two generations of ministers. And now there was Grace to consider.

They walked in companionable silence through gently waking streets until they reached a battered old red van, the hatch defended by a small, wrinkled woman in a pink apron.

'Morning, Betty, two coffees. Anything to eat, Lindsey?'

'Just the coffee.'

'And I'll have two bacon rolls. Makes the best bacon rolls in London, don't you, Betty?'

'Don't patronize me, Sam. That's four quid in new money.'

Sam passed her a fiver.

'Keep the change.'

She thumped down a pound coin and turned away.

'See you tomorrow, Betty.'

'Yeah, right.'

Sam took his food across to a bench shadowed by the statue of a general on horseback – sword pointed forward in victory.

'Loves me really,' he grinned.

'So I see. Your usual haunt?'

'I've known Betty for years. They used to have a

pitch near my old flat in Camden. I'm often here at six when they open up. Betty and her old man, George, somehow keep that old wreck going six days a week. Legendary among cabbies.'

'I'll remember it.' She screwed up her eyes. 'Ugh. Sugar.'

He laughed. 'Do you good. A bit of extra energy.'

She sipped, dubiously.

'What I don't understand,' said Sam, 'is how the car bombings fit the theory that Halliwell was part of Malkie's drug ring. Was Halliwell at the fulcrum of two different, unrelated processes?'

'If Grace's car hadn't gone up, we'd've thought we were looking at a hit.'

'But why? He wasn't grassing them up.'

He sipped his scalding coffee, struggling to enjoy the bitter taste without sweet Carnation milk.

'He wouldn't've been brave enough to steal from Malkie. Bobby tells me he was having an affair.'

'A postgraduate student. Woman in her late thirties called Alma Howard. Doing a master's degree in copyright law. Nice woman.'

'Anything there?' asked Sam.

'Not on the surface. Claims she loved him. He was always promising to leave his wife. Spent quite a bit on her, new car, down payment on a flat.'

'Get her photograph round the pubs in Garton. See if you can shake anyone's memory. Also, see if our Spanish friends have noticed her in Barcelona.'

'Reckon she's involved?'

'Who knows? At this point, we're clutching at straws.' He sipped again. 'Can you think of any reason why we're being followed?'

'What?'

'A car playing cat and mouse with a motorbike as we walked over. Went the strangest route known to mankind to get here. And behind us, the window cleaner is talking into a clip mike.'

Was this to do with Violi? He was becoming convinced that Violi was under investigation from MI5 or SIS, someone who had pull over Charlie Lambie. Or were Malkie's guys keeping tags on the investigation?

'Can't think why.' Stupid of Trevor to tag Sam. He was one of the most brilliant undercover men in the business. In another minute, he'd have tracked one of them down and she'd have had the unpleasant experience of trying to make up a convincing lie as to why two NCS officers were spying on one of their bosses.

'It's so frustrating not being down there. I can't get the smell of this investigation,' he said.

'You're better off here, Guv. There's a ton of work to be done on reorganizing the structure of the squad.'

Sam snorted. He had to write a paper detailing ways in which to achieve a five-year efficiency plan that would deliver savings of at least 5 per cent per annum. *Not* why he joined the Force.

'They need more men down there,' he said. 'Get

one squad focused on the bomber and the other on the drugs. But make sure they have a prayer meeting each morning to keep each other up to speed. We need to cross-match the evidence to see where they tie together. Any more on Leadsmith?'

'Gone to ground. You really make him for the car bombs?'

'Don't know, yet. He's up to something, though. What do we know about Collins' finances?'

He watched as she fiddled with her cup, and something screamed at him: they're holding out on me.

'All above board,' Lindsey smiled – too brightly for her strained eyes. 'Everything checks out. He doesn't live beyond his means. Pays himself two hundred grand as chief executive of his holding company. Enjoys a good lifestyle, but not flashy. Pays his taxes and his bills like a regular citizen.'

'Dig around some more. What's in the name of his wife, child, mother? Oh,' Sam suddenly remembered, 'his best mate's a guy called Frank Brown.' Frank had led the team that tarred and feathered him all those years ago. 'See if there's anything in his name. Malkie trusts him totally.'

Lindsey stared at him. If he was guilty, it was the coolest act she had ever seen. He was daring her to find account 1986 10 404 – Big Planet.

'Will do.'

He looked into her eyes, reading, searching. 'Is there anything else, Lindsey?'

They stood. She felt twisted by guilt and

panic. Her professionalism struggling against her instincts.

'Guv . . .'

'What?'

She swallowed.

'Thanks for the coffee.'

'Sure.'

I'm missing something right under my nose, he thought.

CHAPTER 44

Grace reread the email.

Dr Adams

*Greeting. I've looked at my calculations again.
I must be out by thousands. (You must have had
a good chuckle); – I think you have a brilliant
mind. But you still do not understand our soil
and seasons well enough. I want to help. Please
let me. I'm sorry to have hacked your site. But I
have a higher calling. Like you I have seen too
many of my people die unnecessarily. And I've
seen my father pass out with exhaustion trying
to treat them. Please, please, let me be part of
the team.*

Amir Rahman

He included a CV and a picture of himself. He'd
provided a link to his Web site. She checked it
out and was stunned to discover that he has only
twenty-two. A prodigiously talented mathematician, he had been sent to Dhaka University aged
thirteen, then gone on to complete an Oxford

D.Phil. before returning home to lecture in theoretical biochemistry. He was the son of a doctor who worked not far from the villages in which she had stayed whilst in Bangladesh.

Gitte and Alaina burst into the room, radiating the self-absorbed happiness of new lovers. Gitte deserved some happiness.

'Hi, girls.'

As Alaina pored over the latest research results, Grace longed to hug Gitte, but satisfied herself with a quick clutch of her friend's hand and a small, complicit smile.

Alaina picked up the press cutting about Amir Rahman, 'Bangladeshi Boy Genius at Brasenose', and laughed: 'I wondered how long it would take before Amir would pay us a visit.'

'You know him?'

'Any bleeding-edge research project that deals with micronutrients sooner or later receives a call from Amir. It's a wonder he's taken so long to find you.'

'That's why I worked in private these past two years,' Grace replied, handing over his pathway calculations. 'This is brilliant. Wrong, but brilliant.'

'Typical of the boy. Probably took him all of a day.'

'Why is he in Dhaka? He could go anywhere. Harvard. Back to Oxford.'

'Same reason as you're here at Eastfield,' replied Alaina. 'Idealism. He loves his country.'

'What do you think? Should we rope him in?'

'Your decision, Grace. It's your project. I'm just the midwife.' She turned to Gitte. 'Shall we get some breakfast? I'm famished.'

Gitte grinned, then nodded. 'Can I get you some coffee, Grace?'

'Yes, please.'

Smiling and watching their retreating backs, Grace's thoughts drifted to Sam, then back to the calculations. I'm going to need all the help I can get, she thought, and composed an email to the boy genius.

Johnny Standish was back on the river when Malkie drove up in his mud-spattered car. He had dropped Lilly off with Hal and Sara and had left Frank and the boys at the farm. If he had turned up to meet Johnny with bodyguards, Johnny's suspicions would've been confirmed.

Hal and Sara were obviously in love. And he was glad of it for Sara's sake. Kid needed a bit of good luck. Delawney. What a bastard. He would have to do more than provide a second-hand bike and pay school fees. Hal had told him that they'd a solicitor working on a paternity suit and settlement. Delawney was denying all knowledge of Ruthie, but Sara had been a virgin when he seduced her. And had been celibate since. There wasn't the slightest doubt. He wouldn't hold out for long and the need for a settlement would increase Delawyney's greed and then he would get careless.

Malkie wondered how much Johnny knew or guessed about the scam to buy and inflate the price of the land the Centre had bought. It had been Halliwell's idea and the money had been too good to walk away from. The bomber. I must get the bomber. Something to trade with Sam.

'Malcolm. How are you?' Standish waded from the swirling white water. The beech trees spread out above them and a willow trailed into the river. Somewhere above him the birds were holding a spirited conversation with the sky.

'I'm fine.'

Standish extracted a wriggling brown trout from his hook, held it down on a rock and struck an expert blow just above the eyes. The fish thrashed one last time.

'Want this for supper?' he asked.

'Sure.'

He bagged it and tossed it over.

'I have people out looking for those bastards who came after Lilly.' Standish held him by the arms and looked deep into his eyes. 'We'll get them. The only firms I can think of are the Chinese or those moronic Russians.' New gangs were constantly trying to muscle in on their territory. And they were increasingly ruthless. Another reason to get out, thought Standish.

'We'll get through it. Always have before.' Malkie helped Standish gather his things.

'Let's have an early lunch,' Standish strode over to his picnic basket, where Raul, in a light blue sweater and black designer jeans, sat on a deckchair. Malkie noted his book, *After the Banquet* by Yukio Mishima – more sadomasochistic doom and gloom. Raul was unstable. A worry. Malkie recalled that Mishima had ritually disembowelled himself in protest at Japan's moral decline.

'Lunch, Raul.'

Raul glanced from Standish to Malkie, then flipped open the hamper, extracted Beluga caviar, plain crackers, a bottle of Evian, a half-bottle of Krug and fresh strawberries. He handed a glass of Krug to Standish, spread a snack for himself, then retreated to his chair, thrust on a pair of headsets and returned to his book.

Standish, manners impeccable as ever, placed his glass down and served Malkie. Then they sat on a rug beneath a beech, just two friends chatting amiably, away from the hustle of life. The two bodyguards, Lottie and Louis, waited by the Range Rover, linked by the latest high-tech communication equipment to every security camera within ten miles. Further down the road, they'd stationed new men they'd imported after the failed attempt to kidnap Lilly.

Malkie wondered which of them the Basque had recruited to kill Johnny. Lottie would be swift and take no pleasure in it. It was her job. If Louis, then Standish's tongue would be sliced off and laid on his chest whilst he was still alive. The Basque had made it clear that they wanted Johnny humiliated, so Malkie leant towards Louis as the second assassin.

Malkie had grown to love the creamy, salty taste of caviar. A vast improvement on cod's roe on toast – a major treat provided infrequently by his mother when he was growing up. Poor Ma, he thought, relentlessly upwardly mobile, despite it all. She insisted they ate at the kitchen table, not in front of the TV. Made them clothes from curtains when what they had had fallen off their backs. Saved to buy wine for Christmas dinner. Polished door handles, washed urine off tenement stairs, died at forty-five. Lung cancer. The AIDS of the Glasgow working class. She looked sixty in her coffin, a small bird of a woman, in a black dress grown shiny from use. In death, at least, she escaped Da. She believed in the afterlife and Malkie devoutly hoped that there was a heaven for those who wished for one. He, himself, longed for eternal silence. One life was enough.

'I see our German friend made an unfortunate reappearance.' Standish passed him a strawberry.

'A botched job. I'm sorry.' Malkie felt no guilt over Habermas. The man was scum. Anyone who chose this life had to accept the consequences. Just like the army. Hand-to-hand combat was troubling, disturbing, nauseating. But you did it. As a professional soldier you killed because you were ordered to. Not for a just cause, or patriotism, or love, but because, for the duration of the battle, your consciousness was submerged in the collective will. The enemy was no longer human, to be pitied. They were objects. Habermas had played a dangerous game and was extinguished. That was that. He reserved his guilt for deserving causes. There would be no nightmares about the German. He'd never even met him. Like a staff officer, Malkie ordered death from a safe distance.

'It was a mistake, Malcolm, of significant proportions. I hope you will take suitable action.'

'Already done, Johnny. The team's gone.' He had no intention of telling Standish that he'd simply sent the guys to a small hotel in Crete, away from prying eyes.

'Even I wouldn't've spotted that tattoo,' he'd told Frank, who had come to offer apologies on behalf of the crew and receive and carry out whatever punishment Malkie would hand out. Gestures like that gave Malkie a hold over his men. They knew he was fair. Occasionally, some became greedy or were turned and they disappeared. Boom. No questions asked, no explanations offered.

Let Johnny think he'd punished his guys. He was going to need them. Every one. There was a traitor. There had to be one, because if he were Johnny he'd've planted someone. Stood to reason.

'It would be nearly impossible to trace him back to us,' said Malkie. 'There's enough evidence in his rooms to place him as a drug runner. Including several Ks of smack. They'll assume it's another drug-related hit. I've put it out via some of our friendly guys that Habermas was a mule for the Ivans.'

'Monitor it closely, Malcolm. It would be unfortunate if our sins of omission returned to haunt us. How is the NCS investigation progressing? Little headway, I hope.'

'Running round in circles.'

Standish dug deep into the caviar with his knife, then spread the eggs on a cracker. 'I promise you, Malcolm, I have a great deal of money out there, being pressed into the flesh of informants. No one comes after one of my men. No one.'

Except you, Johnny, thought Malkie. Except you.

'Have they picked away at the problem that is the Earl of Eastfield? He is, I hear, a new father twice over.'

'No. Freddie's in the clear.'

'Is Freddie becoming – how shall we put it? A burden on the project?'

So it begins, thought Malkie. The slow drip feed that'll lead to Hesketh Delawney becoming the new earl before he has even reached his first birthday. Little Ruthie would not have a father for long.

'It may be possible,' he said. 'But I think any move at the moment would look weird. One too many coincidences if they suss out any connection between Halliwell and Delawney.' Especially if they find out about the land deal for the Centre that put half a million pounds in each of their pockets.

'Good thinking, Malcolm. We may have to carry

the weight a little longer. Though I think we should sow some seeds. I believe you and Sam Copeland go back in time. A little issue of a tarred and feathered Scottish bobby.'

'He was a detective constable, actually.' How absurd, Malkie thought, standing up for Copeland's reputation and stature.

'I think,' said Standish, sipping his champagne, 'that we might give him Delawney. A trade.'

'But he'll rat us out.'

'On what evidence? Your British plods could spend a decade trying to tie us down. Not worth it. They'd take Delawney and the glory. We could throw in the student network for spare change. Your media would eat it up. Everyone would be a hero. And your Mr Copeland would be a slam dunk for director general. Now wouldn't he enjoy that?'

Malkie wasn't so sure. But of one thing he was absolutely certain, he was being set up. Johnny wouldn't leave Delawney out there as a loose end, blabbing for the whole world to hear. Not a chance. Standish must know about the Basque contract on him. He's trying to duck. Expose me to the glare. Well, easily remedied. It was time to contact his handler.

'Thank you for your delightful company, Malcolm. One of these days, you and Roni and the lovely Lilly must come out to the Hamptons for a week. The little girl would love it. How is Roni, by the way?'

'Fine, Johnny. Absolutely fine. Bit shaken up by the kidnapping thing. But apart from that, she's as strong as a rock.'

'Glad to hear it, Malcolm. I like my people in steady, happy relationships. Keeps their minds on the job.'

He stood, ran his finger down Raul's cheek and said, 'Home time.'

CHAPTER 45

Sam paced the room. 'What am I going to do?'

'Do what your instincts tell you,' Eileen replied.

'What do you think, Sergio?'

'I never intervene in affairs of the heart, my friend. Not my speciality.'

Eileen eyed the Spaniard with concern. They had known each other a long time. She recalled him as a warm, generous person, handsome and thoughtful. He'd often flirted with her, made her nervous around him. She had always responded to his brand of dangerous charm.

She had invited him to stay with her in the cottage and he told her he would think about it. He needed feeding up and she might have a go at persuading him to control his cigarette addiction.

'This is worse than being underground. At least there I knew what the odds were.'

'No, Sam.' Sergio's voice was sharp. 'I've made a fool of myself many times with women, but the job abandoned me only once.' He hung his head. 'I'm sorry, Sam. This is your big night and I'm ruining it. You go. Ask her to marry you. She'll say yes.'

Eileen straightened Sam's tie, then absent-mindedly patted down his wayward fringe.

'Grace loves you. I know she does. She knows she does. But she's got a lot on her plate. Henry is struggling with depression, and Hal – well, we know about Hal. Lovely boy that he is. On top of that she has a vocation.' She fingered her dog collar. 'I know what that's like. For thirty years I cooked and cleaned for your brother-in-law and worked the farm, when what I really wanted to do was serve Christ and the Church. I realize now that I was doing the Lord's work all the time. I'm using all that experience I gained to help others.'

She kissed Sam on the cheek, then wiped away the lipstick mark.

'If she says no, it's not about you. It's about her responsibilities. It's about life. Not love.'

Lindsey stared at the computer screen, rubbing static from it, listening to the sparks, feeling the electricity run across her hand, then reached for a cigarette, toyed with it, then returned it to the pack.

She didn't believe Sam guilty. She thought the DG was manipulating events for his own benefit. 'Clever' Trevor hated retiring. He had transformed the squad, crewed it up to deal with the drugs crisis, and now he wanted his own people in place – to leave a legacy. He had wanted Hacket to succeed him, a man she considered Trevor-lite – Trevor without the shrewdness or terrifying instincts for human frailty.

What now? Now account 1986 10 404 had a new entry of £60,000, all of which had arrived by wire three days before, the day after Sam pulled the tail off Malkie Collins. The money had been posted by Clyde Securities. Company Secretary, Roni Collins.

Grace fiddled with her starched white napkin, played with the pendant he'd given her many years before, then glanced at her watch. 8:05. Here he comes. Oh, God.

As she stood, awkwardly pushing away the table, her glass swayed then held and she breathed a small prayer of thanks.

'Darling.' They kissed, tentatively. Sam hovered, then sat, glanced through the menu as a way of calming himself down, selected a bottle of wine, then thought; Just do it man. He reached into his pocket as Grace rubbed her forefinger gently round the rim of her glass, staring at a space somewhere above his left shoulder.

'How's Sara?'

'Oh, you know. Well. Coping.'

'And Ruthie?'

'In a little pain still, poor kid. But she's got great courage.'

After they'd ordered, they sat in silence for some seconds until Sam said, 'I'd like you to have this.'

He pulled a worn jewellery box from his jacket, put it on the table, then opened it.

'That's your grannie's ring. You love that ring. I can't accept it.' She'd seen and admired the jewel often in the past. The diamond wasn't huge or expensive. It was just beautifully cut, simple.

'Please.'

'No, Sam. It's too special.'

The waiter came over with their starters and they fell silent once more.

Sam put the ring on her side plate. 'Let me tell you a story, then you can decide whether to accept it.'

'OK,' she replied, dubiously.

'You know that my grannie was German.'

She nodded.

'In 1940 the police scooped up every German or Austrian national in the UK, despite the fact that most were refugees from Nazism. They deported them to Canada or Australia. Although Grannie had been at the forefront of the anti-Nazi movement and had been living in Scotland for the best part of fifteen years, they turned up for her. Big Tam McDonald came up from Tulloch. He was the local policeman. Died a few years ago. I went to the funeral with Eileen.'

'But he arrested your grannie!'

'Patience. Two men we'd never seen before flanked him – hard-faced guys, according to my dad, who was hiding behind her skirts at the time. She was allowed ten minutes to gather her things, and drop the kids off at the Kirk, where Grandpa was leading the Boy Scouts in home defence classes.

'As you would expect, Grandpa blew his top. Sent telegrams to half the government, pulled every contact he had. No use. She was due to be shipped out the following week. Finally, he faced defeat, wondering how to follow her to Canada. Dad says he'd never seen Grandpa cry until that night.'

She reached over to touch his fingers, so white against the brown table.

'Following morning, he dropped off the kids at his sisters, and headed down to see Big Tam in the village. She was being held at Inverlair Lodge, a big place not far from Ben Nevis. It's wild up there, the most beautiful breathtaking country in the world, but wild – more so then, with the blackout. Pitch black at night. Tam bought Grandpa's plan. He, Tam and Jocky McAlpine, a friend of theirs, turned up at the camp.' He laughed. 'Jocky was dressed as a nun.'

'No.'

'I swear. There weren't many Catholics around when I was growing up, but Grandpa knew them well. It hadn't been that difficult to get hold of a habit. The three of them talked their way into the camp, Tam waving round his warrant card. Grannie was sitting out by some miserable hut, her face haggard. As Big Tam told it, he and Jocky had to avert their eyes, the love was so intense between the two of them. Jocky stripped, handed the habit to Grannie and lit off across the moor, knowing exactly where to escape. The others waltzed out.'

Grace grinned.

'The following day, the rest of the internees were shipped out on the *Andora Star*. A U-boat torpedoed the ship. Over six hundred Germans and Italians died. Some had lived in the UK for over forty years.

'In 1942, when Grannie was pardoned, Grandpa had his mother's engagement diamond reset and gave it her as an eternity ring. Now do you understand why I want you to have it?'

Grace gazed at him, her eyes swimming, then she picked up the ring and slipped it on.

'I do.'

CHAPTER 46

They danced naked – Grace's head against Sam's chest, his face pressed into her hair, Elisabeth Schwartzkopf singing lush Richard Strauss lieder on the CD.

'D'you have to go back in the morning?' he whispered. She was due on the seven thirty train.

'Mmm. Don't want to. Don't want to leave you. This. We've waited so long, Sam.'

'Too long. Nothing'll stand in the way this time.'

Lindsey was still racked by indecision. Why would Sam do this? She had admired him for years, but been too shy to tell him. She was always like that. Reluctant to show emotion. Christ, this can't be happening. This is mad. *Mad.* She glowered at the screen again. All a lynch mob needs is a tree and some rope, she thought, then she speed dialled a phone number.

Sam's phone rang.

No. Not now. He tried to ignore it. No good. Only half a dozen colleagues had access to that particular phone – each of them would only use it in an emergency. The phone's number-recognition system called out, 'Not registered.' Impossible. Lindsey had programmed it so that no one got through without the phone recognizing the number.

Sam hit the speaker phone option.

'There's something in the system that could destroy you,' a scrambled voice said.

'Who is this?'

The voice repeated its statement.

He shook his head, trying to process the information, bring to mind details, fragments of his suspicions over the past few days. It began to drop into shape.

'You know you're being followed,' intoned the voice.

'Who *is* this?'

'Look for the Big Planet.'

'Say again.'

The metallic voice repeated its instruction, then clicked off.

CHAPTER 47

The taxi was freezing as Grace nestled into Sam, burrowing for warmth, sensing his ferocious concentration.

'We want to go to Betty's,' Sam told the driver. 'Then down to the river. Albert Bridge.'

He closed the window.

'Do you remember when we used to play sleeping lions when we were larking around up at your dad's cottage?'

'Sure. Each person had to lie flat out and not respond to anything, no matter what the provocation.'

Sam saw the driver check them out in his mirror, and laughed to indicate that nothing was wrong, then kissed Grace and said, 'Think of the next few weeks like a game of sleeping lions. No matter what they say in the media, no matter what my colleagues insinuate, do not respond and do not rise.'

'You're scaring me, Sam.'

'I know. But I need to prepare you.'

The driver stopped outside Betty's van and Sam, aware of the half-dozen people milling around and the two minicabs parked casually in the alley next to the tube station, exhaled gently. Everything had to seem normal. A couple in love. An early morning adventure.

'Bit early, Sam.' She handed him two coffees and a couple of bacon rolls. 'That's six quid.'

Sam felt in his pockets. No cash.

'Don't worry, Sam. I've got it.' Grace handed over a tenner.

'Kept man, now,' grumbled Betty.

'Take care, Betty.'

As they returned to the cab, Sam sensed the imperceptible lines of surveillance shift around him.

'Albert Bridge, mate?'

A little later, they stood in the middle of the bridge watching the Thames flow thickly beneath. The girders above were lit with thousands of electric lights that cast watery colour. Sam sipped his coffee, his arms around her waist, then kissed her neck and watched the surveillance teams reassemble. They were squad. He knew the signs.

'When this is over, we'll come back here at midnight with a bottle of champagne,' Sam said.

'When *what* is over, darling?'

'When I find out, I'll know. In the meantime, we act normally.' He hugged her again. 'Well, as normally as any newly engaged couple.' He needed time to prepare. 'Whatever happens, know that I love you.'

CHAPTER 48

Back at the lab, Gitte and Alaina grinned as she entered.

'How was dinner?' asked Gitte.

Grace held up her engagement finger.

'He asked you to marry him!' exploded Gitte.

As Grace and Gitte hugged, Alaina said: 'Amir has sent us a gift.' She handed over a sheaf of papers.

Grace scanned the documents. 'My God,' she whispered, 'do these calculations check out?' When the others nodded, she sat quietly in the corner, gently rocking in her chair, eyes closed, noise filter on. Eventually she returned to the workstation, and ran her fingers down the paper in front of Alaina. 'It's possible, isn't it?'

'Yes.'

'Why didn't I think of it?'

'Think of what?' asked Stef as he strode in.

'This.' Grace handed the paper and he examined the results. 'It's from Amir Rahman, a young Bangladeshi molecular biologist. He's found a way to break down the phytate that ties up ninety-five per cent of dietary iron and prevents the gut absorbing it. It'll be a huge help in developing the wheat.

'It's good – great – work and I think we should bring him further into the fold. Give him more of the picture.' Only she and Gitte had the full formula. She wouldn't even give it to Alaina, and had forbidden Gitte from doing so.

'No. On no condition will you involve Rahman.'

After an implosive silence, Grace said, 'It's my research, Stef.'

'And I will do everything in my power to help you achieve the breakthroughs necessary to achieve your aims. But on no account will our data be put on the open Internet.'

The women stared at him, anger and incredulity in their eyes.

Stef smiled, ruefully. 'Sorry, didn't mean to explode like that.' He shifted nervously. 'I've just seen too many great projects ruined through bad security. May I see you, Alaina?'

As Alaina joined him, Grace groaned, 'And I thought he was different.'

CHAPTER 49

Sam knocked on Trevor's door. 'Evening, Ian.'

'Come in, Sam. Good to see you. Pull up a pew.'

'Thanks.' Sam placed a large bundle of papers on Trevor's desk and sat down.

'What can I do for you?'

Sam tapped the document. 'This is my interim report on next year's budget submission.'

'That wasn't due for another two weeks, Sam. You're a bit keen.'

'Don't like things to drag on, Ian.' Sam had huddled all morning with six of his admin people, ignoring all other calls on his time. He wanted a reason to talk to his boss and sense the atmosphere.

'Nor do you, Sam. That's what the General told me when I wondered about your suitability for the squad. He's a convincing man, is the General. Convinced most of us about you.'

Sam picked up the nuances, the shades of meaning. Trevor was distancing himself from Sam's appointment, but also subtly putting Sam off guard. Trevor must have something.

'How's your manse coming on?' asked Trevor.

He had to admit Trevor was brilliant. A totally innocent question on the surface, containing all sorts of implications underneath, not least, how could he afford it? Well, that was private. He had no intention of telling anyone.

'Fine, Ian.'

'I'm partial to a bit of DIY myself.' Trevor peered at Sam. 'You can't get up there much. We're keeping you busy down here.'

'I have a good builder.'

'I hate builders,' Trevor grumbled, 'expensive bloody buggers. Never get things done on time. Always over budget. The missus forced me to agree to a new patio. Still, be worth it when I'm retired. Sit there. Nice Scotch, good tune on Radio Two, letting the next generation take the strain. Eh? Heaven.'

Sam laughed. 'You'll be busier than ever.' He patted the pile of paper: 'I'd value your advice on these. I'd better be getting off.'

'Thanks for popping in, Sam. You should do it more often. You've been a bit of a stranger since that Eastfield stuff started.'

'You know what's it's like, Ian. Things get so busy round here.'

'I do indeed.'

'For instance,' Sam continued, 'I can't track down Lindsey Hamilton for love nor money.'

'Is that right? Think I should institute one of those life/work balance schemes? Get in the shrinks to check out the quality of people's work experience?' Trevor's features settled into a stony crag. 'Shut the door on the way out.'

As Sam left, Trevor pulled out Lindsey's file on Big Planet and the mysterious account that tied Copeland to Collins, grunted, then settled down to read it again.

CHAPTER 50

S am, deep in thought, perched on the edge of an armchair in the General's office. The polished oak desk radiated soft warmth and authority. Charlie Lambie's family pictures clustered beside the thin PC screen, alongside regimental memorabilia. The twin pillars of the General's life.

As Charlie entered, Sam straightened.

'Darjeeling or Assam?' asked the General.

Sam was about to say he didn't really mind, then remembered that Charlie cared about tea the way others did about wine.

'Assam, I think.'

'Good choice. Light tea for early evening.'

Whilst they waited for it to brew Charlie said, 'I don't have long, I'm afraid. I'm due at a reunion dinner.' He checked his watch. 'Ten minutes OK?'

'There's something not right, Charlie. At HQ.'

'Not your Eastfield thing? I told you to leave that.'

'No. I don't think it's that.' Or was it? No one was blocking him access to any Eastfield surveillance information. Why would they?

Charlie poured. 'You are behaving yourself over our scientist friend.'

'Does Ian know what's going on with Violi?'

The General's face expressed his disappointment at Sam's lack of restraint in using Violi's name, but Sam was beyond caring.

'For the last time, Sam. It's not a squad issue. Let it rest.'

Sam took that as a 'no'. So Trevor wasn't sidelining him because he was ignoring the General's warning.

'Ian's turning me into an island,' Sam said. 'I can feel it in the atmosphere. Everything is flowing round me.'

The General looked at him – his eyes troubled.

'Is this just a bureaucratic bun-fight, Sam? Because if it is, I'm not taking sides. You and the Director General can sort it out between you. You're both grown men, for goodness' sake.'

The General is rattled by something, Sam thought. The lineaments of the spider's web of influence and power were quivering, sending out tiny pulses of information about the location of new prey. Sam now knew he was smack in the middle of the silk and that the General knew at least one thing. Someone, somewhere was unhappy with Sam.

'Don't do this to me, Charlie. You know me too well to play games. I don't deserve it. What's happening? Ian was dropping big hints that you'd made a huge mistake recommending me. And he was doing it in such a way that (a) he knew something I didn't, and (b) he wanted to knock me off balance. Why?'

The General sipped his tea, then abruptly shot the white cuffs from underneath the sleeves of his dinner jacket.

'Ian has decided not to confide in me about a major operation,' he said, his mouth pursing into a small 'O'.

'But . . .'

'Patience, Sam. What I do know is that this operation involves the corruption of a senior officer in a European police force and possible damage in the squad itself.'

'Someone's gone over?'

'I don't know, Sam. I'm being drip-fed. And believe me' – the General abruptly smacked the table; his cup rattled the saucer – 'believe me, I have been happier in my time with the squad.'

Sam controlled himself. It was possible that it was one of his people who had been corrupted and therefore Ian was controlling access to the information. But that would make no sense. No sense at all. Ian would bring him into the investigation *and* he wouldn't run the risk of upsetting the General.

He stared at the General, who returned the look. Both seasoned professionals, they knew deep down what was going on. This was about Sam.

'I suggest you go back to the office, Sam. And let me, er,' he coughed, 'ascertain the situation with the Home Secretary, whom I am meeting for a drink this evening. I want to talk to him about a certain job offer I believe you are expecting, and which I fully anticipate you will turn down.'

Who else knows about this closely guarded secret? thought Sam. Bloody politicians – leak worse than a tailings dam.

The General accompanied him to the door and shook his hand. 'Stay calm, Sam. It's one of your greatest strengths. Don't do anything, er, that we would regret. You and I.'

CHAPTER 51

St Mary Magdalene's had a mock-Gothic ceiling, a purple carpet that ran the length of the nave, and an altar bedecked with evangelical slogans. Remnants of Victorian Catholic piety clung to the walls – in particular, the gloomy, washed-out Stations of the Cross. Each painting was a study in sepia sentimentality in which a Pre-Raphaelite Christ trudged towards his hyper-realist crucifixion. Malkie shuddered, memories flooding back of his nightly childhood nightmares about his own crucifixion.

On the lintel of the fourth confessional were carved four dour Anglicized Apostles. The wood had turned a deep, troubled brown underneath a hundred and ten years of varnish. He pulled open the door, and pushed aside the velvet curtain that fell between the confessional's interior and the church aisle. As he settled on his knees, breathing in the distinctive smell of dust, incense, sweat and candles, he wondered how many dark sentiments and actions had been divulged in this small space: incest, adultery, murder, hatred, unwise love. God forgave all, in the end. More than he could do.

271

The small door between himself and the priest slapped open.

'Bless me, Father, for I have sinned,' said Malkie.

'Haven't we all, my son?' He recognized the voice: dark, guttural, Basque, the product of a million cigarettes and centuries of pain and frustration. And the smell. The smell was unforgettable – as if someone had bathed in nicotine. They had met no more than five times: Madrid, Bilbao twice, London, and now Garton. Each time the requests – commands, if he were honest – had grown harder to achieve, the promises more extravagant, the hope of release more profound. The reward bigger.

'Is it time?' Malkie asked. Johnny had to be taken out on their precise instructions. No sooner, no later. That was understood.

'Not yet.'

Malkie breathed out slowly. These bastards were playing with him. Both them and Johnny. He was now entirely convinced that Johnny knew that ETA intended to kill him if he stepped out of line. Malkie had initially believed he was the primary assassin. Now he knew better. He was the backup. Dispensable.

'You must have me here for a reason,' said Malkie.

'I have two requests. I want to meet your English partner.'

Malkie was puzzled, but after a few seconds he said, 'Fine.'

'And I want you to kill Sam Copeland. Find out what he knows then dispose of him after you've dealt with Standish.'

'Come off it,' replied Malkie, incredulously. 'Touch him and the world'll cave in on us.'

'After today, they'll be grateful. As will we. We'll double your payment.'

Christ, thought Malkie. Three million quid. Escape.

'But what makes you think he'll come to me?' he asked.

Just then, a hand rattled the priest's door.

'Come out of there,' an Irish voice hissed. 'I told you. No sleeping in the confessional.' This was followed by a jangle of keys and a surprised, 'Who are *you*?' from the caretaker. Malkie opened his door a fraction. His Basque handler was a slight man, old beyond his years, slightly stooped, dressed in a smart shirt. His eyes were hawklike and with a start Malkie recognized him. He was the man who had been staying with Sam. Malkie's people had staked out the flat and checked out everyone who visited. Malkie recognized him from the photographs.

Sergio answered his accuser in rapid Spanish, then slid away, leaving the caretaker muttering about 'bloody foreigners'. Malkie waited a few minutes, then left, passing a handful of old women and teenagers saying the rosary. Remember me in your prayers, he thought.

CHAPTER 52

'**L**ook for the Big Planet.'

Sam sat in his office, staring at the stars, listening to his answering machine tape through headphones, mulling over the warning. Lindsey Hamilton was the only person with access to his restricted number and the technical knowledge to overcome the recognition system. On the other hand, she would not or could not reveal what was going on. Nor could he acknowledge her hints by talking to her face to face. That would alert Trevor. He briefly considered that she was luring him into a trap, but quickly discounted the possibility. Didn't fit.

Lindsey, if it was Lindsey, had given him one more boost. She said there was something in the system that would destroy him. So, whatever it was, it lay in the squad's database.

He called up the case log on his computer, delved deeper into the most secret area using his password and then tapped *Big* . . . onto the screen. He stopped, a sudden shock running through his system. He had to step through the looking glass into Wonderland. If they really suspected him, then they would have installed tracking software to tell them precisely what he had been doing on his PC. If Big Planet meant something, then he would incriminate himself. He had to be more careful.

Lindsey was woozy. She'd needed two vodka and tonics in the wine bar across the road before she could come back to the office. From her room across from Sam, she watched him through a set of binoculars. He looked weary, confused. She had never seen that look before. He was always strong. This is bullshit, she thought. There must be an explanation. I just can't find it. I can't be looking in the right place.

Sam swung round in his chair and walked to gaze out of the window. His email pinged and he turned to check it out. It was from someone called Tycho Brahe. He clicked it open. No message. His mind ran down a hundred channels of memory. Tycho Brahe. *Come on*, Sam. He closed his conscious mind down, breathed deeply, and emptied himself of everything, then allowed a memory to grow in his imagination. He sensed the roots go down, down, deep. Got it! Brahe was a Danish astronomer, the first of the modern breed, discovered Brahe's Supernova – a new star. Whoever warned him about Big Planet was on the other end of the email.

He had to choose his words carefully, knowing

full well that the surveillance team would log everything he typed on the screen. *How's Kepler?* he asked, knowing that Kepler was Brahe's equally famous assistant.

His personal organizer beeped. He scrambled for it in his gym bag, opened it and a message dropped into his personal email. Another secret blown, he thought. The account was registered under his mother's maiden name. Whoever was on the other end of these messages knew the technology inside out. He read the note from Brahe.

Dead. How U? The message replied.

Then his mobile signalled that he'd received a text message.

You're as secure as a baby on a banister ;)–
Help me.
WHY?
Because you believe me.
I've got your number puzzle man.
What number is that?
1986 10 404
Don't understand. Help me.
Ask Roni Collins.

Sam stared at the small blue screen on his phone then typed:

Why?

He waited for five minutes. No reply. He switched off his machines and set off for Lincolnshire and a visit to Malkie Collins.

✱   ✱   ✱

In her sweltering office, Lindsey swallowed bile.

'Well done, DI Hamilton,' said Ian Trevor. 'Well done indeed. That should smoke him out.'

She stared at him with bleak, dark eyes.

CHAPTER 53

Grace felt weary as she pushed through the front door of White Hill House. The confrontation with Stef had drained her, but she could not back out of the 3-Cube project. With Alaina, they had pushed on to a new plateau. Bloody Stef.

The aroma of the fresh almond, lemon and ricotta cake filled the air. It sat golden, crisp and inviting on the kitchen table. Sara was by the pasta maker extracting fresh tagliatelle. Grace looked round the kitchen – nothing out of place. When she poached eggs, she made more mess than this.

'How are you?'

'Good,' smiled Sara. Her arm had healed, but was still painful.

'Want a hand?'

'Be great. Would you wash these?'

As Grace washed six kilos of mussels, she asked, 'Have you thought about what you're going to do next? You're welcome to stay here, you know.' She was sure that her father's current good mood had a lot to do with Sara and Ruthie. They'd brought new life to the house.

'Hal and I were talking about it last night. We're going to move into his London flat.'

Grace wondered how much Hal had told her. He could live till ninety or die tomorrow. The complications of his birth cast a long shadow.

'Great. Have you decided about visitation rights for . . .'

'For her father? No. Not really. He hasn't shown much interest so far. I put up with a lot so she could be near him.'

Grace cut a knuckle as she scrubbed a mussel shell with renewed intensity.

'Will you tell Ruthie about her father?'

'D'you know what she said to me yesterday?' A smile tugged at Sara's lips. 'She said, "Now that we're living in the same house as Hal, will he be my daddy?'

'What did you say?'

'I told her that that Hal would love her like a daddy.' She poured two tablespoons of olive oil into a large pan and added the mussels. 'I'll tell her about Freddie when the moment's right.'

I must talk to Hope, thought Grace. She must be devastated. It was obvious that she knew of Freddie's affairs – he was hardly discreet – but his girlfriends lived in London and therefore did not impinge on her world. But to have Freddie's child living in her family home, and for the entire county to know about it, would wound her deeply.

A few seconds later Malkie came into the kitchen to pick up Lilly.

'Hi, Malk,' said Sara, as she kissed his cheek.

'They're playing very happily with my dad,' said Grace. 'We thought you'd like to stay for an early supper.'

'Nothing special,' murmured Sara. 'Bit of pasta and some cake.'

'Yeah, right.' Grace's eyes sparkled at her new friend. 'Knocked it up in ten minutes.'

Sara smiled. 'Chop the tomatoes,' she said, then added, 'Grace, will you get moving on the tag.'

As Grace boiled water in a large pasta pan, Malkie asked, 'How's it going at Standish?'

'Sometimes it's great. And then today . . .' She shrugged, then dropped the tagliatelle into the water. 'Do you know Stef Violi?' she asked.

'I've met him a few times,' he replied as he stirred the sauce. 'Seems a good guy. Straight. Why?'

'Oh, I don't know. There's something weird about him. I can't work it out.'

Violi is playing complicated games with both Sam and Grace, Malkie thought. Very, very dangerous.

'Sometimes people *are* what they seem,' he replied. 'What's worrying you?'

'Security,' she said.

'Hey, that's my department. You tell me what you want and I'll get it for you.'

'You any good on advanced mathematical modelling for biochemistry?'

He laughed.

'I know a guy who is.' She ran a fork through

the pasta, separating the strands. 'Trouble is, Stef won't give him clearance.'

'Might be a good reason for that.'

'What?'

'Guy might not be on the level.'

'Who? Stef?' She checked his eyes to see if they were smiling. They weren't.

'The other guy. What's he called?'

'Amir.'

'If I were you, I'd follow Violi's instincts. He's been around.'

Lilly rushed into the room, growling. She was covered from head to foot in red, gold and black face paints. 'Raaaaah,' she roared. 'We're tigers.'

'Good grief,' groaned Sara.

'Daddy.' Grace scowled at her father.

'I only provided the means, not the motive,' he replied, then tasted the sauce. 'Needs more salt.'

'Bathtime. Now.' Malkie picked up his daughter.

'Raaah,' said Lilly.

'Raaaah yourself.'

Grace tried Sam's landline, then mobile. Nothing. She sent him an email telling him she loved him and asking him to call. How could they suspect Sam of anything? After all he'd done. She recalled his parting words – 'remember sleeping lions'. Act normally. It was hard when she was sure she was being watched.

She turned her mind to her own problem. She needed to check out Amir and decided to call

Evangeline, her old boss in Bangladesh. Minutes passed as she dialled and redialled. It wasn't unusual to take anything up to half an hour to make a connection in Bangladesh. She had learned patience. She had written to Evangeline the week before with the good news about 3-Cube, but had heard nothing back as yet.

Click. Click.

'ORS. Sister Evangeline Rush. What can I do to help you?'

'It's Grace.'

'Gracie, honey, how in Hades are you?'

'I'm fine. Did you get my letter?'

'No. I thought you'd forgotten me. Was getting a bit grouchy, to tell the truth. Thought of asking the Big Guy to send you a plague of locusts or somethin'.'

Grace frowned. She'd sent the package via the internal post five days before. She'd included a relief pack of shampoos, Hershey bars, a bottle of lime vodka and a beautiful scarf she'd picked up in Liberty. It should've got there by now. The phone cut off.

'Damn,' she said.

'Grace, honey, you there?' She was back.

'Yes, here.'

'Honey, this ain't no good for a social call. I'll call you from Dhaka next week.'

'No, hang on. D'you know a doctor called Rahman? Got a brilliant son, Amir.'

'Oh, yeah. Died. Real shame.'

'His dad's dead?'

'No, Amir. Car crash. Head on.'

Grace froze. What was she talking about? She must have misunderstood.

'When?'

'Two months ago. His pop's still incredibly cut up about it. It was all over the papers. I gotta go, Gracie. I've a village meeting to prepare for.'

'Let me get this straight. Amir Rahman died two months ago.'

'Yeah.'

'But that's impossible.'

'Why?'

'I've been emailing him for a week.'

'Only if you believe in ghosts, hon.'

CHAPTER 54

Tumultuous rain battered the windscreen as the speedometer nudged 100 m.p.h. Sam barely noticed his surroundings as he drove on instinct, his mind focused on the problems facing him. He needed to talk to Malkie – to have someone shed some light on Big Planet and *1986 10 404*. He scrambled for his phone, began to call Malkie then stopped himself. What had the voice said? 'As secure as a baby on a banister.' His heart skipped a beat and he checked his speed, sluiced across to the exit and pulled off the motorway into a series of narrow country lanes. Now he understood.

Whoever was following him would also have paused, unsure of his movements. He got out, the harsh wind whipping his body, and leant on a five-bar farm gate. The landscape between the three motorways was bleak undulating scrub and he could see for hundreds of metres in all directions. Trees groaned in the night and the chill calmed him as he watched car headlights carve holes in the velvet sky, the mist clearing in his mind. This is a set-up, he thought, as he ran through the electronic conversation again in his mind. Whoever alerted him to Roni Collins' involvement had to be in the squad. Even the most experienced hacker would have needed more time to gather Sam's passwords and private accounts, even assuming they knew where to look. The squad, by contrast, could run the Hoover over him in a matter of hours.

'As secure as a baby on a banister.' How many times had he heard Lindsey Hamilton say that? It was one of her favourites. Why had she let him know that the squad was pushing him? She must know what evidence they had against him, would have gathered much of it herself. But she threw him a lifeline because her instincts were troubling her. Look for patterns, he'd taught her. Patterns are more important than detail. She can't see the pattern, so she's following her instincts, and these tell her that I'm innocent. Trevor, on the other hand, would be fighting the pattern and focusing on the detail.

He put himself in Trevor's shoes. Near retirement; a great career; rebuilt the squad after the scandals – a lot to lose if the squad had been seriously penetrated. The General told him that Trevor had a warning from a reliable foreign source that someone senior had gone over in their force, so Ian must be assuming that he had the same problem. But why me?

They must know about his bank account and about the payments for the renovations to the manse. They would know about Jock MacAlpine, his benefactor. Telling them about Jock would be embarrassing, but there was nothing else for it. But that couldn't be enough. They must have something more substantial. Would Lindsey talk to him? Was there a secure way of reaching her?

He turned back to the car. One thing was certain. The last person he should talk to was Malkie. He drove home, aware of the complex interchange between two motorbikes, a blue Mondeo, green Passat and maroon Golf. The drivers would know that he'd spot them. Trevor must be trying to knock him off balance, force him into making a mistake. He'd spent two years undercover in Belfast and knew that fear was his worst and most terrible enemy. He had to be calm.

Grace glowered at the telephone handset. How could Amir Rahman be dead? She stared at Malkie standing in the hallway with a bedraggled Lilly, her wet hair dripping water onto his shoes.

'You look as if you've seen a ghost,' he said.

She looked through him, then put the phone back on its cradle. Yet again she dialled Sam. Where *are* you?

CHAPTER 55

S am lifted his half-drunk beer and put it down again. On the table in front of him was a note from Sergio.

Gone to stay with Eileen for a few days.

He missed his friend. As he walked around the flat it seemed filled with dead zones. He put Verdi's *Tosca* on the CD and turned up the amplifier, filling the rooms with sound and beauty. The phone rang – his private one, the one that had signalled the beginning of this weird nightmare, and the number recognition software said, 'Grace Adams.'

'Hello, Grace.'

'Darling.' She sounded relieved. 'I've been phoning all day. Where've you been?'

'Busy. How can I help?'

'I . . . Is everything all right?'

'Fine. As I've already told you, I'm busy. Can this wait? I'm waiting for a message from Mr Lion.'

'No, it can't wait. What is this? We've been

engaged for one whole day and you already think the job is more important than me.'

'But . . .' he replied.

'Oh, get lost, Sam.' The phone abruptly cut out.

He stared at the receiver, his heart thumping. You brilliant woman, he thought. She got it. She'd picked up his signal that the line was bugged.

He turned off the lights, cracked open the curtain and looked at the two squad cars parked in plain sight at either end of the road. This can't go on, he thought. He had to bring it to a head.

After years of undercover work, Sam had trained himself to find unexpected exits from any building. He changed into black jeans and a leather jacket, then tucked a woollen hat, small voice-distorting machine, and digital voice recorder into his pockets. He had to talk to Lindsey. From the safe hidden under the rug beneath his bed, he extracted two pay as you go phones. He was about to close up, when his fingers brushed the Glock G18 automatic, a presentation weapon from the US Drug Enforcement Agency. He picked it up, thought about it for a few minutes, then returned it to the holster.

Behind the 1930s boiler in the basement of Sam's block was a little-used door to the back of the building. Originally it had led to the coal cellar, but since the introduction of oil in the 1960s, its only purpose was to serve as an exit for successive generations of cats. The current model,

288

a large neutered ginger called Rory, rubbed against him. Sam scratched his ear, dropped a handful of chocolate to the ground, and as the cat wolfed down his treat, he fished a key from his pocket, stolen from the janitor within a week of moving in. He slipped into the dungeon-like alley that ran the length of the block. A rat darted out of his way, pursued with surprising agility by Rory. Sam was grateful – he hated rats.

He shut the door and moved towards a set of dank, mossy stairs, ignoring the sounds around him. He surfaced behind a set of garages, unlocked one, stepped inside and turned on the light. In the middle stood a customized black Harley Davidson Intimidator. He had rebuilt it himself and it had sat there for years. It was registered to Dr Jonathan McAlpine of Grant Street, Truro.

He pulled on a crash helmet, opened the doors into the alley and pushed out the bike. Traffic was hurrying up towards Camden and soon he would be part of it. He glanced back and saw the lights in his flat. He had programmed them to light up randomly until midnight when they would shut off altogether. He had left all the windows open and curtains flapped, sending confusing shadows around the rooms.

Pulling down his visor, he roared into the traffic.

A little later, he parked in an alley in Soho and dialled Gitte, using his pay per use phone. 'I need your help.'

'Just ask.'

'I need to talk to someone who, like you, is a computer genius.'

'I wouldn't say that, Sam.'

'If I gave you her numbers, could you get in touch with her somehow – without other people knowing?'

'I can try.'

He gave her half a dozen telephone numbers for Lindsey – some he knew, some he had had a friend in BT find that afternoon.

'Tell Grace I love her.'

He dropped the phone into a bin, then gunned the bike, weaving through the midnight traffic. Around half an hour later, he slipped off the motorway and phoned Gitte.

'Any luck?'

'Your Lindsey's a hard girl to crack. Everything serious is locked away. Not one number would allow me a back channel.'

He could hear the 'but' in her voice.

'But?' he asked.

'But she's a gamer. Computer games. Everquest, mainly. She's online now.' He knew that Everquest was a fantasy role-playing Internet computer game played by thousands of people.

'That's amazing. She doesn't seem the type.'

'Your girl is hard core. Could take me out in ten minutes.'

'Can you get me into her?' he asked. It was the perfect cover to talk. The squad would not track her in the virtual world.

'What kind of connection are you using?'

'There's an all-night Internet cafe close by. I'll go there.'

'You've got to get into Everquest, then sign in using *livebait*. That's my password. Her handle is *squadgirl*. You've got to track down her clan.'

'Thanks, Gitte.'

'Be careful, Sam. Grace needs you.'

Around twenty minutes later, he hunched over a computer in a downbeat cafe with three students and a sleepy waitress for company. A cup of coffee steamed by his side as he entered the game – a world of princesses, trolls, elf thieves and dwarf merchants. Sam thanked God that Hal had taught him to play multiplayer games years before. It had been a way of staying in touch with the boy as he grew up.

He turned on his immunity to Pkilling. Pkilling, or person killing, was the object of the game for the hard core and he was sure that *squadgirl* would be in Pkill mode. He didn't want any distractions as he moved through the world. He searched for and found *squadgirl* in a castle dungeon in Odus.

'Squadgirl?' He spoke into a thin microphone attached to the computer, using the Internet to talk to her.

'Who's that?'

'Tycho Brahe.'

'How did you find me?'

'Everyone has one weakness. I need to see you. Are you under surveillance?'

'Yes,' she replied.

'Where can we meet?'

Silence. Sam watched and prayed as his character bobbed aimlessly on the screen.

'Please help me, Lindsey.'

'There's a wood half a mile from my house,' she replied after a long pause. 'I often go there to jog. I'll meet you at the entry to the golf course in an hour.'

'I'll be there. Listen, Lindsey, you know this is nonsense, don't you?'

'No, I don't, Sam. The evidence against you is comprehensive and damning.'

Sam watched as his avatar, a lonely elf, slumped inactive against the wall, whilst *squadgirl* hovered and shimmered as Queen of the Wizards.

'See you soon.'

CHAPTER 56

Al Imam listened to the BBC World Service, his eyes peering into the darkness. Beside him, his niece snored gently, her arms thrown protectively across his chest. Increasingly, he needed her innocent warmth. He smiled at the faintest of twitching in his groin. Even now, even this close to death, the flesh demands life. The radio reporter announced the business news:

'*As expected, Aventis, the world's third largest agribusiness, has fallen to a consortium of Saudi businessmen. The Chief Executive of Aventis will be asked to stay on for the foreseeable future.*'

Al Imam *had* foreseen the future. Nothing would change at Aventis for the next eighteen months and then they would ease in their own man. A man they could trust. A brother.

He closed his eyes, imagining the rolling killing fields of the Midwest. That evening Standish had sent a coded message that they had almost broken Dr Adams' code and they were already working on ways to integrate the cancer-causing chemicals into the seeds. In the morning, Al Imam would send out letters to four researchers working in

European research labs who would prepare to take up high-level posts at Aventis. These men would create his bread of heaven.

A surge of pain ran through his body. Allah be praised, he murmured.

Sam watched Lindsey sit on a concrete bollard next to the ornate gates of the golf club, patient but watchful. She was wrapped up in well-worn dark running gear, her shoes battered with use.

Fifteen minutes had passed and he hadn't detected any sign she was being followed. He dialled the number of a phone he'd hidden beside the fence. She searched, then picked it up.

'There's a pile of cut timber in a clearing about four hundred yards due south from where you are. I'll wait for you there.'

When she reached the logs, she didn't glance around as she unzipped her top, revealing a jogging bra. No microphone wires. Seeing she was clean, he appeared from the woods.

'Hello, Lindsey. Thanks for coming.'

She zipped her jacket and shivered. He looks great in leather, she thought, takes years off him. She wondered again what she was doing here. Risking everything. Mad. And yet, the second she saw him again, looked into his eyes, she could not believe in his guilt.

He pulled a book, his bank statement and a computer from the black satchel at his side.

'What's this?' she asked.

'The source of the money I spend on the manse.'

She turned the volume over in her hands, then studied the title. *Dark Convoy*. The author was J. McAlpine. She shot him a quizzical look.

'Read the blurb.'

Captain Tom Graham's toughest assignment yet. He has to command a destroyer from Murmansk at the height of the U-boat campaign in 1941 and track down a Russian killer who is trying to assassinate his precious cargo — a German nuclear scientist who is defecting to London.

'Sounds good. Whodunnit?'

'I've written five books about Tom Graham.' After his divorce, Sam had begun to write. His first effort was a compulsive dissection of his own marriage, which he ditched. Then he established a series about Tom Graham, a Scottish naval captain living in the Western Highlands and operating out of Holy Loch.

'You *are* joking, aren't you?' she said.

He looked almost sheepish.

'Afraid not. Didn't tell anyone. Thought it would be a bit embarrassing.'

'But, Sam . . .'

'I know. I should've declared the cash payments for the farm. But that can't be all Trevor is worried about.'

As she gazed at him, he could see her make up her mind.

'You got a mobile Internet connection?'

He nodded and handed over his Palm Pilot.

She typed quickly, then pulled down the details of Big Planet and the sound files containing his conversations with Fernandez and Malkie.

'Listen to these, and then we'll discuss account 1986 10 404.'

Sam heard the 'conversation' between himself and Fernandez.

Sam – *We must be careful.*

Fernandez – *Always. But they are not on to us. I would swear it on my mother's eyes.*

Sam – *Have you sent my latest instalment?*

Fernandez – *Waiting for you at Big Planet. A double helping.*

Sam – *I need it. Running tight on resources at the moment.*

Fernandez – *Tell that to the Barracuda.*

The sound of laughter, followed by Copeland cutting the connection.

He ripped the phones from his ears. 'Damn.'

'Exactly. You can see Trevor's problem, Sam. It's not a pretty moment when your number two is in a dodgy conversation with a corrupt Spaniard.'

'What've they got against Fernandez?'

'Everything but a signed confession in blood. They're waiting for us to clean out the stables here before they take him down. They want the whole net. At least, that's what Trevor is telling us. We aren't allowed to contact anyone outside the squad. Even the General is off limits.'

'It's two conversations.'

'What?'

'I did speak to Fernandez about the Barracuda. That much is true. I'd had a sniff and wanted to find out what he knew. That's the first two sentences. Fernandez is a good guy. I would swear it. I've known him twenty years. I don't believe he's gone over.'

'But the evidence . . .'

'Is corrupt. These sentences –' he pointed to the screen, *Have you sent my latest instalment? I need it. Running tight on resources at the moment* – are from a conversation with my agent. I had sent her the final draft of my new book and was asking her to nudge the publishers to part with their cash. I made the call to Fernandez from the office and the one to Carole, my agent, from the car. There must be differences in background noise and connection quality, even in something as well spliced together as this.'

'Jesus. I checked. I promise, Sam. If this is a fake then it's perfect.'

'There'll be a flaw. Always is.'

'What about the calls to Collins?' she asked.

'Never made them. Someone has compiled them from a number of conversations to someone else.'

'Whoever is behind this has access to some extremely sophisticated gear. Why are they doing it?'

Sam shrugged. 'I have absolutely no idea. I've been chewing it over for days. But I need you to help me find out.'

She folded herself into his arms. She was frail and shivering. 'I'm sorry, Sam. Sorry for doubting you.'

She looked up into his face, longing to be kissed. He pulled her tight as the wind howled around them.

CHAPTER 57

Roni Collins crooned to her restless daughter who had been bouncing all night, unable to sleep, constantly chattering about going to London with Ruthie. As Lilly finally settled, she pulled on her dark glasses and walked into the hall. Frank met her on his way from the lavatory.

'Sorry, Roni. Know you don't like us up here, but somebody's in the bog downstairs.'

'That's OK, Frank.' She dismissed her previous attempts to protect what was left of the sanctity of her home with a flick of her hand. 'Fancy a drink?' She couldn't face drinking alone tonight. Even Frank would be better than nothing.

'The boss's warned us off the sauce, like. Whilst . . .'

Whilst you protect my daughter from some unknown evil, she thought. An evil invoked by her father's so-called business.

'That's fine, Frank.'

His huge bulk trundled down the stairs behind her; each step creaked under the pressure.

She was shocked to find Malkie poring over a sheet of numbers in the sitting room. He'd gone out earlier, telling her there were things he had to sort out. She headed straight for the drinks cabinet and poured a vodka and tonic. Alcoholics know their place – beside the bar. She shook her head. How many times had she told that lousy stupid joke, propped up against some crappy wine bar wall, whilst Frank sat there nursing a still water, waiting for her to collapse so he could pick her up and take her home.

She folded herself onto the sofa, her body as small as she could make it. Malkie glanced up, finished his calculations and came over to join her. She flinched as he rubbed the back of her neck. He sighed then poured himself tonic water with bitters. He brought over a hard-backed chair, sat, and leant towards her.

'I need to see your eyes.' Gently, he lifted off the Armanis and she did not resist.

'You know I love you, don't you?' he asked.

She nodded, afraid to speak. Malkie didn't love her. He owned her. That was all. Love. There *was* a man who gave her love. Unconditional love. And he didn't live in *this* house.

'I know there's some part of your soul that still loves me,' he said. 'I never disguised what I was. You know that.'

Oh, I knew, she thought. But I was in love. Shout it out to the court, to the priest, to the mother of a child dead from adulterated E. I was in love. Don't you understand? I WAS IN LOVE. Doesn't love justify all? Conquer all? Excuse all? No it fucking doesn't. Then I saw through a glass darkly, now face to face. She looked at Malkie, at his wonderful eyes locked on hers, his gentle hard hands, and sensual full lips. I was in love. Two miscarriages and a stillbirth told me all I needed to know about God's punishment. She reached out to the bottle and began to tip more vodka into her glass.

'No.' His voice was firm. 'No more. You're going back into rehab.'

'There's no point.' She shrugged him off, but he put the bottle on the floor behind him.

'You've turned me into this,' she sneered. Her body ached for more. The buzz hadn't kicked in properly. She felt a hundred ants run across her fingers.

'You know better than that. You are what you choose to be.'

'What's that,' she asked, 'existentialism for fucking beginners? GCSE Sartre?'

She watched his arms tense, his neck muscles tighten. She knew how to wound, to punish. She ran a nail down a vein, opening up an old cut.

'Don't do that. Please don't do that. Don't hurt yourself.'

Causes me more pain than it causes you, Malkie.

He held both her hands, preventing further damage. Those eyes. She closed her lids. Malkie's eyes could seduce God.

'I want to make a deal with you,' he said.

She drifted, calming her anxieties. Soon he would tire of her, retreat to his daughter's room, fall asleep on the floor. Then her night could begin. Vodka in the glass, REM or Nirvana in the headphones, the Turner Movie Channel transmitting ghostly icons twenty-four hours a day: Monroe, Bacall, Garbo. He would put her to bed in the morning, and she wouldn't have to face him again for another twelve hours.

The smack she'd bought the night they tried to kidnap her girl lay undisturbed in her makeup bag. She felt too guilty to use it. It had almost cost too much. But perhaps tonight. Tonight he was being especially disgusting. Those eyes. Look at those eyes. Only Satan handed out eyes like that.

She felt water on her forehead. It trickled down into the corner of her eyes. She opened them and he was sitting close to her, his fingers dripping.

'I will give you Lilly,' he said, his voice soft. 'And I'll walk away.'

She struggled with the fog that had gathered around her consciousness.

'I want you to go into counselling. If you do that, and stay off the juice, I will put two million quid into a private account for you. You can live off the interest for the next five years, and if you are clean, then you get the whole lot. Another million will go into trust for Lilly to inherit when she's twenty-five. But if you fall off the wagon, Lilly goes to my sister, along with all but a hundred thousand pounds of the money. That you can keep.'

She took his water, gulped it, then poured more.

'Why?' she asked.

'For Lilly.'

She peered at her half-full glass of vodka and tonic. She wanted it so badly. Never more, now that she wanted it to be her last. But could she trust him?

'Finish it,' he smiled.

She looked directly into his eyes, picked up and drained her drink, savouring the flow of alcohol into her veins, her brain. Her last drink felt like the final kiss of a dying lover.

CHAPTER 58

Grace sized up the ubiquitous security cameras as she strode into the lab. The room was filled with intense activity. They had leapt forward in the past few weeks, and the familiar feeling of a team close to cracking something important filled their conversation. She had become friendly with Raj, an Indian biochemist in his twenties who specialized in quantitative genetics and biometrics.

'Coffee?' She made drinking gestures with her arm.

'Sure.'

They walked down to the cafeteria, situated in a fake street within a small Mediterranean biosphere. 'Double de-caff mocha with a twist,' Raj ordered.

Grace asked for filter. Black.

'Have you ever met Johnny Standish?' Grace asked. No one she knew had, other than Alaina and Stef, and both were very circumspect.

'No, no.' Raj was very beautiful in an Anglo-Indian way. His mother had been an English mathematician and his father a politician. He had refined features and thin agile fingers. 'Johnny

Standish only turns up once a year to give out the award medals and large cheques at the Standish Conference in Boulder, Colorado. People say he's charming. Why?'

'Very little about him online.'

'Doesn't need the publicity, I suppose.'

Grace sipped her coffee.

'What d'you make of this Rahman thing?' she asked.

'What do you mean?'

'Don't be coy, Raj. Alaina tells you everything.' She watched him over the rising steam.

'He's a brilliant guy,' replied Raj.

'So why doesn't Stef want me to talk to him?'

Raj shrugged.

'Look,' she said, 'I don't want to be disloyal to Stef. He's been good to me. Would you phone Rahman and ask if he would either come here or if there's another secure way of talking to him?'

Raj shook his head. 'I don't think I can do that.'

She put a hand on his. It was soft and the colour of oak bark. 'Please. We both know that the project will take another leap if we bring Rahman on board.'

'Let me think about it.'

'Talk to Alaina. See what she thinks.' Grace drained her coffee.

Half an hour later, he turned up in Grace's office and signalled for her to join him. They walked along the corridor, watching the herons landing on the artificial lake. 'Amir was really understanding,' whispered Raj conspiratorially. 'He says there's a simple method of dealing with the privacy issue. He'll email you this evening.'

'How did he sound?'

'Pretty cheerful.'

For a dead man, thought Grace.

'Thanks, Raj. I owe you.'

'Think nothing of it. For the good of the project.' He walked rapidly back to the lab.

When she returned to the office Grace's spirit dropped as she glanced at Gitte. Her heart will break when she finds out that Alaina is behind this. And where does Violi stand? She had to talk to him, but not before dealing with 'Amir'.

An email had arrived from Dhaka University.

Dr Adams,

Greetings. I understand and applaud the need for privacy. The last thing we want is for your research to fall into the hands of the agri-industrial complex with their patent lawyers and rapacious behaviour.

I don't know how much you know about the Internet, but it is possible through a private link to set up a DCC connection.

She vaguely knew about direct client to client

connections, but she was going to need Gitte's deep understanding of the Internet to pull off the operation she had in mind. He continued.

Use this IP number – 123.909.879.

She replied.

Thanks, tonight. 1900 GMT. Looking forward to it.

She clicked *send* and glowered at the screen. How could she break it to Gitte? Could she deal with it herself?

She read the email again. Deception inevitably destroys love and Gitte had to be told. Three times she opened her mouth to speak and three times failed.

'What are you looking at?' Gitte asked over her shoulder.

'An email from Amir Rahman.'

'What does he want?'

As Gitte read it, Grace thought, There's no other way. She handed her the press cutting about Amir's death that Evangeline had faxed to her home that morning.

At first Gitte was puzzled, then her eyes opened wide with pain as the implication sank in. Tonight there would be rage, thought Grace.

Grace glanced up at the security cameras. 'Don't let the bastards see you cry.'

CHAPTER 59

Lindsey Hamilton was exhausted. Her eyes were red-rimmed as she ran the Fernandez tape through another software package, reading the spikes and troughs of sound, trying to sort out background noise. If Sam was telling the truth, then there was something on the tape that would help him and the sound waves would reveal the different environments in which the two conversations took place.

This case hadn't been right from the beginning. Perched on her desk and the floor around her computer were coffee cups, cold pizza and a congealing plate of cornflakes. Sam had said he would meet her at midday at the office. She was glad it was Saturday. There wouldn't be many calls. Hacket was shooting clay pigeons with an under-secretary of state. Ian Trevor had called her a few times in the morning, but she had been able to fob him off with bits and pieces. He was a shrewd old bugger, though. He would soon know if she was off-side.

It was coming up to ten. A couple of hours and she might crack this. She rolled the software again, watching and listening. The powerful headphones cut out all noise and she didn't hear the footsteps behind her.

Sam sat on the pile of logs where he and Lindsey had parted the previous evening. His head was turned up to the sun, letting the warmth pour over him. The scent was fabulous – pine, early flowerings of irises – his favourite time of year. Lindsey sent him a text message.

Need you here, now. Found it.

She can't expect him to go to her house, he thought. Then came another message.

Safe. Don't worry.

He was cautious. But he was tired of this nonsense and longed to be investigating the events at Eastfield. The bomber had gone quiet, and the surveillance on Malkie suggested he was lying low. But Sam didn't believe it. Malkie had to exact revenge for the attempted kidnapping. Otherwise he would appear weak and in his world weak meant dead.

He cautiously approached her street, checking for surveillance, slid into the field, waited behind a yew hedge, then after a few minutes cautiously entered her open back door.

'Lindsey,' he called, as he wandered up the

stairs. The first room was Lindsey's bedroom. The door was open and as he expected it was delicate and disciplined at the same time. A large double bed, with brass bedstead; pale lilac walls, books set at precise angles on a round table in the centre of the room. Pictures of what looked like nieces and nephews took pride of place on the dresser, on which little pots of makeup were lined up like soldiers.

Next door was her study. The room was a mess. Blood spattered the walls, floor and computer.

'Lindsey!' he yelled, then quickly gathered himself. Think. He checked the room again. The blood distribution showed that she'd struggled and then been shot close to the door. There were two bullet holes on the wall beside her Mac. A third was embedded in the lintel.

He felt sick. What pain had he inflicted on this courageous woman? He flipped open his mobile and called Gerry Mulligan, the NCS Duty Officer, and ordered him to get a team out immediately. Someone must have her, must want her for some reason, or her body would be lying here. She was alive. He knew it.

Sam retraced his steps, careful not to disturb any evidence. In the hallway, he phoned Ian Trevor, explaining where he was.

'Back to HQ,' Trevor ordered.

'But, Ian, I can do more good here.'

'Now. That's a direct order. You wait for the team to turn up. Do you understand?'

'Yes, Guv.'

Sam's stomach churned as he watched cars converge on the quiet street.

'Tell me again, because I don't understand,' Trevor ordered. He sat on the sofa in Sam's flat, whilst Sam perched on the hard chair Trevor had summoned from the kitchen. Blinding sun poured through the large plate windows. Hacket sat behind Sam in the shade. The sitting room was a mess of torn cushions, tumbled books and ripped floorboards. Squad investigators were systematically ripping it apart.

'Lindsey was working on the Collins case for me,' said Sam. 'She told me she had something good and asked me to visit her.'

'Were you in the habit of visiting DI Hamilton?'

'First time.'

Trevor placed both hands flat on his lap. Sam knew the gesture well. It meant that Ian was trying to bring his temper under control.

'Do you recognize this?' asked Trevor.

Trevor reached down, extracted an evidence bag, and then placed it on the coffee table. Inside was the Glock G18 automatic the DEA had given him – that or its twin.

'A citizen found it next to a jogging path used regularly by DI Hamilton. Do you recognize it? It has your prints on it.'

Sam nodded.

'It was fired three times today,' Trevor continued.

'The bullets are embedded in DI Hamilton's wall.'

Sam felt Hacket behind him.

'What the fuck have you done with her, Copeland? You devious piece of shit.' Trevor slammed his fist on the glass coffee table.

Sam's mind was spiralling in a hundred different directions. Questions crowded in on him as he stared at Trevor's explosive face. They were about to arrest him. The evidence against him was circumstantial but overwhelming. He sprang to his feet.

'Sit down,' ordered Hacket.

Sam ignored him. Trying to make it add up.

'I said sit down, Copeland.' As Hacket pressed down on his shoulders, guiding him back to the chair, Sam chair allowed himself to drop by a few centimetres, then his elbow shot back and slammed Hacket's chest. He sprawled on the floor.

Trevor was on his feet screaming at him, but Sam was oblivious. Everything had become background noise. Hacket leapt at him, but was felled by a head-butt. Sam ran through his front door, brushing aside a shocked policeman, then sprinted into the narrow corridor that led to the fire escape. He needed time. And time was running out. Fast.

CHAPTER 60

S am heard the clatter of feet behind him as he jumped down the twisting stairs. More policemen were rushing up the stairwell towards him. He was being sandwiched, but he had the advantage of knowing the building. On level ten, he scrambled a resident's security key from his pocket and opened the fire door, his pursuers seconds behind. Trevor yelled, 'Get him. Get the bastard. Bring him down.' They must be armed. His training took over and he dropped to his knees, evading the bullet that clanged on the metal door, then rolled into the corridor beyond, kicking shut the exit. That would hold them.

He sprinted to the other end of the building, ran up four flights then rejoined the fire exit. Cautiously he took each floor, listening to the crowd below as they summoned the janitor and issued orders to search the building. They wouldn't expect him to go up. The stairs gave out onto a flat roof. On the horizon, a Twin Squirrel chopper from the Air Support Unit swept over from Lippitts Hill. He squinted at the gap between his building and the one opposite. Two metres. He'd jumped

313

it in his mind when planning this escape. The real thing was much harder. Nothing for it, though. He sprinted and took off, falling through the air.

Word had begun to seep out of Scotland Yard that a senior figure was AWOL. It didn't take Malkie long to work out who. His informant told him that the rumour was that Sam had been turned. And was on the take. The official line was that Sam was on a scheduled holiday. That would hold for about a day.

He looked around the table. Alongside Frank was Jason Gregg, a tall, thin, fast-talking Londoner. Thirty-eight. Sharp. Never put a foot wrong. Next to Jason was Martie Etienne, a black guy in his early thirties. Bodybuilder. Hard. Liked money. Tight-lipped. And finally, there was Ali Johnstone, the only woman to run one of his companies. Compact, reserved, but focused.

Through his sleepless night, Malkie had pored over his plan. He needed to be free to float above everything, disappear for days on end without worrying about the company. If he was to take care of Sam, he needed two things, the bomber and Sam's body.

His dining room had been swept for bugs and those found destroyed. The room was spacious, with simple country Chippendale chairs and a long polished dining table. A portrait of Roni and Lilly hung above a fireplace in which logs were burning.

'I've decided to organize us a little differently.'

Their interest picked up, as did the tension.

'It's an age for federalism and devolution. Each of you are company directors, with specific responsibilities. I suspect that this is holding you back. You need to spread your wings.'

Eyes glued to him. Waiting.

'I'm going to split the company on a regional basis. Jason, you get Glasgow and Edinburgh. Martie, Liverpool and the West. Ali, Birmingham and the Midlands.'

He could feel the shock, each of them stealing glances at Frank, the person who had served longest and was closest to Malkie.

'Frank will head up International Relations. That OK, Frank?'

His old war-horse looked down at the table, unable temporarily to speak. Then he looked Malkie in the eye. 'Whatever you say. You're the boss.'

Malkie nodded and placed a hand on Frank's.

'Whatever happens to me, you have Frank to deal with. And Frank will act on these precise orders.' He handed Frank a note. The big man opened it, read it, then slowly looked round the newly anointed chiefs.

'As the holding company, Frank and I will be entitled to forty per cent of what you make. Not a penny more or less. How much you make is up to you. Each of you will be given title to the security businesses in your area. The national companies will become shells. Do you agree to the terms?'

Each in turn nodded. They had no alternative. Either agree or be carved out. Malkie had always compartmentalized in the past. Each of them knew a bit of the story but never all. Even Frank. Now he was giving them a big chance. Sixty per cent was worth it. To begin with. Then we'll see. Malkie read their minds. Yes, we'll see, he thought.

'OK. I don't need to detain you further.'

After they had gone, Frank lit a small cigar and gazed at Malkie.

'Are you disappointed, Frank?'

'Can't deny it, boss. I'd like to run my own firm.'

'You do me one more favour and I'll carve you out something bigger than those three could dream of.'

'What's that?'

'Protect Lilly and Roni.'

'Goes without saying.'

'With your life.'

Malkie sat on the table next to his old friend.

'You need to travel alone. I can't risk anyone knowing where I'm going to send them.'

The big man nodded. 'No question.'

'One more thing. One of these three is a Judas. When he or she shows, kill them.'

Sam put his tube ticket through the automatic barrier and melted into the crowd.

He had ditched his bike in a garage in Hackney, then gone to the barber's and had his head shaved bald and his eyebrows died blonde. He bought a short, neat blonde wig and a priest's black suit from a clerical outfitters.

Throughout the circuitous journey round London, he thought of Grace and of how to contact her. The story hadn't broken yet. Clearly, Charlie had managed to grab hold of the situation and calm Trevor down. It would be disastrous to let something like this into the media, especially as Charlie must know he was innocent. What would the PM think? Surely he can't believe this nonsense. Sam didn't fool himself. Much as he respected the man, he was a politician and would sit on his hands until Sam was proven innocent.

The NCS would be on top alert and their very best people would be searching for him. Grace would be under twenty-four-hour surveillance, as would Malkie and Eileen. He thought of Sergio with Eileen. Sam needed allies. People he could trust. He must find Sergio.

CHAPTER 61

Gitte lay on the floor, her wild, hurt eyes peering into the distance.

'How could she do this to me?'

Grace continued gently to rub her friend's temples. 'I don't know. She must . . . I just don't know. She must be in on whatever Stef and Standish are up to.'

'Maybe,' Gitte sat up, her eyes sparkling with hope, 'they could be forcing her.'

Grace hesitated. 'Maybe.'

Gitte gulped. 'Not true. Is it? She's one of them.'

'I think so. I don't know. I don't know who "they" are. It's obvious they're trying to get the rest of our research. Amir was simply a blind ruse and I fell for it.'

Gitte rubbed tears from her eyes. 'Not your fault. We're so used to communicating by Web sites and email that the fact both were fake just didn't occur to you.'

'Well. Let's do the same to them,' replied Grace. 'What?'

'Let's poison *their* wells.'

PART THREE

HARVESTING THE WHIRLWIND

For they have sown the wind, and they shall reap the whirlwind

The Book of Hosea, 8, 7,
King James Version

CHAPTER 62

May 3 18:58 server kernel: packet log: input accept eth0 proto=123.909.879.

Gitte bit her lip, her concentration intense as she typed in commands to track the computer from which 'Rahman' was operating. From her office, she'd set up a fake port and established a back-door connection.

Alias port19a (echo port 19 DCC CHAT detected from Amir}
*port 19b {/ [$ [*1]] }*

Despite her pain, she'd been quick to grasp Grace's idea of using the chat with 'Rahman' to find the enemy.

At White Hill farm, Grace sat in her mother's study and watched the cursor blinking on her Mac. She was linked via Gitte to the University's servers. She worked through the dialogue in her mind. She had to maintain a relaxed tone in the conversation with 'Rahman.' Nothing must alert them.

Gitte checked out the Standish Building. Light

from half a dozen windows – including those of Stef, Alaina and their own lab. Seven o'clock. It was time. She phoned Grace.

'Go now,' she said.

Grace glanced at the time on her screen. *19:00.*

How are you, Amir?

He replied immediately.

So good to hear from you, Grace. I was worried. Is it urgent?

No. I have a slight political opposition to involving you in our work, but I'm sorting it.

Good. You are doing great things and I'd like to help.

How is your dad? she asked. Silence. Thirty seconds later, he replied.

Fine. I've told him about your research. He's very excited.

Gitte sent tiny fragmented Internet probe packets past the firewall protecting 'Rahman's' computer.

I'm glad he's pleased. I'd like to meet him. You could play an enormous role in taking us forward. Grace's face looked back at her from the window as she typed, a well of anger in her eyes.

Whatever I can do to help, I will.

Gitte's fingers flew over the keyboard as she searched for the computer's location by running a reverse identification scan – *ident protocol rfc 1413.* The results came back. *Computer 13, Standish.*

They're getting careless. Using a Standish computer. Good. Perhaps Alaina would be relaxed and off guard. Whatever happened Gitte would have to return to Alaina's flat and bed. Grace's plan depended on 3-Cube and Standish believing they had access to all their information and calculations. Nothing held back. She ran a command to find out the IP address of the person who owned computer 13. It was Violi's PA. Gitte picked up her phone.

'It's Violi,' she whispered to Grace.

Grace hissed. He had conned her from the start.

They moved on to the second stage of the plan. Gitte walked down the corridor in her usual bustling manner. She had told Alaina she was working late at the lab. Nothing unusual there. But the security cameras would pick up her every move.

I would like to use you to help us with the maths, Grace wrote.

Glad to.

Try this. Grace sent a file containing calculations that she and Gitte had dismissed a few days before. Both had been excited by them initially, and therefore so would 'Rahman'. Especially as Alaina would be able to connect them to the work she had been doing on Grace's behalf.

Gitte entered the lavatory on the fifth floor directly across from Violi's room. His building rose in a bubble twenty metres across the compound and appeared to float on the surrounding lawn. She plugged a scrambler to the bottom of the security camera that would allow blurry and indistinct pictures of the room, nothing for a security man to worry about. Especially as they would be corrected every sixty seconds.

She hauled herself onto the high, narrow ledge, cracked open the window, trained the powerful zoom and focused on Violi's PA's window. Inside the room, laughing, were Alaina and Violi. Sitting at the PC was Raj, their friend from the lab. She fired off some shots, clambered down, withdrew the scrambler, washed her hands and left. Then she sent a text message to Grace. '*Gtg.*' Got to go. She returned to the office, emailed the digital pictures of 'Rahman' to Grace, then went to Alaina's flat to cook fish stew with couscous. Her lover's favourite. A last supper.

Hope this keeps you busy, she typed.

Grace gazed at the pictures that had just popped onto her screen and imagined Violi's and Alaina's pleasure at duping her.

Let's talk tomorrow. LOL, Gitte xx

Grace clicked disconnect and punched the screen with the flat of her hand. 'Damn, damn.'

A phone rang next to her. She recognized the tune – 'Layla' – it matched that on her own machine, but she couldn't locate its muted ring. It seemed to be coming from a package that had arrived in the post that afternoon. She read the address – The Sleeping Lions Theatre Company. Sam. It's Sam. She hit receive.

'Is Father McAlpine there?' asked a female voice.

'Who?'

'Father Jocky McAlpine. I'm due to meet him at nine o'clock.'

'Wrong number, I'm afraid,' replied Grace, her heart beginning to swell.

'Isn't that the Green Man?' asked the woman.

'No. It's White Hill Farm. But if you see Father McAlpine, send him my regards.'

CHAPTER 63

Gitte cradled Alaina, forcing herself to fondle her hair, her lover's betrayal tasting lemon-bitter in her mouth. She wanted to run from the room, but she also wanted answers. How could the fascinating, beautiful, intelligent woman she had fallen in love with do something so shameful?

'Hmmm,' Alaina crooned, then reached up and trickled her fingers across Gitte's lips. 'I feel good. Let's go to bed.'

Gitte yawned. 'I'm sleepy.'

Lazily Alaina traced a line across Gitte's breasts.

You think you own me, don't you? Gitte thought. I'm easy prey. Gitte lifted Alaina's hand and bit into the soft flesh around the mons.

'Oww. Fighting dirty.' Alaina laughed and struggled to sit, but Gitte tugged at the small hairs at the nape of her neck.

'Let me up.' Alaina's laughter caught an edge. 'Let me *up*.'

Gitte's felt a tear trickle down the side of her face, then the cataract burst and she wept silently as Alaina murmured to her, 'What is it, my love?'

Gitte, rubbing her eyes said. 'It's Grace. I think she's gone mad. She's accusing you of stealing our research.'

Alaina kissed her again, this time with more passion. 'Foolish thought. We've done nothing but support her.'

'I know. I know. But she wants me to leave with her. Tomorrow. She's going to pull out of Standish altogether.'

Alaina sat upright and took Gitte's cheeks in her hands.

'She can't. She won't. There's too much at stake. We're almost there. You must persuade her to remain with the project. She can achieve greatness.'

'I'll try,' Gitte kissed her with a deathly ferocity. 'I will try.'

Jenny Appleyard, the landlady of the Green Man in Earl's Langley, stood outside the back door of the pub smoking her last cigarette of the day. She thought she could hear a fox chittering in the distance. Nasty little beast, she thought. Somewhere in the still night a wood pigeon was disturbed and clattered from the trees. Her private moment was wrecked by the revving of bikes at the other pub in the village. 'Bloody vandals,' she grumbled.

She stubbed the cigarette on the wall, then ground it with her heel. From the corner of her eyes, she was suddenly aware of someone moving swiftly towards her. Automatically she raised her hands to shield her face.

'Those things are going to kill you,' Grace whispered, as she ghosted past.

'Not if I die of fright first.'

They hugged in the narrow back hall between boxes of crisps and a crate of beer.

'Good to see you, darling. It's been a while. You'll be careful, won't you?'

'Of course, Jenny. We won't do anything that would harm you. You know that.'

'He's upstairs. Room 3.'

Grace took the stairs two at a time then rounded the landing and knocked on the door. As Sam pulled it open, she stepped back in shock. He looked so different, a bald exhausted giant, and she felt suddenly shy and anxious. She looked up into his face and knew he understood.

They fell on the bed face to face, her lips centimetres from his, then they kissed gently – butterfly kisses.

'You shouldn't be here,' she whispered.

'The answers are here,' he said, his voice hoarse. He hadn't slept properly in days and her presence brought an extraordinary comfort and release. He pulled Grace in closer and she shivered.

'What is it?' he asked. 'What are you afraid of?'

She did not want to burden him further, but he was right. The answers were in Eastfield. There must be a connection between whoever was trying to discredit Sam and what was happening to her.

Grace kissed him again.

'It's Violi,' she said. 'He's crooked. They've been trying to rip off the project. They want to steal the patent. I don't know why they want it so badly, but they do.'

Sam stared at the ceiling. 'I've been warned off Violi by the General,' he said.

'Why?'

'I don't know, but it all seems to come back to him.'

They fell silent, lost in their thoughts as moonlight creased across the quilted bedspread.

'Sam?' she whispered.

Silence.

She opened her eyes. He was sound asleep, his face gentle against the pillow. She burrowed deeper into his body, feeling its enveloping warmth. Dark thoughts filled her head as the moon rose higher carrying away its light.

CHAPTER 64

Hal was working on a new sculpture, hewing an intense torso from black granite. He was sitting on a three-legged stool – the exhaustion of the past days had caught up with him and he'd taken a double dose of painkillers. He needed to work. To clear his head.

'It's brilliant.' Malkie ran hands across the stone. Although the sculpture was abstract, Malkie could see the shape of Sara's breasts, but the other side of the body was twisted, bent, hump-backed.

'How can I help?' asked Hal, putting down his chisel.

Malkie walked round the emerging statue. 'How would you like to go on holiday with Lilly and Roni? The five of you. I'll pay you and Sara a hundred grand and put another hundred into a trust fund for Ruthie. What you do with your money is up to you. You'll get it in exactly one month.' He handed him a post-dated cheque.

Hal looked at him. 'You're serious, aren't you? This has got to do with the kidnapping. You know who did it.'

'I can't give Lilly the attention she deserves. I

need her to be somewhere safe, where she's happy. Will you do it for her?'

Hal thought for a moment, then said, 'I don't know if I can deal with Roni.'

'She's off the booze, and I promise she'll stay off.'

'Where are we going?'

'I can't tell you that.'

Hal turned the cheque over in his hands. 'Make this out to Sara and you've got a deal.'

CHAPTER 65

S am watched Grace as she slept – her face paler than Casablanca lilies. Dreams grumbled through her mind and she kicked the quilt to the floor. He lifted it, wrapped it round her long, lithe body, stroked her cheek, and then returned to the desk by the window.

The blinds were drawn against the revealing morning and he sipped instant coffee and munched a banana. He would ask Grace to contact Sergio later that morning. He needed his friend's help to unravel the puzzles knotted together in his mind. And Sergio must know about Fernandez.

Then he began to jot down notes.

Malkie + Halliwell.

Malkie + Delawney.

*Delawney + Leadsmith – the bomber? Motive??
– violent activist???*

Delawney + Halliwell?????

Something clicked. What was the connection? He was sure there was one.

Leadsmith + Malkie????

Bomber operating on his own. Bombing stopped whilst Leadsmith gone. Where?

He closed his eyes to focus on a nagging memory. A picture. Local newspaper. Lying around in Lindsey's office. He sharpened the image. A formal dinner of some kind. No, it was a charity event. Delawney and Halliwell in dinner jackets, cigars half-smoked between indulgent fingers: wine-drunk smiles – arms around shoulders.

Sam tugged open his rucksack, pulled out and fired up his portable, then searched Google for a link between Delawney, Halliwell and Eastfield University. He found it. A press release from two years before announcing the name of the new Chairman of the Board of Governors – Sir Frank Tillyard, a retired software executive. His predecessor, the Earl of Eastfield, wished him luck.

'Busy?' Grace folded her arms around his chest and kissed his neck. He hadn't noticed her rise.

'Freddie Delawney was Chairman of the University's Board of Governors until two years ago,' he said.

'Yes. I went to the inauguration ceremony. Long and dull.'

'Standish bought that land up by the Centre two years ago, a few months before Freddie's retirement.'

Grace thought about it. 'And Halliwell did the deal. I remember Dad talking about it.'

'Halliwell was suddenly rich two years ago.'

Sam trawled the minutes of the council Planning Committee. There it was, permission granted to change the status of the land: agricultural to development. The owner of the fields was a company – CMI Devco. Halliwell had stepped down from that planning committee meeting, acknowledging a conflict of interest. The chair passed to Councillor Rod Leadsmith.

'Rod and Halliwell came to our place for dinner a couple of times, before the glasshouses were built, of course. Rod hadn't set foot in the house again until my party.'

Sam gazed at her thoughtfully. Unwilling to ask the question forming in his head. Sick at the thought of it.

'How well did Henry get on with Halliwell?'

'They were friends for a long time, then they had a falling out about . . .'

'Two years ago.'

CHAPTER 66

Malkie waited by Hal's jeep as his daughter and wife finished jamming clothes, toys and a portable TV into the back. Lilly rushed back and forth, sucking Blankie.

'Daddy, please come, please.'

He hoisted her chest-high and kissed the top of the head. 'I'll see you in a month.'

'How long is a month? Is it the next day's tomorrow?'

'Yes, the next day's tomorrow.' He pulled the door open and sat her next to Ruthie, who was bouncing with excitement. 'Mum says we're going on a mystery tour.'

'We don't know where we're going, but it will be magical when we get there. It will be magical, won't it, Malkie?' asked Sara.

'Uh huh.' He thought of the Scottish keep, a narrow fortified tower perched high on a cliff overlooking Loch Aline, with a view of Mull, purple on the horizon. He had hitched there when he was released from Barlinnie prison, desperate to taste fresh air. He'd spent three weeks sleeping rough in the then wrecked castle, earning enough for a pint of beer and bag of rolls by helping the farmers collect in the harvest.

Then, on the night of his birthday, two girls with upper-class English accents came into the small hotel bar in which he was drinking. They were dressed in expensive jeans and shirts. He was reading *Richard III*. They laughed at his clothes, accent, smell – visibly amused by the fact that someone like him was reading Shakespeare. Every so often they would disappear and return with the residue of cocaine powdering their noses. 'So, Mr Intellectual, would you like to fuck?' said one after her fourth trip. 'We fancy a bit of rough, don't we, Mo?'

Malkie stared at her, the old venom returning. She turned away, suddenly frightened. The barman took away his drink. 'Out before there's trouble,' he said. Malkie returned to Glasgow that night and became a dealer. No one would ever look down on him again.

Ten years later, he bought the keep and renovated it, renting it out to visiting American tourists anxious to trace their highland roots. For four months it had been lying empty, waiting for a moment he hoped would not come.

'Follow Frank, Hal. He knows where you're going. It's a ten-hour trip, so make sure the kids get plenty to drink. Not too many crisps or chocolate for Lilly, makes her hyper. And make sure she wears sun block. And . . .'

'I think we'll manage, Malkie,' said Sara, with a smile.

Roni leant against the Jeep, smoking a last cigarette. As always, she was wearing dark glasses to protect her red-rimmed and sleepless eyes. She couldn't sleep without alcohol in her system and didn't want to become reliant on sleeping pills.

As he hugged her, she stiffened in his arms. 'Be good to yourself,' Malkie said. 'I want to protect you and Lilly above all else. If you break and you need a drink, get yourself off the peninsula. Don't endanger the rest of them.'

She nodded, then took the final passenger seat.

'I trust you,' he said.

Roni pulled the door closed, and Hal followed Frank down the drive onto White Hill Lane.

'I love you,' Malkie whispered.

CHAPTER 67

'It's me.'

Sam stared at the phone. What kind of trick was this?

'It's Lindsey,' said the voice.

It can't be, he thought. Someone is playing head-tricks with me.

'What's my National Insurance number?' he asked.

Silence, then 'YS842795D.'

'And my private phone number?'

'0441 367 389.'

'What was Tom Graham's rank?' Apart from Sergio, she was the only one who knew that Tom Graham was the main character in his novels.

'Captain,' Lindsey replied without hesitation.

His mind reeled with questions.

'How are you?' he asked.

'Been better. A bit sore. I've been patched up by a friend.'

'Where are you?'

'Garton. The Splendid,' she replied. 'I want to meet you.'

'Can you ride a bike or a horse?' he asked.

'Just about manage two wheels.'

'There's a war memorial two miles from Bishop's Peak. You can't miss it. A large slab of black granite with the names of the men of the submarine Harpoon. Went down in the Second World War. Next to it there's a shelter. I'll meet you there in an hour.'

Gitte stood in the middle of Alaina's sitting room, a room saturated with her scent. Deep, musky, sensual. It was nauseating.

Grace watched whilst she fidgeted with a small box. Inside were three storage devices, each capable of storing ten gigabits of data, enough to suck every piece of information from Alaina's hard drive. Gitte would take them home and run encryption packages on them, looking for passwords and openings into Standish's worldwide computing network.

Gitte had brought a scrambling device that would intermittently break up any internal electronic security, making it an unreliable witness of her burglary. She was looking for physical evidence. Alaina would not commit everything to the PC. She was good at hiding. She hid her true self from me, Gitte thought. The rented flat was relatively anonymous and impersonal. What had Alaina brought with her? And how would she protect her secrets?

A pile of paperback novels sat on the floor. Gitte discounted them. Too obvious. On the wall was a map of ancient Moscow, Alaina's home city. She had already checked the frame for bulges or cracks that might reveal the source of something behind. Nothing.

'What would she need quick access to?' asked Grace. 'Money? Passport?'

'No. Violi would get her out of the country. It'll be a security code of some kind. She's neurotic about being on time and knowing where she's supposed to be. The only occasion I've seen her nervous was when we were in London and might miss the last train back to Garton. She was practically punching the cab seat in frustration. She would want to know precisely when and how they were getting out of Eastfield if anything went wrong. She is *very* thorough.'

Gitte's eyes drifted to the clock and saw beside it an award from the old Soviet Academy of Science for their famous daughter. Shaped like DNA's double spiral, it looked like a pair of twisted stepladders.

She pulled on a pair of thin gloves and gingerly touched one of the rungs. Each had a letter engraved within, **a** for adenine, **g** for guanine, **c** for cytosine and **t** for thymine – the chemical building blocks of life. There were twelve rungs and at the base of the ladder was a thick chunk of metal containing a citation honouring Alaina.

'She must have dozens of these at home,' Gitte said. 'Why has she carried this one across the Atlantic?'

Grace joined her. 'If there is a code here, it'll take us weeks to crack it.'

'Same with her, if she forgets,' said Gitte.

'Would she forget something like that?'

'Memory is strange. She can reel off mathematical formulae, but she writes down her PIN numbers for cash machines. So, I would guess yes,' replied Gitte, her eyes darting round the room, 'she has a code written down somewhere.' She glanced back to the map and retraced her steps. Alaina was a firm nationalist. Like many determinedly *ex*-patriates she was deeply committed to the future of her country, Gitte thought bitterly.

'Turn off the lights and close the curtains,' she instructed Grace.

Gitte shone a halogen torch at the glass. Centimetre by centimetre she crawled over it. Her mobile rang. She checked the number. It was Alaina.

'Hello, darling.' Alaina sounded happy. 'Let's go out for lunch. You seemed so down this morning. I've booked the American Dream – burgers, fries and shakes. Perfect to cheer you. I'll be with you in a few minutes.'

'Look forward to it.'

Gitte threw her mobile on the sofa and stared at Grace.

'You musn't be here. Go now.'

Grace gave her friend a quick hug, then slipped from the flat.

Gitte, heart racing now, continued her meticulous probing. She heard a car pull up outside. Alaina. Damn, damn. She pulled open the curtains, stuffed the gloves into the back of her jeans, then dragged open a book and lay flat out on the sofa.

'Are you ready, darling?' Alaina entered and Gitte's heart almost split again. She looked so beautiful.

As Alaina knelt to kiss her, Gitte's eyes slid off to the side as she struggled with her emotions. She glanced up at the map once more and then spotted tiny scratches at the top right. She could just make them out: *a12, g3, t1, c4.* She would not have seen them standing up. Would have missed them altogether if it hadn't been for Alaina's Judas kiss. Everything depends on perspective, she thought.

CHAPTER 68

Grace drove home, wanting to hook up with Sam and talk to Hal. Being with her brother always brought her much needed clarity. Besides, she thought, I need a hug. She smiled at the thought of Ruthie. She'd read her a book – *The Jolly Postman* or *Blue Kangaroo*.

In her bag were the portable drives containing the contents of Alaina's hard disk. She intended to load the contents onto a new Powerbook she had bought from the local computer shop.

When she arrived, Hal's Jeep was gone, as was Henry's Jag. Where were they? She had a million questions to ask Henry. But did she want to know that her father was part of a property scam with Halliwell? Is that what Halliwell wanted to tell her? She thought back to his phone call. Halliwell had said, 'I need to talk to you about your bloody wheat . . . Don't replant it, love . . . For your own sake, don't. For the sake of your family.'

It was the wheat he was worried about. No reference to property. But why was he killed?

As she came closer to the farm she saw Malkie Collins at the gate. He sat on the boot of his car,

343

legs and arms crossed. Behind him stood a tall, wide man with several scars on his face. Malkie had a brief word with him and he disappeared.

'How're things at Standish?' he asked. Sam had told Grace something of Malkie's past and his possible connections to Halliwell. And Henry. But Malkie and Henry had shown no signs of having met.

'Oh, things are fine at the lab. We're on top of everything.'

He let it pass.

'I need your help.' He handed her an envelope with her name on it. She ripped it open.

Grace,
   I'm helping out Malkie at the moment. He'll explain. Will phone in a few weeks. Everyone sends their love.
   Halxx

Underneath, in coloured ink, scrawled signatures ran across the page.

Love,
Lilly and Ruthie
xxxxxxxxxxxxxxxxxxxxxxxxxxxxxxxxxxxxxxxxxxx
xxxxxxxxxxxxxxxxxxxxxxxxxxxxxxxxxxxxxxxxxx

'What's going on?' Grace asked.
'He's helping Roni dry out. Somewhere quiet.'

344

'He's a kid, for God's sake. What do you think you're doing?'

'He's an adult, Grace. He's tough, resourceful.'

'You don't understand how ill he is. Or might be. Why are you dragging him into this?' She dropped her bag to the ground and grabbed her mobile.

'You won't get him.' He raised his hand and she recognized Hal's phone. 'I asked him for it before he set off. It's too easily traceable.'

'You bastard.'

Malkie crossed his arms and waited for the storm to blow over. He had expected it. 'He'll be fine for now. But I do need to talk to Sam.'

Her eyes went blank. 'I haven't heard from him in days.'

'I don't want us to fall out, Grace.' His voice was calm, but the menace jolted her. 'Just tell Sam I need him. Let him choose where to meet me. But tell him I'm under close observation.'

He walked back towards the car and his body-guard appeared as if from nowhere.

'Take care of yourself,' he said.

CHAPTER 69

Delawney and Standish rode well in their different ways, Delawney high in the saddle, like a hunter, Standish Western style, easy, prepared for long journeys. Warm drizzle gently floated from scattered black-tinged clouds and washed their faces. Below them, the Bain valley spread out, hazy in the late afternoon sun.

Delawney sat still on the top of the escarpment leading up to the chalk hills.

'My father's grandfather owned all of this.' He waved an arm from White Hill House to the sea. 'Stolen by death duties.'

How much can I leave Hesketh? he wondered. How much of our land can I buy back? He was confident that White Hill House would be returned. The cripple couldn't live there and Grace would marry Copeland and move on. The drunk would die soon. And then they would have it back. He closed his eyes and saw his free-range herd roaming the White Hill fields, his family living close by him through their adult lives. His grandchildren taking responsibility for the valley. They would learn to love the land, as he had. Their land. Bit by bit, they would reclaim what the government had stolen.

'One of your Basque chums came to see me.'

'Really.' My God, thought Standish, why are they bypassing me? They've never done that before and certainly not with someone as unreliable as Delawney. He could feel the noose tightening. He'd have to speed up the Malcolm plan.

'Yes. Wanted a special delivery.'

'What did you tell him?' asked Standish, edging his chestnut stallion back onto the track down through the Scots pine and the broad fields leading to Eastfield House.

'I told him I only operate through you.'

Liar, thought Standish. You're only telling me this so as I know you now have a direct line to the suppliers. The request for an increase in Delawney's take would come again very soon.

'When was this run going to be?' asked Standish.

'Wouldn't tell me,' said Delawney, spurring his horse into a gallop.

Standish followed, riding side by side. Why do they need Delawney? Whatever they're up to, it's about more than drugs. Now I have ammunition, he grinned, adrenaline pumping into his brain. Now I can trade with Sergio. And the Syrian.

CHAPTER 70

S am rode his Harley Davidson over the top of Bishop's Peak. The wind was up and the sea sparkled like shoals of silver herring. He loved days like this. He remembered a picnic with Grace high up on the hills. She'd ridden Soulman and he'd scrambled up in an old Honda. She'd beaten him by minutes, her face red with exertion, hair tangled, lips cracked. His marriage was a year old and already empty. But he prized loyalty above everything. Believed in the vows he had taken. The moment had passed, as had so many before.

He left the Harley chained to a gate, disabled it and then set off to walk the two miles to the isolated war memorial. It was a perfect meeting place. From the hills above, he would be able to see for miles. There was no way Lindsey could have backup without him knowing. His bag contained a flask of coffee and two Danish pastries he'd picked up in Garton's best bakery.

He watched Lindsey walk slowly up the long isolated path and enter the shelter. He waited for a while then scrambled down.

'Sam.' Lindsey was hunched in the corner. She

leapt to her feet to hug him, then stepped back in embarrassment. 'Sorry. I've been . . .'

Her cheek was bruised and her neck bandaged at the nape. He held her tight against his chest.

'So have I,' he said. 'So have I.'

They sat on the wooden bench and stared out to sea. On the floor was a hypodermic syringe and the walls were encrusted with graffiti. He resolved to come back and clean up the shelter. It could have been his grandfather who'd drowned in the cold murk of the North Sea. The men deserved a better memorial.

'What happened?' he asked.

'I . . . I . . . Someone tried to garrotte me.' Unconsciously she fingered her neck. 'I was working on the tapes, proving they were fake. I was too preoccupied. He broke through my security systems.'

'I saw blood on the floor, as if you had been dragged downstairs.'

'I was. I managed to twist away from the wire, but whoever it was knifed me.' She smiled grimly. 'But he hadn't quite reckoned on the fact that I've done fifteen years of t'ai chi.' She was fourth dan black belt. 'I became a snake.'

'What?'

'The story goes that the founder of t'ai chi, Chang San-feng, had a revelation when he saw a snake conquer a bird trying to lift it into the air with its claws. He realized that something so soft and pliable could win victory over something

349

so powerful but inflexible. In t'ai chi, we take the way of the snake.'

He poured her coffee and she sipped gratefully, nibbling on a Danish. 'He didn't know what hit him. I broke his nose and he took off. I ran after him but he disappeared.' Her eyes drifted, recalling the pain of the previous few days. 'I was . . .' She shook her head. 'Scared and didn't know where to turn. I phoned a doctor friend, got fixed up and lay low. I was out of it for two days. Drugged up to the eyeballs. When I came to, you were on the run.'

She reached over and touched his gloved hand. 'I didn't realize it would rebound on you, Sam. But when I heard about someone framing you, I didn't know what to do. These people are running us round in circles. If it's someone inside the squad and I make an appearance, then I'm dead. If they can get me in my home, they can take me down anywhere.'

Sam watched a trawler battle against increasingly violent waves. 'You should go back.'

'I can't.' She hugged her arms into her body.

'You must. Ian Trevor is a good man. Unbending. Careless at times. But good. He was appalled when you went missing. He'll look after you.'

'Is someone corrupt inside? Has somebody betrayed me?'

Sam nodded.

'But why . . .'

'Tell Ian you suspect it was me who hired someone to kill you,' Sam said.

'Wha . . . ?'

'Say that I'd almost convinced you that the tapes were fake, but you changed your mind and I found out.'

She looked at him wide-eyed. A ship's horn sounded and echoes circled towards them, dying slowly. Sam held her again and whispered, 'We must fight back. Otherwise they win. With you back at HQ, we have the resources to beat these people, whoever they are. We can't do it all from the outside. If whoever did attack you thinks you're blaming me they'll be more relaxed. Off guard. It's our best shot at finding who is behind this. Will you do it?'

She stared at him for a moment, then nodded and picked up her coffee cup. 'Fill me up, Sam.'

CHAPTER 71

The Observatory was perched like an onion dome on the top floor of a white stone watermill that had fallen into disrepair when steam-driven factories opened up in Garton. The council had taken it over and built a fashionable camera obscura in the late nineteenth century as a tourist attraction. Malkie noticed the small inlaid mosaic of Ahura Mazda, the Persian god of light and fire, above the arched lintel.

These days, the Observatory was little visited and badly maintained and Malkie took the winding whitewashed stairs cautiously. Dull lights flickered overhead, each corner cast in shadow. He was meeting his Basque handler, whose face he now knew intimately, but not his name. That remained a mystery.

Malkie had set up the conversation between the Basque and Delawney in a safe house in Garton, but he had been excluded from the meeting and felt deeply troubled. Delawney was too greedy and ultimately too vain to understand that he could not handle the Basque. They would've asked him to do something extremely dangerous, something that might bring the house down.

He reached the viewing area at the top of the Observatory. The door was padlocked and he tugged a chain that gave easily. He edged his way in, sensing a presence in the corner. In the middle of an otherwise pitch-black room was a metre-wide flat plaster table on which the life of Garton was reflected like a movie via a silvered mirror and optical lenses on the ceiling above. Malkie knew the science well enough. Light travels in a straight line, but when the rays bounce off a bright plane through a small hole the images are reflected upside down on a flat surface. A topsy-turvy world, he thought, as he inspected Gartonites as they went about their business below.

'It's a bit like being God,' Sergio said in the darkness.

'I've never had such ambitions,' replied Malkie.

'It's good for a man to understand his limitations,' acknowledged Sergio.

Malkie turned and saw two guns pointing at him. The other man's face was shaded in shadow. He was smoking – red light from the tip flickered like a full stop in the darkness. The weapons were wrapped inside clear plastic containers. Big Glocks. Probably .45s.

'When?' asked Malkie.

'Tomorrow night.'

'Where?'

'Johnny will be attending a concert at Eastfield

House. At the conclusion, he'll go to his bedroom on the first floor where he will be anticipating a message.'

'What kind of message?' Malkie asked.

The Basque handed over the guns. 'These.'

He drew deeply on the cigarette.

'He must die violently. No other course is left open to us in the pursuit of our freedom. And when you have taken Standish, we want Copeland. He is at his most vulnerable and will seek you out. When he does, kill him.'

'Who is to be my partner?' Malkie asked. He needed to be certain about the second assassin.

'Watch and learn,' said the man and left.

On the obscura's round table, Malkie saw the Basque saunter down towards a red iron bridge that crossed a river on the way towards the city centre. To the left was a car park. The Basque stopped at a nondescript black Vauxhall Cavalier and the driver stepped out. They hugged and then the Basque looked towards Malkie peering down from Godlike space and nodded to the second man. It was Raul – Standish's lover. He was the second assassin.

CHAPTER 72

After being debriefed by Trevor, Lindsey had been driven out to a safe house and some hours later was jogging in the woods behind an elegant sandstone Victorian rectory. She could count the squad muscle surrounding the main gate – they were taking no chances. She called Sam from a scrambled mobile line. 'I'm being treated like the prodigal daughter,' she said.

'What did they say about me?' he asked, riding the Harley down a rough track.

'Confirmed Trevor's worst fears that you're public enemy number one. They're setting me up with some serious equipment that they want me to use to work out where you are. I'm thinking the Orkneys at the moment.'

'Try Marseille. They'd never find me there. And besides, Ian hates the French so he won't trust their information. What's going on with the bomber case?'

'They're no further on. They're no closer to finding Leadsmith, the guy you were worried about. He's disappeared. Apart from that they have nothing.'

Sam watched the low sun throw dark shadows across a field of wildflowers.

'Do me a favour, run a search on Henry Adams, look for anything that might tie him to the bombing.'

'You're joking, Guv.'

'Only when I laugh.'

'Why?'

'Little nags. Could be nothing.' I hope it is, he thought. 'Any leads as to who is behind the fake tapes and bank accounts?'

'I've got some feelers out.'

'A lot of this connects up. First, everything turns back to Spain – Barcelona in particular. See what you can get on Fernandez. Second, Halliwell has led us to some kind of land scam – possibly involving Malkie Collins and Delawney.' He paused. 'And I think Henry Adams was part of the conspiracy.'

'Oh, God.'

'I'm trying to track him down now. On top of that, we know that Halliwell was a front for a drug-import business, probably on behalf of Malkie. For one or both of these activities he was killed. And there's another thing. The General warned me off Stef Violi, but he's stealing Grace's work in collaboration with some outfit called 3-Cube. He's one of the keys to this. Can you dig a bit deeper?'

'Got to go, Guv. Clever Trevor's just turned up. I'll talk to you tonight. Take care.'

CHAPTER 73

O ne of the fruit loaders slapped the back of a van bearing the slogan

Eastfield Organic Farms
Pure is good.

The driver, an Eastfield student, yawned, stretched and turned up the music on his car stereo.

'Ready?' he asked his co-driver.

'Roll 'em, cowboy.'

They headed into the night in a van filled with five hundred kilos of nitroglycerine carefully syringed into tonnes of organic apples.

Standish and Delawney were playing tennis on an indoor hard court nestling within a clearing of pine trees. Delawney had surprised Standish by playing well, power making up for agility and speed. It was five-all in the final set when Standish's phone rang. Raul, his nose in Graham Greene's *Heart of the Matter*, lifted it, muttered something in Spanish, then waved towards Standish.

'It's Lottie.' He handed over the mobile. Lottie

Grun was probably the best bodyguard Johnny'd ever had – never panicked – and when she called he listened.

'Well, find her, then,' he said. 'And quickly. Raul will help.' Raul looked up and Standish caught his eye. He offered an exaggerated sigh and headed towards the door.

'I'll be there in ten,' Standish called after him.

'What happened?' asked Delawney.

'Malkie's sent his daughter away.'

'He's devoted to that child,' said Delawney, wiping his face on a white towel, his crest on the corner, and sipping still water. 'What's he up to?'

'He's expecting trouble.'

'From whom?'

'We'll find out soon enough. Whose serve is it?'

'Yours, I believe.'

'Oh, by the way, your daughter is with them,' Standish shouted as he whipped a vicious topspin swerve to Delawney's backhand.

CHAPTER 74

Hal and Sara carried the children towards the tall, square fortress towering above them, Lilly weighing heavily on Hal's shoulder. What will become of you? He admired Malkie's devotion to his daughter, his calm strength. But he was a villain, a serious one – serious enough for someone to attempt to kill his child. And what of Roni? Would she hold up?

As she smoked another cigarette, Roni gazed out over the loch towards the Sound of Mull – the island shimmering mysteriously in the dusk, a flotilla of small sailboats dancing in the wake of a ferry. She missed her lover desperately, couldn't bear a week without hearing his voice, and had smuggled a phone inside one of Lilly's dolls.

Frank clambered over the drystone wall next to the door.

'Couldn't've picked a better place myself,' he said. 'Only one way in – that small bridge. Very difficult to scale the cliff face on the other three sides. He's got sensors on the deer fence to trigger alarms and heat-sensing lights on the Keep's walls. Malkie's done a thorough job.'

'Malkie always does a thorough job,' she retorted. 'That's what Malkie is. Thorough.'

Frank stared at her, disquiet written on his face. 'I'll make a pot of tea,' he said.

'Yeah. You do that, big man.'

She squashed the end of her cigarette. She never smoked in front of Lilly, hated herself for doing it at all, but needed to be calmed.

'Bathtime, young lady.'

'Don't want a bath. Want a story,' she mumbled sleepily.

Sara had Ruthie slumped against her. 'Let's just put them to bed. They can have a bath in the morning.'

With Lilly asleep, Roni sat by the kitchen table nursing a cup of Earl Grey. This was the worst moment – the sober night spun out before her like an unlived nightmare. She had spotted the hotel in the village. It was only two miles away. Her inner voice whispered that one drink wouldn't make a difference – a white wine spritzer. That's not alcohol. Is it?

'There's some sea trout in the freezer. I thought we'd have it with lemon aioli.'

'Let me help.' Something to do.

The castle's walls, pink on the outside, white within, were ten foot thick and chilly even in summer. The kitchen was twenty foot high.

Sara dragged the fish from a plastic bag. 'There's a story that one of the old laird's mistresses went mad and built a shack in here when the keep had fallen derelict. She still walks the floor at night cursing her faithless lover.'

Roni sensed nothing in the kitchen. It was anonymous. Posed no threat.

'How did you cope?' she asked, preparing to light another cigarette, then remembering she'd agreed not to smoke in the house. She searched around for eggs.

'With what?'

'With Delawney's affairs. I mean, he's slept with half of Hope's friends.'

'You can persuade yourself of many things about a man,' Sara replied. 'I fell pregnant by accident. But he knew I would never have an abortion. He told me he wanted our child, that he loved me, that Hope was unhappy and unstable, having miscarried twice. Eventually he would ask Hope for a divorce. When he could, he would give Ruthie little presents. He seemed genuinely to love her. He's like that with kids – incredibly attentive.'

'But why did you believe him?'

'He was my daughter's father.' Sara gutted the fish. 'He was the first, and until Hal, the only man I had made love to.' She washed her hands. 'I was in love with him the way Malkie is in love with you. Blindly.'

Roni recoiled as if slapped. 'What do *you* know? Malkie wants to *own* me, not love me.' The egg she was carrying fell from her hands and cracked on the blue-veined granite work surface.

'All I know is that I was stupid to stay with the wrong man for so long. And I know that I punished myself too much and too long for trying to break up a man's marriage. And that Malkie would do anything to have you back again.'

Roni's hands were shaking. 'You have *no* idea. Never think you understand someone else's marriage. And never judge.'

She ignored Sara's shocked apologies and ran down the hill to the wall beside the lake. Frank was leaning on the gate, a shotgun in his arms.

'Fag?' she asked, holding out the packet.

He took one and they lit up in silence.

'What's he up to, Frank?'

'Protecting you.'

'But what's he really up to?'

Frank shrugged.

'You know him better than anyone,' she said.

'Nah. Malkie's outgrown me, girl. He's not the same geezer as he was a couple of years ago. I reckon he's sick of it.'

'Are you sick of it?' she asked.

'Look at me,' he replied. 'What am I going to do if I leave the business? Brush floors in a fucking hypermarket? Wash bogs? Nah. I'd rather die on the job.'

'Don't say that, Frank. Life's too precious.'

'If you believe that you should sort yourself out, love. You're no use to Lilly the way you are.'

What is this? First the earth mother has a go, now

I'm being criticized by a man with an IQ the size of his feet.

Roni walked back to the castle. She was desperate for something to take the edge off the night and she'd smuggled in some tranquillizers. She groaned inwardly at her unconscious choice of the word 'smuggled' – a word appropriate for someone living under the rule of someone else's law. Now alone, she dared to pull out her mobile. Raul would have left a message and she needed her fix of his voice as much as the tranqs burning a hole in her pocket. The phone buzzed as she turned it on. She glanced round anxiously. She knew Malkie would be furious that she'd disobeyed him, but the phone was her lifeline, just in case . . .

Raul had left three passionate messages pleading with her to call; saying how much he missed her. She thought about it. Could she breach security? The last said he'd call at nine. She fumbled with her watch-face, punching the illumination button. Two minutes to go. Her hands shook as she drew on the cigarette and counted down the seconds until his incoming number scrolled across the screen. Her heart lifted for the first time that day. That week. The silence was overwhelming.

'I've missed you,' she said. He had not managed to make their last date. 'Where've you been?'

In the library at Eastfield House, Raul watched himself in the mirror as he spoke – his face impassive. Lottie Grun was in charge of the monitoring equipment that was tracking down the location of

Roni's cellphone. Delawney gnawed at the side of his lip, his eyes betraying his anxiety.

'It's been difficult to get away,' Raul replied. 'You've no idea how possessive Johnny can be.' Raul's icy features melted into a pout and his gaze brushed across Standish who mouthed, 'Bastard.'

'Believe me, my love,' Roni said, her voice amplified for all in the room to hear, 'I know what it's like to live as an object.'

'We are not like that, you and I,' said Raul. 'We recognize the need for freedom, that love can be complete without oppression.'

'I'm longing to see you,' said Roni. 'I want to be with you.'

'But how can we? Malkie would kill us both.'

'No. He'll give me a divorce, said he would.'

'That's fantastic. Where are you?' He glanced at Lottie, who motioned him to keep going. She had the cell. They knew where she was to within 800 metres. 'Darling. I want to be with you now,' Raul said. 'Tell me where you are. Wherever you are, I'll come.'

'I . . .'

They heard a scuffle and then the muffled sound of Frank shouting – 'Are you off your fucking head?' The connection died.

Raul threw the phone to Standish. 'How was I?'

'You make a very convincing heterosexual. It's almost as if your heart is really in it.'

Raul kissed him. 'You know how much I like pain,' he smiled.

'As long as it's other people's,' Lottie said.

'The only bearable kind of pain is other people's,' Raul said as he pulled Standish towards the door, desperate for sex.

'They're in Scotland. A little place called Ardtornish on the Morvern peninsula,' said Lottie. The door closed. 'If anyone's interested.'

Delawney stared up into the evening sky, distress gnawing at him like a rat. He gazed out of the window, sickened by the idea that Ruthie and Sara were caught up in the crossfire. He wanted them back. Ruthie was his, after all. He'd send Roy Griffiths and Alex, Sara's cousin, to Ardtornish. She was fond of Alex. He'd make her see sense, but if she didn't, Roy would sort out that old idiot, Frank. They'd be brought back, one way or another.

CHAPTER 75

S am mulled over Grace's news about Malkie as he piloted his Harley up an ancient track that snaked across White Hill. He was heading for Henry's old hut in the woods – a two-storey building a couple of miles from the house. He stopped outside and briefly relished the silence. What was Henry up to? His dossier on Leadsmith had been almost too perfect, as if straight from an FBI psychiatric manual on serial bombers. His phone rang, shattering the silence.

'Got some news, Guv,' said Lindsey. 'Could be something. Henry Adams used to work in a quarry – holiday job when he was at university. Turned it up in an old profile of him. The place is still running. Family firm. Grandad remembers him.'

'And?'

'And they used to call him "Steady Eddie" because he was nerveless around explosives.'

Damnation. 'Thanks, Lindsey, keep me in touch.'

He pushed the hut door – locked – then retraced his steps to an ancient oak and extracted a large old-fashioned key from a bird box. Grace'd told him that Henry'd spent a lot of time up here recently.

He unlocked and stepped inside. 'Henry?' The room, newly painted and varnished, smelled clean, sweet – innocent. A small TV set flickered by the fire, Bugs Bunny laughing silently on screen. He prowled through the kitchen and out the back door. There was a new addition – a small outbuilding, from which classical music filled the afternoon air. He recognized the huge orchestral piece as Bruckner.

Edging inside, he asked, 'You here, Henry?' Tools were stacked in neat order – screwdrivers, tweezers, hacksaw, timers. The workbench had been scrubbed and Sam ran the flat of his hand across the wood then brought his fingers to his face and inhaled the acrid, powdery scent.

On the table next to a mug of cold tea, was a volume of R. S. Thomas's Collected Works that he had sent Henry. It opened on a poem called 'Threshold'. Henry had underlined '*I am alone on the surface of a turning planet.*'

Sam took a deep breath, and then he heard an explosion, followed by a roar. He recognized the voice and ran towards a clearing where he saw Henry standing next to a huge, upturned oak root, smoke billowing round it, his hand punching the air in triumph.

When Sam touched him, he swung round, shock in his eyes, his arms raised, then relief washed over him. 'Sam. It's you. God, you startled me. I've been trying to get rid of that bloody thing for years. Finally ran out of patience. I want to plant some rhododendrons. Want a cuppa?'

A high, chill evening wind drove them inside and Henry lit a log fire whilst Sam poured tea.

'What brings you here?' asked Henry. 'You haven't been up to the hut in years.'

'I'm taking a break – thought I'd see how you were. You look well.'

'Feel good. Been chopping logs. Clearing out rubbish,' he gestured towards some cans of paint, 'spring cleaning.'

'Place looks good.'

'Seen Grace?'

'Spent a couple of hours with her. We're planning to meet up later. She seems worried about you – and Hal. Scared that the bomber may return.'

'I don't think he will, Sam. I'm told that Rod's disappeared. Not surprising, really. He was pretty unstable. The visit from your guys must've sent him over the top. He was very angry with me when I retired and could no longer treat him. I think he was doping himself on Valium. Too much makes people very unstable and irritable. Liable to blow without warning!'

'Do you know if he worked with another therapist?'

'I tried hard to pass him on to an old friend, but he resisted. He may have changed his mind. Would you like the name?' He scribbled down the information and handed it to Sam, who tucked it in his pocket.

'Not sure I like you bald, Sam. What's happened to your hair?'

Sam ran a hand across his scalp and smiled. 'Be better when I have a tan. I hope you know what you're doing with that gunpowder. Might blow yourself up.'

'Don't worry about me.'

'Where did you learn how to use the stuff?'

Henry laughed. 'God, a long time ago. Scares me witless, to tell the truth, but sometimes it's the only way to shift things.'

Their eyes locked.

'I wish I had your expert knowledge,' Sam said. 'I still can't make head or tail of the attack on Halliwell's car. I'm told that his death was an accident. Whoever set the bomb had expected it to go off in the boot, causing minimal damage. Bit of a botched job.'

'But what had he done? He was just my finance director, for God's sake.'

'Unfortunately, Halliwell had been taking lime home for the garden.'

'That'll do it every time. Poor bastard. What a pathetic way for his life to end.'

They fell silent, then Henry yawned. 'Been a long day. Fancy one?'

'Sure.'

A few minutes later, Henry returned from the small kitchen with two glasses of local ale.

'Here's to finding Rod,' Henry raised his drink and they sank their beers. 'How much do you know about the bomber?'

'Nothing much.' Sam suddenly felt exhausted, his head heavy.

'I can help you.'

Sam's eyes closed. Henry seemed a blur in the middle distance.

'I'm your friend, Sam. You can tell me. Tell me . . .'

A few hours later, Sam woke violently. It was dark in the hut and fragments of Henry's words swirled around his mind. '*What do you know? Tell me.*'

Sam felt an overwhelming sense that something was wrong. In his nightmare he'd told Henry that he suspected him of being the bomber and that he was connected to Malkie's cartel. His mouth tasted bitter, chemical.

'The beast awakes.'

Sam shielded his eyes as light flooded the room and Henry stood over him. He was exhausted, drifting, clutching at consciousness.

'It's just broken on the radio that you're "on the run", as the reporter called it. You're big news.'

CHAPTER 76

Ian Trevor read the Spanish Ambassador's note again. *He'd done it.* He'd persuaded the King of Spain to join the Prime Minister in opening the European Anti-Terrorism Conference. The Spanish government had been giving him lots of hope, but no guarantees. Until today. He fought against his pride. Such emotions were dangerous in a copper, led to mistakes.

He scribbled a quick letter of thanks and handed it to his PA, then addressed himself to the team. Hacket was leaning against a wall chewing a toothpick. Trevor had expected more from his chosen successor. Copeland had led them a dance. Correction. Led Hacket a dance. Each man faces his defining test, and so far Hacket is flunking.

'I take it there are no sightings of Copeland in the UK?'

'No, Guv,' replied Hacket. 'Lindsey makes him for Marseille. Someone down there used a cash card in the name of Eileen Daniels.'

'His sister,' explained Lindsey.

'Why Marseille?' Trevor asked, beaming quickly at Lindsey. Brave girl. Could've run for cover after that attempt on her life. But decided to stay on duty. He liked that. Guts. That's what made his squad great. Guts and brains. She had both.

'Sam knows how to hide,' replied Lindsey. 'He would've had a stash of cash somewhere – fake credit cards, the works. He knows France well from his anti-terrorist days. Stayed in Marseille for six months on secondment as a Europol liaison officer.'

'Bloody Europol. Leakier than a tramp's boots. Well done, Lindsey. Casper,' he turned to the cadaverous financial analyst Hacket had pulled into town from the Eastfield investigation, 'anything more on Malkie Collins?'

'He's going bust.'

'What?'

'He's defaulting on bank loans and his companies are crashing. His gang are breaking away. Must be in deep hock to Copeland, though. There was a two million payment into 1986 10 404 yesterday.'

'The Big Planet account?' asked Trevor.

'Yeah. Wired straight back out again to the Caymans. Someone took it out in cash.'

'Incidentally,' Hacket intervened, clearly unsettled that Trevor was ignoring him, 'the bent Dago's done a runner. No one's seen Fernandez since last Friday.'

'Two days after the phone call to Copeland,' said Casper. 'Might've been him on the end of the money trail.'

Bugger, thought Trevor. He hated the multinational nature of this thing. It was out of his control. He turned to his Head of Communciations.

'How did this bloody thing leak?'

Trevor had talked to every man and woman involved in the hunt, looked in his or her eyes and told them that the pride of the squad was at stake. He was sure of their silence. No one was going to give the jackals a story for a couple of hundred nicker when they knew he would hunt them down and destroy their career. And they knew he would.

'The Yard, I would guess. Or it's come out of Garton. It was always impossible to keep the lid on this. I'm surprised we've managed thus far. I'm telling the jackals that Sam has had a nervous breakdown. Best I can do.'

Trevor nodded. 'We should've had him by now. Hacket, my office.' Lindsey watched him wince, then turned to her PC. When she got home, she'd move 'Sam' from Marseille to Morocco. Then she turned her attention to Casper, who smiled at her. He was good, probably better than she was; but he'd forgotten one simple thing – a trapdoor. She'd fed the money in and out of the Big Planet account, and as he traced it, she'd followed him back down a rabbit hole that led all the way back to him. Why had Casper been putting money into Big Planet? And for whom? She needed urgently to talk to Sam.

⋆   ⋆   ⋆

Roni rode the last ferry back to Ardtornish, her cellphone stuck to her hand.

'I need it now, doll,' Frank said.

She swallowed tears of humiliation, then handed over the phone. He threw it high over the rail and into the dark waves. They'd spent the evening driving south, stopping four times to call Raul and say she was on the move, heading towards Glasgow.

After finding Roni whispering on the smuggled mobile, Frank had called Malkie, who'd told him that whoever was on the phone might've tracked them down. Malkie refused to talk to her or accept her assurances that she'd just called a friend, especially when she refused to name Raul. More paranoia, she thought. More suspicion. Her hatred deepened.

She wanted Raul desperately. He'd given her the kind of freedom Malkie would never understand. When Raul talked about poetry, you knew it was more than just a surface reading. He knew. He really *knew*. She wanted her child brought up with a man like that, not someone who might die in a club, cut down by some up-and-coming thug.

At the pier, Hal was waiting for them in a jeep, ready to take them on the hour-long journey to the castle. Frank cast anxious glances at the brown hills – endless waves of earth and stone which could swallow them up – and recalled Malkie's parting words: 'Remember, Frank, if any of our men show up, they'll be there to kill you. I will not, I repeat *not*, send anyone to Ardtornish. Let the castle protect you. Trust it and you'll be fine. Look after Roni. Don't let her do anything stupid again. I should be with you in a couple of days, then we'll take off.'

CHAPTER 77

Henry watched Sam sleep. He'd been drifting for hours, the heavy dose of Valium taking its toll, but even in his weakened state he'd held out against Henry's probing, hypnotic voice. Eventually, Henry had resorted to intense narco-hypnosis, a technique he'd learned in the 1950s, but used in only the most hopelessly repressed cases. He'd administered Thiopental Sodium – popularly known as the truth drug – and eventually even Sam crumbled. Henry realized he had little time to stamp out the evidence against him.

Tears welled in his eyes as depression's black dog gnawed at him. He'd worked so hard to escape this fate. Killing Halliwell had been a bitter mistake. When Halliwell had told him he was going to the police, Henry had decided to scare him out of the decision. He couldn't bear the idea that Grace and Hal would know that he was corrupt. He could face prison – death was close anyway – but not the pain he would cause to his family. He wanted his memory, his final legacy, to transform the evil he had caused in his family's life. He'd never forgiven himself for the death of both of his wives, and grieved each day for Hal's mother.

When the car bomb had killed Halliwell, everything had spiralled out of control. He'd made a fundamental decision not to confess and had put everyone off his scent by blowing up Grace's car and creating 'the bomber'. He'd made sure the car park was empty when he detonated the controlled explosion. He couldn't live with anyone else's pain on his conscience.

By leading Sam to Rod, he knew that Leadsmith would disappear. Not only did Leadsmith have a pathological fear of the police from his teenage years as an arsonist, he was also closely connected to Delawney and was, according to Halliwell, a drug dealer. Also Henry had a deep suspicion that Rod was behind the glasshouse fire.

He slumped on a chair, feverish and restless, then downed another handful of antidepressants. Two other people knew of his involvement, Collins and Delawney. Two evil people. Drug dealers. Corrupters of souls. Collins was the key. Sam would go after him and in the end Collins would do a deal to save his own skin. He'd give up Henry. Henry wondered how much the American, Standish, really knew about Collins' land scam and what he would do if he were told of his partners' treachery.

He heard Sam stir and cracked a few eggs and rashers of bacon into the frying pan. He had to keep him drugged, confuse him, make him doubt his memory.

'Hey, sleepy head,' he shouted. 'What kind of visitor are you? Come up all this way to sleep? You can do that at home.'

When the Eastfield couriers pulled into a large empty warehouse on the outskirts of North London, someone jerked open the van door and shouted – 'Out, out, out.' It was the police. Armed police. 'Oh fuck,' the driver wailed.

They were escorted to a long trailer and a small office dominated by three burly detectives.

'We know what you have in the back of the van,' said one – a pock-faced man with a face like a pug.

'Apples,' said the courier. 'Organic apples.'

'And enough marijuana to keep London going for a month.'

The courier looked shocked. 'Come off it.'

'Don't piss me about, son. You know and I know that you've been driving round the shitholes of London trying to unload this stuff. We've been tracking you since you left Garton. We've a proposal for you. We'll wipe the slate clean if you give us a bit of cooperation.'

Silence. The students exchanged glances, then shrugged. 'What do you want us to do?' asked the driver.

'Good lad. We only want you to deliver your, er, apples,' he smiled, grimly, 'to a different address.

The thing you don't know is that there's a bit more than blow in the back of your transit. There's a dozen Ks of coke.'

'Shit.'

'You deliver on Saturday, then you can bugger off, no questions asked. Stay at this hotel for a couple of days, but don't leave your room. Wait for a call from someone named Picasso. He'll tell you where and when.'

'Done.'

'Spoken like a true patriot.' The detective broke into a gap-toothed smile.

CHAPTER 78

Madness is like a horizon, Henry thought. One day, without knowing, you cross the line and look back at your journey from the other side of the world. He was terrified of the nightmares engulfing him, of the daytime sweats, the tremors, but this physician had to heal himself. He stared in the mirror, then threw cold water on his face. I must not allow guilt to overwhelm me. I *can* leave something good.

By now his anonymous letter would've reached Standish. It provided enough telling details to implicate Delawney and Collins in the theft of millions of pounds of Standish's money. From what he understood from Halliwell, Standish was not a man to take that lightly.

Grace couldn't sleep. The house sounded hollow and empty and she could sense her mother's disconsolate spirit. Looking back, she realized that her mother must have known about Henry's affairs but she'd coped, as most of her generation had. Then Henry fell passionately, deliriously in love with someone else, and her funny, generous mother had effaced herself month by month until she faded into nothing. Grace had vowed then that no man would do that to her. She would always be in control.

'But Sam's the real thing, Mum,' she said into the darkness. 'He's not Henry. Or Freddie.'

She felt restless. Was Sam *with* Henry? She longed to see him, but couldn't take the risk. As dawn crawled over the hills, she threw on some clothes, made coffee and wandered into her father's study. She still found it impossible to believe he was wrapped up in anything so sordid as a land scandal.

As she sipped, she ran her hand across his books, thinking of Sam. They'd agreed to speak at eight thirty. She picked up Steinbeck's *East of Eden*, one of Henry's favourites, read a few well-thumbed passages, then moved on, restless. Glancing at her mother's portrait, she tipped her cup in salute, then spotted a copy of Ted Hughes' *Birthday Letters* on the shelves next to her father's books. She shivered at the thought of the bomber and his quotes from 'God Help the Wolf After Whom the Dogs Do Not Bark'.

Nobody wanted your dance.

She forced herself to open the volume, wanting to read the full poem. Sam had told her that in his view it was about love and desire, not death. She leafed quickly, couldn't find it, then checked the index. Page 26, between 'The Machine' and 'Fidelity'. She flicked through pages 23, 24, then stopped. 'God Help the Wolf' had been cut from the volume. As she ran her finger down the seam, pages fell to the ground as the book disintegrated. She stared at the fallen leaves. 'Oh, God, Henry. Oh, my good God.' She ran to saddle Soulman, then galloped into the woods.

The hut was quiet – Henry would still be asleep in the upstairs bedroom. She was rushing to the stairs when she saw a figure on the sofa. Henry must've decided to sleep down here. She scrabbled for a match and as it flamed, the sleeper turned and groaned.

'Sam,' she whispered. 'Wake up, Sam.'

'We are alone on the surface of a turning planet,' Sam mumbled.

'Wake up, darling. You're not safe here.'

He hauled himself from a deep place, climbing higher and higher, crawling through slime until at last he surfaced and clutched her. 'You're here.'

'I'm here, darling.' She stroked his hair, kissing his mouth, his eyes, then looked up as Henry loomed over them.

'Oh, Dad. What've you done?' she whispered.

CHAPTER 79

Sam couldn't shake free of the confusion in his mind. His memory was fuddled. He'd come to talk to Henry, but couldn't recall about what. As he shook his head, trying to clear the buzz, Henry handed him some aspirin and a glass of water.

'You'll need these, you've been feverish.'

Grace drew her knees to her chin, shivering, as her father reached to touch her face.

'What've you done, Dad?'

He looked puzzled. 'I've been looking after Sam. He's had some kind of collapse.'

'Don't lie to me, Henry.' She pulled tatters of *Birthday Letters* from her pocket. 'It was you, you bombed my car. I don't understand. Make me understand.'

'You're not making sense, darling. Why would I do such a thing? I'd put out my eyes rather than see you hurt.' He stroked her again. 'You must know that.' His hand shook. 'I ripped out the poem in disgust. Rod borrowed the book from me some time ago and when he returned it, he had underlined the words he sent to you. I couldn't stand having them

383

in the same house as me. You must believe me. I've told Sam all of this. I've told him that Rod is the bomber. You believe me, don't you Sam?'

As Sam scrambled around in his mind, Grace sobbed, 'I . . . I, oh God, Dad, I don't know what to believe. What about Halliwell?'

He looked puzzled. 'What about him?'

Sam strained. Halliwell. Henry. What on earth was the connection?

Roy Griffiths and Alex Cross, Sara's cousin, were dressed in combat fatigues, their faces blackened, Griffiths peering through night-vision binoculars at the Keep below. Dawn was half an hour away and they would have to work quickly.

'Look, I don't want Sara frightened,' said Cross. 'Why can't we just talk to her?'

''Cause that old fuckwit Frank'll blow your skinny face off, that's why.'

'She'll see sense, course she will. She knows the Earl loves her. He wants to stand by her, doesn't he?'

Griffiths licked his lips. 'She may need a bit of persuasion.' He loaded his rifle – an M16, standard SBS issue. 'Now sort out your brain, because Frank may be getting old, but he's still a mean motherfucker.' He gathered his gear and slithered down the hill towards the road.

Frank struggled to keep his eyes open, three nights without much sleep was taking its toll. Hal was a good kid, reliable, but he wouldn't be able to deal with whoever was coming after Lilly. Those guys were pros. Serious. He'd trusted Hal with a few hours of the night watch, but had relieved him half an hour before. His third double espresso had left him wired but still spaced.

Upstairs, Roni sat in the cold lavatory staring at a pregnancy kit she'd bought a few days before when she realized she was ten days late. It was positive. She willed herself to believe that the child was Raul's. But they had always used a condom. She wept as she recalled a desultory, drunken fuck with Malkie about a month before.

Frank checked the monitors, cursing the darkness. No building was impregnable. He turned on the searchlights and flooded the yards.

Griffiths stood by the edge of the arc of light then extracted a crossbow and a dart that he loosed at the tower, twine streaming out like a blue streamer. He'd practised this for hours at the House, snagging the chimney four times out of five, but still crossed his fingers as the rubber dart landed on the third-floor ramparts.

'Have you done it?'

'When I set out to do things, son, they get done. Now, I want you to give Frank a little heart attack. Will you do that for me?'

Cross nodded morosely. This wasn't what the Earl had asked him to do. But Griffiths was in charge. And when Roy said jump, the normal question was 'How high?' He'd seen too many broken faces on people who'd crossed Roy.

'Do your job, son, and the Earl'll see you all right. You got your pea-shooter?'

Cross unpacked his .22 air rifle and Griffiths trained his glasses on one of the floodlights on the roof.

'When I get to the bridge, take out that light. I know you're nervous. I understand that. But just relax; think of it like a pheasant and you'll be fine.'

Griffiths flexed his fingers, cracked his knuckles, loaded his pockets with a flash-bomb and hook-tipped blade, and then slung an assault rifle round his shoulders.

'Three minutes, then fire.' He slipped into the darkness.

Frank prowled, restless, checking doors, monitoring equipment, waiting for the comfort of daylight and 360-degree visibility.

'You OK, Frank?' asked Sara, rubbing her hair dry as she wandered down the cold stone stairs in her pyjamas. 'Can I get you some breakfast?'

'Could murder a sausage sarnie, doll.'

'You ever heard of cholesterol?'

'Down Devon way, isn't it?'

She laughed. 'Sausage it is.'

Griffiths reached the bridge and checked his watch. About fifteen minutes till dawn. Not much time. He waited for the shot, the seconds sweeping past.

The boy was a minute late, two minutes. Amateur. He focused on the twine floating on the breeze and adjusted the long rope he held in his arms. C'mon, kid. Do it. The light switched on then abruptly disintegrated as the bullet hit. That should get Frank's attention. He'd be confused, herd his brood into one room, leave the cripple in charge; then he'd be forced into a defensive position. Perfect.

Griffiths sprinted to the twine, attached the rope, depressed the start button on an electronic fob and the dart sprouted three hooks. He pressed again and watched as the twine whizzed upwards carried by a small electrical motor attached to the dart. A few seconds later, he tugged hard and the makeshift grappling hook held.

Another shot pinged off a window. Good boy, he thought. You keep that up. Harmless little pinpricks to keep Frank occupied.

He clambered up the wall, estimating four minutes to the top.

'What's wrong, Frank?' asked Sara, depositing his breakfast on the desk, and fielding Ruthie, who'd wandered downstairs searching for a glass of water.

Frank listened. Was that a gun? He turned and smiled. 'Nothing wrong. Light's broken. Going to check it out.'

'I'll keep this warm for you.' She scooped up her daughter. 'C'mon, you. A quick drink and we'll get your clothes on.'

*   *   *

Griffiths was near the ramparts when Frank turned the corner towards him. He froze, pointed urgently to Cross, whose shot cracked across the road, splintering on the wall of the keep and sending Frank sprawling to the ground. You stay there, Frankie boy, thought Griffiths as he leapt onto the third-floor balcony. Best place for you.

Frank's mouth was filled with dirt and tasted sour as he quickly scanned the rocks on the hill. Where was it coming from? How many were there? Ten, minimum. That's how many I'd send. So why aren't they charging? They've got me on the ground, so why am I alive? Tentatively he slithered back, keeping his body low, making the smallest target possible. A bullet whipped the ground several metres away. Not even close. Not even trying. What was that? A .22? Must be an amateur. What's going on? Here we go.

He rolled onto his knees, spraying rounds in the general direction of the shooter, relying on the other man's naivety and fear, then sprinted up the stairs and tumbled into the hall.

'Up. Everyone up. Get down to the basement. Now. Now.'

'I think everyone *is* up, Frank,' said Griffiths, prodding Hal and Roni forward, Lilly cowering behind. 'Put down your gun, old man, and play dead.' He did a quick headcount. 'Where's the other two?'

CHAPTER 80

Sara and Ruthie were scrunched inside a priest hole in the recesses of the kitchen. In the seventeenth century it had hidden Catholic priests from Presbyterian fanatics, and was narrow and dank. Ruthie shivered in her mother's arms as Sara stroked her.

She heard him shout, 'Where is she, old man?'

The silence was followed by the crack of wood on bone and Roni shouting, 'Oh, my God, Malkie'll kill you.'

'I seriously fucking doubt it. He's a dead man walking. Now tell me, you old tosser, before I slice off each testicle.'

'We don't know,' screamed Roni. 'Honestly. Sara's gone out. We don't know where. That's it. That's all. She's gone shopping.'

'Funny that. Shopping round here. Local branch of Selfridges, is it? Come here, lover boy.'

Sara peered through a crack in the hidden door and saw Hal being shoved into the kitchen, followed by Griffiths and Cross. Oh, God. What's Alex doing here? What's he mixed up in now?

'Sara,' shouted Griffiths, 'lovely Sara. We have

389

your boyfriend here and the thing is, I don't want to hurt him. But I have a problem. The father of your child for some unaccountable reason would like you back.'

Ruthie trembled and Sara whispered, 'Shhhh . . .'

'Alex here has a letter to give you, special delivery. Come on out now and we'll talk about it. Whatever your decision is, the Earl'll live with it. But you must read the letter.'

A few seconds passed in silence.

'Thing is, Sara, I don't like your boyfriend. Never have. Arty-farty intellectual type. Always looked down on me and the likes of me.' He grabbed Hal's hair and forced him to stand on tiptoes. 'So it'll give me pleasure to hurt him, and in the end you'll come out because you won't want to hear the sound of his pain.' He elbowed Hal in the stomach and he fell groaning to the floor.

I have to go, she thought. Have to.

'Mummy.' Ruthie tugged at her arm.

'Shh . . .'

'But, Mummy, look,' the child whispered, and pushed the panel at the back of the hole. It slid sideways. 'It's our secret place. Mine and Lilly's. We found it yesterday. It's ever so scary.'

Griffiths kicked Frank in the face. 'Where is the bitch, old man? What is she to you? Give her up.'

Frank spat blood onto the floor and whispered, 'I'll kill you.'

'Yeah, yeah. Big scary words, Frankie. Thing is, I'm the one with the gun and you're the one needing stitches. See what I mean? It's a balance of power thing.' He turned to Cross. 'Try upstairs again. Search the rooms. Impress on your cousin the need for common sense.'

'Oh, God, Roy. Is there any need for this?'

'The Earl's paid us to get the girl, so do as you're told, there's a good lad.'

Cross ran up to the landing on the first floor and pushed open the door in the sitting room. Sara was standing by the fire. 'There you are,' he said with relief. 'C'mon. You're causing all sorts of trouble downstairs.'

'Not me,' she said, raising her shaking hand and pointing Frank's Smith and Wesson .38 automatic. 'It's you. You're doing this.'

'The Earl wants you back.'

'Funny way to go about it.'

'This isn't him. It's Roy. You know how moronic he can be.' Cross pulled a letter from his pocket. 'It's all in here. A new house. School for Ruthie. An allowance. Recognition of the kid in his will. It's a great offer, Sara. You've got to think about it. For her sake.' He glanced at Ruthie.

'You always were naive, Alex.' A tear rolled down her cheek. 'It meant so much to me that you stood by me when the rest of the family walked away. Now, look at you. Did you only support me because the Earl told you to?'

'No. Of course no. He just . . . told me to

391

look after you, like. Make sure you were happy and all.'

'Look at me, Alex. Do I look happy? Now get out of my way.' She advanced towards him, gun outstretched.

'What the fuck are you doing?' he pleaded. 'He'll kill you.'

'Stay here and look after Ruthie. Do one sensible thing in your life.'

'Don't.' He reached across for the weapon and she stepped back.

'Help me, Alex,' she begged. 'Don't let him do this to me. I love Hal. He's all I want.'

'I can't. You know I can't. He'll kill *me*.'

'Don't be weak, Alex. Don't be a coward. *Help me*.' She pushed past him, slid onto the stairs and back through the narrow tunnel to the priest hole. Through the crack, she saw Hal tying Frankie's hands behind his back and heard Griffiths issuing instructions to tighten the bonds. Roni and Lilly were huddled on a chair beside the recess. She had only one chance.

'You found her yet, boy?' Griffiths shouted.

No response.

'Alex? You got the bitch?'

He backed towards the door, his weapon pointing at Frank, tugged it open and bellowed, 'Get your arse down here.'

Sara took her chance, cracked open the hole and slid the gun to Roni, who jumped in surprise, then quickly grabbed the gun and threw it to Hal. 'Hal,' she hissed. He reached forward to catch it, but staggered and the gun clattered off his hand onto the floor.

Griffiths turned. 'Back away. Now.' He crouched into a shooting position, lunged forwards and grabbed Hal, who back-heeled the gun towards Frank.

'Still a balance of power thing, old man,' Griffiths said as he held Hal in a neck choke. 'I can cause him serious brain damage just like this.' His thumb pressed against Hal's throat and he began to fight for breath as Frank jumped to his feet, aiming at Griffiths' head.

'Drop it, Frankie.'

'No, you drop it, you moron,' said Alex and Griffiths felt a barrel pressed against his forehead.

'Don't do this, boy. The Earl'll be furious.'

'Fuck the Earl. Let him go.'

Hal dropped to the floor.

'You wouldn't hurt me, Alex. You're too chickenshit.'

'*I'm* not,' said Frank, rising. 'Son, give your gun to Hal, there. He's got every reason to shoot this motherfucker in the balls.'

'What? The cripple? Do me a favour.' Griffiths swung and pointed his weapon. 'He couldn't hit a fish in a jam jar. Besides, one shot in here will ricochet round the place. Who knows what'll happen? But we can always find out.' Griffiths pulled the trigger, followed instantly by Frank.

For a few terrifying seconds, bullets cracked

against walls. A mirror shattered and then there was silence. Sara burst from the hole and rushed to throw her arms around Hal. 'Are you OK?'

'I'm fine.'

They heard a throaty groan, quickly scanned the room and saw Griffiths on the floor, the top of his hand blown off. Frank staggered over, kicked away Griffith's weapon and said, 'Let's talk balance of power now, shithead.'

CHAPTER 81

Standish scowled as he read the anonymous letter. He now understood the scam; those bastards had stolen millions from him and it made his plans for Malcolm all the more sweet. Revenge is a dish best eaten cold, as Delawney, too, would discover. When I have the Syrian's cash, I'll pay off some debts.

'The interesting question is,' he handed the letter to Raul, 'who sent this? And why?'

'Was it that little weasel Leadsmith?'

'He's disappeared, so it's possible. But he's a coward and there's no way that he'd play this game. He'd know I'd want the money back – with interest.'

'Why don't we ask Delawney?'

'I think I shall, Raul. I think I shall.'

Frank sat with Griffiths in a dungeon in the depths of the castle. The kidnapper was suspended, naked, from an ancient hook in the ceiling. Bags of coffee, tins of fruit, and general supplies produced a fresh, warm household scent. On a table in front of him, Frank had laid out a large sharp knife, a pair of pliers, a nail file, a metal toothpick and a claw hammer.

Griffiths had refused to talk and Frank needed information. Now. He slowly lifted an olive, inserted the toothpick and gouged around until he extracted the stone, which he placed very carefully in a white saucer in front of him. It rolled a little before settling.

'See,' he said, 'I'm a very simple person and I don't like complicated stories.' He lifted another olive and repeated the exercise. 'A man I knew once,' he ate the olive, 'blind now, made the mistake of telling me two lies. The first one I could live with. It was understandable. He was under pressure. But two, now that was a different matter, two had to be dealt with severely.'

Frank spun the stones from the saucer onto a wooden board, then lifted the hammer and brought it down with controlled ferocity. They shattered.

He lifted a pair of pliers, showed them to Griffiths, then placed the ends round one of his testicles and squeezed. Out of the corner of his eye, Frank saw Alex's terrified stare.

'You got something to say?'

'The Earl . . . he . . . told us we had to get Ruthie out. That's all, I swear.'

'Why?' asked Frank.

Alex pleaded with his eyes.

'Why?' Frank's voice was barely a whisper.

Alex shook his head, terrified at what he'd already done.

Frank exhaled. 'Boys,' he said, 'you've got to understand. I'm a professional. I don't like doing this, but I do it for a living. And I'm good, really good.'

He returned with a large roll of tape and cut four pieces. He then stuck Griffiths' eyelids to the top of his sockets, exposing the orbs. Alex was weeping as Frank brought the toothpick over and jabbed lightly on the surface of Griffiths' retina. His screams ricocheted along the ceiling.

'Some guys coming to kill you,' spat Griffiths. 'And I want to watch when they do, you old bastard.'

'When?'

'Fuck off.'

'When?'

'Tomorrow,' said Alex, dully. 'Tomorrow.'

CHAPTER 82

Malkie listened to the horn player. She was very good. He liked Mozart, cleared the head. The rest of the quintet were equally vibrant.

There were two hundred people gathered in the Great Hall at Eastfield House, each worth at least two million – cash. Hope had spent months organizing this charity evening in aid of the Lincoln Cathedral Restoration Fund. Following the music, there would be dancing and supper. She aimed to raise £200k, she'd told Malkie, pressing him gently but firmly for a contribution. He'd offered a thousand pounds and been rewarded with a radiant smile.

Standish sat three rows in front of Malkie and when the music finished, the crowd applauded warmly and rose. Raul looked back at Malkie and nodded. It was time. As Malkie set off across the crowded floor, his phone buzzed in his pocket. Quickly, he scanned the message from Frankie that Delawney had sent up some goons, who were to be followed by Standish's men. He had to take out Standish. Now. He reached the

Churchill Room on the first floor and knocked on the door.

'Come.'

When Malkie entered, Raul was on his knees in front of Standish.

'You're welcome to stay,' Standish smiled.

Malkie stumbled back into the corridor. Minutes later, Raul opened the door, brushing his teeth, his eyes dead as he bent forward to reveal the shoulder holster under his dinner jacket.

'Witnessing an act of homosexual lovemaking will probably scar you for life,' Standish grinned wryly.

'I'll live, Johnny.'

He crossed to the open window and sat on the sill feeling for the Glock the Basque had told him would be taped to the drainpipe outside.

'I believe you have a message for me,' said Standish.

'Yeah. It's from our lords and masters.'

'And what do they want?'

Malkie spotted figures on the lawn – Lottie Grun and Louis Highfield – then pulled in the gun and aimed in one quick movement.

Horror registering on Standish's face.

'Now, Raul,' Malkie shouted.

Raul smiled, listening to some internal music.

'Do it, Raul,' Malkie screamed.

Raul seemed transfixed, his Glock aimed at Standish's temple – then he turned and a bullet smashed into Malkie's chest.

CHAPTER 83

Louis Highfield lashed out at Malkie's limp body as it lay on the lawn beneath the open bathroom window, then extracted a long-handled knife and felt inside Malkie's mouth for his tongue. Malkie's bite almost severed the man's upper finger. As he screamed in agony, Malkie fought for control of the blade, then butted Highfield on the bridge of the nose – bone met flesh in a juddering impact. The American launched a snap kick at his legs, but Malkie rolled over and grabbed the knife.

As Lottie Grun ran towards them, Malkie sliced through the tendon in Highfield's left thigh. His animal howls penetrated the night.

'What the hell's going on?' yelled Delawney rushing from the House trailing security guards. Torchlight poured through the darkness, followed by the yowling of guard dogs. Malkie ran for the woods, bullets whipping past his body. Twisting and turning, he reached the trees and paused for breath.

The pain in his chest was agony. The impact of Raul's bullet on the Kevlar ultra lightweight body armour had caused major bruising. The soft, wet turf had cushioned his fall, but he felt dizzy and breathless. Keep going, he thought.

The dogs were close. Too close. He stopped. They wouldn't be trackers. Guard dogs wouldn't be sniffers. He needed to hide, not run. Think, Malkie. Think. He dialled a number.

'Grace Adams.'

'Help me. I need your help.'

'Malkie?'

'I'll be at the little stone bridge. Get Sam to come,' he whispered. 'Now.' Grace heard the sound of baying dogs – then nothing.

Some time later, Malkie was wading downriver, head lowered against the rain plummeting down in sheets, shock flowing through his veins. His hands shook. He heard the dogs howl.

As he sheltered, he saw Raul giving orders to the security guards. He now knew why Delawney had taken on a new firm the previous month. He and Standish were in on this together. What happened? Why had the Basque betrayed him?

He sank beneath the water as Raul stopped nearby, then as Raul turned back towards the woods, he rose, water dripping from his face, hands, clothes, and stuck a .22 in the back of Raul's treacherous skull.

'Why?' Malkie whispered in his ear. 'Why?'

'You're nothing to us,' Raul replied. 'You're like Standish. Just a drug dealer.'

'And what are you?'

'A patriot.'

Lottie's kick exploded on the side of Malkie's temple. The rain had masked her movements. He rolled sideways, then scrambled to his feet and ran blindly into the night. A split second later, Soulman appeared out of the murk.

'Up,' yelled Grace. Malkie grabbed the pommel, swung himself onto the stallion's back and threw his arms round Grace's waist as she urged the horse across a stone bridge. He craned back as a four-wheel-drive jeep screeched onto the road behind them. Lottie was urging the car on as Raul leant out of the window and aimed at Soulman's head.

'Hold on tight,' shouted Grace. 'Up, Soulman, up,' she yelled and dug in her heels.

The stallion completed an arc in the thin dark air, landing on the other side of a wire stretched five feet off the ground. The jeep's windscreen shattered, sending it careering into a tree.

Soulman veered right, took a four-bar gate into a field, galloped up the track silhouetted against a full moon, then down to the bottom of the lane where Sam was waiting, his Harley growling. As Sam lifted Grace down and kissed her passionately, Malkie slithered to the ground and buried his head in his hands.

CHAPTER 84

Henry stared at Malkie resting on the sofa and gripped a carving knife. Collins was planning to ship out to Scotland at first light. Grace and Sam were asleep upstairs. He closed his eyes and leant against the still warm fireplace. She can barely look at me. She wants to believe me innocent, but there's so much evidence. So much truth. He glared again at Collins. I could kill him now, bury his body in the woods. The others would think he'd disappeared. No one would ever find him. Then Standish would silence Delawney and it would be all over. Grace would come back to him.

'What're you doing, Henry?' Malkie looked up at him – relaxed, unconcerned, his hypnotic blue eyes gazing into Henry's.

'Get up,' hissed Henry, waving the knife.

'What do you want?'

'I want you to get up.'

Malkie felt the cold, sharp edge against his artery. 'You're not a killer, Henry.'

'Tell that to Mrs Halliwell. Now get up.'

Malkie's hand tightened round the gun he'd

slept with. So Henry was the bomber, poor bastard. Out of his depth. A civilian.

'That was an accident,' he said.

'I know what it was. Get up.'

'Don't do this, Henry. I'm not your problem.'

Henry shivered as a tear snaked down his face. 'You took my soul, my self-respect. You turned me into you.'

'You're not me, Henry. Put down the knife and walk away. I'll not cause you any trouble. I just want to get out of here. I've things to sort.'

'Too late . . . Damage done. If you don't get up, I'll, I'll . . .' He drew blood.

Slowly turning his head, Malkie said, 'Grace'll find me. You'll die in prison. Is that what you want?'

Henry sliced deeper.

'Think, Henry. Think very, very deeply. What kind of man are you? What do you believe in? You're just about to make a big choice. Would Hal agree with it? Grace? Sam?' Under the blanket, Malkie eased his gun until it pointed at Henry's chest. 'Don't do something you can't live with.'

Henry's hands shook. You deserve to die, Collins. Street scum. Pander.

Malkie counted down from five, staring into Henry's eyes, desperately trying to read his mind. When he hit one, he intended to fire. Five, four. Henry was rocking back and forward. Three. I'm sorry, Grace. So sorry. Malkie's hand tightened, his lips fell open and he could sense his heartbeat slow.

Two, One. He tried to fire, but couldn't move his fingers. Tried again. Nothing.

'The tip of the blade is awash with tubocurarine – a muscle relaxant,' smiled Henry, suddenly calm. 'Now what am I going to do with you?'

Malkie tried to plead, but his lips refused to form words. With wide eyes he begged Henry as he rolled him onto a rug and dragged him to the door. 'Plshh,' murmured Malkie. 'Needshh get Lillly.' His head smashed against the concrete doorstep and he passed out.

Sam woke with a start. His dreams had been troubled and yet again he'd heard Henry's constant, probing voice. '*Tell me what you know, Sam.*' Henry had planted post-hypnotic suggestions that he knew would not hold long in a healthy mind, but he was relying on Sam's confused condition to buy time.

Since Grace woke him the previous day, Sam had been force-feeding his brain number games, puzzles, riddles, allowing his damaged mind to recover fragments of memory, pictures, images. His instincts told him one thing. He had to talk to Henry.

'Hmmm.' Grace ran her hand down his back. 'Come back to bed. It's not dawn yet. We'll help Malkie when it's light.' They intended to smuggle him up to Scotland.

'I need to talk to your father.'

She was suddenly awake and following Sam

downstairs. The sofa was empty. Where was Malkie?

'Dad? Where are you?'

The back door was open a crack and Sam peered out as the sun's rays swept low along the ground, highlighting the track of the rug as it disappeared into the woods.

'Henry,' he yelled. 'Bring him back.' His voice echoed, then died.

Malkie regained consciousness and saw his grave. Henry was weeping again, running dirt-caked hands across his face, smearing mud on his cheeks. They were in a dense, soundless thicket of beech. No one would see or hear them. He must get through to Henry. Lilly might die unless he flew to Ardtornish that morning.

Henry grabbed him by the collar, hauled him into the deep hole, and then shovelled dirt onto his face. Malkie's skin crawled as he realized he was being buried alive. With one last act of will, he practised the words he was desperate to yell – forming them in his mind, projecting them to the point of his tongue, bailing them into a sentence. He could taste the dirt in his mouth as tried to scream, 'Standish'll kill Lilly.' He heard the words trickle softly from his lips like exhausted bubbles.

CHAPTER 85

Sam and Grace ran through the trees, following the trail until it stopped. Dead.

'Dad,' she shouted. 'Please come back.'

'Shhh,' Sam urged her, listening, eyes focused intently on the woodland floor. 'You know what to do. This used to be our second home.'

She froze, allowing the woods to come alive in her mind – a deer crashed through the undergrowth and rabbits scurried across the path as she strained to hear something alien, something human.

'There.' Sam pointed at a broken holly branch swinging in the gentle breeze. 'They went into Cain's marsh.'

Oh God, she thought, you could hide in there for months.

They ran towards the foetid shore of the marsh, then stopped. It had been over a decade since either had tried to negotiate the treacherous marshland, with its hidden pools and mud. There used to be a safe path that snaked across to various copses in the middle, but was it still there? Marsh gas drifted, giving off sulphurous fumes.

'Oh, God, which way?' groaned Grace.

$\star \quad \star \quad \star$

Henry lifted Malkie's gun and hesitated. Should he shoot himself in the leg? Would that convince Grace that Malkie had kidnapped then tried to kill him? He'd say that he'd discovered that it was Collins who'd set the fire in the glasshouses. That was pretty much true, anyway. It certainly conformed to Sam's suspicions.

What was Collins saying about Lilly? He felt desperately sad about the child. She was lovely. But she'd be better off without Collins – the man would transmit his poison to the next generation.

Malkie moaned and Henry extracted another dose of tubocurarine, the cumulative effects of which would shut down Collins' heart. It was the kindest way. Wiping dirt from the cartoid artery, he found his spot.

'Standish'll kill Lilly,' he was sure he heard Collins say. That was impossible. That man can't speak. His lips can't be moving. Not with that amount of drugs in his system.

'Plssss.'

Henry scrambled from the pit. Oh, God. No. No. Don't do this to me. Don't make me responsible for anything that might happen to your daughter. His hand shook as he pointed the gun at Malkie. It had been fifty years since he last fired a weapon, rough shooting in the woods round the quarry. It was easy, you just flick off the safety and pull the trigger – the bullet does the rest.

'You bastard. You scheming lousy bastard. You came to me, bought me.'

A single tear rolled down Malkie's face.

The gun exploded in Henry's hand as an involuntary shudder ran through his body. The bullet ricocheted from a tree and in the silence that followed, splinters floated in the air like mites.

As the shot exploded into the still air, sending rooks cawing into the sky, Sam shouted, 'You go left, I'll go right.'

Henry put the barrel in his mouth, tasting the hot metal, allowing it to burn his lips. Dear God, what have I become? Can I condemn this innocent child? Would Standish harm her to get at Collins? And Henry couldn't tell him that Collins was dead. No one must ever know.

Oh, Christ, save me. His finger again tightened on the trigger.

'Don't do it, Henry,' shouted Sam, crashing into the clearing. 'For Grace's sake. For Hal.' Sam halted beside Malkie's grave and saw his exhausted, tearful eyes. At least he was alive. Just.

Henry gagged. Sam knew the truth. And Grace would know. As would Hal. And Hope. Poor, lonely Hope.

As a young hospital doctor, he'd closed the eyes on many patients – their eyes were vacant, gone, life extinguished. Death was nothing. All he required was the courage to leave life.

He watched Sam edge towards him. Good man, Sam. Glad to see him hook up with Grace at last. Sam was metres away, whispering, pleading. He reached him, wrapped his hands around Henry's and pulled the barrel gently from his mouth. The old man's legs gave way and he collapsed against Sam's chest. As he embraced Henry, Sam slumped to his knees, the gun falling between them.

Grace broke into the glade. Her fingers flew to her mouth and in that second Henry could see his terrified, imprisoned future. Consumed by anger and self-loathing, he crawled to his knees, shrugging Sam off, then pushing him into Collins' grave. Henry stumbled into the woods and the marsh beyond, blocking his ears against his daughter's pleas.

The marsh gas swallowed him, as he knew it would. He was heading for the one place he felt safe, a hidden refuge he'd built years before when he needed to escape from everyone. I need to think. To plan. I need help.

CHAPTER 86

Grace sat grim-faced on the sofa in the hut. Sam held her close. Malkie had passed out as Sam carried him, and was recovering upstairs.

'Henry's been self-prescribing Valium,' Sam said. 'And if the amounts in his bedroom are anything to go by, he's massively overdosing. And now he'll be in agony. Going cold turkey.'

She squeezed her eyes shut, struggling against more tears.

He wanted to shield her from this, to take the burden, to find Henry himself. But that was impossible.

'You must phone the squad,' he said. 'They need to find Henry before he hurts himself. Or others.'

'Oh God, Sam. I can't. I can't . . .'

He stroked her hair, sunlight pouring through it like golden thread.

'He's getting worse, Grace. Henry's at war with himself and there's no telling what he'll do. And the concoction of drugs he's taking must be producing powerful delusional effects.'

She shuddered and buried her head in his chest,

411

then picked up her mobile and dialled the number Sam had given her. 'I'd like to speak to Assistant Chief Constable Fiona Cassell,' she said.

Malkie staggered downstairs, his breathing shallow and laboured.

'We must get to Ardtornish.'

'You're in no condition.'

'You don't *understand*, Sam. Standish has sent his men there. They're after Roni and Lilly. They'll be there today.'

Grace said, 'Of course I can be there at noon,' cut the connection, then ran to Malkie. 'Is Hal still with them?'

'Yes. I must go. Now.'

'I'm coming with you.'

'You must stay here,' pleaded Sam. 'Henry needs you here in the hut. He'll come back. I know he will. He must. I'll go with Malkie.'

She gnawed her lower lip.

'Call me as often as you can. I need to know you're OK.'

As Sam linked his arms around Malkie and guided him through the door and on to his Harley, she kissed him gently. 'Be careful.'

CHAPTER 87

At a small airfield a few miles from Garton they were met by the pilot of a twin-engine Fokker, who handed Malkie a black bag. Inside were five heavy-duty guns and hundreds of rounds of ammunition. Malkie watched a rain cloud gather like a huge black pig on the horizon, buckled in and they took off.

A few hours later, the plane skimmed below clouds that clung to the top of peat-dark hills, then bounced through swirling turbulence before landing unsteadily on a patch of green field. They could almost taste the rain in the air.

Spruce and fir jutted through the mizzle like cathedral spires, and far below, Loch Aline brooded. Slashes of light illuminated tawny bracken, chocolate bark and nutty peat, and then, every few miles, a brilliant, affirmative green field stood out against the gloom.

A Land Rover waited for them, engine running. As Malkie sped onto the single-track road down towards a narrow bridge, Sam phoned Grace and they managed to snatch a brief conversation, his gut tightening at the thought of her facing this trial on her own. He knew Henry would not harm her. In the end he would not hurt innocents. The same could not be said of the vermin who'd attacked Lilly Collins and were set to do so again.

'How long?' he shouted as the guns clattered at his feet. He prayed they wouldn't need to be used.

'Five minutes.' On the horizon, Sam saw the castle appear like a sentinel, then the heavens roared and the building disappeared in a torrent of rain.

Fiona Cassell, in her designer suit, blouse and shoes, sat opposite Grace, in jeans, battered sneakers and well-worn jacket, and knew that she would never look as good. But she had long given up comparing her plain looks with those of beautiful women. As she moved through her forties, it all seemed to even itself out.

They were sitting either side of a cheap table, the closed orange curtains casting an uneasy glow over Cassell's pale features as she said, 'We need to get in touch with your father. Where might he have gone?'

'I honestly don't know.'

'I realize you want to protect him. But we need to find him before . . .'

'Don't you think I know that?'

'I'm sorry. You're our best hope.'

Cassell studied her. The woman looked strong. Capable.

'He's an emotional furnace,' she said. 'You'll need to give him a reason for living. He'll be in touch, we're sure of it.'

'I'll do whatever it takes.'

CHAPTER 88

Hal spotted the attackers first. He was tucked into a bay window at the loch end of the high-ceilinged sitting room that hundreds of years before had housed archers and watchmen peering nervously out over the loch waiting for the Norsemen. He felt like their heir as he stared down a powerful telescope at three speedboats pounding over the restless waves. They had come, just as Alex had said. Oh, Christ. He sent a warning to Frank, Malkie and Sam, then dragged himself towards the oak door, calling for Sara and Roni. As they joined him, his heart sank when he looked into Roni's eyes – she was spaced. As he took Lilly from her arms, Roni barely noticed.

'Ready?' he asked the children. 'What game are we going to play?'

'Hide and seek,' shouted Lilly. 'Hide and seek.'

'You ready, Princess?' asked Frank.

Roni sat by the extinguished fire, her head nodding to internal music.

'Oh, Christ, Roni, what've you done?' Frank knelt beside her.

'I just needed a bit of, you know, help.' She

416

looked up defiantly. 'I haven't broken my promise. You tell Malkie I haven't broken my promise. I haven't touched a drink. It's only tranqs. Harmless. Come to Mummy, darling.' She reached out for her daughter. 'Mummy loves you. Come here. I want a hug.'

Lilly broke from Hal and ran to her mother, clambering onto her lap.

Hal whispered in Roni's ear. 'Don't live someone else's life. Lilly needs you.'

Her eyes filled as she grabbed his arm. 'You understand. See, Frank, Hal understands.'

Frank stared out of the window at the advancing gang. 'We all understand, sweetheart. It's survival I'm worried about.'

He flipped off the safety on his Uzi.

'Let's motor.'

CHAPTER 89

'Good of Johnny to give you a second chance,' said Raul, his hair matted with rain, emphasizing the sculpted beauty of his cheeks. Raul was oblivious to his looks the way a bird was to flight. 'Think you have enough men to take the child this time, Jason?'

Jason Gregg had been Malkie's enforcer for decades and had gone to jail when he could've taken the deal offered by the Crown Prosecution Service. Malkie had been good to him in return. Promoted him. But now Malkie was weak. Standish had made it clear that if he delivered Lilly Collins, then Malkie would be assassinated and his assets transferred to him. He had also supplied the fake policeman who'd picked up the two couriers.

'Don't take the piss, Raul. Every job is worth doing right.'

'First time?' asked Raul, his face upturned towards the rain. It sluiced down his skin and dripped from his hair.

Why is this mad bastard here? Jason asked himself. Compromising the mission. Malkie would never've put up with it. Liked discipline, did

Malkie. Well, the time'll come when the Basque won't dick me around. He looked up at the tower, shielding his eyes from the slanting rain. Fuck, he thought, whoever built that meant business. He was glad he was only up against Frank. He sensed his crew assembling at his back. Seasoned pros – the most loyal of his own guys plus half a dozen mercenaries. None of them owed Malkie – no confused emotions.

'Let's go,' he ordered.

As Frank led them down a narrow twisting staircase the children sang, 'Hi ho, Hi ho, it's home from work we go,' and clung to the thick rope banister. Hal peered out the narrow window at the shapes making their way up the bank.

'They'll be here in a few minutes, Frank.'

'OK,' said Frank. 'We're going to play a new game, my little princesses.'

He disappeared round a corner and whispered, 'Follow me, if you dare.'

The children squealed when Frank's arm shot out from a hidden entrance and Hal handed over Lilly, then Ruthie. Sara followed, then Roni. Hal was last.

The tunnel was pitch black – apart from slashes of light from windows the size of single bricks, placed at ten-metre intervals down the tunnel.

'You go first,' Frank ordered Sara. 'Hal, you take the rear. This is an old escape route, built five hundred years ago. Malkie had it restored. It comes out on the other side of the hill, next to a waterfall. There'll be a van waiting for you. Get in and go. I'll catch up.'

'I'll stay, Frank,' said Hal. 'You can't deal with those bastards on your own.'

'I can look after myself. You take care of the wee lassies.' Frank crawled back along a space that could barely accommodate his bulk, then waited on the stairs. The invaders would be at the end of the drive. He needed a better view. As he raced up the stairs, arms snaked round his chest and pulled him backwards.

He felt hot breath on his cheeks. They've come early, he thought.

'Well done, Frank. You're a star.' Malkie hugged him. 'Who is it? Who is the traitor?'

'Jason.'

'Jason. Damn. Damn. Had to be, I suppose. His was always the most businesslike approach.'

Above him on the landing, Frank saw Sam.

'Hello, Frank,' said Sam, shaking his hand. 'How's the tar business?'

As Malkie entered the sitting room, he briefly recalled the ease and contentment of being here for the first time after the restoration. He had taken something man had destroyed and given it to future generations. The future is all we have, he thought, as he stared through the telescope.

'Ready?' he asked Frank, who held an electronic fob in his hand.

They're going to kill them, thought Sam – blow them up.

'Ready,' replied Frank.

'Don't do it, Malkie.' Sam spun him round and stared into his eyes. 'Turn this into a bloodbath and your last chance is gone.'

'Go,' Malkie commanded Frank, and an explosion ripped through the air, followed by a cascade of red and blue sparks that flooded the sodden landscape and cast a million rainbows.

'Yessss,' hissed Frank, his binoculars raised.

Sam tore them from his hands and peered into firework-illuminated gloom. He could just make out two screaming men hanging from pine trees by their feet.

'Come on, Frank.' Malkie ran down to the dungeon. Huddled in the corner, their wrists tied, were Delawney's would-be kidnappers.

'You're running with bad company, Alex.'

He lowered his eyes whilst Malkie hissed at Griffiths, 'I'll deal with you later.'

'There won't be a later,' said Griffiths. 'Later, you'll be dead.'

Malkie smashed his fist against Griffiths' nose. 'Consider that a message from beyond the grave.'

He opened a trapdoor and slid full length along a narrow ledge. 'If you want to be helpful, Sam, there's some boiling oil on the roof. Pitch it on the buggers below.'

'Are you nuts?'

'Only joking. Come with me.'

As Malkie crawled further along the ledge, Sam ducked into the narrow confines of the chamber.

The air was warm and stale. He smelt dead something.

Malkie called, 'Come *on*, Sam.'

They were a metre under ground, shuffling along an aluminium tunnel that was about two metres wide and one metre high. Above them, Sam heard more muffled explosions.

'I did a lot of research when I bought this place,' said Malkie. 'Over the years the defenders had put in a honeycomb of tunnels. I had them restored. When I say pull,' he said, 'tug this.' He indicated a cord attached to the wall.

'What is it?'

'Was there ever a time in your life when you didn't ask questions, Copeland?'

'When I had tonsilitis, couldn't speak for two days.'

'Happy days,' said Malkie. 'Pull.'

Sam tugged, a door opened, and as rain slapped against the wall, Malkie glanced down. They were on top of a stone shed. He signalled to Sam to follow. Another starburst firework boomed to their left, illuminating two of the attackers sheltering below. Malkie leant down and coshed the first, whilst Sam dropped on the second, knocking him unconscious. They dragged the senseless men into the shed and locked the door.

'Eleven to go,' Malkie said as he sprinted for the trees, his rain-soaked trousers sticking like seal skin. He heard a muffled cry, then murmured. 'Ten.'

CHAPTER 90

Raul waited on the road watching the waterfall tumble and cascade. As quickly as the rain had come, blinding white sunlight followed, clouds hurried from the sky by a fierce, fresh wind. He could see Gregg's stumbling gang as one by one they disappeared. Fireworks exploding at their feet herded Gregg and his two remaining lieutenants towards the pond. One of his men lay screaming on the ground – the victim of a star-bomb that had exploded at his feet and ripped through his flesh. Gregg was panicking, shooting at the wind.

Raul pulled a palm-sized device from his pocket and fired it up. It was a heat-seeking monitor connected to a low-powered satellite. He honed in on the coordinates of the hill until he found himself – a red dot flashing on the electronic relief map. He stretched the shape of the search zone until he saw four flashes of light moving slowly under the hill, heading for the exit in a cave below the top of a five-metre-high waterfall. Raul sprinted to meet them.

★　　★　　★

'Are you OK, Hal?' asked Frank on the mobile.

'Fine. Almost at the end of the tunnel.'

'Take the van to the Coram ferry. I'll meet you there in an hour or so.'

Hal opened a metal grille and crawled onto a cave ledge. The waterfall cascaded over their heads into the river below. They needed to jump across to firm ground opposite.

'I'm scared,' said Lilly, clamping her hands to her ears, blocking out the thunderous water.

Hal scooped her up. 'I'll carry you across.'

'Like a hand?' said Raul. 'Or two.'

'Darling,' smiled Roni. 'Is that really you? What're you doing here? You've got to help us.'

'Of course I will. Give me the child.'

'Get lost.' Hal backed against a flat black rock, spray rattling against his face.

'You're incapable of defending the girl, so, please, be sensible, don't make things unpleasant for yourself.' Raul's blade flashed in the sun.

'Piss off.' Hal leapt onto a slippery ledge, aiming to double back into the tunnel.

'You're beginning to annoy me, cripple man.'

'What're you doing, Raul?' Roni tugged at his arm. 'You're scaring the kids. Stop it. Let's just get down the hill.'

Raul shook her off, but she jerked again, and he thrust back his forearm, catching her on the cheek, knocking her to the floor of the tunnel. He leapt onto the ledge beside Hal. Lilly was shivering, rocking dangerously in Hal's arms.

'OK,' Hal said. 'OK. Just let me get her off the ledge.'

'Give her to me. Now,' ordered Raul.

As Hal handed her to Raul, she wriggled and fell.

'Mummy,' she wailed as she tumbled towards the lip of the ledge.

'It's all right,' soothed Hal. 'Stay there. Don't move.'

She froze – her eyes huge – as he hooked his fingers around her and pulled her back into his chest. He lifted the child and took her across to the path. As Raul followed, Hal leapt at him, punching and pushing him backwards. Surprised by Hal's strength and ferocity, Raul staggered, then steadied himself on the lip of the drop to the river.

'You're brave,' he said, 'but experience counts for everything.' He dropped his shoulder, feinted with his left, then sliced upwards with his knife. For a moment, Hal stood, numb. Then pain seared through him and as he passed out Raul calmly reached for his arm, spun him into the air and watched him fall.

CHAPTER 91

'Shall we take Gregg, boss?' asked Frank.

They were hiding in a ditch running the circumference of the pond and saw Gregg cowering behind a green oil tank.

'How many did you say?' Malkie asked.

'Fifteen.'

'Sam and I took out six, Gregg and another two are over there. How many did you score?'

'Five,' said Frank.

'Shit. Where's the last one?' said Malkie.

He swept the area with his binoculars and saw a woman and a child staring down into the river, then three other figures scrambling down the hill. He zoomed in and his heart thudded. It was Raul with Lilly and Roni. He started to run and was immediately pinned down by crossfire from Gregg and his men. Malkie rolled onto his stomach and fired. The first bullet ripped the metal, the second exploded inside the boiler, the third pierced the heart of the tank, ripping it apart.

'What are you doing, Raul? For God's sake, what have you done?'

426

Roni's eyes were wide with the horror and discordant flashes of red flooded her mind. She could still hear the sound of Sara's screams as she and Ruthie sprinted down the path, desperate to reach Hal.

As Raul shoved them into the boat, an explosion rent the air. He looked back and saw Malkie with two other men sprint desperately towards them. He fired rapidly into the hulls of the two other speedboats, then sped into the mirror-calm water of Loch Aline.

'What are you doing?' Roni yelled again.

Raul heard the roar of another engine. He hadn't damaged the other boats sufficiently, but they wouldn't last long in the water. Nearly four hundred metres, through a narrow inlet, sat the broad sweep of the Sound of Mull where a large yacht was waiting. He glanced back. There was one person in each speedboat, and a Land Rover sped along the road that ran the length of the loch. He grinned. This was living.

Malkie's vision had narrowed as he concentrated on his daughter huddled against Roni. He could sense their confused terror. Sam manoeuvred the other boat beside him, then pulled narrowly in front and signalled a pincer movement. Malkie nodded and spun off to the left. Freezing loch water poured in from holes in the hull and lapped his ankles. It would be a matter of minutes before the boat sank.

They were gaining on Raul, as Roni momentarily distracted him by punching the back of his head. Raul reached out and slapped her down. Dazed, she rolled in the bottom of the boat as Lilly scrambled to reach her. Ahead of Raul was a large black ferry, halfway across the Loch, blocking their way. The captain blew a warning blast as he watched the speedboats head towards him at full throttle.

It was touch and go, but Raul gambled that if he made it through the gap the others wouldn't.

'No!' screamed Roni as Raul squeezed another ounce of power from the engine and steered for the gap between the ferry's hull and the rocky outcrop of the mainland.

Malkie concentrated on the closing space. The ferry didn't count. Only the opening. As Raul slipped through with half a metre to spare, it narrowed and Malkie thrust his foot to the floor, sensing the ship loom over him, feeling his keel judder in the swell, fighting for control. But then he was through and heard a full-throttled roar beside him. Sam must've slip-streamed. Sam sped ahead and Malkie, too, managed more power as they swallowed up a little of Raul's lead. But not enough.

Malkie saw the Sound of Mull ahead and in the middle distance Standish's yacht. As Raul headed into the Sound, a loud crack ricocheted across the water. Frank fired from the top of the Land Rover on the last spit of land before the sea took over. But he's out of reach, thought Malkie. Surely Raul was out of reach. Frank squeezed off one more shot. Raul reeled as the bullet snapped his right shoulder.

Raul felt shock more than pain. He'd been hit before, but that had been a flesh wound. This was real. Shit. He slumped against the wheel.

'Get Lilly,' Sam shouted to Roni as he pulled alongside. As she leant over to pick up her daughter, Raul's arm shot out. He lifted Lilly one-handed into the air and threw her into the dark waters.

CHAPTER 92

Malkie and Sam leapt into the loch. It sucked them down as they swam frantically to the spot where Lilly sank. Malkie's lungs burned, but he could not see her. He screamed within himself, helplessness beginning to paralyse him. Then he saw a shape, bulky in the shadows. It was Sam, kicking desperately towards the surface, pulling Lilly in his arms.

Heaving desperate gulps of air, they floated briefly before Malkie reached for his daughter. Her eyes were open and she was screaming. As he swam towards her, he heard the roar of an engine and looked up as Raul gunned towards them.

Roni scrambled to her knees, reeling with pain, then dragged herself forwards. She leapt on Raul, bit deep into his neck and twisted the wheel away from the swimmers, holding it tight as he punched her face. They narrowly missed, but still she wouldn't let go, biting deep, tasting his blood, hearing the gurgle in his throat. Still she held on as the speedboat roared round in circles. As his fingers dug into her eyes, she suddenly straightened the

430

wheel and they shot towards an outcrop of rocks.

The boat disintegrated, spraying blood, oil, body and wood across the loch.

Malkie held Lilly in his arms, treading water, as Sam whispered, 'Out of the depths we have cried unto thee, O lord . . .'

CHAPTER 93

'Get more of the boys up to lock down Gregg,' said Malkie as he stood on the steps of the Fokker, its engine revving. 'Now that we've flushed out that treacherous bastard, we can trust everyone else. You can let him go when I say so.'

'What do you want me to do about Roni?'

Malkie fought the bile in his throat. 'The police'll be up here in an hour. Tell them that she was out of her face on E and had gone joy-riding.'

They were silent for a second, listening to the howl of the wind and the whine of the engine.

'Will do, Malkie.' Frankie made as if to hug him, then shook his hand and ran back to the Land Rover.

Malkie settled quickly into his seat as Sam finished talking to Sara on the phone.

'How is he?'

'Not too bad. A bit bruised. They're in A and E in Fort William, claiming that he cut his shoulder falling from the cliff when he was larking about. They won't ask too many questions.' He'd been lucky – his twisted face had protected him.

Raul's blade, aimed at his throat, had slashed his shoulder and Sara and Ruthie had managed to scramble down the winding path to pull him out of the river.

The plane took off and they travelled in silence to Garton, Lilly staring at nothing, Malkie and Sam, their shoulders touching, each lost in thought.

Malkie felt that he was being ripped apart. A gut-wrenching emptiness seemed to weigh heavier by the second as Lilly burrowed into him like a frightened animal. Now, more than ever, his duty was to his daughter. Who set him up at Eastfield House? Had Sergio sold him out to Standish? What could be more important to them than Standish's treachery? Either way, Standish had sent Gregg for his child and they'd come after him again, even more relentless now that Raul was dead.

Malkie was torn. If he told Sam about Sergio, then he'd hunt down the Basque; but in prison, the Basque could issue the order that would kill Lilly. The Basque still wanted Sam dead, and still the contract lay with him. The choice was as stark now as it was when the hit was authorized. The Basque wanted him to kill the man who'd now saved both his life and that of his child. Oh, Christ. *I can't.* Won't. There must be another answer. His brain reeled.

Sam, too, was lost in contemplation. Malkie is holding out on me. He closed his eyes and focused on the face of the speedboat driver. He had seen it before. Sergio's office. Madrid. Raul, that was the guy's name. Raul was introduced to Sam as a bright young member of Sergio's team in the Grupo who had won an honour for anti-terrorist activity. So what was Raul doing in Scotland? Why Standish's organization? Was he still working for Sergio? Surely no undercover agent would willingly take part in a major crime like abducting a child, let alone trying to drown her.

He needed desperately to talk to Sergio, but hadn't been able to contact either him or Eileen in days. Could Sergio be running a dirty operation? Since autumn of 2001, the rules of engagement with terrorists had changed. More risks were taken with the legal process, more agents felt that the rights of citizens to a peaceful life more than outweighed the legal rights of those in terrorist networks. Raul would not have been the first to cross over the line so many times that he no longer knew the line was there.

Malkie knew the answers to these questions, but still refused to talk. Who could exert that much pressure on him? And what of Violi? Malkie and Violi were the double helix of this problem, the DNA of the answer.

CHAPTER 94

The courier watched porn on late-night TV and drank his fifth beer of the day.

'Why are they doing this?' he asked.

'They told you,' replied his companion, 'they're fitting up the guys running this scam. The guys above Roy Griffiths.'

Griffiths was the points man in the Eastfield Organic operation and the only person any of the mules ever saw. The phone rang. 'It's Picasso. Be at the underground car park in Regent Street. Eight p.m. tomorrow. Look for a uniformed policeman standing next to the post-box. Do as he says.'

Sam and Grace sat in the sitting room of a safe house in Garton, a large warehouse flat Malkie had rented months before. Malkie lay motionless in bed listening to the clank of a half-dozen cranes, thoughts reeling around his head. Sam was trying to involve him in his plans, but he couldn't take the risk – Sam's legal route led to jail and jail led to death at the hands of someone paid by Standish or Sergio.

Sam hugged Grace. 'You OK?'

'Holding up.' She'd spent an hour talking to Hal, dissuading him from flying immediately to Garton. He was still not ready to travel and she wanted him out of harm's way, so Malkie had arranged for them to stay in a remote cottage in Lewis.

'We need to talk,' Sam whispered.

Her head dropped, then she nodded and he steered her towards the table beside Lindsey and Gitte, then taped a large piece of white paper to the wall.

'This is a hard time for all of us,' he said. 'Unbelievably hard. Some of you have families at risk and each of us is under the threat of death. Malkie has lost his wife, and Henry is running. And we still don't know why. Each of us understands only a little of the story.'

He wrote the names of Violi and Delawney at the top of the paper.

'What we know so far is that there are links between Violi,' he underlined the name, 'and Delawney. They are tied by the land deal that connects the Standish Centre to the University.'

Underneath Violi he wrote

Alaina Prokovitch, Habermas – **Intellectual property theft.**

And under Delawney he scribbled,

Halliwell, Henry, Leadsmith – drugs and land.

Grace briefly closed her eyes, sickened to the pit of her stomach that her father's name was on the list. There was still no word from him. Oh God, Dad. Please phone.

Then Sam wrote

SPANISH CONNECTION – Fernandez?

'Someone has gone to a lot of trouble to frame me and get me out of this investigation. Lindsey has found out that one of the squad's financial specialists – codenamed Casper – has been manipulating the money supposedly flowing through my bank account. And we know Roni had been authorizing the transfers. Malkie is too traumatized to explain what's going on.'

He wrote Casper and Roni Collins next to Fernandez. 'So who is paying off Casper? And how did Roni get involved? There's a connection with a Spanish security agent called Raul Rodriguez.' He scribbled Rodriguez next to Fernandez. 'Who was he working for?'

'If this was my research,' said Gitte picking up a red pen, 'I'd be looking for a new causal variable. Something generating the rest.' She wrote TRUE CAUSE and drew arrows between it, Delawney, Violi, Fernandez, Rodriguez and Casper.

'Is Malkie Collins the true cause?' asked Lindsey, glancing towards the closed bedroom door.

Sam wrote Malkie on the chart above 'cause'.

'Malkie's a smart guy. But he doesn't have the clout or resources to mastermind this.'

'If you stay with my approach,' said Gitte, 'then Collins is too obvious. You must think laterally when approaching intractable scientific problems. Most people believe that science moves in an orderly fashion, that methods discover facts and theories follow. Or that imaginative scientists dream up theories which are then proven or disproved by facts. In fact many of the great leaps are accidental. Look at Fleming with penicillin. What most people don't know is that it took fifteen years to purify penicillin and Fleming had nothing to do with that. Even then, success was down to chance. The researchers chose to test it on one of the few animals for which it wasn't toxic. If they had selected something else, the results would've shown that the wonder drug was too dangerous to use.'

She returned to the chart. 'Crick and Watson were as surprised as anyone else when they cracked DNA. And what would have happened if James Watson had stayed in the US? Their quixotic partnership was crucial to solving the problem.' She ran a red line up from Malkie to an empty box. 'You have to look for something deeper.' She drew a large question mark. 'And when you find it, you'll have your true cause.'

Sam stared at Violi's name. You know, don't you, he thought.

CHAPTER 95

The following afternoon, as Gitte listened to Alaina singing in the shower, she ran her fingers down the double ladders of the DNA model, pressing gently on the numbers – first *a12*, then *g3*. When the water stopped, she paused, her fingers trembling.

'Would you pour me a drink, darling?' cried Alaina. 'There's some white wine in the fridge.'

Nearly there. She hit *t1*, her lips dry.

'Hold the wine,' Alaina shouted. 'I'll get dressed first. Be there in five.'

Gitte relaxed and popped the ball numbered *c4*. When a thin drawer opened, she lifted out a piece of plastic no bigger than a sliver of garlic, slid it into her breast pocket, then grinned.

A man's hand clamped her mouth.

'Don't make a sound,' Violi hissed as he dragged her across the room.

As Violi bundled Gitte into the back of a black Lexus, he said, 'She's got the Doomsday Codes in her top pocket.' Julie, his PA, transferred her gun to her left, fished in Gitte's shirt, extracted

439

the plastic and dropped it into an envelope.

'That was really foolish, Gitte,' shouted Violi as he sped round a corner. 'Alaina's a dangerous and unforgiving woman. We must make you disappear.'

She heard Julie muttering instructions about a 'chopper' and 'rapid reaction' into a mobile as Violi turned into a series of country lanes, doubled back, stopped, then drove again, eyes flicking to the mirror. Finally, he skidded to a halt in an isolated grassy clearing by the sea. A low wind pressed down on them as Violi, grim-faced, urged Gitte forward. Then the air filled with the beat of helicopter rotors.

She pulled away, but he tightened his grip. 'If I have to knock you senseless I will.'

As the helicopter began its descent, Violi shielded his eyes from the storm of dirt and leaves, then the world turned black. When he regained consciousness seconds later, his head was hooded and he was being dragged into the woods.

'Julie!' His muffled cries struggled uselessly against the machine's noise.

A pistol was thrust against his flesh and he fell silent until his hands were strapped to a piece of metal.

'Where am I going? Where's Julie?'

'Get on,' shouted a voice. 'Now.'

Hands guided him onto a seat and a motorbike revved beneath him, branches whipping his face as the driver sped up a rutted path. A short while later, he was forced to walk, his arms roped to the person in front, a guard on either side and another behind. Julie?

'In,' said the voice.

Heat and the roar of a log fire hit him as he was guided through a door.

'Sit.' He was lowered onto a sofa and the hood lifted.

It took a few seconds to adjust to the light – then relief briefly flooded through him when he saw Julie on the chair opposite, her eyes darting, looking for escape.

'Sorry about the cloak and dagger. Would you like a cuppa?'

He glanced in the voice's direction.

'Copeland?'

'Back like a bad penny.'

Violi caught Gitte's eye and she nodded grimly.

'This, you may recall, is Detective Inspector Lindsey Hamilton,' said Copeland.

'You don't know what you're dealing with, Copeland. I suggest you get us back before you do any more damage,' said Violi.

'Damage is such a relative concept. Depends on who's doing it, to whom and why. Arresting a criminal does damage to their liberty, but it's necessary in a well-ordered society.'

Sam poured tea from a brown china pot.

'Darjeeling?'

Violi shook his head.

'I have a problem, Dr Violi. A serious problem

and you are one of the keys to unlocking it. Let me lay it out for you. May I have the file, Lindsey?' She reached into her case and handed him a portfolio, which he passed to Violi, whose heart sank as he read transcripts of conversations between Grace and 'Amir Rahman', then the details of his own role in the deception, taken from the documents Gitte'd stolen from Alaina's flat.

'I don't know anything about this.' He dismissed the evidence with a wave.

'Why did you kidnap Gitte?'

Silence.

Sam produced a series of digital images of Violi hustling a struggling Gitte into the Lexus and of the helicopter coming into land.

'Oh, and then there's this.' Gitte handed Sam a small tape recorder that'd been sewn inside her jacket. He hit the button and played back the conversation about the Doomsday Codes.

'Now, I've no idea what the Doomsday Codes are. Or what's going on here,' said Sam. 'But I would guess that if I hand you over to Lindsey as a suspected kidnapper and thief, a lot of people would be very unhappy – Charlie Lambie, for one. You know Charlie, don't you?'

'Don't get involved, Copeland. You're out of your league.'

'How did you know Gitte was trying to steal the Doomsday Codes?'

Violi crossed his legs and fell silent. Copeland would cause him no harm, and even if he were arrested, he'd be out again in half an hour.

'Was it because of this?' Sam nodded at Lindsey, who depressed the start button on a tape machine. Alaina's voice boomed from a speaker.

'Stef, it's me. Gitte is nervous. She knows something about the contents of my DNA model. You must keep an eye on her. Make her disappear if necessary.'

It was the message left on his machine a few hours earlier, after which Julie'd put a 24/7 surveillance team on Gitte.

'The message was a fake composed by Lindsey. A necessary lie,' said Sam. 'Alaina has no idea what we know. But Lindsey has enough to arrest you on suspicion of kidnapping.'

'Go ahead. I'm pretty sure you have entrapment laws in this country.'

'And then there's Halliwell's murder. The press would have a field day with that – "Research Centre's Director in Drug-Death Shock".'

'That's a crock of shit, and you know it,' replied Violi, visibly reddening.

'I've got a lot of friends in the press who'd kill for a story like that. But let's see what else we can add into the mix.'

Sam turned to Lindsey. 'Let's find out who Julie was calling in her haste.'

Producing a box the size of a telephone charger, she plugged it into a USB port at the back of her laptop, then ran the numbers stored in the mobile, including that of the last call made.

'When you're under pressure,' said Sam, 'one of the first things to go is secure communication.'

There was a loud beeping noise as the software unscrambled and honed in on the last number dialled.

'CIA,' she said. 'Specifically, the office of Assistant Director of Tactical Support, Gerald Ruttger.'

'Well, well,' Sam smiled. 'Gerry Ruttger. One of the General's best pals. Served together in Nato. How long have you worked for the CIA, Dr Violi?'

CHAPTER 96

The couriers followed orders and waited by a Ford Transit on the second floor of a concrete car park. One of the detectives they'd met before tapped his watch. 'You were almost late, son. And you must've realized by now that I don't like to be pissed about with.

'This is Jake,' he indicated a second figure, 'otherwise known as DI John Starr. He'll accompany you.'

'Where are we going?'

'You'll know when you get there. Here.' He handed over a block of cash. 'Five K apiece. Simplest job in the world. You've got a legitimate contract with the Conference Centre. No one will ask any questions. Deliver the goods. Unload the apples. Walk away. We'll do the rest.'

They looked at one another. Nervous.

'Put these on,' said Starr, who was wearing a red uniform with Jake written on the name-pad. He passed over similar clothes and passes for the Queen Elizabeth II Conference Centre across Victoria Street from Westminster Abbey.

'Saddle up,' said the policeman. 'It's going to take us a while to unload.'

Sam smiled at Violi. 'Right now, all hell is breaking loose at your HQ. You've been here for five hours. They have no idea who has you or why. What will they do?'

Violi gnawed his lip, reached for a cigar and lit up. The operation was dead in the water unless he went along with Copeland. Either Ruttger would pull the plug, or he would go for Standish too early without sufficient evidence to take him down or discover the shadow project. Violi had not been able to penetrate the real reason for Standish's intense interest in 'Perfect Wheat', but he knew there was more to it than simple commercial gain. There was a hidden agenda known only to Standish and Prokovitch. He glowered at Copeland. The Scotsman had him and he knew it.

'Give me the phone. I'll tell Ruttger that we're OK.'

'Give me two days. That's all I ask.'

Despite the circumstances, Violi decided that he didn't dislike Copeland. And he could be right, Standish might walk without Collins' evidence. And if he walked, they'd never track him down again. As he made the call, Sam said, 'Gitte, what's that term you use when you're talking about complementary DNA sequences?'

'Reverse transcription?'

'That's the one. The genes reverse themselves. Right?'

'In a manner of speaking. Reverse transcriptase is an enzyme that carries out the process of reverse transcription.'

'Grace told me that this sequence means that viruses can enter host cells. Is that right?'

'Yes. It's one of the biggest problems with the AIDS virus,' said Gitte.

'That's how we're going to trap Standish and his paymasters,' said Sam. 'We've already used a trapdoor to get us Casper, and you've tracked down Standish, now we're going to do in reverse what they did to me. Send the money back, Lindsey. Push it up the chain to where it came from. Make certain that lots turn up in a special numbered account established by Standish. Understand?'

'Standish is under our protection, Copeland,' said Violi. 'We need him.'

'He's not going to deliver,' said Sam. 'And more to the point, whoever is trying to get me out of the way has something bigger up his or her sleeve. The only man who can tell me what it is, is falling apart at the seams. I need to remind him of his priorities.'

He grabbed his jacket.

'Incidentally,' he said to Gitte, 'what are the Doomsday Codes?'

Gitte smiled – a slow, delicious smile.

'With these codes, Gitte can melt down the whole Standish database,' said Lindsey.

CHAPTER 97

The courier was sweating by the time he unloaded the last box of apples. He was feeling great, money in his pocket and his girlfriend had agreed to spend the night with him in London. He barely felt the pinprick in his neck and was only dimly aware of the paralysis in his legs and arms as he dropped unconscious to the floor.

As Grace waited outside the House she pulled her mother's old jacket more tightly around her – a scent clung to the fabric like an echo of better days. The police had insisted that she wore stiff body armour that shifted uncomfortably as she moved. In the hills and by the river, the police waited for Henry to show. He'd contacted them that afternoon, saying that he would surrender himself at the House.

The squad's psychiatrist had told her that in his opinion Henry was capable of turning against his family. Why did he want to come to the farm to give himself up? she asked herself as she watched a Volvo drive up the lane. He had told the police that the car would explode if they approached him, that he would surrender only when he was ready.

As his Volvo came closer, she saw that it was being driven cautiously but erratically, hugging the verge, its lights flashing across the valley. She ran forwards as an electronic voice in her ear commanded – 'Stop. We don't know if the suspect is armed.' The *suspect*, she thought. They had already turned him into an object. Henry would never harm me. *Never.* She ignored the order and pulled open the car door.

Jenny Appleyard, the landlady at the Green Man, sat very still as policemen edged towards her, guns drawn.

'On the ground,' shouted one. 'Now.'

'You're joking. With my arthritis, I wouldn't go down on my knees for Tom Cruise.'

'Drop,' yelled a red-faced copper. She'd had enough of being shouted at and bullied by men and women half her age. From now on, she would stand up for herself.

'Drop yourself, fatso,' she said. She sat rock-still on the car seat, next to the package Henry had asked her to deliver. Grace leant against the Volvo, breathing heavily.

'He left this for you, love. It was in the snug, on the seat he always used when he came for a glass or two.'

Grace pictured him tucked in the corner of the bar, reading. No one bothered Henry. They knew he liked his privacy. A policeman tugged her away. Not much privacy now, Henry.

As Jenny was forcibly escorted from her car she slapped a tall, gangly policeman on the shoulder. 'I served you your first pint of beer, Smithie. And cleaned up your sick. Don't you *dare* push me around.'

Fiona Cassell, followed by a squad of bomb-disposal specialists, walked up to Grace.

'We need to make the car secure, and find out if the package contains anything suspect. Let's wait inside.'

An hour later, they sat quietly at the kitchen table, on which were spread two locks of white hair, a watch and a pair of satin baby shoes.

Grace held a letter in her hands. It was encased in clear sheeting and Fiona was about to take it away to run lab tests.

Darling Grace,

I'm sitting here thinking of the day you were born. I held you up to the sun at the front door of White Hill Farm and dedicated you to Good. And throughout your life I knew you had a good heart. I, on the other hand, was not a good father. I know that. Too many demons and not enough strength to exorcize them. Weak, my mother called me when I was growing up. She was right, my Mam. Not that she was right that often.

I took a man's life because he was going to take mine. Is that immoral? Yes. Halliwell played on my vanity and my weaknesses. But I had no reason to seek his death. Indeed, I didn't intend it. It was a mistake. I meant only to scare him. What fools men are.

I'm so glad about your marriage to Sam, and I hope desperately that you have a child. You are a woman of passion. More so than Hope who, much as I love her, had too much of my own mother in her. Self-righteousness and beauty are a dangerous confection. They've produced some coldness at the centre of your sister's heart. I've sent her a letter, telling her how much I love her. Please don't reveal the contents of this one. She needs your help, Grace. Don't abandon her, no matter how often she seeks to reject you.

Give this watch to Hal. It belonged to my father. That boy is testimony to your love, Grace. Without you he would've shrivelled up. Whatever happens to him, now, he has lived. And for that I send you a father's gratitude.

These locks of hair, I would like you to bury at your mother's and Sue's grave. I'm afraid the boots are an old man's indulgence. Sorry they're a bit tacky. All I could get round here. But I wanted something I touched to touch my grandchild.

One last thing, darling Grace, I know the price rationality extracts from the soul. I, too,

451

followed the hard purity of logic, but as I reach my death I realize that the truth has always been just out of reach. You have been blessed with a powerful mind. Use it for good. Destroy your perfect wheat. Mankind cannot flourish under the dictatorship of science.

I love you. Always.

As her tears dropped onto the table, Grace didn't notice Fiona Cassell gather the letter and leave.

CHAPTER 98

'Why did you volunteer for this?' asked Sam. 'You had a brilliant career. Why take the risk?'

'You have no monopoly on risk, Sam,' replied Violi, taking a swig of water, lost in thought. Then he said, 'Thirty years ago, my older brother, Guido, was a brilliant public prosecutor. Some say fearless, others foolhardy. He went after Roberto Di Gambetta, who was then the heir apparent, on a rape charge. Di Gambetta had violated a young girl, no more than fourteen, in full view of six of his men, who of course saw nothing. Guido died in a *freak* accident, hit by an avalanche of rock on a small country road. With him was his wife, Sophia. She was six months pregnant.

'My other brother and I vowed we would do everything in our power to break the Gambetta family. The Gambettas have been allies of Standish and his ETA men for fifteen years. They are the brokers between the 'Ndrangheta and the Barracuda. So when the CIA approached me to go underground at the Standish Centre, I had no hesitation. I had no wife, no family. Now I find myself on the brink of taking Standish down, and with him Roberto Di Gambetta, I ask myself – what will I do when I no longer have hatred to fuel my world?'

'Fill it with something better.'

'Pain hollows you out, Sam. You know that. People like you and I have no capacity for love.'

'I used to believe that. But I refuse to be that person. I believe in redemption.'

Sam's thoughts drifted to Sergio, his hollow friend, ruined by an obsessive pursuit of the hydra-headed ETA, then he returned to his logic tree and followed Gitte's advice to think laterally.

Standish--------Malkie
Raul------------Sergio

Of course Raul knew Sergio and Malkie. He joined the dots differently and created a faint, dark, unsettling picture.

Standish----Raul-----Malkie-----Raul-----Sergio

Suspicions tumbled on top of one another. Sergio was in his flat when Sam was being set up. Sergio knew Fernandez, the Bilbao policeman. He knew about Sam's secret writing. And the gun. He knew about the gun. Oh, good God. He's living with Eileen. He hit the phone. No one there. Where was she?

He spoke to Lindsey. 'I need an APB on my

sister. Get someone outside the cottage 24/7. Try to track down her mobile. Also, find out Sergio Colinas' whereabouts.'

Malkie stuffed the pillow into his mouth until he was dizzy with suffocation. *There is only one answer. I must run. Take Lilly with me. But where? The Basque or the Barracuda will find me – and Lilly. And they'd kill Lilly in front of me. They'll slice her up slowly, just for fun.* He threw the pillow against the wall, his hands shaking.

'Christ, Roni. I'm sorry. I'm so sorry.'

Feverishly pulling clothes from drawers, he thrust them into two bags, then he glanced at the pregnancy kit he had scooped up from the lavatory at the Castle. *She had been pregnant. Roni had been having his child.*

'Run. Must run.'

A silver frame tumbled from the chest, the glass shattering on the wooden floor. He glanced down at the picture. It had been taken the day Lilly came home for the first time. Roni was exhausted, but beaming as she held her – their – baby. He slumped against the wall and closed his eyes. He saw again Roni's anguish, her anger and fear, the explosion that took her. *I killed her,* he thought. *I took my wife's life just as surely as if I'd put a gun to her head and pulled the trigger.* He felt for the pistol in his pocket. *It's the only answer. They won't touch Lilly if I'm dead. Sam'll protect her. It's the only answer.*

'Sam,' he yelled. 'Sam, I need you.'

The bedroom door pushed open and he looked up at Sam, who froze.

'Please look after Lilly for me,' said Malkie. 'She deserves more than I can give. Tell her I love her, Sam, and I wish I could've been more like you. Promise me, you'll adopt her.'

As Sam knelt and pleaded, 'Don't,' Malkie drove the pistol into his mouth and fired.

CHAPTER 99

That evening Sam sat by Malkie's body, the blinds drawn, the room mournful. Sam sighed and buried his face in his hands, exhaustion gnawing at him. At least Malkie was alive. Sam had taken the bullets from the gun when they'd arrived at the flat from Scotland, afraid that Malkie might make an attempt on his life. Malkie had passed out when he fired the weapon and had just woken. Sam had insisted that he take tranquillizers. He knew Malkie was traumatized and would remain so for years. When the strong crumble, all they see is dust.

Malkie looked into his eyes, then muttered weakly, 'Sergio wanted – wants – me to kill you, Sam.' He sipped water, then collapsed back into the pillows. 'You've saved my life and Lilly's. And still I'm supposed to assassinate you before the Basque will let me and my child live.'

Sam's spirit was heavy. Sergio had long been a friend, a good one. And yet he would sacrifice me for some abstract principle. He fingered his phone. Still nothing from Eileen. He could not believe that Sergio would harm her. Come on, Eileen. Phone me.

'Why did Sergio want to take me out?' he asked.

'I honestly don't know. Initially, he wanted me to kill Standish because he was talking to the CIA. Then the focus switched to you.'

'Did you know about these talks?' Sam asked Violi, who was sitting on a soft chair by the bed.

'Yes. He was offering us some serious fundamentalist terrorists in the US. They were the big prize. We were prepared to let him walk if he used his contacts to give us the renegade Saudis and their Barracuda suppliers.'

'But what about your brother? Revenge?'

'There are many ways to find vengeance.'

'But I still don't get it,' Sam rubbed his right arm. 'We have no real issue with ETA in this country. There are still some residual links with IRA dissidents, but nothing that would involve me.'

'What am I going to do, Sam?' asked Malkie.

Sam looked down at his haggard, drawn face.

'You must die, Malkie.'

Henry sweated as he stumbled on a root, but still he pressed on, his hands burning from nettle rash, his face pocked by scrapes, hair matted. All night, the helicopters had circled, searchlights probing. He'd retreated to Cain's Marsh, knowing its winding, hidden trails, understanding its deceitful waters.

Even the locals seldom ventured into the interior. If he could, he'd stay in his retreat for ever. But he had to take his own life in his own time. He owed himself that.

They were coming for him again. He could hear them sloshing around in the shallows, their torches flashing. Then silence. He could sense them now, quietly gathering in a circle. He retreated into a crack in a rock wall, a fissure not much bigger than his body. Pressing himself against the stone, he held his breath.

'Dad.' He heard Grace's voice. Must be in his head. 'You've got to give yourself up. We need you. We need you to help us. No one else can.'

I'm of no use to anyone. No good. I told you that in my letter.

'It's over, Dad.' He felt her soft fingers on his cheek. 'Over.'

She took his hand and he tumbled from the rock, staring at the blackened faces of CIA agents.

'We've got Badger. Repeat, Badger is in trap,' an American voice called. He was helped to his feet, walked through the shallows towards a helicopter then thrust inside.

Grace hugged him close.

'We're going home, Dad.'

CHAPTER 100

Standish drove his horse through thickets. His anonymous correspondent had promised him Malcolm – that treacherous bastard. Standish had punished Raul for Malkie's escape by sending him to Scotland. And now Raul was dead. When he'd finished torturing Collins, his last breath would be the one he'd welcome most.

He broke into a clearing near a hut, Lottie and Louis behind. Louis's face was contorted with pain, his slashed leg encased in bandages. But still he'd ridden with him. Good man. He'd enjoy killing Collins slowly. It was nearly nine, the appointed moment. He looked up and saw a horseman negotiating a path that snaked down the hill beyond.

'It's Delawney,' said Lottie, handing him binoculars.

What does he want? Standish had still to confront him about the deal. That moment would come and it would be pleasurable. I might force him to sign over his beloved House to me. I might return and live here someday. The Syrian's untraceable bonds will pay for five years of restless movement, shifting identities and plastic surgery. By the time I return, the world will be a very different place.

'I see we've been invited to a concert party,' said Delawney, reining his chestnut stallion and dismounting.

'Mutual friend, obviously.'

Delawney's face flushed. The letter that had arrived the previous evening had told him bluntly that Standish would be informed about the land deal unless he showed up at Henry's old hut at nine. His stomach churned as he saw Standish already there.

The hut door opened and Henry, looking tired and frightened, appeared. 'Gentlemen, thank you for coming. Please join me.'

Standish nodded to his bodyguards, who backed first against the door, then slipped inside.

'I think you might want to see this,' Lottie shouted.

'Clear,' yelled Louis from his place at the back.

As Standish entered, it took a second for his eyes to adjust to the gloom, then focus on the figure on a chair next to the fire. He grinned. It was Collins, trussed like a Thanksgiving turkey, thick tape wrapped across his mouth.

'Mercy me. What have we here?'

'My gift,' said Henry. 'For a small price.'

Delawney's heart beat furiously as he looked into Collins' flat eyes. He rubbed his palms together vigorously.

'And what can I give you for such a jewel?' asked Standish.

'A way of explaining away the half-million bribe I took for signing over the university's land to the centre,' said Henry.

'You old fool,' exclaimed Delawney. 'What bribe? It was a perfectly legitimate deal assigned by the council.'

'Halliwell kept the papers outlining the true valuation. They're in a safe deposit box in Garton. Eventually, Mrs Halliwell's lawyer will unearth them. And a detailed account about your drugs operation.'

'How do you know all this?' asked Standish.

'That's why I . . . killed him.'

Silence.

'So it was you,' whispered Delawney.

'I think I can accommodate you, Mr Adams,' said Standish, with a smile. 'How about a letter acknowledging that I had discussed the issue with the Chairman and the Head of the Planning Committee and was willing to pay a premium over and above the price I'd already offered?'

Delawney smiled with relief, he was off the hook. Then he glanced at Standish and knew that for him there would be a heavy price to pay.

'The half million is yours to keep,' said Standish. 'Call it a finder's fee. I'll put it through our accounts as consultancy. I'm afraid, however, the others will have to return the stolen funds.' He smiled at Delawney. 'With considerable interest.'

He turned towards Malkie and whispered, 'Now, may I have my prize?'

As Henry nodded, Standish ripped the tape from Malkie's mouth, then spat in his face.

'Louis. Do you have your knife with you?'

'Ready and waiting.'

'I believe you have a delayed date with Malcolm's tongue.'

'Fuck you,' spat Malkie.

'Infamous last words.'

Henry stepped in front of Highfield as he unsheathed a long, wicked-looking blade. 'You must think clearly about this,' he said to Standish.

'Get out of my way, old man.'

'The Eastfield bomber didn't deface anyone's body. We want Collins' death to be part of the bomber's modus operandi. The police mustn't find anything unusual.'

Standish regarded him with an amused eye. The man had hidden talent.

Henry opened Collins' jacket and revealed a dozen sticks of dynamite attached to his body.

'I've put quicklime beneath him, a clear echo of Halliwell's killing. Be sensible.'

Standish's desire for inflicting precise, controlled pain on Raul's killer battled with his need not to compromise his deal with the CIA. He needed their help to disappear before the Syrian's plans clicked into place. And he could tell the Basque that he'd taken revenge on Collins. Silence flooded the room as he brooded.

'You're right, Mr Adams. Very wise. How are you planning to detonate this?'

'Remotely. At the end of this –' Henry tugged at a long thin wire snaking out of the door – 'is the detonator.'

'Very ingenious.'

Standish leant down and whispered in Malkie's ear. 'For what it's worth, Roni was a lousy fuck. We both had her. She was just another lousy junkie lay. Deserved to die.'

He inhaled the pain he saw in Malcolm's eyes, turned and left, Delawney trailing in his wake.

As they reached the door, Standish stopped. 'One problem, Mr Adams. I'm afraid you're surplus to requirements.'

'What?'

'I can't trust you, unlike your son-in-law. From what I hear, you're pretty unstable. I'm afraid I must rescind my offer. You make a very plausible bomber. And with your fingermarks all over this hut, I think the police would be able to close the book very easily on this case. No, I think you must stay and commit suicide. Lottie. Do what's necessary.'

Lottie's kick snapped Henry's head and he tumbled unconscious into the sitting room.

Delawney felt trapped as the cords tightened around him. Now he was party to Hope's father's death. He sweated. What could he do? Nothing. Nothing.

'Ready?' asked Standish, as they sheltered behind the trees.

Highfield held up the plunger.

'Kill the bastard.'

He depressed the button. No response.

'Do it again.'

Once more his thumb hit the red knob. Again, no response.

'Damn it. The old fool. Why did I think he was up to this? Back to plan A, Louis.'

As he hobbled across the clearing, the hut exploded, flames shooting up like fingers, consuming leaves and grass, tumbling him over. Standish mounted his horse and trotted into the woods without a backward look. It was time to disappear.

CHAPTER 101

Al Imam analysed Standish's news that Sergio Colinas planned to destroy the Queen Elizabeth II Centre. Allah had sent a new opportunity.

His niece pushed the wheelchair along the Cornish beachfront and stopped on a pathway overlooking the sea. Al Imam listened to the birds and the waves, breathed the scents of the wet beach, and recalled childhood games among the gritty sands of Aleppo. The warmth of the sun on his face restored his spirits. Preparing for death was an art, he concluded.

'Have you ever heard of caesium 137?' he asked.

'Can't say I have,' said Standish, sitting on a green bench next to him.

'It's a radioactive metal. In 1995, Chechen separatists left a 32k dirty bomb containing caesium 137 in Moscow's Ismailovsky Park. They didn't detonate it. Simply offered it as a warning. A similar amount of caesium left with the ETA bomb would contaminate a large part of central London.'

'Colinas'd never do that. ETA would be destroyed without mercy. They would lose all support in their homeland.'

'The world would have another focus for its hatred and under that cover our project would flourish.'

'But . . .'

'You can see the logic of what I'm saying, my dear Mr Standish.'

Pause.

'Clearly.'

'And with ETA gone and Colinas exposed and captured, you would have little to fear.'

Al Imam broke a piece of dark chocolate and placed it in his mouth, where it sweetened his parched tongue. His children must have time to grow undisturbed. Let chaos reign around them.

'You will find a suitcase in Room 312 at the Ritz. Can you arrange for it to be placed in an advantageous location?'

Standish stared at the sun glittering on the waves and nodded. 'Fly away, fly away over the sea,' he hummed.

CHAPTER 102

Grace was worn out but couldn't sleep. Each time she closed her eyes, she saw again her father's hut explode and felt anew the rush of fear. Someday he would die. Not like that, though. Thank God. After the explosion, Sam, Violi and she had hauled Malkie and Henry from a makeshift reinforced cellar below the hut and had stowed them in a motel near London where Violi's people were looking after them.

She sat in her study staring at the computer screen, trying to focus. She needed to work in order to quell the shivering she felt in her bones. Besides, she was curious as she loaded up more of Alaina's data. How close had she come to understanding 'Perfect Wheat'? Burrowing into the numbers, she stopped abruptly as a heavily passworded file blocked her. What was there? She phoned Lindsey, who took over the computer online and ran a hacking sequence that broke the code.

Grace peered at the shape of the molecule, then rubbed her eyes. Can't be, she thought. It's impossible. She retraced her steps, calculating quickly in her head. There it was again. What could it mean?

'Gitte. Come quickly. I need you.'

'Explain it again,' said Sam urgently.

'Look,' Grace said, stabbing the screen with her finger. 'They've taken my seeds, then subtly altered the DNA by inserting a poisonous compound called ptaquiloside. It's found in bracken.'

'What's the problem with that?' asked Violi.

'Bracken can cause stomach cancer if you eat it in any quantity. It's a serious problem in Japan, where bracken tips are a delicacy.'

'But surely this'll be found out at the test stage?' said Sam.

'Not if the "Perfect Wheat" technology has already passed the most stringent of tests. It's possible to disguise these traits and then activate them in subsequent generations of the wheat.' She stared at the screen. 'But I don't understand. What did they intend to do with this research?'

Violi shook his head. 'Standish has been working on something that even I didn't know about. But this beats me. I don't get it.'

'I can tell you something,' said Gitte, her voice tight. 'If ptaquiloside is disguised in GM wheat and gets into the food-supply chain, it'll kill millions.'

Violi grabbed his mobile and called his boss. 'I don't care if he's meeting God himself,' he hissed when told that Ruttger was with the President, 'get him.' He turned to Sam. 'We *must* find Standish.'

'No,' replied Sam, staring at the screen, 'we must destroy this research.'

CHAPTER 103

Violi pushed Gitte, bound hand and foot, through the front door of Alaina's flat. She tumbled to the floor and curled into a foetal position.

'What are you doing?' asked Alaina, rushing to pick up her dazed girlfriend. 'Are you OK, my darling?' She tugged down the gag and Gitte snarled 'Leave me be.'

'She's got your copy of the Doomsday Codes,' said Violi.

Alaina's eyes flicked to the DNA model on her fireplace. 'Impossible.'

Violi held up the file. 'She's been in contact with the National Crime Squad. We checked her phone calls. We must abort. Standish's orders.'

Her face blanched and she bit nervously at her lip. The database contained so many incriminating thefts of other people's research. And, she thought, my own glittering career will be revealed as the fraud it is. I was the harvester of other people's genius. But what about the Syrian? She could not let him down. He was a man of integrity. She thought of her parents, both brilliant mathematicians reduced to selling their clothes on the street when that wretched fool Yeltsin had let in the American advisers and devastated her beloved country – impoverishing her writers, her philosophers and her scientists. Surely, they could not give up the wheat.

'I need to speak to Johnny.'

'Do you have a secure line?' asked Violi.

'Yes. We have a direct link. Someone staffs it 24/7. Wherever Johnny is, they'll find him. It's also the number that activates the Doomsday process.'

'Do it. Quickly.'

With a glance at Gitte, Alaina dialled from a phone in her study. As she did so, the CIA's best crackers traced the number and an actor trained to sound exactly like Standish waited to respond to her.

Gitte lashed out at Violi and he slapped her.

'No. Don't,' shouted Alaina. 'Please. Leave her.'

'Have it your way,' growled Violi. They had bought more precious seconds as his colleagues rerouted the call. 'Come on. Let's get this over with. I don't intend to go to jail. Kill the data.'

Alaina heard Standish say, 'Yes? What is it? Is that you, Alaina?' The actor precisely mimicked Standish's idiosyncratic vowels.

'Violi's here. He says you want to activate Doomsday.'

'I'm afraid we must. The NCS and the CIA are on to us. We must destroy the evidence.'

'But . . .'

'No buts. Just do as Violi tells you.'

'Oh God, not everything? What about the "Perfect Wheat"? We're very close to breaking Grace. One more push and we'll give the Syrian what he needs.'

'There'll be another day. Do as I say.'

She nodded, closed the connection, and then joined Violi at her desktop.

'It'll take me a few minutes to get through security.' She realized she was weeping as she gazed into a retina-checker. She wiped her eyes, then placed her thumb on an electronic pad that relayed her unique print to the security sensor, then finally the computer asked –

DO YOU WANT TO ACTIVATE THE DOOMSDAY CODES?

'I wish to activate the Doomsday Codes,' she replied. Two thousand miles away in Manila a program analysed the data, cross-referenced the voice, print and iris and sent back a message.

WHAT ARE YOUR PASSWORDS?

In Cyrillic she typed the revolutionary slogan, All Power to the Soviets, then sat back, knowing that her work was being chewed up, dissected and destroyed. The West would continue as before. She glanced at Gitte and pain seared through her.

I could've been great, she thought. I had the talent. I could've made it on my own. A tear slid down her cheek. But I wanted it all. And Johnny had promised to make it all possible. Even revenge.

The computer screen noted,

DOOMSDAY COMPLETE.

Violi hugged her.

'Well done,' he said. 'I know that was tough. I've made arrangements for your departure. At twelve fifteen a plane will take you to Portsmouth, where you'll join a chartered yacht that'll take you across the Channel. From there, you'll pick up a new passport and a commercial flight to Manila, where a cruise ship is waiting. I want you to contact the network, they'll take care of you.'

'Thank you,' she said, her heart racing.

She knelt beside Gitte, touched her cheek and said, 'I'm so sorry. I wish it could've been different. I loved you. I wish I could explain about my mother and father. You would have understood. You would have loved me.'

'Go, quickly,' Violi urged her. 'I'll deal with her.'

'Please, don't hurt her. I couldn't bear that.'

'Don't worry. She won't suffer.'

Alaina turned towards the door. 'Thank you,' she said, and left.

'Are we on her tail?' asked Violi on his cellphone.

'Sure are,' replied Julie.

He knelt and quickly untied Gitte.

'You were great.'

The Doomsday Codes burrowed like a neural mole. But instead of devouring information, the CIA crackers sucked the data into a server farm in Colorado. Sam sat back. At least they had the information somewhere safe. But who was the Syrian? And what did he want with carcinogenic wheat? He called Violi.

'Well done.'

'Thanks. Your idea. I just carried it out.' Violi sounded anxious.

'Who is the Syrian?' asked Sam.

'Don't know. We've got people on Alaina's tail. Let's hope they turn something up.'

'Pick her up, Stef. She's all we've got.'

CHAPTER 104

Sam peered again at the digital pictures. Although they were crystal clear, it was impossible to make out the face of the man talking to Standish: his eyes were covered in large sunglasses, and a white silk scarf was pulled across his face. Was he the Syrian?

A CIA agent had taken the images from his perch on a fishing boat. The agency had been keeping increasingly close tabs on Standish since the attack on Malkie. Although Standish was still dangling a deal in front of his handler, the careless and personal nature of the assault suggested that Standish was preparing to run. The information about the mysterious Syrian made it even more important that they maintain contact. Violi had told Sam that even the CIA top brass was nervous of Standish's real intentions.

On the PC screen, Sam enhanced the man's emaciated hand as it reached back to touch the woman pushing his wheelchair. Was she a nurse of some kind? She was wearing a veil, and a long black dress.

'Lindsey. Do a check on every clinic in London.

We need information on all registered patients, then we must match the names against Syrian databases.'

'Will do.'

'I'll be back in ten.'

Alaina Prokovitch sat on a plain wooden chair. Her heart was racing, but she willed herself to be calm.

Sam entered and joined Stef Violi.

'We know about the wheat, Alaina,' said Sam. 'We need to know the name of the Syrian.'

I'm sure you do. But why would I tell you? Her tongue flicked and dug at the back of a molar, a thin plastic membrane covering the cyanide inside.

'We have all of the information from your computer, Alaina. It's only a matter of time.'

Time is what the Syrian has. He knows enough to continue even without Grace's wheat. He'll find another way. She had given him options with her work on the bracken. That was high-class research. As good as Grace's. Better.

Flick, flick.

She pictured the day she had found her father dead in front of the fire, pills littering the table next to the bottle of expensive lemon vodka she had sent him. On his lap was Chekhov's *Lady with a Lapdog*. In the bedroom, her mother had been laid out in her graduation gown. Another triumph for the West.

Flick. There it is. She could feel it now. It had

been there for so long, waiting for this day. She smuggled the capsule into her cheek. Only two people outside his circle knew of the Syrian, she and Standish. And Johnny would disappear. Once he realizes he cannot contact me he'll go into hiding. The Syrian will be safe if I do not talk.

'Sam.' Lindsey put her head round the door.

Alaina tipped her neck back, allowing the capsule to roll into her throat, then dropped her head, feeling it against the back of her teeth, then she bit hard. The sweet taste flooded her senses, then the cyanide-seizure exploded in her brain.

'Oh, Christ,' said Violi as Alaina collapsed on the table. He hit the phone. 'Crash unit. Crash unit.'

Sam ran his finger down the list.

'No recognizable name?'

'None on Interpol, CIA, NCS or FBI databases,' said Lindsey. 'I had an idea, though. Cross-checked the names against trains and buses to Cornwall.'

'And?'

'Nothing.'

'Damn.'

'On the other hand . . .' She produced a credit card receipt. 'Someone by the name of Fatima Al Imam bought fifty quid's worth of petrol at an Esso place on the A39. And,' she circled a name on the clinic list, 'there's a Burhan Al Imam registered at the Harley Street Hospital.'

'What's he got?'

She ran her finger across the page.

'Stomach cancer.'

'I know that name,' he said. He did a quick online search and came up with ten thousand references to Burhan. 'The guy's practically a modern saint. What's he doing with Standish?'

'Only one way to find out, Guv. Let's go ask him.'

Sam, dressed as a postman courtesy of his American cousins, knocked on the door of Burhan's white house in Regent's Park.

'No answer,' he whispered into a microphone on his lapel.

'We've got heat sensors aimed at the building. No warm bodies,' replied Violi from a van parked around fifteen metres away.

'Neighbours say that he was taken away in an ambulance last night. Not returned yet,' said Lindsey, who was holding a clipboard and conducting a market-research survey at other houses in the street. 'I'm going in the back door. I'll deal with security. See you inside.'

A few minutes later, Sam stood in Burhan's study, ran his fingers across the desktop, then sniffed the air. It had been professionally cleaned – practically airbrushed.

'The Syrian bird has taken wing,' said Lindsey.

Sam stared at the bound volumes of GM research reports on the fourth shelf of the library. Then he looked at the neat pile of papers on the desk, sifting quickly for something unusual among the articles on development economics, Arabic poetry and German philosophy. His eye alighted on a broker's report for Aventis, the agribusiness acquired by Saudi businessmen a few days before. Why would a short-story writer have such a report?

I need some answers. Go for the weakest link. Delawney.

'Guv,' said Lindsey, listening to a message on her phone, 'we've tracked down your mate, Sergio.'

'Where?' His stomach muscles crunched.

'He's riding shotgun for Trevor at the Security Conference. Apparently, the Spanish insisted.'

He'd forgotten all about the Conference. This was to be the night the PM announced the launch of the European Anti-Terrorist Unit, and that he was to be the first DG. Now he knew why Sergio wanted him disgraced or dead.

CHAPTER 105

Malkie lay in a pitch-black hotel room, his head throbbing and the smell of explosives still on his body after a multitude of showers. He popped more antidepressants, chased by two powerful painkillers. In the other bed, Henry groaned and held his head. Christ, that had been touch and go. He should've anticipated that Johnny wouldn't leave Henry as a witness, but he hadn't been thinking straight. In the minute available, he'd managed to shear his bonds with the concealed blade, then drag Henry down to the basement and the makeshift bomb shelter.

At least he was now officially dead. Sam would get him into a witness-protection programme when this was over. The Basque would never find him.

The phone rang. It was Sam.

'How's the head?'

'Playing techno-thrash.'

'Do you know who else Sergio saw apart from Standish when he was here?'

'Give me a context.'

'Sergio is second in command of security at the Anti-Terrorist Conference in London. What's he up to? It's connected with his trying to kill me. He didn't want me as his partner. I was supposed to run protection for the PM.'

'I don't know, Sam. He didn't mention the conference.'

'Did he see anyone unexpected?'

Malkie thought, trying to untie the previous few weeks, to make sense of them. 'Delawney. He saw Delawney.'

'Why would he do that? Did they have business together?'

'No. Never. His people were couriers. That's all.'

'Did Delawney have a legitimate contract with the Conference Centre?'

'Dunno, Sam. It's possible.'

'They're out to attack the conference. But with what? If they have penetrated security, what're they carrying?'

'Could be anything. Sarin. Anthrax. Bombs. Christ, Sam, the possibilities are endless. These days you could carry a thermonuclear device in a truck and still have room for a hundred kilos of Granny Smiths. I'm coming to help you.'

'No. Stay there. You're dead.'

'And dead men don't bite,' said Malkie, bitterly.

Sam and Violi rode a helicopter towards Eastfield House, Lindsey scanning data on her laptop.

'Got it, Sam. Eastfield Organics have had a

contract to supply fruit to the Conference Centre for the past two years.'

His head spun with possibilities. 'Check whether an Eastfield van has delivered in the past few days.'

He hit a speed dial number. 'Jo. It's Sam.'

'Oh, my God, Sam. Are you all right?'

'Fine. Get me Ian. Emergency. I don't care where he is. Track him down.'

'He's not going to believe you,' said Violi.

'I can try,' said Sam. 'I must.'

Ian Trevor waited in the wings wearing his dress uniform, medals marching across his chest. Beside him stood the PM, composed, head bowed, people whispering in his ear. The King was on his other side, surrounded by a contingent of Spanish security. In Trevor's earpiece, voices chattered – everyone on full alert. He was confident he had everything under control and in ten minutes he would step out and introduce the PM and the rehearsal would be over. In another hour, he'd do the real thing.

Fiona Cassell whispered in his ear. 'I've got Sam Copeland on the phone.'

He grabbed the receiver. 'Where are you, lad? You've got a lot of explaining to do.'

'Did Sergio Colinas feed you any information that compromised me?'

'Just come in, Sam. We'll sort this out.'

'Answer me, Ian. Did Sergio compromise me?'

483

'Just get your arse to the nearest syndicate and turn yourself in. I'm not answering any questions.'

'Listen closely, Ian. Sergio Colinas is a double agent. He works for ETA. He's planning something big at the Conference. Something serious. You must, I repeat, must track him down.'

'For your information, Colinas returned to Spain this afternoon on urgent business. I don't know what fantasy life you're living, Copeland, but you're doing no good out there. Come in. We'll talk.'

'Hang on,' said Sam, 'I've got someone I want to speak to you.'

'Guv. It's Lindsey. Sam's right. There's something hooky. Get everyone checking for a van labelled Eastfield Organics.'

'What are you doing there with him?' Ian asked incredulously.

'He's innocent, sir. You must trust me.'

What the hell was going on here? 'Fiona,' he turned. 'Get me double the number of officers. I want this place tighter than a duck's arse. Check for anything remotely suspicious. Clear the area of vehicles for half a mile around.'

This conference is going ahead, he thought grimly. And no bugger is going to stop it.

CHAPTER 106

Hope Delawney stood back in shock as Sam with two companions entered the hall. He had been top of the news for the past two nights. 'A renegade copper', the newspapers called him. She'd never really liked Sam. Grace could do much better if she'd only try.

'Where's Freddie?' asked Sam.

'I'm afraid . . .' Her words trailed off as Lindsey produced her warrant card and said, 'We need to speak to him urgently.'

'He's in Paris. A symposium on sustainable agriculture. I'll be sure to ask him to get in touch.'

Sam ran for the stairs.

'Come back here,' Hope shouted as Violi and Lindsey followed. 'This is *my* house.'

Sam found Freddie in his study.

'Copeland. How are you?' asked the Earl, rising unsteadily from his chair. 'I hear you're in a spot of trouble.'

'Not as much as you,' said Sam.

He turned to Hope, who'd appeared at his arm. 'Rustle up some coffee.'

'Don't take that tone—'

'Now,' Sam ordered. 'Lindsey. Go with her. See if she knows anything. Do your guys know where Standish is?' he asked Stef.

Sam watched Delawney wince at the sound of Standish's name.

'To the inch.'

'Have your guys pick him up. See what he can tell us.'

A young woman, Sara's replacement as Hope's assistant, brought in coffee and said, 'The Countess has retired to her rooms.'

'What's going on with Sergio?' asked Sam.

'Who?'

'Don't have time for this, Freddie. Sergio Colinas is an ETA agent. He has done some kind of deal with you. It involves your couriers.'

'Don't know what you're talking about. Never heard of the man. Would you like a drink? I've a lovely Montrachet.'

'Drink your coffee, Delawney. You're going to need it. The Earl is going on a trip. Get Ruttger to phone the PM's office,' he said to Violi. 'He must listen to sense.'

Sam joined Violi in the rabbit warren inside the QEII Conference Centre. Delawney's face was red with anger.

'The VIPs are due up in a few minutes. We don't have time for bullshit. Where is it?' Violi hissed.

'Get me out of here,' pleaded Delawney. He'd known nothing about the bomb until Standish had told him that morning. He had been told that his couriers were simply carrying 'a special assignment'. Oh Christ, what have I done?

'You're here until I know what Sergio sent in your van. Where is the load?' Sam checked his watch. Why was Trevor delaying the evacuation? He phoned Lindsey. 'Ian's not listening, Sam,' she said. 'He doesn't believe that anyone could've broken his security ring. He's sent the Bomb Squad and sniffer dogs in, but they haven't found anything. And he's convinced the PM that he can't give in to terrorism.'

'Is he mad?' hissed Sam.

He turned again to Delawney. 'This is simple. You'll die here unless you tell me what's going on.'

'I have no idea what you're talking about,' he replied. 'Now get me out of here.'

'Malkie told us about the side deal you made with the Basque.' Violi grabbed Delawney by the throat. 'Now, tell us where it is?'

Delawney's face was pale and wretched, then tears rolled down his cheeks.

Sam checked his watch again. Seven o'clock. He heard the strains of the National Anthem and pictured his colleagues on their feet, waiting for the PM to open the conference.

'Get me out of here,' pleaded Delawney.

'You're not going to tell us, are you?'

Sam turned to Stef. 'Let's go. We're out of here.'

'Now you're talking sense, Copeland,' said Delawney.

Sam extracted a pair of handcuffs from his coat pocket, then he dragged Delawney across to a heating pipe and cuffed him to it.

'What the hell?' he screamed.

'No one else'll ever know, Stef,' said Sam. 'Only you and I will know that one of the victims of this catastrophe had committed suicide. Poetic justice for Malkie and Henry. Let's go.'

'You wouldn't,' said Delawney as Sam and Violi ran towards the stairs. When they reached the door, Delawney shouted, 'I want a deal. D'you hear me? A deal.'

Sam turned. 'Where is it?'

'What's the deal?' asked Delawney, his eyes wide.

'You get to live. Now, where is it?'

Delawney looked deep into Sam's eyes, appraising, assessing, then his spark faded.

'It's nitro, hidden in apples. Eastfield organic apples,' he said. 'Green boxes. Look for bright green boxes.'

Sam glanced again at his watch. Five past. The Spanish National Anthem was playing. The King would be speaking in a few minutes. Sergio would have made sure that the bomb went off with maximum advantage. He hauled a wooden crate into the middle of the floor and filled it with paper.

'You got your cigars?' he asked Violi.

'Yeah, here.'

488

'Give me your lighter.'

Sam poured cooking oil onto the crate, tossed in the cigars, then the burning lighter. Seconds later the sprinkler system kicked in, as did a wailing alarm. The evacuation would begin. Now.

Sam ran towards the kitchens, talking to Lindsey on the phone. 'Where are the storerooms? Where would they stockpile fruit?'

She checked on the electronic map of the building.

'There's a cool room on the ground floor – G4. That's the fruit room. But get out of there, Sam. If it's nitro, anything unstable will set it off. Please back off. Everyone's running for the exit.'

He ran into the corridor and stopped at the door to G4. It was padlocked. He pulled out his Glock and fired, shattering the metal; then he shouldered his way into the room. The couriers were slumped in the corner. Then he saw the boxes. Dozens of them. Enough nitro to take out half a city block.

'How would they detonate it?' he asked Lindsey. There was a momentary silence on the other end of the line then she appeared behind him carrying a remote scanner. 'Got it from one of the Bomb Squad guys.'

She turned it on and pointed it at the boxes. 'The initial bomb won't be big, but it's still lethal on its own.'

The machine emitted one beep and then a series. 'There. Top centre. Small metal box. Crude timer.

Two minutes to go. Christ, what's that suitcase on top?'

'Does it contain explosives?'

She ran the scanner. 'No.'

He flipped it open.

'Oh my God.' Her hands flew to her mouth as she saw the caesium wrapped in clear plastic. 'It's a dirty bomb.'

As Sam rushed to gather the detonator, she whispered, 'Careful, Sam. Tip over any of those boxes and the timer'll be unnecessary.'

'Please go,' he insisted. 'Now.'

As she dragged one of the couriers to safety, Sam knelt on the bottom layer of cases, then crawled to the top and grabbed the detonator. A minute left. He huddled it into his body like a rugby ball and ran.

The stairs seemed endless, his breath laboured. Up one flight, then another, searching for an exit. He kicked open a door and stepped onto a balcony. As fifty guns held him in their crosshairs, he threw the bomb into the air and collapsed to the concrete, bullets peppering the walls around him.

CHAPTER 107

Ian Trevor slumped in the corner of his office, his tie loose, jacket undone, medals on the desk in front of him next to his resignation letter. Sam fretted by the window. Where was Eileen? Police forces all over the UK and Europe had pictures of her and of Sergio. He knew Sergio would go to ground as effectively as he had done himself. But Sergio was the key to Standish, and Standish the key to Burhan. The CIA and the FBI were already on the case with the Aventis deal, tracking down the men behind the operation. But, of course, it was clean. No crime had been committed.

Desperately Sam dialled Eileen's mobile phone number yet again. One ring. Two. Three. Four . . . Then his sister's distinctive voice said, 'Look, Sam. You can tell Sergio to get stuffed. I'm not coming back to London even if he does apologize.'

'Eileen? Are you OK? Where are you?'

'I'm in a cab on my way home. And you can tell Sergio that I'm not one of his Spanish doormats. He can – well, frankly he can p.i.s.s. off.' She cut the connection.

He redialled. 'Where is he?' he asked.

'Isn't he with you? He told me you and he were due to meet at seven and that I was to go home and wait. He dismissed me, Sam, as if I were a servant.'

'I haven't seen him. Where were you staying?'

'The Langham Hilton. Room 226.'

Sam ran for the door, closely followed by Lindsey and Violi.

The hotel corridor stretched and curved as they edged along it, not knowing what Sergio had in store for them. By now Sergio would know his assassination attempt had failed and he would be either on the run or dead. The Basque would not tolerate his catastrophic failure and would be looking for scapegoats and traitors. The money Lindsey had placed in Sergio's bank account would be difficult to explain. ETA would be told by the Spanish double agents that it was a pay-off and enough of them would believe it.

Squad detectives fanned out and waited whilst Lindsey using a fibre-optic camera checked on activity inside the room.

'Two people on the bed. They're not moving. Nothing else happening,' she said.

Bobby ordered up a sniffer dog to check the door for explosives. The handler gave a thumbs up.

'OK, let's go,' said Sam.

One of the men attached a small explosive charge to the door, trusting that the shock and diversion would give them a crucial few seconds of surprise.

'Go,' ordered Sam, his back to the wall.

As the dust rose from the explosion, they rushed into the suite, guns ready. 'Clear,' echoed voices as they searched the rooms.

On the bed were Lottie Grun and Louis Highfield. Both had been garrotted and deep, red welts bit into their necks.

'Sam.' Violi pointed to an envelope. 'Something for you.'

Sam picked it up, recognized Sergio's cramped writing, and moved to slit the seal.

'No chance,' said Lindsey, 'not until we've run a thorough check on it. God knows what could be in there. Don't want to lose you to anthrax. It's been a busy day already.'

He looked at Standish's dead bodyguards. ETA would hunt Sergio down and his punishment would be long and painful. Assuming they could ever find him.

Sam stood by the window in his office and read Sergio's letter.

My Dearest Sam,

We have been friends for many years. Good friends, I believe. But there is an intense love beyond friendship. My love for my country and my people is my deepest commitment. You will not understand. You're far too rational, my friend, to feel the intensity of the oppressed.

You must also believe me, Sam. We had no intention of setting a dirty bomb. We have no moral difficulties killing the men and women oppressing our people, but we have no animosity towards the English people. We were betrayed.

This has been a strange and difficult period in my life. In my heart I love you, but I ordered Collins to kill you. I hear from others that Collins is dead. The world will not mourn. Drug dealers deserve no more.

Killing you is rational, Sam. When you think about it, you will understand. At first I thought merely discrediting you would be sufficient. I did not want you running security for the conference. You are too good. But when I heard that you would be offered the European anti-terrorism job, I knew I had to act. You will take the post, I know you will. And you will be excellent. Again my heart wishes to spare you, but I'm afraid I must continue to pursue my mission. I cannot let you hunt my people down.

You must understand, Sam. As long as I live your family will be safe. But if I die, you must resign. My friends will come after them. I salute your attempt to smear me. It was clever. But it won't work. My brothers and sisters know me. They believe in me. And I in them. Together we are strong. Together we will liberate our homeland.

Give my love to Grace and, in particular, to

494

your lovely sister. I was rude to her. I wanted
her out of London and harm's way. I must go
now. As you see I leave death behind me. They
came at Standish's instigation.

 With respect and regret,
 Sergio.

Sam handed the letter to Lindsey who bagged it and sent it to forensics for further analysis.

'Ian has handed in his resignation,' said the General. 'Will you take over as director general on a temporary basis?'

Sam stared out into the afternoon, then turned back to the General.

'I've something to do first.'

CHAPTER 108

Al Burhan found it difficult to breathe, the oxygen barely reaching his starved lungs. He had heard the news about Aventis and that the policeman, Copeland, was an international hero. But none of my people have been touched, he thought. They have nothing on us. I have planted an intellectual seed and it will grow.

The room in the Damascene hospital was small and quiet. Darkness settled peacefully in the air. He smiled at his niece. I will die surrounded by love. Allah be praised.

The door opened and a cleaner entered, noisily rattling a plastic bucket on the wooden floor.

'No, no.' His niece ushered him out. 'It's late. Leave him. Do it in the morning, please.'

The cleaner looked at her, then pulled her into him and thrust a pistol into her mouth, breaking her front teeth.

'No,' pleaded Burhan. 'She's innocent.'

'Innocence is relative in warfare,' said Sergio. 'I thought you knew that.' He pulled a pillow from a chair by the bed, placed it in front of her face and fired twice into the back of her skull.

Burhan struggled to reach her as she dropped to the floor, her eyes wide with shock and despair.

Sergio lifted the body and placed it at the bottom of the bed, then turned and locked the door.

'Kill me,' groaned Burhan. 'Kill me.'

Sergio turned off the oxygen mask and gathered up the painkillers into a bag.

'You will die tonight. But I will not kill you.'

Pain surged through Burhan's body as the cancer began its last assault.

CHAPTER 109

Three Months Later
Rio, Brazil

Standish lay on the operating table for his second operation. His nose was to be flattened and his eyes narrowed. Already the first bout of surgery had taken ten years off his face. This one would make him look Spanish, from the plains where the Moors and the Spanish interbred. He would live there.

He was calm as the bustle around him settled and the anaesthetist came over to gas him. He looked up and smiled, then his brow furrowed. He'd never seen this one before. The doctor dropped his mask and Standish saw that it was Sergio. He tried to yell, to warn the surgeon, but no words would come.

The mask was strapped over his face and he held his breath until he was dizzy, then he began to breathe in the poison. He choked and vomited, but still no one came to his rescue. They stood watching. 'He deserved it,' said the surgeon, turning to the door.

Standish clutched at his throat, pulling at the

mask, feeling himself dragged into oblivion. Suddenly, he gulped air and woke up, sobbing as he realized he was in bed in the clinic. Oh Christ, it was just another dream. He'd had them each night since he'd heard of the Syrian's death.

He lay back on the bed. In time these nightmares would go. The Syrian's money would see to that.

A match struck in the darkness. He sat upright, reaching for the gun by his bed. Gone. Oh Jesus. It's Colinas.

The intruder lit a candle and Standish saw the face appear through the flickering light.

'Hello, Johnny,' said Malkie. 'You've been a hard man to find.'

CHAPTER 110

Eighteen Months Later
White Hill Farm

'C'mon,' Hal shouted. 'It's time for the annual Sparky challenge.'

'Noo,' chorused Ruth and Lilly.

'You are a chump, darling,' said Sara, Sam, her year-old son, laughing in her arms.

'Oh yes, Sammy,' said Hal. 'Today your dad will tame the beast.'

Sparky backed into a corner as Hal saddled her. 'OK, Sparks, you old sow. Here we go.'

Soulman, Grace's horse, trotted away from the madness as Hal urged Sparky on. The pony seemed docile for all of ten seconds, before it tipped Hal over his head and onto the ground, much to the delight of the children.

'I'd stick to sculpture if I were you,' laughed Grace, returning from one of the three restored glasshouses, behind which was an experimental field of 'Perfect Wheat'. Violi had kept his promise and found her funding, this time from a legitimate philanthropic fund he was now running, his CIA days behind him.

500

Her baby kicked inside her and she rubbed her womb, thinking sadly of her sister struggling to cope with the sale of the House and its assets, preparing to move into a small house on the outskirts of the estate. She'd refused to divorce Delawney or to talk to any of them since Henry had given evidence against him at the sensational trial. Henry was due to be released in a few weeks. She smiled as she recalled her last visit to him in prison hospital. He'd responded brilliantly to treatment and had come to terms with himself and his future. With Henry back, she'd try again for a family reconciliation.

Sam came over with two glasses of homemade lemonade and handed one to Grace and the other to Gitte. 'Good results?'

'Early days,' replied Gitte. 'Got to get it right. Got to stay confident. Only way we'll win the battle of public opinion.'

'Amen, sister,' said Grace. 'Is he here yet?'

'On his way.'

Sam shielded his eyes and gazed into the hazy afternoon. He'd offered Malkie an escort and protection, but Malkie'd insisted on walking from the maximum-security prison in which he'd spent the previous two years helping them track down Standish and put together the case against Delawney and the drug-running cartel. Sergio was still on the run, but when they found him, Malkie had helped ensure that they would have enough evidence to take him down.

For this cooperation he'd been given a new name and a place in the witness protection programme, but Sam knew that would never be enough for his restless friend. He was going to offer Malkie a job in the European Anti-Terrorist Unit. Set a thief to catch a thief.

He watched the lonely figure breast the hill and walk towards them. Sam hadn't told Lilly her dad was coming, but he had booked a holiday for them at the beach starting the following day. Father and daughter would need time to get together again, heal wounds, create new memories.

Malkie hesitated, tempted to turn back. To disappear. But something drew him on, a stronger impulse than shame. He recalled the searing heat as he and Henry sheltered in a shallow concrete bunker whilst the fire raged above. Everything had worked out as Sam had promised. He thought he could feel Roni's frail hand in his, as cold as frosted glass, and knew he owed his daughter a mother's love.

'Hello, Malkie,' said Sam, approaching him. 'Lilly's waiting for you.'